A Rural Affair

Catherine Alliott

Published by Sourcebooks Landmark, an imprint of Sourcebooks, Inc.
P.O. Box 4410, Naperville, Illinois 60567-4410
(630) 961-3900
Fax: (630) 961-2168
www.sourcebooks.com

Originally published in 2011 in the UK by Michael Joseph, an imprint of
Penguin Group.

Library of Congress Cataloging-in-Publication Data
Alliott, Catherine.
  A rural affair / Catherine Alliott.
      pages cm
  (pbk.)
  1. Widows—Fiction. 2. Life change events—Fiction. 3. Villages—England—
Fiction. I. Title.
  PR6051.L543R87 2012
  823'.914—dc23

                          2011045468

            Printed and bound in the United States of America.
                    BG 10 9 8 7 6 5 4 3 2 1

For Fiona, Jenny and Ruth

Chapter One

IF I'M BEING TOTALLY honest I had fantasized about Phil dying. Only in a mild, half-baked, Thursday morning in Sainsbury's sort of way. I'm not talking about lying awake at night plotting his demise, no, just idly cruising those aisles, popping in the Weetabix, or driving to pick Clemmie up from nursery, dreaming a little dream, that sort of thing. Like you do when you're bored and you've got two small children on your hands and you've been married for a while to an irritating man. Wondering what life would be like without a husband. And always the life afterward bit, the nicer bit, not the horrid bit of the death itself.

Having the house to myself appealed. Getting rid of those ghastly leather sofas in tummy-upset brown, never having to hoover them again and get right down into the cracks, or keep the house immaculate as he liked, and as his mother had so assiduously done. No more wiping the skirting boards weekly, or turning the mattress monthly. No more meat and two veg and a lot more pasta. Or just a boiled egg. No more frantically raking up autumn leaves, I mused to myself now as one fluttered onto my windscreen, a beautiful, blood-red sycamore, spiralling down, winking at me. They could just lie where they fell, in a red and gold carpet on the grass as nature intended, instead of having to rush out like a lunatic when the first one dropped, Phil shouting, "Quick! They're coming!", raking furiously. These sorts of thoughts—innocuous, harmless ones, that crested, then sank, only to resurface some weeks later. Being alone with my babies, for instance; I glanced in my rear-view mirror at my toddler son as I drove along, watched as his thumb dropped wetly from his mouth and his eyes slowly closed. I reached back and deftly took the carton of juice he'd been clasping.

And OK—I straightened myself back at the wheel—just very occasionally, very fleetingly, my mind had inevitably turned to the mechanics of it. A piece of scaffolding perhaps, falling on his head from the construction site he walked under every morning, on his way from Charing Cross to Ludgate Circus: the one outside the Savoy, where they'd been at it for months. One of the workmen dropping a hammer. Clunk. But after six months, the scaffolding had come down—I'd checked. So…what about a mosquito bite? Turning septic? Quickly and painlessly, on one of our annual trips abroad—always Spain and always cycling. Same hotel every year, with other cycling enthusiasts. I read, mostly, and looked after the children. But the summer would slip by and Phil would remain un-bitten, so, to embrace the winter months, I'd fondly imagined him slipping on ice as he went to get the paper in the village shop.

"It all happened so quickly," Yvonne, who ran the shop, would say, her saucer eyes seeing everything before it happened anyway. "One minute he was breezing out with the *Telegraph*; the next, he was flat on his back, blood pouring from his head!"

No, not blood, that would be horrid. All internal. I turned down the lane that led to my house, so narrow in places the hedges brushed the sides of the car. And unlikely too, because since when had an icy fall actually killed anyone? So then I'd had him falling off ladders while clearing gutters, but Phil didn't do much gutter clearance so that didn't really work; but then, it wasn't supposed to work. It was just a run-of-the-mill, quotidian fantasy most housewives surely toy with occasionally when they're married to—not a bad man, and not a complete fool, but not a terribly interesting or exciting man either.

I narrowed my eyes at the low autumn sun, pulling the visor

down in defense. And since the cycling bug had bitten—he'd taken it up with messianic zeal a few years ago—he was almost permanently clad in blue Lycra, which didn't help. Even to Clemmie's first parents' evening, complete with extraordinary Lycra shoes. He'd arrived in the classroom, where Miss Hawkins and I were waiting, looking like Jacques Cousteau emerging from the depths. Miss Hawkins had dropped the register she'd been so flustered, and as he'd sat down beside me on an infant-sized chair, peering over his nylon knees like a garden gnome, I'd thought: not entirely the man I'd envisaged spending the rest of my life with. But then again he paid the bills, worked extremely hard, was faithful, didn't beat me, loved his children—despite sometimes behaving as if they were annoying relations of mine who'd come to stay: "Your daughter thinks it's a good idea to throw her food on the floor!" Surely his daughter too? And even though he liked to be in complete control of our little household at all times—even taking the TV remote to the loo with him—I didn't really hold it against him. Didn't really want him dead.

It was a shock, therefore, to open the door to the policeman.

"Mrs. Shilling? May I have a word?"

While he'd been cycling along the Dunstable Downs, the ridge of hills above our house, an easyJet plane returning from Lanzarote had simultaneously prepared for its descent at Luton. Dropping from freezing high altitude into warmer air, it had relieved itself: had fall-out. A chunk of ice, eighteen inches in diameter, had broken off from the fuselage and, five thousand feet below, found Phil, pedaling furiously. As my husband strove to render his body a temple, God, it seemed, had had other ideas.

I remember struggling to comprehend this, remember gaping at the policeman as he perched opposite me on my sofa, twisting his hat in his hands.

"A piece of ice? From where exactly?"

"From the undercarriage." He cleared his throat uncomfortably. "From the toilet, as a matter of fact."

"The toilet?"

"Yes. Blue Ice is how it's known. Being as how it's mixed with detergent."

"What is?"

"The urine."

I stared. Not in a million years could I have dreamed this up. Fantasized about this in Sainsbury's. Phil had been killed by a piece of piss. A hefty, frozen block of pee, travelling at spectacular speed and velocity—and which, it later transpired, hadn't actually claimed him as he'd been cycling but, as bad luck would have it, when he'd stopped at a stile, taken his helmet off to scratch his head and wonder how to get the bike over. A freak accident, but not the first of its kind, the coroner would later inform me sympathetically over his bifocals as I sat at the back of his court in a navy-blue suit, hands clenched. "Thirty-five similar instances in the last year alone."

"Although in the last forty years, only five fatalities," the man from the Civil Aviation Authority had added stiffly. Six, then, with Phil.

"Right. Thank you so much. I mean—for telling me." This, to the policeman in the here and now, in my sitting room. I stood up shakily.

The officer got to his feet, uncertain. He spread his hands helplessly.

"Do you…want to see him?"

My mind reeled. "Where is he?"

"In the hospital morgue."

I caught my breath. Oh, God. On a trolley. In a bag. "No," I gasped instinctively.

"No, not everyone does." He hesitated, unwilling to leave so soon. "Well, is there…anyone you'd like to contact? Have with you?"

"No, no one. I mean, there is. Are. Plenty. But—not now. I'll be fine, really."

"Your mother, perhaps?"

"No, she's dead."

He looked shocked. So many dead.

"Really, I'll be fine." I was helping him, now. But he was only young.

"And the children?"

"Yes, I'll pick them up from school."

And pick them up I had. Well, only Clemmie. Archie was asleep in his cot upstairs, and I'd taken him with me and driven very slowly, because I was pretty sure I was in shock. I was a quiet mother at the gates, but not a distraught one, so Clemmie didn't notice anything, and then I'd driven back and given them tea. Chicken nuggets, I remember, which I only serve in extremis. At the table Clemmie had told me about Miss Perkins, Mummy, who's an assassin. "Assistant?" Yes, and got a moustache. And later I'd bathed them and put them to bed.

And then I'd walked around the house on that chilly, blustery evening, clutching the tops of my arms, gazing out of the window at the shivering late roses, the clouds rushing through the dark blue sky, flashes of sunshine casting long shadows on the lawn, waiting, waiting for something to happen. For the sluice gate to open. For my hand to clap my mouth as I gasped, "Oh, God!" and fell, like Phil must have fallen, I told myself looking for a trigger, in a terrible heap to the ground. I tried to imagine him lying in the bracken, his bike a tangled mess, his face broken, shattered. Nothing. So I walked round the house some more, the house we'd lived in together for several years—happy years, I told myself sternly. This lovely cottage, in this beautiful village, which we'd stretched ourselves to afford, had done up meticulously, sourcing terracotta tiles from Italy, Victorian light switches from Somerset, cast-iron door handles from Wales, and from whence Phil had commuted into London every day, toiling in on a packed train, to bring back the wherewithal to raise our children. A selfless, dedicated man. I waited. Nothing.

Shock. Definitely shock. I'd read about it.

On an impulse, I hastened to our wedding album, found it tucked away among the books by the CD player. My eyes flickered guiltily over Phil's Neil Diamond CDs, his Glen Campbell collection, which I'd never have to listen to again. I pulled the leather tome onto my lap. Tissue paper fluttered and a bit of confetti fell out. There I was on Dad's arm, coming up the church path in a mistake of a dress: leg-of-mutton sleeves, the real things happily hidden away under shot silk. Dad looked a bit worse for wear already, perhaps under the influence of a pre-match tincture. Then me and Phil coming out of church, but Phil had his eyes shut, so that didn't help, and neither did the gray morning coat he'd hired from Moss Bross, a totally different color to the rest of the male congregation's, much paler, and which he'd accessorized with a red carnation, while his ushers, in black, had favored discreet white rosebuds. I flipped the page quickly. Me and Phil cutting the cake—shame about the pink icing, but then his mother had made it. And next—oh, no. I shut the book hurriedly, aware that the following shot might be of me and Phil going away. Not in a glamorous vintage car, or even a pony and trap, but, as a surprise from Phil, a tandem: a bicycle made for two. So that accompanied by shouts of "Go on, Poppy, get your leg over!" and other hilarious quips, I had. And split the pink pencil skirt I'd bought for the occasion from top to bottom, and then had to cycle behind my new husband the half mile from the country club to here, white pants flashing, rictus grin on my face, waved off uproariously by our closest friends, and most of the village.

It was getting chilly, but I didn't seem able to put a match to the fire, the one Phil, who got up at six, laid punctiliously every morning with firelighter, kindling, logs and a drop of coal, for the evening. I stared at the log on top. For me, I told myself. All for me. And my children. A caring man.

Perhaps I should tell someone? The moment you vocalized these things they became much more real. Tears would flow, it was well documented. The moment I picked up the phone and said, "Hi, Dad, look, Phil's dead," that would be it. Phil wasn't my father's dream son-in-law but he'd nevertheless be shocked and horrified. Drop everything—probably a horse's reins—and beetle down from Flampton in his ropy old pick-up to be at my side, still in his breeches and flat cap. But he wouldn't cry. He'd sit beside me on the goose-poo sofa and take my hand and not know what to say. And together, dry-eyed, we'd stare glumly at the carpet. I picked up the phone. Punched out a number.

"Jennie?"

"Oh, hi, Poppy. Hang on, I'll just take the sausages off. Jamie, stop it. No, you cannot have it in front of the telly, come and sit down—now!" Then back to me. "Sorry. Nightmare day. Frankie had a party here last night and naturally one or two teenagers were sick. I cleared up most of the puke but at two a.m. I found another on the landing and just bloody hoovered it. Error. Mrs. B. beat me to the hoover this morning and now the entire house is giving off the most spectacular pong, can't think why Glade haven't used it as an air freshener."

"Um, Jennie, the thing is, Phil's dead."

Things happened quite quickly after that. Within seconds my back door had flown open because Jennie only lived next door. Within minutes it had flown open again, because Angie, who lives up the road at the manor, had been texted by Jennie, and in the space of another few minutes a gust of wind heralded the front door flying as Peggy, who lives across the road, heard from Angie. Beads jangling, cigarette still clasped in her jaws, she'd hurtled up the path, velvet coat flapping.

Angie wept, clasping me to her expensive cashmere breast, my face pressed to her pearls, Chanel wafting up my nose. Jennie walked round and round, arms tightly folded, saying, "I cannot believe it. I *cannot* believe it." Peggy helped herself to my Famous Grouse, pouring one for me too, which, when I didn't drink it, she polished off as well.

One thing they were all agreed on, though, was that I was in shock.

They agreed again an hour later, when I was still sitting composed and silent and I don't think particularly white-faced, whilst they'd been bustling around boiling kettles and checking children and going into huddles and sitting and stroking my back muttering, "poor *poor* Poppy."

A bit later on, they wondered, tentatively, if I'd like to be alone? Jennie's children had been heard making merry hell through the wall, which she'd banged on a few times, and now there was an ominous silence. She'd texted frantically, but no response. Angie started muttering in her cut-glass accent about a parish council meeting which, as chairman, she was *supposed* to be addressing, but of course she didn't have to, and Peggy had been seen glancing at her watch on account of *Corrie*. "Although Sylvia might have recorded it," she murmured into space when no one had moved.

"Do go," I said, suddenly realizing; coming to. "I'm perfectly all right."

Angie and Peggy were already on their feet.

"Sure?" said Jennie anxiously, still stroking my back on the sofa.

"Positive."

"You'll ring if you need me? I'll come straight round. You can call me at three in the morning if you like."

"Thank you." I turned to my best friend, her hazel eyes worried in her pretty heart-shaped face. If my eyes were going to fill, it would have been then. I knew she meant it.

She gave my shoulders another squeeze and then they trooped silently out, shutting the door softly behind them. The cheese sandwich Angie had made me curled in front of me on the coffee table, the dusk gathered coldly outside the windows, the fire Peggy had put a match to smouldered in the grate.

I gazed above it to Phil's cycling medals and trophies on the mantle. Got stiffly to my feet. My legs had gone to sleep beneath me.

It was still early, but I wanted it to be the next day. Not the day my husband died. So I went upstairs, checked on the children, who were sleeping soundly, and went to bed.

At precisely three in the morning, having stared, dry-eyed, into the darkness for six hours, I sat bolt upright and seized the phone. Jennie answered immediately. Drowsily, but immediately.

"The children!" I wailed. "My children won't have a father!" Tears fled down my cheeks. "They'll be fatherless—orphans, practically!"

She was there in the time it took to throw a coat over her nightie, fish in her fruit bowl for my spare key, run down her path, up mine, and leg it upstairs. She hugged and rocked me as I sobbed and grieved for my children, gasping and spluttering into her shoulder, choking out incoherent snatches about how their lives would be wrecked, asking her to imagine distorted futures, scarred psychological profiles, looming criminal tendencies, broken homes of their own and dysfunctional children. Eventually, when my body had stopped its painful wracking and my hyperbolic ranting had subsided, Jennie sat back and held me at arm's length.

"Except he wasn't exactly a huge presence in their lives, was he?" she said quietly. "Wasn't around a lot."

"No," I admitted with a shaky sob, a corner of my mind rather shocked. "But he did love them, Jennie. There'll still be a vacuum."

"Oh, sure, he *loved* them. He loved Leila too."

Leila was Jennie's dog. A crazy Irish terrier who liked nothing more than to accompany Phil on his bike rides, lolloping along for miles beside him.

"Yes, he loved Leila," I conceded, wiping my eyes on the duvet.

"Spent a lot of time with her."

I knew where this was going. "More than he did with the children?"

She made a non-committal not-for-me-to-say face: cheeks sucked, eyebrows raised.

"Not everyone embraces fatherhood," I reminded her. "Particularly when the children are little."

She looked me in the eye. "No, but he almost resented it. Remember when you used to bundle Clemmie in the back of the car in the middle of the night and head for the M25 to stop her crying? So Phil could get some sleep?"

"He worked so hard. Needed his sleep."

"True. But at the weekends, did he ever change a nappy? Push a pram?"

"Once or twice," I said, wishing I could remember him doing any of those things. But Phil was dedicated to his work, his bike and his body in three equal parts; he didn't like other distractions. We didn't really see him. It was just me and the children. Which was how it was going to be now. No change. I shut my eyes. Prayed for courage. Wondered if I could tell her. Eventually I opened them and took a deep breath.

"The thing is, Jennie," I said in a low voice, "I'd fantasized about it."

"About what?"

"About Phil dying."

"Yes."

"What d'you mean, yes?"

"Quite normal."

"Is it?" I was shocked.

"Oh, yes. How did you do it?"

"I didn't!" I gasped.

"No, but in your dreams."

"Oh. Well. I—I had him being hit by falling masonry, at building sites."

"Ah, the old scaffolding ruse. A rogue hammer?"

"Yes," I admitted. "And I had him bitten by a mosquito in Spain."

"Nice," she said admiringly. "I've only ever got to dodgy prawns on holiday."

"And then I had him poisoned by bleach when I was getting stains off teacups."

"I've left the bleach *in* the teacups. Poured it out later, naturally."

"Really?" I peered anxiously at her in the gloom. "You've thought about it too?"

"Of course! Life would be so much simpler without Toad." This, her husband of many years, whom I adored and thought the funniest man alive—fall-off-your-bar-stool funny—but of whom she despaired.

"But, Jennie, I'm lying here thinking: perhaps I thought it so much, I made it happen. You know? Maybe…maybe whatever it is that causes bad luck—a glitch in the solar system, Teutonic plates shifting, an elephant stepping on an ant in the Delta—everything that makes stuff happen, did so because I willed it to. Maybe I actually killed him? I mean, how bizarre was his death? It was like one of my very own fantasies—could have been my next one!"

"Don't be silly, you haven't got the imagination. Of course it wasn't you. Did you beetle off to the airport and strap a lump of piss to a 747?"

"No, but—"

"Well, then." She paused. "Did you pray?"

"Pray?"

"Yes, did you get down on your knees and pray to God? Plead for his demise?"

"Of course not." I was startled. I felt my eyes widen in the darkness. "Why, have you?"

"Oh, yes." Jennie sniffed. She sat up straight and shook back her dark curls defiantly. "At the foot of the bed like Christopher Robin. Eyes tightly shut. Doesn't mean I'd *do* it, Poppy. But that time he wrote off two cars in one week, let the bath overflow through the ceiling into the new kitchen, came back pissed from the office party and told Brian Cunningham on the train that his wife was having it off with our builder, then used Jamie's tracing paper from his geography project, on which he'd laboriously traced the Great Lakes, to wipe his bum, that night I got down on my knees and asked God for deliverance. I did have a nervous moment when he crashed the quad bike a few weeks later, remembering my crash-and-burn plea, but we're only human, Poppy. We can't make these things happen. Did you imagine the funeral?"

I stared at her, horrified. "Yes," I whispered finally.

"I do that too." She drew her knees up chummily. Hugged them to her chest. "What did you think you'd wear?"

"That Whistles skirt with the kick pleat and my good wool jacket from Hobbs."

"Over your gray silk shirt?"

"I thought a cami."

She made a face. "Bit louche."

"With the jacket done up?"

"Oh, OK." She nodded; looked thoughtful. "I'm going to wear my Country Casuals dog-tooth number to Toad's. Elegant, yet restrained. Did you flirt?"

"What, at Phil's fantasy funeral? No! Did you?"

"A bit. Only on the way out. Just a few vulnerable glances through tear-stained lashes, and only with Passion-fueled Pete." This, the local farrier, who shod Angie's horses and was tall, blond and gorgeous. He caused quite a stir whenever his mobile forge rumbled through the village.

"Why would Passion-fueled Pete come to Toad's funeral?"

"Oh, I don't know. I haven't worked out the logistics, Poppy." She passed a weary hand through her hair, looking tired. "Perhaps he had a horse-drawn hearse?"

"What, like they do in the East End? Like the Kray brothers?"

"It's only a fantasy, for heaven's sake."

We sat companionably in silent contemplation for a moment,

the only light shining through from the hall, where she'd belted up the stairs.

"You'll have it in the village church, I presume," she said at length. "I mean, the real one?"

"I suppose so. Yes. Definitely."

"Everyone will come," she warned. "You know what they're like round here. Any excuse."

"I know."

"Sunglasses?"

"I think so."

To hide the dry eyes, we both thought.

"And actually," she said slowly, "it will be quite ghastly. You will need those glasses. Trust me, you'll sob."

"Really?" I looked at her anxiously, hoping for grief.

"Really." She regarded me steadily. "A human life has been taken here, Poppy. A young man cut down in his prime. And that's very sad. You'll cry. But don't you go feeling guilty about not feeling or weeping enough. You never wanted to marry that man, you just slid into it. You made a decent fist of your marriage because he was the father of your children, but let's not get carried away here. A few years down the line, you wouldn't have been with him."

"You don't think so?"

"I know so. You'd have flown, Poppy. This way, you'll just fly a little sooner."

As she said it, I felt some faint metaphorical itch between my shoulder blades where, one day, I might sprout wings. It was instantly followed by a lorry load of guilt tumbling on them like rubble, which had me cringing on the bed. We sat there side by side, Jennie hunched in her old camel coat and hugging her knees, me in my baggy Gap T-shirt, crouched under the duvet. Through the wall, we could hear Toad, or Dan as I preferred to call him, gently snoring. Not so gently, in fact; he was gaining momentum. She turned to me, appalled.

"I didn't know you could hear him!"

"Only occasionally."

"I'll put a pillow over his head!"

"Do not. I don't mind. Quite like it, actually. Sounds…masculine." And automatically I thought how Phil had been quite feminine. Fastidious. Clean. Two showers a day. Nail brushes. And slept like a mouse.

"Well, at least there's no danger of you hearing anything else," she remarked darkly.

I didn't reply. Jennie's increasing lack of interest in the physical side of her marriage could wait for another night. And anyway, this wasn't entirely true. On the odd occasion I had employed ear plugs.

"Go, Jennie," I said quietly, at length.

"Sure?"

"Sure."

"I'll be back tomorrow."

I nodded, gave her a weak smile. Then she hugged me and slipped away. I listened to her footsteps going down the stairs, the door closing behind her. I knew she would be back, first thing. Knew I was blessed with friends like this, knew that moving to this village was the best thing I'd ever done. That it had been a huge compensation for my marriage and would now stand me in very good stead. And although my heart was heavy as I went to the loo and then crawled back to bed—I dreaded my next hurdle, which was telling Clemmie in the morning—as I lay down and shut my eyes, a part of me was already thinking about how I'd clear the medals from the mantle above the fire, take down the Tour de France pictures in the loo, sell the rowing machine on eBay. Not have to wake up to him doing press-ups by the bed in the morning. Not have to go downstairs and find a note in the kitchen headed "Poppy—Things to Do." And part of me was also thinking: no longer, Poppy Shilling. No longer can you say nothing ever happens to you. Finally, something has gone on in your life.

Chapter Two

HE HADN'T ALWAYS BEEN like that, of course. Phil. Boring, meticulous, health-conscious, dedicated to his own physical well-being—the supreme vanity, in my book. Hadn't always wanted a blood-pressure kit for Christmas or a treadmill for his birthday, hadn't always been so inward-looking. Once upon a time he'd been quite—I was going to say fun, but I'll qualify that with normal. He'd always been around, part of the crowd I'd hung out with in London when I lived in Clapham, but on the edges, the periphery. Somebody's brother had known him at university, not Jennie's because her brother went around with quite a fast lot, but it could have been Tess's brother at Durham. Anyway, there he was, at parties, in pubs with us, probably not on the raucous beery table I was on, but next door with others I vaguely knew but not well. A nice guy. Nice Phil, if you asked. Oh, yeah, Ben would say, Phil's a nice guy. Don't know him that well.

Ben was my boyfriend. Had been for years. Ridiculously, on and off since we were fifteen. In fact it was a bit of a joke. We'd met at school, gone out for a year, split up for a year, got together in the sixth form, got a bit more serious, split up for our gap years, and ended up going to the same university together. We hadn't intended to, but I had to go through clearing because I hadn't got my grades and the only place I could read history was at York, where Ben was. I'd worried slightly that he might think I was following him up there, but he was very cool, totally relaxed, and after the first year we were back together again, and then for the next three. There were the inevitable jokes about us being a little married couple and joined at the hip, and girlfriends asked me if I'd ever been out with anyone else, but we shrugged it off. Then in London we were still together; at parties, concerts, suppers, always Ben and Poppy, Poppy and Ben.

It wasn't that unusual. It was cozy too. But when Jennie came back to the flat we shared in Lavender Hill one evening, pounding up three flights of stairs, coat flying, cheeks flaming, like the cat who'd got the cream, crying, "I've met him! I've met the man I'm going to marry! He's called Dan and he's a wine trader and he's a bit older than me and I love him, I love him—and oh, my God, I've *never* felt like this before. Never!"—when I looked down into her shiny eyes as she flopped on the sofa, I wondered if I ever had. Felt that sheer, unadulterated, in-loveness. That euphoria. And when she'd gone to meet Dan for dinner in Chelsea—Ben and I could only afford the pub—still wrapped up in her happiness, I'd felt a bit flat. A bit jealous. Jennie hadn't had a boyfriend for a couple of years, was always bemoaning the fact, but now it seemed she'd not only landed on her feet, but leaped ahead of me; sprung up the ladder, trumping me with not just a boy next door of our own age, but a proper romantic hero, who sent flowers to her office, took her on proper dates to restaurants, was older, sophisticated, and what's more, adored her.

And then Ben had come round complaining he'd had a shitty day, kicking his shoes off like we *were* married, slumping down in front of the television, while I made us spag bol in the kitchen and while Jennie sat in Tante Claire, toying with artichokes and blushing prettily. And when I brought supper in to eat on our laps in front of *Friends*, Ben had his feet up on the sofa, was yawning widely and scratching his balls, and for some reason I flipped; I snapped at him about not being a bloody waitress. Then a few weeks later, I split up with him.

A guy in my office, in my PR agency, had been flirting with me for months. An attractive guy called Andy: slightly rough around the edges, not strictly my type, but rather thrilling, very good-looking. Hot. Andy and I had a fling. A very exciting one in his flat in Docklands. He was only the second man I'd ever been to bed with, and he whisked me off to nightclubs—admittedly more Brixton Sound than Annabel's—and we had a laugh. We drank a great deal, smoked in Ronnie Scott's, and I thought I was living. I think I knew his family was a bit shady but I never met them, and then one night, over dinner, he admired the jewelry I was wearing; it was quite good because it had been Mum's. A heavy gold chain and a bangle she'd always worn. And he asked me why I didn't accidentally lose them and claim on the insurance? Because it had never occurred to me. But after that—and it took some time for the penny to drop—one or two other things did. Like the way Andy gambled a lot and spent nearly every Sunday night playing poker. And a few weeks later we argued about something, and he pushed me. Not hard, but I fell against the wall. It was enough: we were history.

When I turned around, Ben had gone. To America, it transpired. New York, where his investment bank had transferred him; promotion. So I contacted him. Asked when he was coming back, if we could meet, have lunch. I wasn't unduly worried. In fact I was so casual I think I was even painting my toenails on the stairs in Clapham at the time, phone tucked under my chin. And he'd said not for a bit, not for a good six months, and anyway, he'd met someone in New York. Caroline. An American girl, who worked with him. Same age, twenty-four. A banker. They were going to get married.

Hard to describe the body blow felt at the time. The breathlessness. The pain. Ben, who'd always been there. Funny, clever, beautiful, blond Ben, who of course would be snapped up in New York—would be snapped up in London, but with the accent, the whole Brit bit, would go down a storm over there—but who loved me. Had always been there for me. While I'd been totally complacent about him. My Ben.

Jennie had endured much grief and wailing. Much smoking of too many cigarettes, much talk of shelf life, and eventually, the months having ticked by, much furtive hiding of wedding plans from me after she admitted she was engaged.

She'd meet me after work, samples of shot-silk organza hidden in her handbag, CDs of suitable music for bridal entrances secreted about her person. She'd counsel and sympathize and suggest suitable replacements for Ben, but all were unacceptable. All were second-bests. Will Thompson was nice enough, I supposed, when she told me he fancied me, but he didn't have Ben's charm, his easy manner, and Harry Eastgate was fun too, but, oh I don't know, Jennie, he worked so hard, was very driven.

"What about anyone at work?"

"What, like Andy?" I said gloomily, sinking into my cider without bothering to pick it up.

When Jennie got married it was fine, because I knew she would, to Dan, who turned out to be everything she described and was madly in love with her, but then Tess, a sweet girl on the fringe of our group, got engaged, and the following year Daisy, a really good mate, and then Will Thompson and then Harry Eastgate. Which pretty much just left me. And I can't tell you how panicky I felt. I told myself to relax, but I hyperventilated. I went to spas with girls I knew quite well, but not like Jennie and Daisy, and lay around wrapped in seaweed. I went to the Canaries to get an early tan for the summer. I even went to see Madame Sheriza—not a fortune-teller, you understand, but a proper medium, at a reputable institute of psycho-something in South Ken, and she told me I'd meet someone through my sister, except I didn't have a sister. Sorry, I meant your brother. Don't have one of those either. And all the while my eyes roved around in a crazy fashion at parties, and one day I panic-bought. Those crazy eyes lit on Phil. Phil. On the periphery of society, tall, pleasant-looking, fair-haired, slim—nice Phil, surely?

"Oh, *lovely* Phil," Tess assured me eagerly. A good friend of her brother's. Really lovely Phil.

"*Quite* nice Phil," Jennie said, more hesitantly. A bit sort of… bland, maybe? And don't forget, Tess's brother read sociology.

But I wasn't listening. Off I went on dates with him and he was delightful. He hadn't had a girlfriend for years and feeling, I think, he was punching above his weight, was pulling out all the stops: taking me to country-house retreats, weekends in the Cotswolds, even mini-breaks in Paris.

"Phil's great!" I'd squeak, flying round to Jennie and Dan's in Twickenham, where she'd be reading to her stepdaughter, Frankie, or getting the supper amid packing cases, poised to move to the country. "And he's mad about me, and yesterday I got roses at work!"

"Good. And you're mad about him?" She poured me a drink and we perched on a box.

"Of course."

"And does he make you laugh?"

"Oh—*laugh*. Last night we went to see *Airport* and we couldn't *stop* laughing!"

"I think you'll find that was Gene Wilder making you laugh, but good, Poppy. I'm pleased. Shit. Hang on."

She'd moved like lightning, legging it up the stairs to meet Frankie, aged four, who'd appeared damp and tearful at the top, still wetting her bed at night.

I finished my drink and left her to it; went home hugging my happiness. My settled-ness. My all-organized-ness. And if, for a moment, I had any doubts, they were only really tiny ones, like the way he spoke to waiters. The way he'd said to that young girl in the bistro: "I'd like my salad dressing without vinegar. What would I like my salad dressing without?"

She'd glanced at him, surprised. "Vinegar."

"That's it." He'd smiled. And she'd smiled too, relieved.

"I have to do that," he'd confided quietly to me when she'd gone. "Otherwise they forget, and I can't abide salad with vinegar."

Of course not.

A few months later Phil proposed, and things got even better. We went around Peter Jones with our wedding list and discovered, to our delight, that we had exactly the same taste. We inclined toward the red Le Creuset rather than the blue, the retro fifties toaster, the antique weighing scales, eschewed a dinner service in favor of hand-painted Portuguese plates, more conducive to cozy kitchen suppers which we infinitely preferred to dinner parties, decisively ticking our lists attached to clipboards. Another box ticked. A big one, we felt as we gazed at one another under the bright lights of China and Glass.

We also both agreed we wanted to get out of London.

"Too frenetic," Phil said, frowning thoughtfully, "and too…"

"Superficial," I continued and he smiled. Heavens, we were finishing each other's sentences now.

He favoured Kent, where his mother lived, but I wanted to be near Dad, so we looked at villages in that direction, within an hour's commute of town. Eventually we decided, somewhat sheepishly, that Jennie and Dan really had done their homework. That it was hard to better theirs. Sleepy, idyllic, with two pubs and a duck pond, but a functioning village too, with a shop and a school.

"But do you mind?" I asked her anxiously, when a house at the other end of the village had come up for sale.

"Mind?" Jennie shrieked down the phone. "Of course I don't mind, I'd love it!"

She had made one friend, she told me, a lovely girl called Angie, frightfully glam and rich and great fun, but apart from that was bereft of kindred spirits, and couldn't think of anything nicer than having her best friend down the road. For moral support if nothing else, she said grimly, which she needed at the moment, what with dealing with daily tantrums from Frankie, and Dan's increasing inability to pass a second-hand car showroom without buying a banger—they were a four-car family at present—which he drove at speed down the country lanes, parp parping like Toad. Not to mention the dawning realization that she appeared to be pregnant.

Unfortunately the house at the other end of the village fell through, but then she rang me to say there was one for sale next door.

"Bit close?" I said doubtfully. "I mean, for you, not me. I don't want to—you know, cramp your style?"

"Trust me, I don't have a style. Unless you count heartburn that makes me belch mid-sentence, or piles that have driven me to adopt the post-natal rubber ring two months prematurely. Please come, Poppy, before I change the e in antenatal to a vowel I regret."

I shot down to look at the house: a dear little whitewashed cottage, low-slung, as if a giant had sat on the roof, with bulging walls, a brace of bay windows downstairs—one on either side of the green front door, two more poking out under eaves, a strip of garden that gave onto farmland at the back and the forest beyond. It was attached to Jennie's similar cottage on one side, and next to a sweet terraced row on the other. Inside was a mess: low, poky rooms and an outdated kitchen and bathroom, but Phil and I decided we could knock through here, throw an RSJ up there, just about have room for an Aga over there. "And lay a stone hallway here," he said, indicating six square feet just inside the front door.

"Yes!" I yelped, thinking how uncanny it was that I'd been think-ing the same. "Limestone or slate?" I asked, hoping for the latter.

"Slate, I think," he said thoughtfully, and I almost purred.

We moved in, already engaged, and, once the structural work had been done, got to work. We stripped the walls together, sanded doors, rubbed down floorboards, re-enameled baths, working every weekend, evenings too, radio blaring so not much chat, whilst Dan and Jennie, who'd got a team of decorators in to do theirs, popped round to marvel. Jamie was in Jennie's arms now and Frankie was still sucking her hair and scowling. Well, of course she was, Jennie said staunchly; her mother might have drunk too much and run off with an Argentinian polo player, but she was still her mother, for crying out loud. She missed her.

So Phil and I scrubbed and varnished and stippled and dragged, and even found a window of opportunity one Saturday to get married, arranged with military precision by Phil, both of us agreeing on the music, the number of people, the flowers; as I say, the only fly in the ointment was the tandem to go away on, the surprise googly, as it were. Another year of tireless house restoration followed before we sat back on our weary heels and looked at each other, delighted. With the house, at least. But I do remember, as I regarded Phil that day, spry and fair, putty scraper in hand, slightly narrow lips which didn't smile that often, remember looking at him as if I hadn't seen him for some time, had seen only Designers Guild samples, Farrow and Ball paint charts, and it being…quite a shock. As if I'd taken a year-long nap. Was this my husband? This man, so free of jokes and wit and laughter, but full of plans for the garden? This man who had ideas for opening up the inglenook fireplace, growing roses round an arbour—both romantic notions, I felt—but who made love so quickly and quietly, almost…stealthily? Who was disinclined to linger in bed afterward but wanted to get those tulip bulbs in, wanted to get on?

Joyless was a word horrifyingly close to my lips. And as I sat on my heels and looked at him and he asked if I'd ordered the bedroom carpet, and I replied I hadn't yet, he held my eye. "That's the second time I've had to ask you, Poppy," he said slowly. I went a bit cold.

"There's a sample in the kitchen drawer," he went on. "In the file marked Floor Coverings."

"Right."

"On the back you'll find the John Lewis number," he added patiently, when I didn't move. "Do it now, please."

I got slowly to my feet. Moved kitchen-ward.

In retrospect that should have been my moment. Before children. My moment to take a deep breath and think: what have I done? Marrying this man who knew his way around B&Q blindfold but not the human heart? Who could spot a speck of damp at twenty paces but not a faint tremble of misgiving from his new wife? A small cry for help? But that way horror lay. And anyway, I told myself, getting the carpet sample from the file, one of seven files, all neatly labeled in Phil's precise hand, we were so good together. Everybody said so. Such a good team. I ordered the carpet and then went quickly to boil the kettle with the curly spout, the one we both liked and had bought in a junk shop. I made us some tea.

If this all seems a trifle submissive for a hitherto sparky girl, a typical product of the twenty-first century and not the nineteenth, let me say something about confidence. Mine had taken a battering: first on losing Ben, and then, it seemed to me, losing everyone else. So many happily married. And I'd experienced quite a bit of loss in my life; didn't want to experience any more. Which brings me to family. I didn't have the backing of a big happy one to wade in and give advice, sit around kitchen tables cradling mugs of tea before brandishing motherly or sisterly handbags if needs be. I had Dad. Who was lovely, but—well, a dad. And I'd never missed Mum so much. Never wished so much that I could talk to her, that she hadn't died. Which perhaps explains why I'd flown to my best friend's side. I'm not making excuses here—of course I should have been more punchy, answered back, told him to order the bloody carpet himself. I'm just outlining mitigating circumstances. I'd only been married a short while; I wanted to keep the peace. Wanted us to be happy. Didn't want to throw saucepans at this stage.

And after all, what would I do without Phil? Phil, who pitted his wits against the entire building industry, plumbers who plumbed in radiators upside down, tilers who used the wrong grouting, the distressed-pine kitchen fitter, who disappeared mid job, with four out of seven cupboards unfitted, and who, when we rang, leaving messages on his answerphone, seemed to have disappeared into thin air. Phil eventually tracked him down. His wife, it transpired, had had a miscarriage. But Phil had him back working in an instant, albeit looking as distressed as his cupboards, I thought, as I took him a cup of tea.

"It's the second baby they've lost in two years," I told Phil as I joined him in the garden, where he was tying up runner beans.

"So I gather. But life goes on."

I shot him a look. "I hope you didn't tell him that."

"Why?"

"Wouldn't be terribly tactful."

He shrugged. "Maybe not, but it does."

We continued to do the beans in silence.

Teamwork, that was the key. And of course it would be an even stronger team when we were three. When we had a baby. Even I could spot the sink-estate mentality inherent in that notion, but it disappeared the moment I discovered conceiving wasn't that easy, when nothing happened for a year or two, when we had something else to pit our wits against, another cause to campaign for, besides the house.

Phil read books, went on the Internet, and declared that the first thing to do was to identify the culprit.

"The culprit?"

"Yes. See whose fault it is."

"Bit soon, isn't it?" I said doubtfully. "Shouldn't we—you know—try for a bit longer first?"

"What, and waste more time?"

"Might be fun. I read somewhere that if you do it every night for a month you stand more chance of hitting the egg. Blanket bombing."

I smiled flirtatiously, but he'd already turned back to the

computer. And within a twinkling, had made appointments for us both in Harley Street. Me to have my tubes blown, him to fill a test tube, assisted by a girly magazine. This fascinated me. Not that a smart Harley Street joint provided such a thing, but the idea of Phil looking at one. The results came back and we were both declared innocent, which I could tell surprised Phil.

"Why, did you think you were firing blanks?"

"Oh, no, I knew I'd be OK."

After that our marriage roared into action, with Phil at the helm, morphing swiftly from house restorer to infertility doctor. He knew the temperature of my body to within a whisker, knew when my ovaries were ripe and rumbling portentously, could pinpoint to the hour when conditions were ideal for copulation. He knew when I was hot, in the strictest, David Attenborough sense of the word. There was to be no blanket bombing, but once a month he'd ring me at work to tell me to hustle home sharpish and get my kit off, and if that sounds sexy, it wasn't. Not when your husband is grimly plunging his testicles into freezing-cold water beforehand without cracking a joke—I tried one, about cold fish, and it didn't go down very well—and not when I was instructed to lie doggo for at least an hour afterward, the only laugh coming when I suggested he lie with me. Personally I wondered if the tight Lycra cycling suit he squeezed back into afterward and wore ninety per cent of the time was helping matters, but since I was rapidly losing interest in the whole project, I decided not to mention it.

Why was I losing interest? Why was I finally succumbing to what can only be described as torpor as I rumbled home every night on the train from the West End to what should have been my enviable country love nest? Because everyone has their saturation point. And happy as I wanted us to be, little by little, drip by drip, as the months, then the years ticked by, I was coming to the mind-numbing conclusion that I'd made the biggest mistake of my life.

My epiphany came as I was standing at the kitchen window one Thursday morning, on one of my precious days off from work, looking at the list of "things to do" he'd left me, the last of which read: Have your hair cut.

I reached for the phone to tell Jennie I needed a coffee, pronto, and also to tell her I was leaving him. Her answering machine was on. I knew she was in, though, because I'd seen her in the garden a few moments earlier. I was about to go round and tell her, when I stopped off in the downstairs loo, and saw the pregnancy test he'd left me. It was open, with a note propped on one of the sticks.

Poppy—pee on this today. You're day 14.

I sighed but peed on it nevertheless, thinking it was the last thing I would ever do for him. Then I watched the blue line darken and realized I was pregnant.

As I slowly went back into the kitchen, the telephone rang.

"Poppy? Did you ring?"

"Hm? Oh. Yes, hi, Jennie."

"You OK? You sound a bit down."

"No, no, I'm fine."

"D'you want to come round for a quick coffee? I've got literally twenty minutes before I pick Jamie up from school."

"Er, no. Better not. I've got the ironing to finish."

"This afternoon? Cup of tea?"

"Actually, Jennie, I think I'm going to have my hair cut."

Chapter Three

THE FUNERAL TOOK PLACE a week later and was indeed dreadful. Much worse than I'd imagined or even Jennie had prophesied, but perhaps for different reasons. The brightness of the day and the pure blue sky didn't help, adding poignancy somehow, throwing the occasion into relief. Ancient yews cast long dramatic shadows across the churchyard and villagers were silhouetted starkly as they left their cottages, one by one or in hushed groups, following the haunting relentless toll of the bell, wreaths in hand ready to lay at the church door. Inside a sorrowful aroma of dank stone, polish and candle wax prevailed. Our tiny church was full, as Jennie had also grimly predicted, the respectful silence broken only by the odd hushed whisper or rustle of skirts as people took their seats, casting me sympathetic glances the while as I swallowed hard in the front pew, biting my lip. One week on and I felt utterly drained and exhausted. A small part of me was relieved at that. How awful would it have been to stand here at my husband's funeral singing "The Lord's My Shepherd" and not to have a lump in my throat? Not to have to count to ten and dig my nails hard in my hand as the organ struck a mournful chord, everyone got to their feet, and the coffin processed up the aisle?

Three of Phil's cycling cronies were pall bearers: tall, skinny and anemic-looking to a man. Each what my dad would call a long streak of piss. The fourth was my father himself, who's tiny, so that the coffin, I realized in horror, leaned precariously his way. And his shoulders sloped at the best of times. The congregation collectively held its breath as the coffin made its way, at quite an alarming angle, to the front, Dad's knees seeming to buckle under the strain with every step. The cyclists had to stop more than once to let him get more of a grip, but finally the altar was achieved. I shut my eyes as the coffin was lowered. There was, admittedly, a bit of a clatter and a muffled "fuck" from Dad, but I think only I heard. My father glanced round as he straightened up, unable to resist making eye contact, to suggest he'd done really rather well, under the circumstances.

I gave a small smile back as he puffed out his chest and stood respectfully a moment, head bowed over the coffin. The other pall bearers had dispersed. That'll do, Dad, I thought nervously, as the seconds ticked by. My father may be small, five foot seven in his socks, but he's frightfully important-looking as small men often are. In his youth, when he hadn't been riding point-to-pointers or driving all over the country to do so, he'd done a lot of am-dram, and something in his manner suggested there was still a chance he'd sweep a cloak over his shoulder, hold Yorick's skull aloft and proclaim to the gallery. When he'd milked his moment for all it was worth he turned on his heel and came, head bowed, to sit beside me, clearly relishing this particular performance.

The vicar meanwhile, after we'd sung the first hymn, manfully launched into the eulogy. Manfully because he'd never met Phil, so he was really quite at sea. I'd decided to leave it to him, though, despite his anxious "Really, Mrs. Shilling? Sure there's no one else?" "Quite sure." And now he was telling us what a helluva guy Phil was, what a pillar of the community, what a loss to the village. All nonsense, of course, because Phil had never been involved in village life; had indeed never been inside this church before now, except to get married. But then the vicar said what a marvelous father he'd been and what a loss to the children, and that's when I welled up. He hadn't been marvelous, but any father is a loss. You only get one, and my children would never have another Christmas with him, another holiday with him, not that they'd necessarily want to cycle through the Pyrenees being yelled at constantly to keep up, or… OK, he'd never make speeches at their eighteenths, twenty-firsts, that sort of thing. Actually Phil had only ever made one speech to my knowledge, a best man's speech for a cycling crony, which had gone on for forty-six minutes, and been so turgidly dull that eventually, when everyone began coughing and nipping to the loo or the bar, the bride's father, a bluff Yorkshireman, had got to his feet and said firmly: "That'll do, laddie." I couldn't have put it better myself.

I sighed. Still. My poor babies. Clemmie, in particular. Archie, at twenty months, was too young to understand, but Clemmie had listened soberly when I'd told her the bad news the following morning, sitting her down before nursery school, explaining carefully exactly what had happened. Her brown eyes had grown huge in her pale little face, knowing, by the tone of my voice, rather than the content, that this was bad.

"So is he breathing?"

"No, darling. He's dead."

"Like Shameful?"

"Yes, like Shameful."

This, a ram in the field at the back of our house, who'd been found stiff and cold last month, and was so called because he rogered every ewe in the field before breakfast, which Phil had found offensive when he was eating his muesli.

"It's shameful!" he'd roar, so Clemmie thought that was his name.

"Where is Daddy?"

"He's…well…" I hesitated. The morgue sounded horrible. "At the undertaker's. It's a special place where dead people go before they're buried."

"Not in heaven?"

"Oh, well, yes. Yes, his soul will go to heaven. It's quite complicated, darling, but the point is, you won't see him again. Do you understand?"

She nodded. "Will Shameful go to heaven?"

"Yes. Yes, I'm sure."

"Even though he had lots of girlfriends?"

"Well…yes. I don't see why not."

She finished her cereal in silence. Got down from the table. But no tears, which worried me. But then, she was only four; it probably hadn't quite filtered through. And the thing was, Phil never got home until they'd gone to bed in the week, and at the weekends he'd cycled all day, so how much more had she seen of him than of the ram at the back of the house? In the field where my children played most days, climbing on the logs, splashing in puddles?

When I collected her from nursery, though, Miss Hawkins had caught my eye, scuttled across.

"May I have a word, Mrs. Shilling?"

"Of course."

"I'm so sorry for your loss."

"Thank you."

"I just thought you should know that Clemmie says her daddy was hit by a plane."

"True, in a way."

"And that he's died and gone to heaven."

"Yes."

"And that anyone can go, even if they've had lots of girlfriends. Even if they're shameful."

I blinked.

"Right. Thank you…Miss Hawkins."

She was already hastening away before I could put her straight. I sighed. Oh, so be it, I thought as I watched her departing back. Let the entire village think he was the local lothario. It couldn't be further from the truth. Unless it was in the interests of conception, which appealed to Phil's competitive nature, he regarded sex as…a bit of a chore. A box to be ticked by a workaholic who'd rather be on his BlackBerry. There hadn't been much since Archie had been born, which, Jennie told me darkly, I should thank my lucky stars about. Dan hadn't even let her get to her six-week check after Jamie, and when she was up on the ramp having her overhaul, she hadn't liked to tell the nice young doctor who'd coyly told her she could start giving herself back to her husband, that he'd been helping himself for weeks.

But no, Phil hadn't been much of a bedroom man; indeed the idea of him putting himself about locally was almost as fanciful as him putting his goodwill about, being a stalwart of this parish, where, thankfully, the vicar was winding up now, his material being quite thin. He cleared his throat and enjoined us to stand and sing the final hymn, number one hundred and seventy two: "Jerusalem." We all got gratefully to our feet.

As questions go I've always thought the one about whether our Lord's feet actually walked in ancient times upon England's mountains green to be not only rhetorical, but, if pressed, the answer would be a resounding no. I was still thinking about it as we filed out of church a few moments later. Blake had clearly lobbed it up metaphysically, wryly, not to be taken literally, and yet hundreds of years later it was belted out by congregations across the land and embraced patriotically, the answer a resounding "Yes!" from those who wanted Him to be an Englishman ten foot tall. Would it have amused Blake, I wondered, as I reached the gate on the lane, my eyes narrowed against the low sun which was dazzling, blinding almost, to hear it sung with such fervour? Did it amuse God?

"Mrs. Shilling!"

A voice cut through my reverie, scattering my thoughts. I turned, abstractedly, at the gate.

"Mrs. Shilling?" There was a note of incredulity to it.

Back at the top of the path, in the grassy, undulating area to the left of the church, otherwise known as the cemetery, the vicar was waiting, prayer book open, cassock flapping, saucer-eyed, surrounded by the rest of the congregation. They appeared to be clustered around a huge gaping hole in the ground which…Shit. I'd forgotten to bury my husband.

Shock, naturally, Jennie and Angie both quickly consoled me, as I hastened to join them, to stand between them; that and nervous exhaustion. I nodded dumbly. Horrified and sweaty-palmed I bent my head, which was indeed very muddled, so that as I was passed some earth to throw onto the coffin and nervously did so, Angie, swathed in black mink, had to touch my arm and murmur: "Easy, tiger. Wait till the vicar gets to the earth-to-earth bit. Let's not hurry this along too much, hm?" She handed me some more in her suede-gloved hand.

Later, and it seemed like an eternity—so horrible, seeing him lowered in that dreadful box into the ground, so final—I was back at the church gate again with the vicar. I knew it had been part of the plan at some point; I'd just hastened there rather too quickly. One by one the villagers filed past to pay their respects, to say how sorry they were, pressing my hand and murmuring condolences. Yvonne, the post mistress—whom Phil had once called an interfering busybody to her face when she complained about him leaving his bike leaning against her shop window—said how much she'd miss his sunny smile. Sylvia Jardine at the Old Rectory, who considered herself the local nob and didn't know Phil from Adam but clearly thought she'd done her homework, said, in a carrying, fruity voice that Philip had been an outstanding bell ringer, a misunderstanding courtesy of this month's parish magazine, in which someone had complained about Phil ringing his bicycle bell at six in the morning as he waited impatiently for Bob Groves to drive his cattle through the village. Dan, Jennie's husband, gave me a huge hug and whispered, "You're doing brilliantly, girl," which made me well up, and Frankie, in a black minidress and matching nail varnish, who at sixteen had never been to a funeral and had come out of interest—she later confided she didn't think there'd been nearly enough weeping or black veils—squeezed my hand and said I must be "properly pissed."

Happily many of the condolences were for the children, who I'd deemed too young to come for the whole service, and who were now with Peggy across the road. Peggy, who'd brought the children briefly and sat at the back, but who'd told me in her throaty drawl, as she dragged on her fourth cigarette of the morning, that she wasn't a great one for funerals, and anyway, she'd never liked him. I smiled to myself. Just the one voice of truth ringing in our valley. How I loved Peggy.

She wasn't an obvious role model, being widowed and childless, and cut an eccentric figure in her long flowing coats and beaded scarves, down which she dripped cigarette ash. The only time I'd seen Peggy cook, I'd watched fascinated as two inches of ash had fallen from her cigarette into the Bolognese sauce and she'd calmly stirred it in, muttering "Roughage." But she had a certain objective wisdom. Objective, perhaps because of a lack of blood ties with the world, which ensured impartiality. And a glorious irreverence for anything humbug. Those who cared to sit in the snug at the Rose and Crown and play backgammon with her, drink copious amounts of vodka and listen to her quiet, upper-class voice and her throaty laugh could learn a lot. I loved her refreshing take on life. "When I am old I shall wear purple" could have been written for Peggy, although I suspect she'd always worn purple: it was just that these days it was diamanté-studded.

As we all trooped away from the church and across the green for coffee and sandwiches at my house, my father fell in beside me and linked my arm.

"Well done, old girl."

"Thanks, Dad."

He tactfully left it at that. I might not have rushed to complain to him in the early days of my marriage, but I was close to my dad, and recently he'd known Phil and I had had problems.

"And I'm sorry you're missing Tick-a-Tape run."

This, my father's horse, or leg of a horse, the one he owned in a syndicate, and for whom he hadn't missed a race since he bought him. He was running the biggest one of his life today, at Kempton.

"Don't be silly, it's only a race. There'll be others. He was my son-in-law, for God's sake."

Teetotal, fiercely competitive and allergic to horses: everything Dad was not. We walked on in silence.

"Got the beers in, love?" By now we were following the procession up the path, into the house.

"Well, I thought coffee. And a few bottles of sherry?"

Dad stopped; looked appalled. "Right. Well, no worries. I'll nip to the offy and get a bit more, shall I? Just to be on the safe side. Back in a tick."

He turned and shot off across the road to his mud- splattered pick-up, bound for Leighton Buzzard, and a tick was all he would be, I thought, since he drove at the speed of light. It was one of the things my mother had despaired of. Mum. What would she be thinking now, I wondered, as I carried on into my house, glancing briefly heavenward as I crossed the threshold. What would she think of this fractured little family of hers, this widowed husband, this only child, now a widow herself? Mum had never met Phil, her own car, which she drove as thoughtfully and carefully as she lived her life, having been involved in a pile-up on the M4 long before he'd been on the scene. That terrible Boxing Day evening when I was eleven, and she'd felt compelled to go and see Auntie Pam, who was on her own, and then come back to give us cold turkey and beetroot for supper; generally packing too much into one day, splitting herself too many ways. The pilot light in Dad's life and mine had all but gone out for a long time, but gradually we'd lit the fuse together, with shaky hands. She might recognize Dad, I thought as I turned to watch him go, haring off in an all-too-familiar fashion, one hand tuning the car radio into the racing, but would she recognize me? This hitherto headstrong daughter of hers, who'd sat on her hands in a bad marriage for years? She wouldn't think me capable. But then, she wasn't to know the after-effects of her death; wasn't to know I was a different person. Wasn't to know I now had a very scared, conventional side, one that didn't want to be the one left without a mother, or a husband; one that didn't want to be last. Or perhaps she did know that. Perhaps I'd been like that all along, and maybe she would recognize me, after all.

My tiny sitting room was packed, and some were people I swear I'd never seen before in my life, but with Mum still on my mind I greeted them warmly, gratefully, as she would have done, before going to the kitchen, where more familiar faces were busy taking cling film off sandwiches, boiling the kettle. Jennie and Angie turned as I came in; gave me sad little smiles. Perhaps she'd met him, I thought with a start as I went to the fridge. I stopped, in the light of the open door, heart pounding. Perhaps Mum was even now up there shaking hands with Phil, on a cloud somewhere? I felt a hot flush creep up my neck. I hoped not. I could see her lovely generous smile, see her being studiously warm and kind to him, but, underneath, might she be thinking: heavens, who's this? Whatever happened to Ben?

"Are you all right, Poppy?" Jennie was at my elbow, peering into my face. I seemed to have dropped the milk bottle. It was flooding in a white lake all over the terracotta floor. Someone else, Angie, was quickly wiping it up, crouching in an elegant black shift dress and heels. I saw them exchange a concerned glance.

"Hm?" I came to. "Oh. Yes. Fine. Sorry about that."

Peggy and the children arrived from across the road. The children ran about screeching, darting between adult legs, overexcited to see so many people in their house. Peggy swept in and positioned herself on a stool by my Aga, her usual spot. Once obviously beautiful, she'd kept the streaky blonde hair and the skinny figure and today was in leggings, pixie boots, a long black polo-necked jumper and bohemian beads. She chain-smoked and watched me carefully, her small smile ominously irreverent.

"So everyone's making themselves very busy?" she observed in her gravelly way, as if a laugh was barely suppressed.

"I know, aren't they kind?" I said, ignoring the inference. Much as I adored Peggy I wasn't sure this was the moment for her refreshing take on life. "Oh, Angie, I thought we'd have the sausage rolls later, after the sandwiches have been…Oh." Angie had already swept through to the sitting room on a waft of scent.

"When you're bereaved, people behave as if you can't see or hear," Peggy told me. "It's as if you've been in a tremendous accident."

I ignored her and went to get some more milk from the fridge. As I poured it into a jug, Jennie looked doubtful. "I've smelled it," I told her. "It's fine, just a bit creamy."

"They like to have something to do," Peggy murmured. "Makes them feel useful. Takes their mind off you."

Jennie got a fresh bottle of milk from the fridge, busily poured the first one away, then refilled the jug.

"And anyway," Peggy concluded, "they don't know what to say to you."

"No one ever does at a funeral," said Jennie.

"Particularly one like this," remarked Peggy darkly.

I was glad when Angie's teenage girls burst in, looking windswept and gorgeous: flowing hair, tiny skirts.

"Hi, Poppy. Oh God, I'm so sorry about Phil." Clarissa flung her arms around me. "Poor you."

"And I'm so sorry we couldn't come to the funeral, the train took literally hours." Felicity hugged me too.

Lovely, sweet girls with soft hair and beautiful manners, they knew exactly what to say, exactly how to behave, courtesy of a full-time mother and expensive boarding school. I hugged them back, hoping for the same for Clemmie one day, hoping to enable her.

"Obviously he couldn't get them here earlier," their mother remarked sourly, coming back in with her empty sausage roll plate. She banged it down on the side and hugged her daughters. "Oh no, it would be too much trouble to get out of bed and get them to the station on time. Too much of an inconvenience."

Her daughters looked strained, even their pretty manners not stretching to a response to this, a reference to their father, Angie's estranged husband, Tom, a delightful, twinkly-eyed charmer, who, a year ago, had succumbed to the charms of Angie's girl groom. In fact he'd done more than succumb and the pair of them were now ensconced in a cottage in Dorset, where the girls had clearly just come from. Uncomfortable, they stole silently into the next room.

Tom's sudden defection had shattered this perfect, enviable family and Angie had gone from being a beautiful, slightly pampered woman who shopped in Knightsbridge, played tennis on her court in the summer and hunted her horses in the winter, to yet another abandoned wife who hadn't seen it coming. Hitherto, her housework, garden and horses had all been seen to—and, it transpired, her husband—but if anyone had considered her spoiled, nobody would have wished this on her. The shock had aged her overnight and she'd looked all of her forty-one years. But Angie was a fighter, and recently she was better dressed than ever, more beautifully made-up—even when popping to the village shop for bread—although you didn't have to look hard to spot the pain which flashed across those limpid blue eyes, or the tension around the full glossy mouth. Her daughters seemed as confident and charming as ever, but I couldn't conceive that the ripples hadn't reached them, and Angie told me sadly that they had: they were more tearful down the phone on a Sunday night from school, more demanding. And those ripples would surely reach

Clemmie and Archie soon too, I thought in panic, as they felt their own father's absence. Experienced their own void. At least Clarissa and Felicity had had a family unit for a good number of years; at least it had seen them well into their teenage years. Suddenly the enormity of my children's abandonment dawned on me.

"You don't mind them coming, do you?" Angie asked me anxiously.

I stared at her, uncomprehending.

"I've only got them for one day, thanks to Tom throwing his weight around and saying he wanted to see them. They have to go back to school after lunch."

I came to. "Of course not, I'm thrilled. And mine will be delighted."

I watched Clemmie's eyes light up at the sight of them. She threw herself at Clarissa's legs. Frankie, on the other hand, bit her thumbnail and looked guarded. I turned. Forced myself on.

"Now, what else needs to go through?"

"Nothing," drawled Peggy. "It's all going like clockwork. Everyone's very busy."

"Yes, well, you're not, so why don't you take these round?" Angie put a plate of sausages in her hands, knowing Peggy's mischief-making of old. "Is she being a pain?" she asked when Peggy, sliding off her stool and disappearing with a sly smile, was out of earshot.

I shrugged. "You know Peggy."

"I do. No social code. When Tom went, she said I'd handed Tatiana to him on a plate," she said grimly.

I was silenced, because of course we had all thought that. When Angie employed a smiling, honey-haired, heavily breasted maiden from Auckland to muck out her horses and live in her cottage, we'd all wondered what planet she was on. And then watched in horror as Angie had gone off to yoga on a Monday, and bridge on a Thursday. The curtains in Tatiana's bedroom would close almost before Angie's car was out of the drive. Peggy hadn't known, otherwise she certainly would have told her, and by the time Jennie and I had had endless cups of coffee and dithered and discussed and were honestly just about to break the news—it was too late. Angie was left in the gorgeous Queen Anne manor on the edge of the village with its bell tower and tennis court and gables, while Tom ravaged his nubile New Zealander in the horrifically sexy-sounding village of Bustle-under-Winkwood. Satisfyingly, when the pair of them traveled all the way to New Zealand to tell her parents the good news and then returned, she hadn't been allowed back in the country. But that didn't last long; she winkled her way in eventually, just as she had into Angie's home, and her husband's heart.

"You know what Peggy said to me when we heard about Phil?" Angie paused to turn and warm her bottom on the Aga.

"I bet you wish it had been Tom?" hazarded Jennie.

"Exactly."

"And do you?" I asked, wondering where I'd put the cake knife, if I ever had one.

"Of course." Angie raised her chin. In the light, her lovely, sculpted face was fretted with fine lines. She shook back her flaming red-gold hair. "It would be so much neater, wouldn't it? No messy stepmother only a fraction older than my daughters, no drifting between two houses. I'm deeply jealous. And look at all the sympathy you get." She waved her hand at the gathering in the next room, the flowers, the cards. "All I get is—well, of course she had it coming to her."

"That's not true," muttered Jennie, knowing it was.

"And on a more personal note, if I can't have my man," Angie went on, "I certainly don't see why anyone else should."

"Whereas, you see, I wouldn't mind," Jennie said airily. "I'd quite like Dan to live elsewhere and just visit me at weekends. Someone else could wash his dirty underpants, sort through the insurance claims, the unpaid bills."

"No one believes you, Jennie," I told her.

"Ah, but that's because you don't think I've got it in me," she said, dark eyes suddenly flashing. "Don't think I'll wake up one morning—when the next Troy incident occurs—and say, 'Enough!'"

This, a reference to last Christmas, when Dan, driving home from work after a boozy lunch, pranged his car into a crash barrier on the A41. Sensing he was too pissed to call the AA, he'd left his immobilized vehicle on the hard shoulder and proceeded to walk home. He'd reckoned without a passing motorist calling the police, though, and soon the nearest patrol car—a dog handler, as it happened, complete with Alsatian named Troy—had found Dan's abandoned vehicle. In moments they were out of their car and tailing Dan across country. Knowing his house to be literally over the next hill, Dan was taking the scenic route back to the village where, coincidentally, on that moonlit night, the entire population had gathered around the Christmas tree on the green to sing carols. All of a sudden Dan, in the shaky beam of his pursuer's torch, in a pinstriped suit, briefcase flapping, ran hell for leather over the hill toward us, an Alsatian on his heels. As the handler shouted, "Get him, Troy!" Troy did, and with his children watching wide-eyed on the green, Dan was brought down by his trouser leg, pinned until a back-up police van arrived, then bundled, limping, unceremoniously into the back of it.

"Don't think I won't leave him if a scenario like that ever unfolds in front of the children again," Jennie trembled. "Everyone has their breaking point."

The three of us were in a row against the Aga now—a common enough sight in this kitchen—hovering where we shouldn't be, least of all me. Three women who'd shared a lot over the years, each with a few more lines around the eyes, each with a ubiquitous glass in hand.

"I've done my bit," Peggy announced, coming back to join us. She tossed the empty plate on the side and resumed her place on the stool, lighting up again.

Four women.

"Who's he talking to?" asked Jennie after a moment, craning her neck to peer next door. We watched as Dan tried to crack a nut which clearly wasn't cracking.

"Phil's sister," I told them. "If I tell you she hasn't laughed since 2006 you'll know what he's up against."

Sour Cecilia, her plain, scrubbed face mystified, was on the receiving end of Dan's charm offensive, a practiced stream of anecdotal wit which he usually unleashed on pretty secretaries at work who'd lapse into fits of giggles.

"I'd better rescue her," Jennie sighed, putting down her glass.

"Do not," Peggy told her, staying her arm. "Do her good. She's a pain in the tubes. I've already had two minutes with her. And your Dan's going the extra mile as usual."

It probably didn't help Jennie that we all loved Dan.

"And that, presumably, is the mother," Angie murmured, as an older, but more handsome version of Cecilia hoved into view.

"Don't let her see me!" I squeaked, shrinking back behind Peggy. "I've done my bit. Hours and hours on the phone last week, and then a whole day down in Kent with the pair of them. I'm not doing any more."

"Good for you," agreed Peggy. "Your Dad's not one to let a mouth like a cat's arse put him off, though, is he?"

We watched as my father, having returned from his drinks run to hand round gin and tonics with bonhomie, succumbing as ever to his urge to make a party go, sidled up to Marjorie, clearly of the opinion he'd met her somewhere before, which of course he had, at our wedding.

"It's Margaret, isn't it?" he boomed. For a small man Dad's got a very loud voice.

"Marjorie." She tensed, visibly.

"That's it. Weren't you at the Gold Cup a while back? In a box with the McLeans?"

"I was not," she said tightly.

He gave it some thought. "Didn't we have a dance at the Fosbury-Weston's once?"

Her mouth all but disappeared. "We did not. I'm Philip's mother."

It was pretty to watch. It all came flooding back to Dad. The wedding reception down the road at the country club where he'd greeted her jovially from the top step of that grand house, tightly up-holstered as she was in purple silk, a fascinator on her head. A fascinator's a strange little hat, and this one had a peacock perched aloft, but as he'd lunged to embrace her, the peacock's antennae had somehow become involved in his buttonhole, which the florist had surrounded with some netted confection, so that her head became locked to his chest. A grim struggle had ensued: Marjorie silent, Dad hooting with laughter as he descended the step—which didn't help, rendering Marjorie bent double—then he roared, "She can't get enough of me!"

"My fascinator!" Marjorie had yelped, clutching her hat, which was nailed to her head.

"Why thank you," Dad had quipped back, eyebrows wagging.

Cecilia had finally rushed with nail scissors to part them and Marjorie had stood back panting and unamused, hands clenched at her sides like a boxer.

As her identity was now revealed, Dad looked desperately at Dan, but Dan had been struggling for a good ten minutes with these two and had watched helplessly as my father had flown into their web.

"Lovely…party?" said Dad, in despair.

"Isn't it?" agreed Dan.

Marjorie and Cecilia looked aghast.

"I mean…as these things go," added Dad, waving his hand lamely.

Dan gazed bleakly into his beer; my father at his feet.

The four of us lined up on the Aga viewed this little vignette with interest.

"Those two are the only men in that room who belong to us," Jennie observed. "Take a long hard look, girls. That's what we've ended up with. That's what's left for us in the man pool. Two men still in short pants. No offense, Poppy."

"None taken," I assured her.

"But would you want any of the rest?" Angie murmured.

We took a sip of wine and surveyed the throng thoughtfully. We liked this sort of question.

"I wouldn't mind a crack at Angus Jardine," Peggy said at length.

She was playing to the gallery but we all gasped dutifully. Angus Jardine was the silver-haired, silken-tongued husband of Sylvia, queen bee of the village, who'd praised Phil's bell ringing skills. Retired from the City, where he'd been a big fish at Warburg's, he now just swished his tail contentedly in his river-fronted rectory. He was very much out of bounds.

"You hussy, Peggy," Angie told her.

"I said a crack. Once I'd got him I'm fairly sure I wouldn't want him. The word is he's stingy as hell, a finger of whisky is literally that. And anyway, don't tell me you haven't got a crush on Passion-fueled Pete," Peggy retorted.

"I might have," Angie agreed equably, "but he's not here, is he? You said anyone in that room."

"Oh, we can digress," Peggy told her. "Jennie?"

"You mean hypothetically?"

"Of course hypothetically. This is a wake, dear heart. We're not suggesting you jump anyone right now."

Jennie hesitated. Just a moment too long, I thought. I turned, surprised. "Nah," she said, sinking into her wine. "You know me. I'm off men, full stop."

"Poppy?" Peggy asked smoothly.

I blinked. "Oh, don't be ridiculous," I spluttered. I seized a plate of fairy cakes and stalked, irritated, into the next room. "I've just buried my husband!"

"Quite," I heard Peggy say softly as I left.

Chapter Four

DEATH HAS A WAY of sorting the men from the boys. Some people kept their distance, fearing they'd trigger emotion, be responsible for a nasty scene. There were those who'd walk right around the pond on the green just to avoid me, and if they did have to pass me, they would scuttle on by, heads down. Men, mostly. Others couldn't resist bringing it up at every opportunity. Outside the village shop, for instance, at the school gates, they would positively leap the pond to be by my side. Women, mostly. They'd lay caring hands on my arm: "How are you? Are you all right, Poppy, are you coping?" Looking right into my eyes. Too much sometimes, but so hard to get right. Then there were those who cut the crap and made lasagne for you, picked up the kids, were keen to set you back on track, genuinely wanting to help. Friends, mostly. And Jennie in particular.

Some weeks after the funeral she burst in through my back door on a blast of cold air and let it slam behind her. "Right, money," she announced firmly, putting a blue casserole dish on the side.

"Money?" I turned to her abstractedly, sitting as I was at the kitchen table in my dressing gown, staring into space as Archie had his morning sleep. I did a lot of that, these days.

"Have you thought about it?"

"Not really," I said dully.

"Well, did he have much?" she asked impatiently, flicking the kettle on behind her and sitting opposite me, still in her coat. "Were you doing OK, or was it seat-of-the-pants stuff, like me and Dan? Smell of an oily rag?"

Dan was self-employed, and now that the recession had bitten hard, seemed to go less and less to London. Perhaps people were drinking less wine? I hadn't mentioned it.

"No, I think we were doing OK. I mean, there was always enough in my account and I did very well on my…"

"Housekeeping," Jennie finished drily.

Jennie had always been rather scathing about Phil's financial arrangement whereby he put a certain amount into a monthly account for me, out of which I paid all household expenses.

"But what if you want a new coat or something?" she'd say.

Jennie and Dan had a joint account from which they both helped themselves, not that there was anything in it, as Jennie would remark tartly.

"Well, I either save a bit each week, or I ask him. He'd probably say yes," I'd say uncomfortably as her eyes would grow round.

"Yes, but it's the whole idea that you have to ask. It's so nineteen-fifties."

"It's his money," I'd say defensively. "At least you earn a bit, Jennie." Jennie was a cook and rustled up dinner parties for friends, food for freezers, that sort of thing. "He earns every penny of ours."

"Well, I won't go into the fact that you've given up a career to raise his children," she'd say, "or that my children are at school so I *can* work, and you've still got a baby so can't," and I was glad she didn't. And in turn didn't go into the fact that Phil called my monthly allowance my salary. I could hear her squeal of horror at twenty paces.

Now, though, it seemed I might not get away with keeping too much dark. Jennie had that determined look on her face which meant she intended to get to the bottom of something.

"Did he have a life insurance policy?"

"I've no idea."

"Poppy, has all this completely knocked the stuffing out of you?"

"What d'you mean?"

"Well, even the most grief-stricken widow might, in an anxious moment, have wondered whether her chickens were going to be provided for. Are you going to get dressed today, incidentally?"

I glanced down at my toweling robe. "D'you think I should?"

"I do, as a matter of fact; you didn't yesterday. Who took Clemmie to school this morning?"

"Alice's mum picked her up for me. Has done for a bit."

"Right. Good. But…well, brush your teeth at least, won't you?" she said awkwardly.

I shrugged. So demanding. And so many questions.

She swallowed. Licked her lips for patience. "OK, Pops, back to basics. Money. Where did Phil keep his papers?"

"In there." I pointed vaguely behind me, through the open kitchen door to the sitting room, where a walnut bureau sat under the bay window.

"Would you mind if I…?"

"Be my guest."

She was in like a rat up a drainpipe. Shimmying out of her coat and tossing it en route on the sofa, she hurried across the sitting room and spent the next half hour getting very busy. I watched her flicking through his files, which, typical of Phil, were organized and methodical, but which somehow, even though I'd walked across to the desk a few times and stared at it, I hadn't been able to face opening. I turned and resumed my contemplation of the tiny back garden, the sheep in the field beyond. All ewes now, grazing peacefully. Were they happy to see the back of Shameful, I wondered? Or was any man, demanding or otherwise, better than nothing? They looked pretty content to me, munching away out there.

Behind me I could hear the rustle of papers as Jennie burrowed deeper. I sat on. On the one occasion I did glance around, it was to see Angie peering through the sitting-room window from the road, perfectly plucked eyebrows raised inquiringly under her fur hat. Jennie gave her a quick thumbs-up. Angie nodded and swept by. Apart from the kitchen clock ticking and the occasional snuffle of my darling Archie through the baby alarm, the house was silent.

At length she came bustling back, brandishing bits of paper.

"Right. Well, the good news is, he did appear to have a life insurance policy, but I have no idea what's in it. He also appears to have had a solicitor, who I'm sure can tell you more."

"Oh, good." I tried to raise some enthusiasm.

I looked beyond her. Funny. I'd never noticed that damp patch on the kitchen wall. I might have to put a picture on that.

"No will—at least, not that I can find—but that's quite normal. It's probably lodged with the solicitor."

"Ah."

"Shall I make you an appointment?" she said impatiently.

"Is that necessary?"

"Yes, I think it is. You'll have a lot to talk about. Sometime this week?"

"Couldn't it wait?"

"No it couldn't. I'll have the kids for you."

She'd already whipped out her mobile. Punched out a number which she'd gleaned from the letterhead in her hand. Why couldn't I make the appointment, I wondered. Because she thought I wouldn't do it, perhaps. Would I? Hard to say. The feverish adrenaline which had rendered me almost manic a few weeks ago, arranging the funeral like a whirling dervish, putting a notice welcoming all comers in the village shop, rushing from one thing to the next—beetling away from my husband's grave—had left me now. Something else had moved in. I felt very cold. Very numb. Had done for over a week now. Ten days, to be precise. Ever since that knock upon the door. It was as if I needed to sit here forever, all day, just to conserve energy. I managed quite well when the children were around, forced myself to be chirpy, but most evenings, and in the mornings when Archie was asleep, I sat here, in this chair.

"Right, well, that's all organized. Tomorrow at four. OK?" Jennie went to pocket her mobile, but it rang. "Hello…" She swung away to hide her face. "Yes…yes, I've done it," she said quietly as if the eagle had landed. "Pretty low still, I'm afraid."

"Who was that?" I asked absently.

"Um, Peggy. Wanted to know if I was, er…going to the shops. Now, shall I put it in your calendar?"

"If you must."

Clearly. Within a twinkling she'd flicked over a page muttering something about me being a week behind, and was penciling it in, then underlining it for good measure.

"OK?"

"Couldn't be better."

"And I've put a shepherd's pie in the fridge for you. That's if you're absolutely sure you won't come over."

"Absolutely sure."

Jennie asked me over pretty much every night, as did Angie and Peggy. I'd been to Jennie's a lot in the first few weeks, taken the baby alarm with me, but recently I was happy with my chair.

"Although I couldn't help noticing there was one in there already."

"One what?"

"Shepherd's pie."

Ah. She'd put it there at the weekend. And I'd forgotten to give it to the children.

I sighed. "I like crackers, Jennie. So does Clemmie. But thanks. I appreciate it, really I do."

She gave me that hassled, worried look I'd seen a lot lately. I pulled my dressing gown around me and tucked a lank piece of hair behind my ear. I did hope she was all right. Had Dan been stopped for speeding again? He'd only just got his license back. I must remember to ask her. To inquire. But somehow, dredging up words about anything these days was hard. Where did they come from, all those words? I'd see women gossiping in the street—what about? Such an effort. Like washing my hair. Or going to the village shop. God, it was miles, wasn't it? I'd forgotten we lived so far away. Lucky Jennie, who was just that bit closer. Five yards at least.

"And I thought I'd walk up to the nursery with you later."

"You don't have any children at the nursery."

Jennie's children were older: Jamie, twelve, and Hannah, seven, were both at the local school, which didn't chuck out until three-thirty.

"I know, but Leila could do with the exercise. And I daren't go back into the forest with her."

Leila had been known to chase the deer up there, an offense which carried a fifty-pound penalty from the deer warden, who had threatened to shoot to kill next time. "Can I watch?" had been Jennie's riposte. I'd been with Jennie on this last occasion, when, as usual, she'd foolishly let the dog off the lead, then, as usual, spent the next half-hour crashing through undergrowth hissing, "Leila! Leila, you bitch, come here!" Not too loud, you understand, so as not to alert the warden. We'd crashed about some more, when suddenly, in the distance, there'd been an ominous rumble of thundering hooves. To get the full Serengeti effect you have to imagine the stampeding does, the whites of their eyes, the clouds of dust as we flattened ourselves against a tree, pulling Archie's pushchair in sharpish, and then, in their wake, an Irish terrier, shooting us a delighted look, tongue lolling, galloping joyously. Obviously the warden was crashing through the bracken moments later in his Land Rover, puce in the face with rage, and obviously Jennie was given a fine on the spot and sensibly hadn't been back. But still, a walk to the nursery, two minutes up the hill, hardly constituted exercise for our Leila. And don't be deceived by the terrier word, incidentally. With Irish before it, it's more like a small horse.

I sighed. "OK," I said obediently, as I tended to these days.

"And then, later on, I thought you might like to come to choir practice with me."

"Really? Why?" I felt alarmed.

"Because we're singing the Gloria tonight, and you'll enjoy that."

"But I don't sing."

"Anyone can sing. And anyway, I've stood next to you in church and you've got perfect pitch. Frankie's going to baby-sit for you."

"Right," I said flatly. Sing. I couldn't remember how to talk.

Sure enough, as I set off with Archie an hour or so later, Jennie appeared miraculously from her front door with a straining Leila— I'd swear Peggy's curtain twitched opposite—and we set off up the hill. We collected Clemmie and walked back down the hill, all of which took about fifteen minutes, a little longer than usual as Jennie had a furtive word with Miss Hawkins, but still not enough for Leila, who needed a good hour.

As Jennie said good-bye, she bent down to talk to Clemmie.

"That's a pretty dress, Clem."

"I know. It's got a rabbit on the front."

"It has. And a bit of gravy. You were wearing it yesterday, weren't you, darling?"

"Yes, and every day. Six. I've counted. Mummy said I could."

"Good, good." She straightened up. Looked anxious again. I must remember to ask about Dan.

"Seven o'clock, then?"

"Hm?"

"Choir practice. I'll send Frankie round, but I'll have to meet you there because I need to take Jamie to scouts."

"Righto."

Submissive. Punch bag. Best way.

The children and I had just about finished our tea when Frankie appeared sometime later. She was a sulky, skinny girl with a washed-out face, not helped by heavy, dark eye make-up, and over-long, bleached blonde hair. She was at the local comp where everyone tended to look like that, but where had that sensitive, rather pretty eight-year-old gone, I wondered, as she sat in a heap at the kitchen table, picking gloomily at her black nail varnish. Archie grinned and banged the table enthusiastically. He responded well to her sulky charms.

"Hi, Arch." She took his soggy offering of a masticated biscuit and his eyes widened delightedly. "Crackers and lemonade, yum. We're never allowed that for tea."

The children beamed proudly.

"Yesterday we had a hoola-hoop sandwich," Clemmie in formed her grandly.

"Good for you, Clem. Why bother with the old five a day, eh?" She turned to me. "Jennie says you're going to choir practice with her. That's a bit sad, isn't it? You'll be doing the church flowers with her next."

"Your Mum's very busy, Frankie," I told her. "And someone's got to do it."

"Why?" she said belligerently. "No one would notice if there weren't any flowers in church, would they?"

"Some people would."

"People like Jennie. So she does it for herself, in fact."

I could see she was pleased with that. Was probably storing it away to deploy on her stepmum later, when Jennie came home, tired. Normally I'd defend her, tell Frankie if everyone thought like that there wouldn't be any community in the village, but somehow I couldn't be bothered. Couldn't raise the energy.

"It's like dusting," she was saying. "She's got this thing, right, that you don't do it anymore, don't hoover either, but what does it matter? So what if the dust builds up? Who was it said it gets to a certain level and doesn't get any thicker?"

"Quentin Crisp," I said distantly. Dust? Why were we talking about dust? Oh, as in ashes to ashes.

"You see?" she said admiringly. "You know things like that. 'Cause you read, which is more than Jennie does. Who was he, anyway?"

"The last of the stately homos. At least that's what he called himself. D'you want a cracker, Frankie?"

"No, you're all right. You'd better go, though. She'll get stressy if you don't turn up. D'you want to brush your hair?"

"No, thanks. Do you?"

"Not really. Shall I do Clemmie's?"

"Sure."

My daughter slipped down shyly from the table and ran off to get her Barbie hairbrush. Such was her admiration of Frankie, she could hardly speak for the first five minutes of her visit. I got heavily to my feet and went to pluck my coat from the back of the door.

"School breaks up soon," Frankie said abruptly, apropos of nothing. "Half-term. Can't wait."

"So it does," I agreed. Ages away, actually; but for a sixteen-year-old it was like a drink in the desert. A reprieve from the daily grind winking away in the distance: lie-ins in the mornings, night life in the evenings. Never quite the reality, obviously: lashings of rain and endless boredom with the odd gnomic exchange with an equally bored mate in McDonald's, but the idea was good. Like most ideas. Marriage. Children. In fact, wasn't most of the joy in life derived from the planning, the theory? I must remember that. Plan more, do less.

"So what are you going to do with yourself this holiday?" I forced myself to say conversationally. Never let it be said I couldn't string two words together, something I'm sure I heard Yvonne in the shop say about me to Mrs. Pritchard, as I left her premises earlier today with my pint of milk.

"I thought I might get pregnant."

I was shrugging my coat on at the door, facing away from her. I turned.

"Why not? Mum did it."

"Jennie didn't—"

"No, my mum. She was sixteen."

"Oh."

We stared at one another. She gave a hint of a smile. "You're not that far gone, are you? Not completely mental."

Ah. Shock tactics. "Nice one, Frankie."

"Still, I might, though," she said defensively.

"Got anyone in mind?"

"No," she said sulkily, deflated in an instant, alive to the poverty of her plan. I wished I hadn't asked. "There's Jason Crowley at school, but he'd never shack up with me. Just want a quick shag. That's the whole point," she said, dark eyes flashing.

"What, a quick shag?"

"No, to shack up, get out of there." She jerked her head next door. "Or there's Mr. Hennessy, my biology teacher; he's really fit, but he's got a wife and kids, which isn't ideal, is it?"

"Not…ideal." Where was I going? I stared at the door. Oh, yes, church.

"Single mothers get priority with council flats, though," she told me. "You jump the queue."

I sighed. "Frankie…"

"Anyway, he doesn't fancy me. Mr. Denis does—physics—but he's properly weird; he fancies everyone. Or I suppose I could nick your new intended? Come along to choir practice."

"What?"

"Nothing."

She got to her feet as Clemmie came back with her brush and a mirror from my dressing table, struggling under the weight.

"Oh, salon stuff!" Frankie relieved her of the mirror and hoisted it onto the table. "A French pleat, madam, or shall we cut it all short?"

"All short!" sang Clemmie, jumping up and down, ecstatic with excitement.

Frankie grinned. "Nah, yer mum might notice that. Then again," she grimaced and shot me a look, "in her state she might not. Here, give me that." She took the brush from her. "We're going to go for a pleat, right? And then we'll give Archie a comb-over."

My son had yet to collect much hair, but what he had was long, wispy and very much around the edges. Archie beamed and offered her some more cracker, clenched and soggy in his fist. She took it and put it on her tongue, which was pierced.

"D'you dare me?"

Clemmie nodded. Frankie swallowed. The children roared with laughter, delighted.

"Don't underestimate those harpies, though," she went on as I turned to go out of the back door. "Once they put their heads together, you're sunk. Trust me, I should know. Oh, and you might want to take your dressing gown off under your coat. They'll need smelling salts if they see that." I glanced down to where two inches of pale blue towelling protruded from my navy reefer. "Then again, you might not. Personally I like the layered look. But our Jennie's got ever so bourgeois recently. She's not so into the Quentin Crisp philosophy."

I took her advice, removed the dressing gown, replaced my coat, and putting one foot in front of the other, went off down the road to choir practice. In a small corner of my mind I was dimly aware that Frankie had given me a searching look as I'd left and, for one crazy moment, I'd almost turned and shared with her. Almost come back in, shut the door and blurted out my troubles, just as she'd blurted hers. I hadn't, though. Of course I hadn't. Because there was no one I could tell. Not even Jennie. Not because I'd be mortified—I would—but because once it was out, I'd have no control over it. Dan would know. Then someone in the pub would know. And my children, so damaged already, must never know. Never hear from someone at school. I clenched my fists fiercely in my coat pockets in resolve. It must be a closely guarded secret. My secret. No one must ever know that their father, my husband, hadn't found me enough, emotionally. That he'd had another life with another woman. That she'd been to see me ten days ago, paid me a visit. That she'd been there at his funeral and I'd never known. Been in our lives and I'd never known. Filled a void in Phil's life I hadn't been able to. They must never know that their father had been unhappy, desperate. It was my shame and I must bear it alone. Tears fled down my cheeks, soaking my face as I walked on.

Chapter Five

CAREFULLY WIPING MY FACE as I stood on the church step, I gave myself a moment. Breathed in and out deeply. Then I pushed open the heavy door. The choir were already assembled in their stalls up by the altar, but then I was ten minutes late, having lingered to talk to Frankie. Most people I knew: friends and neighbors, who turned and smiled as I came in. But as I let the heavy oak door swing shut behind me, I wondered what on earth I was doing here. I hadn't been in since Phil's funeral, and the familiar smell of cold stone, candle wax, and damp, which I usually found rather comforting, seemed to ambush my senses as if a hood had been slipped stealthily over my head. I felt even more breathless than usual. I turned and with a shaky hand reached for the door handle again. I could pretend I'd forgotten something, then not come back. But the handle was stiff, and anyway, Jennie was beside me in a moment, having slipped out of her stall and down the aisle. My arm was in her viselike grip.

"Good, good, you're here," she purred. "We haven't started yet because we're waiting for the organist. Come along, I've saved you a place."

She frogmarched me down the aisle in seconds, which wasn't hard, because our church is tiny. And rather beautiful, or so I usually thought. This evening, though, the domed ceiling with its rows of blackened beams seemed ominously lofty and towering; the figure in the stained-glass window, St. John the Baptist, I think, less kindly and benevolent, more threatening as he turned to glare at me over his

rippling shoulder in his rags, eyes flashing. Angie was beckoning hard
from the back row. No Peggy, but then she was a firm nonbeliever.

"Papist nonsense."

"It's C of E, Peggy."

"Still. All those smells and bells."

"Not in the Anglican church."

"I've got my own, thank you very much." And she'd puff on her
ciggie and tinkle her beads.

"Hello, Poppy."

Molly, a widow of about seventy, was sitting in the front row
with her carer. She looked a bit disheveled and smiled toothlessly at
me, most of her tea down her front, shaky paws, slippers on. Molly
wasn't quite like other budgerigars.

"Hello, Molly."

"Would you like to sit beside me, dear?"

"Of course." I moved to do so.

"No—no, because Angie and I have saved you a place, haven't
we?" Jennie's grip tightened on my arm and she shot me, then Molly,
a look.

But, actually, I had a feeling I didn't necessarily want to be
squeezed between my two best friends tonight, and anyway, Molly
would be hurt. I sat firmly where I was. Jennie hesitated—I think for
a moment she considered heaving me bodily to my feet and bundling
me away—then she rolled her eyes and shrugged helplessly at Angie,
who rolled her eyes back. She sat down huffily beside me. This put
her next to Jed Carter, a local farmer from down the valley. Molly
wasn't the only one with an appendage this evening. Jed didn't go
anywhere without his sheepdog, Spod, a randy old boy lying at his
feet who was in love with Leila. The joy in Spod's eyes as he sniffed
Jennie's ankle, got a whiff of his beloved, and realized he could shut
his eyes and pretend her left leg was Leila was hard to describe.

"You see, why we don't sit here?" hissed Jennie as Spod attached himself to her like a limpet, eyes glazed, humping hard. She shook him off furiously.

"Sorry."

"And Spod's not the only reason, as you'll discover to your cost," she muttered grimly, as Sue Lomax, flaxen and inclined to furious blushes, took up her position at the lectern, tapping it smartly for our attention. We obediently got to our feet. Sue, or Saintly Sue as she was surreptitiously known, was attractive in a buxom way, but preachy. Ex-head girl, county lacrosse player and choir mistress, Sue was an all-round goody-goody—although Jennie and I privately thought her frustrated and man-hungry. She cleared her throat and looked important.

"Right. Welcome, everyone. Now since you're all here, I think we'll crack on with just Ron on the piano because Mr. Chambers has just sent me a text saying he'll be a bit late." She gazed down at the phone in her hand with a look I'd seen very recently in someone else's eyes. Ah yes, Spod's.

"The organist," Jennie informed me importantly.

So crack on we did, straight into Mozart's Gloria, with Just Ron, who played mostly at the pub, thumping away valiantly. Everyone belted it out, myself included, surprisingly, bounced as I was into behaving, into opening my mouth and remembering it from school. It was quite a shock, and not altogether unpleasant. I even felt a sensation approaching the warmth of blood in my veins. Molly was a bit distracting beside me, though, because she was singing something different.

"She's singing 'Nights in White Satin,'" I muttered to Jennie when Sue tapped the lectern to stop us because Ron had lost his place.

"Always does," muttered back Jennie. "But she's been in the choir for thirty years, so what can you do? We just don't sit next to her," she added pointedly.

At that moment the church door flew open.

"Oh, good—you made it, Luke!" Saintly Sue swung around delighted, even more flushed than usual, and her color was always high.

A tall, rather attractive sandy-haired man in jeans, a biscuit-colored linen jacket and gold-rimmed specs bounded down the aisle.

"New organist," Angie leaned forward from behind to murmur in my ear, as we lunged to catch our hymn sheets, which were fluttering up like a flock of doves on the blast of cold air.

"Sorry I'm late," he said, bouncing toward us with a wide smile. "Bit of a cock-up at work and I couldn't get away." There was a definite puppyish charm: long legs, floppy hair, eyes that glinted merrily from behind the specs in an open, friendly face.

"Oh, no, not at all," purred Sue, smoothing back her hair and straightening her blue angora jumper over her ample bosom. "We were slightly early, in fact. But then I'm always a bit keen!"

It might not have been entirely what she meant to say—Jennie sniggered—but I find that often happens to me, and as her hand went to her darkening throat, I sympathized.

"Well, I'll pop up, shall I?" Luke said, after a slight pause during which their eyes met, his slightly more amused than hers. He indicated the organ above us, aloft. "Press on?"

"Oh, yes, *do*," said Sue, as if it was a terrific idea, and one that hadn't occurred to her. "Super!"

"You're all sounding great, by the way," he told us. "I could hear you halfway down the street—wonderful stuff!"

He bestowed on us another winning smile, gathering everyone in, and everyone beamed delightedly back. All except one. I might have remembered how to do the Gloria, but I wasn't up to beaming yet. My mouth did twitch politely, but later, after the event, as I find is often the case these days.

"Rather gorgeous, isn't he?" breathed Jennie lustily in my ear as Luke eased himself into position at the organ. He had a lengthy grace, sensitive fingers poised.

"Not bad," I said non-committally.

"He's fresh out of the Guildhall," Angie billowed from behind into my other ear, as if he were a gleaming trout from the river. "Post-grad, obviously. Just bought a cottage in Wessington. He's in insurance now. Got his own business."

I didn't answer.

"Incredibly charming," she murmured again. "I mean, to talk to." As opposed to what?

"All yours, Angie," I said, turning and managing the first half-smile of the evening. "I'll hold your handbag."

"Me?" She reared back incredulously, hand on heart. "Oh, no, he's far too young for me. He's your age, Poppy." She fluttered her fingers dismissively at me.

I turned back. Shut my eyes. Why had I come? Why wasn't I at home in my chair?

Off we went again, only this time not so successfully. As Ron slipped gratefully out of the side door and back to his pint in the Rose and Crown, Luke, up at the organ, got very busy. So busy we didn't know where we were. All sorts of crashing introductory chords rolled into one another like waves, and we'd ejaculate prematurely only to discover Luke was still building up to something big. Only Molly ploughed on doggedly with her shrill, warbling rendition of the number-one seventies hit for Procol Harem. Molly, and obviously Spod, whose look of glazed lust as Jennie tried to concentrate and forgot to kick him off was close to euphoric. As the organ threatened to climax, Spod, it seemed, was closer.

Afterward, as we walked home, or rather as I was escorted, my friends agreed over my head that we needed more practice.

"Which is fine, because we've got plenty of time. The wedding's not for a few weeks," said Jennie.

"Wedding?" I was surprised to hear my voice.

"Well, that's the whole point, that's what we're practicing for."

"Oh."

"Every Monday," Angie told me firmly. "And don't forget, you're all coming to my house tomorrow."

"Are we?" I felt panicky. "Why?"

"Because we're starting the book club. We told you that a week or so ago, remember?"

Oh, yes, vaguely. But it had been that terrible day. The one when everything had changed. All the clocks stopped. Black Friday. When, suddenly, I hadn't been a widow who was finding hidden reserves and coping really rather marvelously, much to the relief of my friends, but in the blink of an eye, in twenty-five minutes to be precise, had become someone different.

"And I said I'd…?" I felt my way cautiously.

"Come," Angie told me firmly. "Definitely come. And pitch in. Everyone's bringing a few nibbles."

"Well, no, we might do that, actually," Jennie said quickly as they exchanged a glance. Nibbles from me might be a bridge too far.

"When you say everyone…"

"Just the four of us," Angie told me kindly. "Us three and Peggy to begin with. The idea is that this week we'll just meet to discuss and decide who to ask along, what sort of books we'll read, that type of thing."

"Oh."

"Manage that?" asked Jennie gently, as we got to my gate.

I nodded dumbly. Stared at my shoes. Felt my body go rigid as they both embraced me. They bid me goodnight.

I realized, as I went inside, that my two friends were still loitering outside, conferring a moment and talking in hushed whispers behind my hedge. I leaned back on the inside of my front door and counted to ten. Then I peeled myself off and, with an effort, propelled myself toward the sitting room.

Frankie was on her hands and knees at my coffee table, already gathering her schoolbooks from it, stuffing them furtively in her bag. For all her big talk, Frankie harbored subversive tendencies: she was a secret worker who did well at school. I gave her a moment, lingering in the hall, taking off my coat and putting my bag on the table. I was fond of Frankie and knew there were some guilty secrets she wouldn't want Jennie to know.

"Thanks, Frankie," I said, going in and handing her some money as she stood up, swinging her book bag over her shoulder. "Everything OK?"

"Yeah, fine. We played for a bit, then they did their teeth and went straight to sleep. How was your big night out?"

"Oh, huge."

"Good. You look a bit, you know—" she peered at me "—better, actually."

I nodded, unable to speak. Angie and Jennie concerned about me I could handle. Frankie, with her multitude of teenage problems, would reduce me to tears.

When she'd gone, I went upstairs and looked in on my sleeping babes, pushing each of their bedroom doors ajar. Clemmie was on her side, elaborate furrows of tiny plaits decorating her head and culminating in something complicated at the back. Her fist was clenched tightly around her rabbit's ears. Archie, in the next room, was flat on his back, arms flung out like a starfish, mouth open, his wispy hair gathered in a top-knot tied in a pink ribbon on his head, like a Flintstone baby. His intense vulnerability almost made me cry out. My hand went to my throat. I stood for a moment, watching him breathe in and out, noticing the way the moon shone through a gap in his curtains, casting a silver sliver on the opposite wall. Then I turned and went back downstairs to the kitchen. Back to my chair.

On the pinboard on the wall opposite was a photo of Clemmie and her best friend, Alice. It had been taken at the beginning of term in their ballet class, a few days before Phil died. In the days immediately following his death I'd looked at the photo a lot. Two little girls, same ballet shoes, same little pink skirts, same advantages—except now my daughter was changed forever. And she didn't yet know it. Half of her unconditional love had gone, half of her quota to get her through life. I was terrified at how reduced she was. She wasn't the same child in the photograph, and whenever I looked at it, it made me panicky with fear. But then somehow, gradually, as the days, and then the weeks had crept by, I'd managed to control the panic. I'd force myself to think positively, think of people who'd survived this lack of parenting, myself included. Peggy, whose father had died young.

I'd even begun to feel that in some small way I was winning: that we'd be all right, Clemmie, Archie and me. What I hadn't accounted for was my own sudden reduction. The shrinking of my own soul as I'd opened that door, looked into a past I didn't know I had, and realized I wasn't a proper person at all.

Chapter Six

SHE WAS CALLED EMMA. Emma Harding. I remembered her coming up the road through the village. Remembered her little black Mini. A Mini Cooper. A cool car. One that in a vague, unformed sort of way, not that I was particularly into cars, but if I was, I'd quite like, if you know what I mean. And I'd seen it clearly, because I'd been dusting the windowsill at the time, lifting a lamp. It stopped outside my house. Out got Emma, pretty, petite, blonde, her shoulder-length hair swinging as she turned to shut the car door behind her. A white smocky top, jeans, beaded mules. Oh, and a flimsy sparkly scarf round her neck, pale blue and silver: nice. Sort of Monsoony. I watched as she came up the path, surprised it was my house she was approaching. She saw me through the window: stopped and waved uncertainly. I went to the door. I remembered her smile. Shy. Nervous. She was ever so sorry to call unannounced, she said, hands fiddling with the strap of her shoulder bag; she knew this was a terrible time for me.

I frowned. "Sorry, do I…?"

"My name's Emma Harding. I was a friend of Phil's. A good friend."

I didn't think anything of it. She followed me through to the sitting room, and as I turned her eyes finally met mine, so nervous, like a scared rabbit. And I motioned her to sit on the goose-poo sofa and then sat down opposite her, duster still in hand. And in that instant, I knew where I'd seen her before. At the funeral. She'd been crying a lot. Head bowed, hanky to mouth, in a black wool suit, quite elegant. And someone had an arm protectively around her shoulders, one of Phil's cycling friends. His wife, perhaps, I'd thought. Perhaps not. And I'd been rather ashamed because I wasn't crying. Not like that.

She started to speak, in a low, unsteady voice, hands twisting. She and Phil had met at work. They'd tried not to…you know. Had resisted each other for ages in fact, denied the attraction, but at a conference in Manchester…well, it all got out of control, seeing as how they were away from home. And then over the last four years…well, they'd completely fallen in love. And of course there was their cycling, which they did at weekends. Nearly every weekend. And she, Emma, knew it was so wrong, but she wasn't married, you see, wasn't betraying anyone. And Phil was so lonely. So sad.

Emma looked anxiously at me. White-faced. Scared. Fingers in her sparkly scarf in perpetual motion.

"Why are you telling me this?" I managed. Found my voice which was hidden deep in my rib cage. Cowering there.

"Because I know Phil provided for me. I know, in his will, he made a provision, because we'd been together so long, and I want you to know," her voice began to tremble, "I want you to know I don't want any of it."

I stared straight ahead into the school playground where I was standing right now with Archie in his pushchair, waiting for Clemmie. My eyes felt dry and gritty with lack of sleep. I remembered *her* eyes, though: full of grief. Full of proper mourning. And I'd been humming as I'd dusted the window ledge that morning. Just a little bit, but still.

"Mrs. Shilling?" Miss Hawkins was beside me suddenly, her anxious face in mine. "Mrs. Shilling, have you got a moment?"

Clemmie was by her side, holding her teacher's skirt. Eyes downcast, she was sucking her thumb, something she hasn't done during the day for ages. Luckily, Archie was crying in his pushchair; had been for some time.

"I just wanted to talk to you about the other day," Miss Hawkins was saying, having to raise her voice over Archie's wails. "When you forgot to collect Clemmie?"

"I'm sorry, Miss Hawkins, I really need to get Archie home. He wants a bottle."

Such a long sentence, but somehow I got to the end of it. Then silently I took Clemmie's hand, which hadn't instinctively reached for mine, and we set off down the hill, Miss Hawkins's eyes, I knew, boring into my back. Archie was still sobbing, but he cried a lot these days. All morning, sometimes. Perhaps he was missing his sunny mother, wondering who this withdrawn, distrait woman was, this impostor.

When I turned the corner at the bottom, my cottage came into view. A familiar red pick-up was parked outside. It hadn't been there when I set off for the nursery a few minutes ago. It did occasionally rock up without warning, but usually after a gap of a few months, and I'd seen Dad relatively recently, at the funeral. Besides which we'd spoken a bit since. Dad and I were close, but we were self-sufficient souls and I'd imagined we were pretty much familied out. He was emerging from the pick-up—still minus its radiator grill, I noticed, which he'd left in a hedge some years since—in his working wardrobe of breeches, boots and an ancient checked shirt. He turned and waited, hands on his hips, as I came down the lane toward him.

"Hello, love." He looked anxious, his bright blue eyes searching mine.

"Hi, Dad. What are you doing here?"

"Grandpa!" Clemmie's face lit up and she let go of my hand to run to him. He scooped her up, beaming.

"That's my girl! Hey, look at you. Been painting?"

"No, we had ketchup for tea last night."

"Did you, by Jove. Well, you need a flannel. You've got it on your rabbit dress too." He prodded her chest.

"Yes and I'm allowed to wear it every day. But I don't want to wear it tomorrow."

"Wise move, Clem." He put her down.

Archie had stopped crying and was smiling and kicking his legs vigorously in his pushchair in his grandfather's direction. Dad bent to tickle his knees, peering up at me the while.

"Everything all right, love?"

"Fine, thanks," I said as he straightened up to plant a kiss on my cheek. "Coming in?"

"Well, I thought I might."

I turned to open the gate and he followed me up the path. "What are you doing here, anyway?" I asked over my shoulder. "This is a busy time for you, isn't it?"

Dad dealt in horses, hunters in particular, and the beginning of the season was usually frantic. He spent every spare moment getting his mounts fit and then was either showing them off to prospective buyers or sending them out as hirelings to go cub hunting, often accompanying his clients if they were nervous.

He scratched his head. "Oh…I was passing. There's an Irish Draft cross near here I might have a look at. Good blood lines, apparently."

"Oh, right. Where?" I let us in.

"Um…" He cast about wildly and his eyes lit on an estate agent's board opposite. "Dunstable?"

"Dunstable's pretty urban, Dad. In someone's back yard, is it?"

"Something like that."

We went inside.

"Everything all right, Pops?"

"You've already asked me that," I said as he overtook me and crossed busily to open the sitting-room curtains in the darkened room, then stooped on his way back to pick up the ketchup-smeared plates from the carpet. He took them into the kitchen looking anxious. And my dad isn't domestic.

I made him a cup of tea except there wasn't any milk, whilst the children leaped all over him excitedly. I had a feeling he'd come for more than a cup of tea, though, so I flicked *Fireman Sam* onto the little kitchen telly to immobilize my offspring for five minutes and handed them each a chocolate bar. Dad eyed them nervously.

"Lunch?"

"Well, you know. Needs must, occasionally."

Gosh, he looked terrible. Really worried. I did hope the business wasn't in trouble. Dad claimed the recession hadn't hit the horse-trading world, but maybe that was just a line he'd spun me, and maybe it had? Or had he come off one of his green four-year-olds and not told me? I did worry about him still breaking in horses at his age, but the trouble was, both Dad and I were so non-controlling, we couldn't begin to tell each other what to do. Back in the sitting room, we sipped our tea, side by side on the sofa.

"I felt a bit bad abandoning you like that after the funeral," he said at length.

I frowned. This was about as deep as it got. "You didn't abandon me. You just went home."

"I know, but…" He shrugged helplessly. "You know. I could have helped a bit. Should have pre-empted this. Anyway." He swallowed. "'You were always on my mind.'"

My father was a big Elvis fan and, in times of stress, drew heavily on his song lyrics. Things were clearly bad.

"'Little things I should have said or done. I just never took the time.'"

I sighed. "Dad."

"Hm?" He looked at me. Blinked in recognition. "Oh. Right." He nodded. "Well, anyway, I'm here now. Better late than never, I suppose. And Jennie and I wondered if I shouldn't…or if you shouldn't…" He hesitated and I waited, surprised. He and Jennie?

He hadn't seen Jennie since the funeral. "Well, look, love," he said, summoning up something really quite portentous, "what I wondered was, whether you'd like to come and stay for a bit?"

I frowned. "What, at Grotty Cotty?" Dad's cottage was so called because it was unfeasibly chaotic: full of half-cleaned tack and saddle soap, riddled with damp and reeking of a heady combination of horses, dogs, Neats foot oil, socks and whisky. It was an extremely ripe bachelor pad and totally unsuitable for children—who of course loved it—but still.

"That's kind, Dad," I said, speechless. "But no thanks."

"Or I could come here?"

Now I really was concerned. Dad couldn't leave his yard for five minutes, let alone stay the night. The mere fact that he'd dropped in for a cup of tea was quite something. Suddenly I went cold.

"Oh God, Dad, has it all collapsed? The business? Gone tits up?"

"No! No, it's going well, couldn't be better. I sold three eventers last week, one to Mark Todd's yard. No, it's just…well, I'm worried about you." He put his arm around me awkwardly.

"Me?"

"And I'm there for you, love. If you need me."

I nodded, thunderstruck.

"'For my darling, I love you. And I always will.'"

I gazed down at the carpet. "'Love Me Tender'?"

He sighed. "Could be. Anyway," he said, removing his arm, "if you're sure you're all right…" He patted my back tentatively and we sat there in silence. "Um…d'you want me to get the kids some lunch?"

"They've just had it," I said incredulously, convinced I'd already told him that. Hadn't we just had that conversation? Literally moments ago? Now I was really alarmed. Alzheimer's?

Dad got up and took his cup into the kitchen. He also spent ten minutes washing up a toppling tower of crockery already in the sink, which was kind but very unlike him, then he came back looking a bit wretched, and then, finally, he left. As he went down the garden path, I watched from the open doorway. He wasn't looking where he was going and nearly collided with a statuesque middle-aged woman in a tightly belted pea-green coat, spectacles and a purposeful air.

"Ah, hello there." She peered around Dad to address me on the doorstep, her smile not quite reaching her eyes.

"Hello."

"I'm Trisha Newson, from Social Services."

I gazed at her down the path. Dad had gone quite pale.

"Um, could I have a word?" he was muttering, drawing her away and around my little beech hedge. I stood there pondering. Giving it some thought. Suddenly it came to me. Ah yes, Mrs. Harper, next door. She went to the Chiltern Hospital every month in an ambulance, about her veins.

"Next door," I called to them over the hedge, as Dad frogmarched her away. "Mrs. Harper is next door."

They didn't appear to hear me, though, so I shrugged and shut the door. *Fireman Sam* was still going strong in the kitchen, and I knew that particular DVD was good for another hour or so and Clemmie knew how to put another one on after that, so I went upstairs to lie down on the bed for a bit.

That afternoon, against my better instincts, I got up off the bed and paid a visit to Phil's solicitor. I'd hoped Jennie might have forgotten, that it might have slipped her mind, but cometh the hour, cometh the neighbor, bustling up my path well before the appointed meeting. I'd considered being out, or hiding in the cellar and shutting all the curtains, or just point-blank refusing to go, but knowing with a sinking heart any such prevarications would provoke awkward questions, I acquiesced. I felt very much as if I were en route to the gallows, though. Surely this was when the will would be read? Color what was left of my life?

"Would you like me to come in with you?" Jennie asked as we

got the children ready. "There might be a receptionist or someone we could leave the kids with?"

"Absolutely not," I told her, so vehemently I think we were both startled. I straightened up from buckling Clemmie's shoes to stare at her, aware my eyes were glittering.

"OK, Pops," she said gently, "that's fine. I'll wait outside."

I could see her thinking it was the most emotion I'd shown for a while.

Nevertheless she insisted on driving me into town, telling me I'd never find it—I can't think why, it was right next to the town hall, slap bang in the middle of the high street. But apparently I needed to be dropped at the door, wear a certain shirt and skirt she'd picked out, wash my face and brush my hair. So bossy. Clearly the man I was bidden to meet did not have a bossy best friend, though, because not only had he forgotten to brush his hair, he had biscuit crumbs all down his front.

I had to climb a few flights of stairs to achieve his office, and although Jennie was going to sit with the children in the car, in a sudden diversion from the script, Archie had refused to be parted from me and had a shouty-crackers tantrum in the car, so that by the time I'd got to the top of the stairs with my son in my arms, sobbed-out now and quiescent, I was panting rather. A couple of doors faced me with very little clue to the content of the rooms beyond, so I pushed through the nearest one and into a reception area. No receptionist, just a rather messy waiting room with a few magazines strewn around and another couple of doors on the far side. Feeling on the verge of a great escape but knowing Jennie wouldn't be satisfied unless I gave it one last shot—might even bound up the stairs and insist on seeing for herself—I decided to push one of them open and if that didn't yield a solicitor I'd call it a day.

The door was stiff, so I turned and used my shoulder to barge it open, employing slightly too much force so that when I flew through with Archie in my arms, slipping on one of many pieces of paper that littered the carpet, it was in a manner reminiscent of a couple from the Ballet Rambert practising a new and complicated lift. The room was small, and our faltering pirouette ended at a leather-topped desk. Behind it sat a muscular man dipping a Jammy Dodger into a mug of tea. He gazed in astonishment as I spun to a halt. His hair was dark and tousled and in need of a cut, and he had very broad shoulders. He looked like a rugby player who'd been squeezed into a pink shirt for the occasion and was slightly uncomfortable with it. Even in my tuned-out state, I could see he was handsome. He hastily put down the biscuit, brushing a few crumbs from his shirt, and got to his feet, hand extended.

"Oh—er, I'm so sorry, I didn't hear you knock."

"D'you know, I'm not sure I did."

"Mrs. Hastings?"

"No, Mrs. Shilling." I brushed some hair from my eyes and shifted Archie onto my other hip to shake the hand he offered.

"Oh." He looked surprised. "Really?"

"Well, I'm fairly sure." I managed a smile but then felt a bit peculiar. A bit…light-headed. Must have been the stairs. And not sleeping for two nights. I needed to sit down. I reached behind me for a chair, which happily existed, and sank gratefully into it with Archie on my lap. The tousled man sat too, hastily consulting an open file in front of him and quickly shoving the packet of biscuits in a drawer.

"Right. Mrs. Shilling. So…your husband hasn't run off with a Portuguese baggage handler, brackets male, from Heathrow?" He glanced up, a rather nice quizzical gleam to a pair of deep brown eyes: amused eyes. "And you didn't snap his golf clubs and then replace them in his golf bag before he flew to Sotegrande for a week with said baggage handler?"

"No, my husband died a few weeks ago."

He looked horrified. "Oh, Christ. Oh, God. I'm terribly sorry." He really looked it. He shut the file and tossed it to one side, running his hands through his hair. "How very crass of me, I do apologize."

"Please don't worry."

He looked genuinely upset. As he turned hastily to consult a computer screen on his desk, no doubt flicking up my notes, I took the opportunity to wonder how he'd squeezed those shoulders into that shirt. The sleeves were rolled up, a tie abandoned on the desk. For some reason he reminded me of Archie, the one and only time I'd tried to dress him smartly, for the funeral. His buttons had flown off in seconds flat.

"I'm so sorry," he was murmuring as he peered at the screen and tapped away with the mouse. "As you might have noticed I'm minus a receptionist at the moment. Janice's mother is ill, so I'm slightly rudderless. She usually points me in the right direction."

"Temp?" I hazarded.

He turned from the screen to gaze at me. "Sorry?"

My sentences were sometimes somewhat truncated these days and I took a deep breath and tried again. "You could get a temporary secretary."

He gazed at me a moment, then his face cleared. "What a completely brilliant idea. D'you know, that hadn't occurred to me." He scribbled it down on a pad, cast me another quick, admiring look, then went back to the screen. "Ah yes, it's all becoming horribly clear. Mrs. Hastings is coming in next Tuesday, whereas you're coming in today. I've got the dates muddled up. Mrs. Hastings probably wants to know if she can change the locks and sell his Jaguar SJS, whereas you're here to talk about a will, which at this precise moment is at home on top of the linen basket in my bathroom."

"Your bathroom?"

"I took the papers home to read last night. Left them upstairs."

"Oh. Right."

"Sorry, too much information, it's just I often read papers in the bath. I find a rush of blood to the head helps the grey matter."

"Fair enough, I read novels in the bath."

"Although I seem to remember I didn't quite get to the Shilling bundle, I only got as far as the dusky bag handler. I do apologize, Mrs. Shilling, you've come on a wild goose chase. Not only hasn't your solicitor read the papers, he's left them at home." He turned from the screen and held out his wrists across the desk. "Cuff. Or slap." He put them down and looked grave. "Or even fire, possibly. I would."

I smiled. "Don't worry, I'm not fussed. I'm not sure I'm up to discussing wills yet, actually, but one of my friends insisted."

"Did she? Oh, well, unless you're totally insolvent there's no immediate hurry. There's nothing that can't wait. Come back when you're ready, if you like."

"Really?" I stood up gratefully. "Thanks. I might do that." I had no idea if I was solvent or not. Just put the bills in a drawer. "It may even be a few weeks yet."

He too got to his feet. "Which gives me plenty of time to retrieve your precious bundle from my laundry basket and give it the attention it deserves—couldn't be better."

We both smiled, equally pleased, I suspect, with the outcome of the meeting: both feeling we'd got a result. He went quickly ahead of me to hold the door as I picked my way back across his floor—him apologizing for the mess and me assuring him it couldn't matter less and that it was a bit like playing Twister with my children—and as I went through Janice's room and toward the stairwell, I was aware of him watching me from his doorway.

Outside in the street, Jennie was hunched at the wheel looking stressed, her car on a double-yellow line.

"Well?" she demanded, as I popped Archie in his seat beside Clemmie, buckling him in. I got in the front.

"Yes, it was fine."

"What d'you mean, it was fine? Oh, piss off!" This, to a traffic warden who was attempting to take down her number plate. She lunged out into the traffic to thwart him amid a blare of horns.

"I mean, it's fine, it's all in hand. But there are a few incidentals to be sorted out, so I'm going to pop back in a few weeks."

"A few weeks!" She turned to look at me, horrified.

"Days. I mean, days. But I'll manage, Jennie, now I know where the office is. I'll be fine on my own." I felt exhausted suddenly. Really lie-down-on-the-pavement exhausted.

"Well, I'm surprised you have to go back at all, to be honest," she said hotly, raking a hand through her hair. "Wasn't it all there at his fingertips? Didn't he just read it out to you? The will? He's not disorganized, is he?" She shot me a quick look.

"Not in the slightest."

"Only someone—I think Laura Davy—said he's a bit chaotic. She went when they took her mother's appendix out instead of her hernia and said he was all over the place. You do realize he's not Phil's solicitor, don't you?" she said sharply.

"Er…" So many questions.

"No, he died. This is the nephew, who's inherited the practice."

"Ah."

"I checked it all out when I made the appointment, because I didn't think the name corresponded to the letterhead. The uncle was well known locally apparently, whereas this one is a bit of an unknown quantity. He was in a big city firm in London, but his wife left him and he came out here for a quieter life, wanted a change of pace, which is all very well, but just because we're parochial doesn't mean we're stupid, does it? And if he can't get his head round a simple will…" She set her mouth in a grim line and shook her head. "He's got to shape up, I'm afraid, or he's toast."

I thought of the pink shirt, slightly strained at the shoulder seams.

"He's in quite good shape, actually," I said vaguely. "And he's extremely organized. I think he'll do very well. What's his name?"

She turned, aghast. "You don't even know his name?"

"Of course I do, I just forgot."

"Sam Hetherington."

"That's it. Don't bully me, Jennie, I'm feeling a bit all-in as a matter of fact."

I was. Truly tired. Relieved to have got that over with but exhausted with the effort. And I certainly wasn't up to my son wailing again from the back seat. Since when had he started to cry so much? He used to be such a good baby. I leaned back on the headrest and shut my eyes.

"There's a carton of juice in my handbag," Jennie told me.

I opened my eyes. Turned my head slowly to her. "D'you want it now?"

"No, but Archie might," she said patiently.

"Oh."

I leaned down and fumbled obediently in her handbag at my feet, found the Ribena and handed it to Archie, sticking the straw in first. He put it to his lips, squeezed the carton with his fist and the juice went shooting out of the straw, all over his face and down his front. For some reason Clemmie, beside him on her booster seat, burst into tears.

"You forgot to say don't squeeze!" she wailed. "You always say don't squeeze!"

Archie gazed at his soaking-wet jumper in dismay, opened his mouth as wide as he could and roared, dropping the juice on the floor. Jennie swore under her breath then reached behind for Clemmie's ankle, stroking it and making soothing noises, reaching for Archie's too. As we drove home, amid the inexplicable cacophony of my fractious children, Jennie shot me an exasperated look which I caught in surprise. Was there a law, I wondered, as I gazed out of the window at the increasingly bare branches of the trees as they flashed past, the sun appearing between them like a searchlight, against just sitting quietly the while? About having a little hush?

Chapter Seven

THAT EVENING, AT EIGHT, the inaugural meeting of the Massingham book club took place at Angie's house. Peggy, Angie, Jennie and I assembled in the vast, beautifully converted barn kitchen where Angie and Tom had entertained so splendidly and raucously over the years: sixteen for dinner sometimes, and a lot of laughs. This evening, however, it was just the four of us who sat at the huge oak table under the high vaulted ceiling criss-crossed with original beams, the twinkle of many tiny down-lights upon us. Outside the huge picture windows, darkness had fallen, but in the soft glow of a coach light, Angie's horses could be seen behind the post and rails, already rugged up for winter, standing nose to tail. Inside, candles had been lit above the fireplace and in great urns beside it, while the fire crackled comfortingly in the grate. Michael Bublé crooned softly in the background.

"So. Everyone got a pen and paper?" Angie, sitting at the head of the table, had clearly decided to take the chair—her house, after all. She was looking particularly stunning tonight in her delicate, Jane Asher way: red-gold hair shining, elegant despite jeans and Ugg boots. We all nodded. "OK. Well, we're here tonight primarily to discuss who we want to join our club," she said importantly, crossing her skinny knees.

"And which books," Jennie reminded her, unused to playing second fiddle.

"Oh. Yes, of course." Angie was deflated in an instant. "Which books to read. Anyone got any ideas?"

"*Who's Who*?" drawled Peggy. We all looked at her. "Then we could determine if there's anyone within a radius of twenty miles worth hitting on."

"Anyone got any sensible ideas?" went on Jennie smoothly, ignoring her. "Angie?" she asked diplomatically, having usurped her so very recently.

"Well, I have given it a bit of thought, actually," said Angie, going a bit pink. She'd clearly rehearsed this. "How about *Silas Marner*? It's by George Eliot, so heavy, but look how short it is."

She just happened to have a copy handy and whipped it out of a drawer from the side, the better for us to marvel. It certainly was delightfully slim. Not more than a hundred pages.

"And then we could say we were reading Eliot," mused Jennie, flicking through.

"Exactly," said Angie triumphantly. "And look, half of it's Introduction, which we don't have to read, and quite a lot of Index. Or there's *Pride and Prej*?" she said, rather warming to her role of literary doyenne in her salon. She leaned back expansively in her chair and waved her pencil about. "I mean, I know we've all read it, but just to kick off with, you know? To get us in the mood and—"

"Who's read it?" interrupted Peggy.

Angie and Jennie looked smug. They stuck up their fingers. Looked rather pityingly at Peggy.

"Poppy, you have too." Jennie nudged me.

"Oh." I stuck up mine. I'd been looking at a spider crawling up a rafter into the roof.

"Really?" Peggy asked. "You've all read it, have you?"

"Of course," said Jennie.

"Or have you just seen the film?"

Three fingers wavered slightly. Then lowered.

"I've seen both versions," said Angie defensively. "The Keira Knightley one and the old one."

"Come on, let's not kid ourselves that we're going to wade through the classics," Peggy said drily. "I vote we kick off with Dick Francis."

Jennie looked pained. "Yes, we could, but the idea is to stretch ourselves a bit, isn't it?"

"Is it?" Peggy lit a cigarette. "I thought we were here to enjoy ourselves. Thought we were doing this for pleasure." She blew out a thin line of smoke. "OK, how about Lawrence, then? He's a bit more stretching, although admittedly mostly in haystacks." She gave a throaty chuckle.

"Poppy?" Jennie turned to me. "Any ideas?"

I came back from the spider. It had gone right up into the rafters, into the apex of the roof.

I stared blankly. "*Anne of Green Gables*?"

How odd. Dad had attempted to read that to me when Mum died. We'd started with *Black Beauty*, but had to stop when Ginger died. I remember the tears rolling down Dad's wind-blown cheeks as he sat on my bed. I even remember my pink floral bed cover. We hadn't liked Anne, though, had never gotten to the end. Found her feeble.

My friends exchanged startled looks. Angie attempted to give this due consideration.

"Yes…we could read *Anne of Green Gables*," she agreed, "but—"

"Oh, let's forget the bloody books and talk about who we're going to ask," said Peggy, wriggling on her bony bottom in her chair. "Far more exciting."

Jennie raised her eyebrows and shuffled her notepad. "OK," she said wearily. "Peggy? You're clearly itching to fire away."

"How about Angus Jardine, Pete the farrier, that smoothie antiques guy Jennie fancies, and Luke the organ-grinder in church."

We looked at her aghast.

"Peggy, this is a book club, not a frustrated-women's dating agency!" Jennie spluttered. "I meant local women!"

"Why do they have to be women?"

"Well, they don't, *exclusively*. But usually, you know…"

"Usually it's the little women who get together? When their hunter-gatherers come home? Bustle out importantly to show they have lives too?"

Jennie and Angie looked at one another.

"Peggy's got a point," muttered Angie.

"But we can't have the four of *us*, and four *men*. How would that look? We need a couple of women, for heaven's sake," Jennie insisted.

"Saintly Sue?" suggested Angie. "If we can put up with her halo. And my sister might come?"

Jennie crossed her legs and sucked in her cheeks. Angie's sister was a scary ex-Londoner called Virginia who worked in advertising. She'd recently moved locally on account of leaving her husband, a wealthy hedge-fund manager. Jennie had cooked Angie a dinner party one night when Virginia and various other high-achievers were guests, but she'd had problems with the turbot and, out of nerves, proceeded to get disastrously drunk. At two a.m. Jennie had crawled into the double bed in Angie's spare room to sleep it off, unaware that Virginia, equally plastered, was already installed. The next morning, Virginia had leaped out of bed bellowing: "Bloody hell—I've just left my husband, and the first person I sleep with is a woman!"

Jennie wasn't necessarily in a violent hurry to meet her again.

"Yes, your sister," she mused, as if giving it ample thought. "Who's delightful, of course. Only I wonder if she isn't a bit high-brow for us?"

"Oh God, yes, she's frightfully clever," Angie agreed. "Got a first from Oxford."

"Fuck me, that's no good," muttered Peggy, stubbing out her cigarette.

"So," Jennie went on, "we could have Saintly Sue, but then again, d'you think that's a good idea, bearing in mind…" She jerked her head eloquently in my direction. It was as if I wasn't alive any more.

Didn't exist. "I mean, if we *do* ask Luke, which I actually think is quite a good idea of Peggy's, although not necessarily the others—"

"Why not necessarily the others?" demanded Peggy.

Jennie sighed. Turned to me. "What do you think, Poppy?"

"About what?"

"About inviting Luke Chambers?"

"Who's Luke Chambers?"

Three pairs of eyes turned incredulously on me. There was a long and meaningful pause. At length, Jennie put down her pencil. She clenched her teeth and blew out hard through her nose, making a faint whistling sound.

"OK," she said quietly and in very measured tones. "OK. We are here tonight ostensibly to talk about the book club. To talk about who we want to join and which books we want to read. But one of our members, one of our very dear friends, is in trouble, and I, for one, cannot go another day, cannot go another minute, without finding out why. What's happened, Poppy? What the flipping heck is going on?"

"What d'you mean?" I felt myself go cold.

"Two weeks ago you were coping. Sad, but coping. Resigned to Phil's death, to being a widow. Then suddenly—and knowing you as I do, knowing your movements as well as I do, I would be so bold as to pin it down to two weeks ago last Friday—something happened."

I felt my mouth go a bit dry. All eyes in the room were upon me. Possibly even those of Angie's children in their silver photo frames on the side: those beautiful poised teenagers, back at school now, whom Frankie derided as snobs but of whom I think was secretly in awe. Not so poised these days perhaps, with their father gone. Felicity, off the rails a bit according to her mother, nothing too terrible, smoking, drinking, but only fifteen. Clarissa, not working for her exams. Their eyes too, it seemed, in frames all over the room, on ponies, on ski slopes, gazed and waited.

"I...had a visitor." I also had no saliva. I couldn't believe I was doing this.

"When?"

"You're right. On that Friday. At lunchtime. You were cooking a lunch for the Hobson-Burnetts."

Miles away, in Buckingham. I knew, because my first instinct had been to go next door, to find her. Find my friend. My second instinct had been to hide, which was the one I stuck to.

"A woman called Emma Harding came to see me."

My friends waited, wine glasses in hand. And although they sensed what was coming was not good, there was an air of expectancy in the room. Of relief, perhaps.

"Apparently she'd been having an affair with Phil. For four years. Since Clemmie was born."

You could feel the air thicken, hold and set. Nobody moved. Nobody blinked. They waited. I remembered Emma's pale anxious face as I'd offered her a drink. A cup of tea, perhaps? Her polite refusal as she sat down, putting her bag at her feet. Swallowing; pressing her hands together to compose herself.

I turned to my friends, their drinks still motionless in mid-air, and, in Peggy's case, her cigarette about to drop an inch of ash.

"She helped Phil set up his private-equity firm four years ago, the banking offshoot. When he left Lehman's and set up on his own, remember?" I certainly remembered because it was just after Clemmie was born. I'd be sitting up bed in the middle of the night breastfeeding and he'd stagger in, exhausted. Working day and night to get it off the ground. "They worked very closely. She was in charge of new investment. She was crucial to Phil. They spent so much time together, it was inevitable. They fell in love."

In my head I scrolled back to Emma telling me this. She'd looked anxious, but hadn't avoided my eyes. "When you're doing deals like that," she explained, "working right into the night, it's so hard."

"So hard," I murmured automatically now.

"What? *What* is so hard?" Jennie was on her feet.

I regarded my friend in Angie's kitchen. "Working in such close proximity—the total absorption, handling huge sums of money, the stress, the excitement. It's business, Jennie, you and I wouldn't know. We've been out too long. Too steeped in children. It takes over their lives. And she knew I'd find out about her," I went on mechanically. "Knew, when the will was read, that she'd be revealed, because he provided for her. He told her so. So she came to see me first. And she doesn't want anything, Jennie. Nothing at all, that's what she came to say. Quite brave, really."

I remembered Emma gazing up at me from under a pale silky fringe. Looking so frightened, unsure.

"Little chit," spat Jennie.

"Oh, no," I said, surprised. "No, she wasn't like that."

"What d'you mean, she wasn't like that?" cried Angie. "She was sleeping with your husband!"

"I mean—she wasn't the mistress type. She was soft, vulnerable, even. Said Phil had been so lost. So sad. And she'd just comforted him originally."

"Lost?" Jennie's incredulous voice.

"After Clemmie was born. Said I'd withdrawn into the world of my child. The world of babies. Excluded him."

"Just a bit…" Emma had said nervously, hunched forward on my sofa. "You were a bit preoccupied, Phil said."

"And he'd felt left out?" sneered Angie.

"Well…yes. Yes, he had. And—I think that's true." I turned to them. "I had been preoccupied."

I thought back to Clemmie's birth: my unbridled joy at having her, my darling daughter, my beautiful bright-eyed little girl, who'd brought so much joy into what was a rather dim world. Turned the light on in my marriage.

"So Phil felt excluded and turned to a secretary at work," scoffed Angie.

"Finance manager," I told her.

"Right, and this 'finance manager'," she said, making ironic quotation marks in the air, "no doubt told you it wasn't the sex that her new lover had missed, but the love and affection?" She got up and began to pace around her converted barn kitchen. Her arms were tightly folded, chin tucked in her chest, like someone looking in the eye of a storm.

"Yes. Yes, she did. And the thing is, Angie, if I'm honest," I was having trouble breathing here, "I did pour so much love into Clemmie, I was so consumed, that maybe he did feel rejected. Maybe he cast around helplessly for some affection—"

"And maybe he got a stiffy in the office," Peggy said caustically, tapping ash into a pot plant beside her. It was the first time she'd spoken. "Maybe his wife had had a difficult birth and he was a bit impatient on that front."

"Yes," I agreed, "but some men do need it. I mean, look at Dan and Jennie." I hadn't stopped looking at Dan and Jennie since Emma had been to see me. Normal service resumed within a twinkling of Hannah's birth. Hadn't stopped thinking what a selfish cow I'd been.

"Oh, don't be ridiculous," stormed Angie. "Jennie had two caesareans! Hers came popping out of the bloody sunroof, not bursting through the engine room like ours!" Peggy, childless, crossed her legs and looked pained. "Don't you be beating yourself up about *that*, my girl, that is *no* excuse!" Angie wagged her finger.

"I wouldn't say 'pop'," muttered Jennie stiffly.

"And this Emma," went on Angie, still pacing. "She was no doubt dressed down, hm? In a sort of sweet peasanty top and flat sandals? No makeup? Freshly washed hair?"

I looked up at her, surprised. "Well…yes. As I say, she wasn't the mistress type—"

"Well, she's not going to strut around to your house in her basque and fishnets, is she? Twanging her suspender belt!"

"Oh, I'd find it *very* hard to believe she was like that."

"Believe it," snapped Angie, stopping suddenly to slap the palms of her hands on the table in front of me, making me jump. Her eyes were like flints close to mine. "You believe it, Poppy." They looked very fierce, these friends of mine. Very grim. "Don't think she didn't move seamlessly into mistress mode the moment your husband was in her bedroom."

I had a sudden mental picture of Phil walking into her bedroom in his suit, briefcase in hand. Emma waiting on the bed, reclining perhaps in a silk robe. I felt myself rock.

"Really?"

"Really. And as for blaming you, with your lack of sexual favors—how low can you get? I know darned well you felt very rejected in the bedroom."

"Yes, but if I'm honest I didn't really care."

"None of us care!" squealed Jennie. "A few children down the line, none of us care if we ever have sex again, but it doesn't mean *he* can go off-piste!"

"Doesn't it?"

"NO!" they all roared in unison, fists clenched.

There was a silence. The room felt very charged, very tense.

"This is not your fault, Poppy," said Peggy gravely, at length. "Is that what you've been thinking, my love? These past few weeks?"

"Well, I've…" Suddenly I felt I might crumble. Her term of endearment hadn't helped. It seemed to me I were made entirely of ancient parchment which could disintegrate to the touch. I thought back to Emma, getting up hesitantly from the leather sofa in my sitting room. Twisting her hands about and saying how sorry she was to be the bearer of bad news. I remembered feeling so shocked as I looked at her. I'd already lost a husband, my children's father. I'd already been dealing with that. But…how can you lose someone who wasn't there? *Phil had never been there.* I'd been on my own for a very long time. I just hadn't known it. The sense of abandonment had threatened to overwhelm me. I remembered not being able to breathe.

Somehow I'd got to my feet, followed Emma to the door, where she'd stumbled out some more apologies, saying she'd only wanted to comfort him, in what he felt to be a sterile marriage.

"Sterile marriage!" shrieked Angie. I'd said it out loud. "And no doubt she said you'd been cold and unfeeling, and that, oh dear God, the poor man had felt driven away? Poppy, have I not talked to you about Tom? Run you through his lines?"

"Well, I—"

"This is all mighty familiar," she hissed. "And it is nothing whatsoever to do with this," she slapped her hand to her heart, "and everything," she seized a large courgette from the vegetable rack, brandished it priapically, "to do with this."

There was a silence.

"So she said she was sorry, did she?" mused Peggy.

"Yes, she did." I cast back to Emma. By the front door, eyes downcast. Shoulder bag on.

"And that she never meant to cause trouble, particularly when there were children involved?"

"Yes."

"And that she was mortified you had to find out this way. That you had to find out at all, even. She never wanted to add to your grief?"

"Yes, she said all that."

"And then she left, trying to walk slowly and calmly down the path, but unable to resist scuttling a bit at the end."

"She did…scuttle, a bit." I frowned as I recalled her quickly shutting the garden gate; leaping into her Mini. Glancing back over her shoulder as she pulled out sharply, not bothering with the seat belt, eyes flitting up to the rear-view mirror, to me.

"And she left you, the widow, feeling like a heel."

"More than a heel," I whispered.

"Like a cold, unfeeling, heartless wife, who'd driven her husband into another woman's bed."

Buckled as I was, I caught the ironic tone.

"She doesn't want any money," I told them, almost defensively. "That's what she came to say."

"So she's got a conscience. Or so she says. But she's running scared, Poppy. She knew you'd be banging on her door the moment the will was read, so she thought she'd bang on yours first. She came to see you to pre-empt the situation, before the shit hit the fan. No doubt Phil made provision for her assuming he'd die at eighty, and incidentally, how cynical is that? To plan on cheating on you forever?" Peggy paused. "Your husband was a bastard, Poppy." I looked up. Peggy's eyes were unnaturally unamused. No benign, sardonic twinkle to them now. "He treated you appallingly. In fact he made a mockery of your marriage. He controlled you, he told you what to wear, he lowered your self-esteem and confidence, he handed you money as if you were a child, and then he compounded the crime, added insult to injury, by sleeping with another woman."

I breathed in sharply. "I never thought of it like that," I muttered.

Jennie put her head in her hands and moaned low. As she looked up, she let her fingers drag theatrically down her face. "Poppy, Poppy, where have you been?" she whispered.

"In a fairly dark and horrible place," I said in a quavering voice. I didn't tell her there'd been moments when I'd wanted to hide forever. Moments, like that one on the way back from the shops the other day, when I'd thought I could just drive the car into a brick wall.

Jennie leaned forward. Gripped my wrist. "Most women would

look upon this recent revelation, this visit, as a salve to their con-science. Proof that they need not feel too guilty about their lack of widow's weeds."

"And yet, for someone like Poppy, I can see it could also be a crushing blow," said Peggy slowly.

I looked at her. Someone like Poppy. What did that mean? Someone just the tiniest bit malleable? Suggestible? Riddled with insecurities and inadequacies, prone to be a wee bit downtrodden, over time? I felt scared at what she might say next.

"It was rejection on a grand scale," she went on. "Not just widowed, but cheated on too. By someone she felt she'd accommo-dated, put up with out of the goodness of her heart. How shameful is that? By someone like Phil the Pill," she spat darkly.

"Phil the…"

"Pill. Short for Pillock. It's how he was known, locally."

Jennie and Angie bent their heads and studied their fingernails. Locally? I gazed at my friends aghast, but their eyes were averted. How far, I wondered. As far as Aylesbury? My heart started to beat. Slowly at first, but then it gathered momentum. Something dry and withered was uncurling fast within me, thrusting out green shoots and drinking, finding some nourishment. Phil the Pill. *My husband.* And in a corner of my mind, I'd known. Known he was a pillock. Had overheard Angie once say to Jennie he was a bad draw at a dinner party. But I'd ignored it. Covered up for him. Like you do when you're married to a slightly dull man. Out of loyalty. Personal pride. Told myself he had hidden depths that my friends couldn't know about. Concentrated on how hard he worked, how dedicated and selfless he was. How he brought home the bacon. But, in my heart, I knew I'd sold out by marrying him. I just didn't realize ev-eryone else knew it too.

Words were finally forming in my brain, like fridge-magnet letters swirling around in a furious kaleidoscopic anagram.

Simultaneously, in the pit of my stomach, which latterly had been a bit ashen, a bit shrunken, there was a rumble, as if Vesuvius, dormant for years, was making a comeback, deciding it was time for a tremor. But it had been a while. It had its work cut out. I'd been in denial for years and, for the last eleven days, severely crushed. But fury was finally on its way. Roaring in from afar like the seventh cavalry. All those long lonely evenings. All those solitary weekends with the children. He hadn't just been working, hadn't been cycling—recharging the batteries, as I'd tell myself stoically: he'd been sleeping with another woman. Before coming home to me. And always a shower. Two-showers-a-day Phil. Now we knew why. I looked at my friends, my three good friends, grouped tense and watchful around me.

"How dare he?" I breathed, softly at first. It was a surprise to hear the words. They waited. Jennie nodded eagerly.

I dug deeper, right into my very soul. As I gazed into it, his treachery stared back. I saw it very clearly, like a roll of film. Saw him coming in late, midnight sometimes; me stumbling downstairs in my dressing gown to pop his dinner in the microwave, ask how his day had been, sympathize. I saw me sitting in the audience at Clemmie's first nativity play, an empty chair beside me, then a text: "Sorry, can't get away." I saw me eating with the children at teatime so as not to eat alone. I saw a one-parent family. Why had I felt so ashamed these last few days, so fearful the world might discover I hadn't been enough for my husband? Because he was dead? Death was no excuse. He'd let me down. *He'd* betrayed *me*. Not enough for him? He'd *never* been enough for me! I wasn't so much seeing the light as having a full-blown epiphany.

"HOW BLOODY DARE HE!" I roared, the force of my ejaculation jerking me back in my chair.

"Atta-girl," breathed Peggy softly.

I seized my wine glass, blood storming through my veins and

knocked the Chablis back in one. Then I slammed the empty glass down on the table. "Fill it up," I demanded.

"Lordy, Poppy," Angie murmured in consternation, but Peggy was already on the case.

"Atta-*girl*," she repeated admiringly as she filled it right to the top.

Chapter Eight

OF COURSE IT TOOK more than a couple glasses of white wine to sort me out. More than an evening with the girls. Apparently I hadn't been terribly well. Hadn't been…coping. And evidently going without sleep for nights on end wasn't normal. This was all explained gently and carefully to me by my friends, and then the very next day Angie marched me off to see her GP, a pleasant, middle-aged woman who had seen Angie through her separation from Tom. She gave me some little white pills. They certainly helped me sleep but also made me feel an awful lot better in a matter of days, although that could have been psychological. I took them avidly, marveling at the change in me. After a while, though, I began to feel a bit turbocharged, as if I might take off, exhaust fumes billowing out behind like a cartoon character, so I flushed the rest of the pills down the loo.

Meanwhile I seethed, rumbled and roared around my house. It seemed to me it trembled with me, like the one belonging to the giant, the one with the beanstalk outside. Fee fi fo—I strode about with eyes like saucers, pausing occasionally to ask, "What? He did *what*?" incredulously of the fireplace, or the bookshelves, pacing in circles that got ever larger, and encompassed the upstairs bathroom where I showered every morning long and hard, washed my hair furiously and came down clean and steaming, hair tied back, wearing freshly laundered jeans and a shirt, nostrils flaring.

The house was tackled next. I dusted and hoovered it from top to bottom, then I hired a steam cleaner. I washed the windows, polished the furniture, mended a broken curtain track in Archie's room, scrubbed the tiles in the shower—getting right into the grouting with something so toxic it nearly took my fingernails off—and tidied all the drawers and cupboards. I then removed all traces of my husband. I saved cufflinks, a watch, and his dinner jacket for Archie and a watercolor he'd liked for Clemmie, but I took all his clothes to a charity shop, and the rest, the things no one would want, I burned in the garden when the children were asleep. I stopped short of burning photos or anything hysterical like that and put them in a box in the cellar, but there was, nonetheless, a faintly heretical gleam to my eye as his Lycra cycling shorts (three pairs), his gloves, silly shoes, ordnance survey maps and stopwatch went up in acrid flames. As the tongues licked high into the velvet sky, crackling and popping in the night, I felt a profound sense of exorcism. Of release. Humming—yes, humming—I turned and strode back into the house for more. Trophies and medals had gone into the cellar along with the photos, but all those sci-fi books could burn, along with his self-help manuals—how to be rich, how to be popular, etc.— and one which I'd never seen before and had found nestling under his side of the bed and was charmingly titled: *How to Live Without the One You Love*. Screeching, I ran downstairs and frisbeed it into the flames. Glancing up I saw Jennie's startled face at her bedroom window. She took in the situation in an instant, gave me a huge thumbs up and went about her business.

The children were next, spruced to within an inch of their lives. All clothes were washed and hung out to dry on the line, faces scrubbed, sweets and crisps banned, the television turned off, and there were lots of cuddles at bedtime and chat at teatime, which included broccoli and carrots. In other words, business as usual. The smiles and laughs came back too, not slowly as they might with adults, but instantly, children being so forgiving and immediate, which made my heart lurch. But if I had any temptation to beat myself up about their past eleven days of enacting life on a sink estate, I told myself it had been only that: eleven days. And that real grief, and the side effects on a family, could last a hell of a lot longer. That hadn't been grief; that had been shock. A very nasty one at that. I rang Dad and told him not to panic, I was fine, and knew he could tell by my voice I meant it. His relief was tangible and he rang off with a cheery good-bye and an assurance that he'd try not to come off the enormous chestnut hunter he was breaking in for somebody else to fall off on the hunting field.

In the mornings, after I'd taken Clemmie to school, I went for long bracing walks in the forest above my house, borrowing Leila, Archie's hand in mine. The three of us would stride through the autumn leaves, Archie kicking them up in his wellies, laughing as colors as bright as jewels—amber, ruby and gold—fluttered down around his head. Just occasionally I'd stop, in this five-thousand-acre wood with not another soul in sight, to clench my fists and shout, "Bloody hell!" to the treetops. "Bloody HELL!" Archie laughed delightedly and they were, unfortunately, his next words. The burnished autumn colors seemed to inflame me more than ever, though, like that fire in my garden: fury was in my heart, my belly, and I'd return refreshed, but incensed. Truly incensed that Phil could have done that to me.

Thank God he was dead, I thought, surprisingly, one morning. At least, it was a surprise to me. I voiced it too, to the bird table, as I had a piece of toast at the kitchen window, then glanced guiltily to the heavens as two sparrows fluttered up to tell. But suppose he hadn't died; suppose he'd carried on with Emma for years, deceiving me, making a mockery of my life—yes, thank God he was dead, I decided fiercely, throwing my plate in the dishwasher.

"Thank God," repeated Archie gravely behind me, eating his Weetabix. Ah. I'd have to watch that.

The following day I saw Jennie in the shop as I went in for my paper. My newspaper. Which I hadn't bought for weeks. Had had no interest in the outside world.

"Choir tonight, isn't it?" I said cheerily.

A couple of elderly women in the post office queue turned, surprised.

"Yes, seven o'clock. Oh, *look* at you, Poppy, you look so much better." Jennie beamed. "You've had your hair cut!"

"Doesn't she look a treat," agreed old Mrs. Archibald, nudging her neighbor, Mrs. Cripps, who agreed with a toothless grin. "Like the whole world has lifted from your shoulders, love."

"It has," I assured them, taking the apple Archie had grabbed from the fruit rack and passing it to Yvonne to be weighed. "In fact," I told them, "I feel blooming marvelous. Better than I've felt for years."

If the old dears looked a trifle surprised at this, it was only to be expected, I thought, as I went on up the hill with my children to nursery: they didn't know the minutiae, the background. Not many young widows could go from catatonic inertia to full-blown euphoria in days, but this one could. Oh, yes.

Miss Hawkins, too, looked delighted to see the three of us looking so clean and sparkling, and for the first day in a long time, Clemmie skipped in with her friend Alice without hanging on to my leg, or Miss Hawkins's, or both.

That evening, when Frankie arrived, I was almost waiting by the door, keen to be off.

"God, look at you," she said, struggling with her enormous bag of books to the kitchen and dumping down it on the table. "You've got makeup on and everything. You look loads better."

It occurred to me she didn't. Her hair was greasy and lank and there were spots on her chin; misery around the eyes. I must talk to Jennie.

"Yes, it's extraordinary what undiluted fury can do for you," I assured her.

"Oh, yeah, you found out he was a love rat, didn't you? Who would have thought. Your Phil."

"Who indeed," I said grimly, seizing my handbag.

"I mean, he looked so, you know…" She bit her thumbnail.

"Dull?"

"Well, I was going to say harmless."

"Nerdy? Unattractive to women?"

She looked uncomfortable. "Except he's dead, isn't he? Perhaps we shouldn't…you know." She shrugged.

"No, perhaps we shouldn't," I agreed, but somehow I knew it would be difficult. And it was heartening to know Frankie hadn't thought much of him.

"What was she like?" she asked, following me to the door.

"His mistress?"

"Yeah. Jennie said she called round. Bloody cheek."

"Quite attractive, actually. Surprisingly pretty."

"And so are you. So he must have had something," she said meditatively.

"I suppose he must," I said, turning to her at the door. "But it wasn't enough, Frankie. Not to excuse that sort of treachery. I'm delighted he's gone." I knew I'd thought it, but was surprised to hear myself say it.

Her kohl-blackened eyes widened. "Check *you* out." She stared. Gave it some thought. "Course, he was a married man, wasn't he, which has its own attractions. For her, I mean. Someone else's property and all that."

"Right." I held her eyes a moment, remembering the biology teacher. "See you later, Frankie. Archie's bottle is in the fridge."

Someone else's property, I reflected as I strode off to the church. Well, she was welcome to him. Perhaps I shouldn't have burned his things? Should have taken them round to her house, dumped them on the doorstep, said: here, have him. Which perhaps I would have done if he hadn't died. If I'd just found out. Yes, how would that little scenario have played out, I wondered as I pushed the gate into the walled churchyard and walked up the path, slippery with leaves, the wind in my hair. Obviously I'd have divorced him and he'd have gone to live with her, but then it would have been so much messier for the children. Alternate weekends, chunks of the holidays, like Angie; plus a stepmother…a stepmother. I stopped. Rocked on my feet on the church step, worn smooth with age and generations of worshippers traipsing through. I glanced up. Thank you, I assured Him from the bottom of my heart as I pushed open the door. Thank you so much for sparing me all that.

Jennie was late, having dropped Jamie at scouts, but I knew the rules now and made firmly for the back row, away from Molly, where I saved my friend a place. As it happened, that put me beside Angus Jardine, he of the silver hair and silken tongue. Angus was a pond-leaper, but protocol required him to turn to me with a look of concern and clear his throat.

"How are you, my dear? I say, I saw the report of the inquest in the local paper today. Hadn't realized his death had been caused by one of those wretched easyJet planes. Terrible thing to have happened. Terrible."

"Oh, no, not really," I assured him placidly, shimmying out of my coat. "Could have been a lot worse."

"Really?" He looked astonished. Paused to consider. To frown. "In what way, exactly?"

"Well, he was having an affair. Phil, I mean. If he'd lived, it would have been a great deal messier, sharing the children, that kind of thing. I was just thinking that as I came up the path."

His rheumy old eyes boggled in shock. "Euh," he muttered uneasily. "Good Lord."

"Yes, *very* good Lord, Angus." I raised my eyes and pointed to Him upstairs. "I was just thinking *that* too!"

Angus didn't know what to say. He looked like he'd swallowed his dentures.

"And sorry to have shocked you," I said more gently, putting my hand on his arm, "but the thing is, I'm not sure I can play the grieving widow anymore when, frankly, I don't feel remotely sad. Not now."

Angus gave me a level stare for quite a long moment. Eventually he nodded. "Quite right. Good for you, old girl. Why be hypocritical?"

"Why indeed."

I held his gaze and then we both faced front in silence, digesting this. I knew I was a bit over the top at the moment, a bit out of control, but I couldn't help it.

"Has Peggy asked you about the book club?" I asked at length, changing the subject.

"Peggy? No."

"Oh, well, a few of us girls are starting one. Thought you might like to join."

He smoothed back his flowing, Heseltinian locks delightedly. "I say…" he purred, mouth twitching. "How sweet of you to think of me. D'you know, I don't know…"

"Oh, come on, Angus, you'll love it." I nudged him. "Nattering away about Robert Harris's latest thriller with a glass of Muscadet on a Tuesday? Got to be better than *Panorama*, surely?"

"Yes. And Sylvia plays bridge on a Tuesday…" You could see the wheels of his mind turning.

"There you go, then. No reheated cauliflower cheese with an enormous baked potato on a tray."

"No." His eyes widened. "Quite. Well, I might." He looked enormously chipper suddenly. "Tell Peggy I might well."

"Might well what?" said Jennie as she slipped in breathlessly beside me, just as, coincidentally, did Sylvia, only she had to sit on the pew in front, as there was no more room. She glared at her husband for not saving her a place.

"I was just telling Angus about the book club," I breezed.

"What book club?" asked Sylvia, quick as a flash.

"Oh, er…I'll tell you about it later, my love," said Angus, as, fortuitously, Saintly Sue tapped her lectern to get us to our feet. We all rose obediently.

"Is he coming?" Jennie asked me softly, alarmed.

"Think so," I told her.

"We'll have to ask Sylvia, now," she said nervously.

"No we don't," I said brazenly. "That's not what Peggy had in mind at all. We don't want Sylvia."

"Keep your voice down," Jennie muttered as Sylvia's head half turned at her name.

"And anyway, she's got bridge on a Tuesday."

I raised my chin. Opened my mouth to fairly shout the Gloria to the heavens, feeling empowered and euphoric. In fact, my voice rang out so loud and clear above the others that Sue glanced at me in delight.

Luke, true to form, was late. This time I took more interest as he bounced boyishly down the aisle, blond hair flopping, music under his arm, eyes twinkling behind his specs. Hm. He'll do, I thought.

Jennie shot me a horrified look. One or two people in the pew in front turned to grin.

"What?"

"You just said, 'He'll do'!" she hissed.

"Did I? Oh, well. Nothing like a bit of clarity, eh?"

More titters at this. Meanwhile Luke bounded up the steps to his organ, raised his sensitive hands and struck a chord which we all dutifully followed, launching into the Gloria again.

Afterward, as we gathered up our hymn sheets and shuffled out, I made purposefully for our new organist as he descended from his instrument at the far end of the church. Jennie was on my heels, though, a restraining hand on my arm.

"Steady," she muttered.

"What? I'm just going to see if he wants to join."

"I know, I can tell, but some people might not understand the eager gleam in the young widow's eyes. Might misconstrue it for callousness."

I frowned as I hastened on. "Phil was having an affair, Jennie. For four years. I hate him for that. I hate him for lying to me, deceiving me and betraying me. I didn't have a life, not a proper one; he saw to that. I just want to get on with what's left of my life now. See what else is out there." I shook her off and strode toward the door, our organist ahead of us.

"Yes, yes, I know," Jennie was saying, scurrying after me. "It's just that social conventions being what they are, people will expect a *tad* of grief nonetheless and—"

"Well, they shouldn't," I told her firmly. "Not under the circumstances." I beamed as I bore down on Blondie.

"Hell-o there! It's Luke, isn't it? I'm Poppy Shilling."

He turned, a sheaf of music under his arm; smiled, surprised. Then, as the penny dropped, so did his countenance. He regarded me gravely.

"Oh, Mrs. Shilling. Oh, yes, I heard. I'm so terribly sorry. Please accept my sincere condolences."

"Oh, don't worry about that," I said, waving my hand airily. "That's all over and done with now, dead and buried even—hah! Now look, I don't know if you've heard, but a few of us gals," I waggled my eyebrows jauntily, "are forming a bit of a book club. Didn't know if you'd like to join?"

He gazed, startled. Was he all there, I wondered?

"It's on a Tuesday night," I went on more slowly, kindly even, in case he couldn't keep up, "at Angie's place. That's Angie, the very attractive divorcee, who's not here tonight although she's usually in the choir. And her house is the pretty manor house you pass just as you go out of the village. We'll have drinks and nibbles at seven and nothing too serious book-wise. In fact we might not even have books at all!" I turned to grin at Jennie, who was looking strangely horrified. Odd, my friend Jennie: one minute she wanted me to snap out of it, the next, to snap right back in.

"What Poppy means," she purred, shoving me out of the way and walking beside Luke as he went to get his bike from the church porch, "is that we won't be tackling Dostoyevsky immediately, if you know what I mean."

"Oh, right. Jolly interesting, I expect, but a bit heavy, I agree."

Was it my imagination, or was he shooting me interested glances over his shoulder as he bent to apply bicycle clips to his trousers? I could overlook those, I thought as I posed coquettishly on the church step, one arm stretched high above my head on the door jamb, the other on my hip.

"Who's jolly interesting?" Oh Lord, Saintly Sue was looming from the shadows, breasting her music, cheeks very flushed. The Only Virgin In The Village, Peggy called her; desperate to be plucked.

"Dostoyevsky," Luke told her, straightening up. "Jennie and, um, Poppy here, are starting a book club."

She almost bounced on the spot, cashmere embonpoint jiggling. "Oh golly, how exciting! Can I join?"

"No," I said quickly. Jennie shot me an aghast look.

"Of *course* you can!" she gushed.

I blinked. "Can she? I thought we didn't want any more women? Bearing in mind…" I covertly inclined my head Luke's way.

"No, no, I meant too many *older* women. Didn't want it getting too, you know, pensioner-ish." She cast Sue a collaborative look. "But of course *Sue* can come, Lord yes. See you both next Tuesday, then." She had my arm in a viselike grip. "Seven o'clock. Oh, and it's going to be at Peggy's house, not Angie's—the one with the white picket fence. Toodle-oo!" She frogmarched me off down the path at speed, leaving Luke gazing after us blankly; Sue, as if she'd been shot.

"Have you been drinking?" Jennie hissed.

"No, why?"

"Because you're behaving as if you are completely and utterly pissed. You're being outrageous, Poppy!"

"Am I?"

"Yes, and I end up looking like some ageist bigot just to get you off the hook!"

I stopped in the lane. Felt my forehead. I did feel a bit inebriated, actually. A bit light-headed. I was aware that my timorous desire not to rock the boat had been replaced in some fabulously epiphanic way by a desire to be true to myself whatever the consequences. The trouble was, my feelings had been suppressed for so long without the valve being even slightly loosened, that now the lid was off, the contents were not so much out, as all over the walls.

"Sorry. Sorry, Jennie." I walked on, slower now. "But the thing is," I said carefully, feeling my way, "I feel the truth is so…well, crucial, suddenly. Of such vital importance, you know?" I turned to face my friend earnestly. I felt faintly visionary about it; might even get a bit evangelical. "I mean, it's so liberating, isn't it?" I urged. "Why don't we all just say what we mean all the time? Always?"

"Because polite society dictates that we don't, that's why," she said heatedly. "Just because you're a widow doesn't mean the bridle can come off, you know. Doesn't give you carte blanche to say whatever comes into your head. You still have to exercise restraint; can't just trample on people's feelings!"

I blinked, suitably rebuked. "No, I suppose not," I conceded. "Except…everyone tramples on mine?"

"Phil, trampled on yours," she reminded me. "Not everyone."

"Why are we going in here?" I ducked as we made a sharp right turn and went into the pub under a low beam.

"Because if you haven't had a drink," she told me as she steered me into the snug of the Greyhound bar, "then perhaps you should. Two large gin and tonics, please, Hugo." This, to the barman, a local teenager in his gap year, as she parked me firmly on a bar stool. Still looking distinctly harassed, she flourished a ten-pound note at him. "And even if you don't need one," she told me, collapsing in a heap on a stool beside me, "after that, I jolly well do."

Chapter Nine

A FEW DAYS LATER I received a surprisingly efficient missive from my solicitor in the form of an e-mail, apologizing for our disorganized inaugural meeting and wondering if I had time to "pop in for a second attempt." I did, as it happened, the following afternoon, and since he too was free, a meeting was arranged. As I sat in his supremely tidy waiting room, watched over by a pleasantly plump blonde matron with pussycat-bow chiffon blouse, navy skirt and red nails, I realized something of a sea change had occurred here since my last visit. When I was shown into his office it became all the more seismic as Sam Hetherington stood up to greet me, spotty tie firmly in place, suit jacket on, papers and files previously littering the floor now neatly aligned on shelves behind him, no half-empty mugs of tea, and no sign of the very dead spider plant wilting on his windowsill.

"You've scrubbed up," I said in surprise as we shook hands across his desk.

He raised his eyebrows. "Funny. I was thinking the same about you. Didn't know one was allowed to voice it."

I laughed. "I meant your room, actually."

He looked taken aback. "Oh. Right. Sorry, it's just Janice insists I wear a tie so I assumed you meant…However, you do look better," he concluded awkwardly as we both sat down.

I smiled. "Thanks. I'm feeling much better."

I realized the last time I'd been in here I'd been sporting clothes that had seen better days and hair that hadn't seen a brush for a while.

It also occurred to me that his own dark wavy hair together with eyes the color of good sherry was my most favorite combination.

"Janice makes you wear a tie?" I said as I settled back into my seat.

He sighed. "Janice rules my life in very many ways. And thank the Lord she does. And that her mother's recovered. You saw how slovenly I was without her. She has an uncanny insight into the mind of the prospective client and their sartorial expectations. Apparently shirt sleeves and an open collar simply will not do, suggestive as they are of a chaotic mind and careless approach to business and not a tireless toiling over the brief. So yes, she makes me wear a tie." He smiled. "Now. What can I do for you?"

"You asked me to come in."

His dark eyes widened in surprise. "So I did. So I did." He hastened to collect himself and shuffled some papers around. "It's all coming back to me. Of course. There's a will."

"And where there's a will, there's a relative," I quipped.

He frowned. "Sorry?"

"Oh, er, bad-taste joke," I said hastily, remembering Jennie's terse reprimand to behave. I sat up straight. "You're right, I'm here about my husband's will."

"Which I've got right here."

He picked up a wad of papers from his desk and flourished it triumphantly, almost as if that in itself was something of an achievement. Then he put it down and gazed reflectively. Glanced up and met my eye.

"You're a wealthy woman, Mrs. Shilling."

I blanched. "Am I?"

"Well, compared to me you are. Compared to most people. Your husband ran a flourishing private-equity firm and made a lot of money, which you're now entitled to. Added to which he also took out an insurance policy in 2002 which has quadrupled in value in the last eight years." He passed a piece of paper to me across the desk, swiveling it simultaneously. A sea of figures swam before my eyes. "Bottom right," he said kindly, pointing.

There, nestling in the column he indicated, was a figure so colossal I wondered for a moment if it had been translated into drachmas. If Phil, who after all had had a secret mistress, was also secretly Greek? But there was a pound sign before it.

"Good grief. Have we always had that much?"

"No, it falls in on his death. It's insurance."

"And is it all mine?"

"On an annual basis, yes."

"Annual. You mean…not a lump sum?"

"No, that's what you'll receive every year."

I looked up. Stared. He gave me a level gaze back.

"Blimey," I said somewhat inadequately. "I had no idea."

"He provided for you very well."

"Yes. Gosh. Didn't he?" I said humbly. I realized I'd been less than complimentary about my late husband recently. "But you're sure it's all entailed on me?"

He retrieved the paper. Whisked it around to peruse it. "'In the event of my death,'" he read out, "'all my estate to be bestowed on my wife.'" He looked up. "That's you, isn't it?"

"Yes."

"Seems clear enough."

"No other dependents?"

"Well, your children, obviously, if you die."

"Obviously."

"But no bequests to other relatives, no." He shrugged. "It's not a detailed will, but then it wouldn't be. People don't expect to die at thirty-four." He started to shuffle it all back together.

"You've read all of it, have you?" I said nervously. He was a bit more on the ball today, but he had struck me as slightly shambolic, previously.

He paused. Looked up. "Yes, I've read all of it. I passed my law exams too."

"Sorry. It's just…"

"There's a mother?"

"Well, yes, but—"

"There often is." He glanced at the papers again. "No, not provided for."

"A sister too," I said, playing for time. "Cecilia Shilling?"

He ran his eyes over it again. "Nope."

"And, um, someone called…Emma Harding."

"Emma Harding." He frowned. "Why do I know that name?" He read again. Took his time this time. When he'd finished, he looked at me more intently. "Not here."

"Sure?"

"Positive."

"May I see?"

"Be my guest."

He passed the relevant page across, and I scanned it quickly. Then I breathed out slowly. When I looked up, he had his head on one side. He was regarding me closely, brown eyes watchful.

"Relieved?"

"Very."

"Special friend?" he said gently.

"So…I was led to believe." I swallowed. Passed the will back. There was a poignant silence.

"Mrs. Shilling…"

"Poppy."

"Poppy. Often people—well, men, in particular—promise all sorts of things, all kinds of—provision, and then never follow through. I've seen it before. Family, inevitably, comes first. Most people are careful about that."

"So it seems. In fact it seems…" I hesitated, "that he's been extremely…careful." I felt a stab of guilt, remembering how I'd recently maligned him. Very publicly. In church, no less, to Angus. Said I was delighted he'd gone. Told Mrs. Cripps in the shop I felt blooming marvelous. I had felt marvelous. Euphoric even. But suddenly I felt wretched. Could feel myself shriveling. Life was so complicated. My feelings were so complicated. Mood swings, violent ones, flung me this way and that as if I had no control, as I lurched from one revelation to the next. A good revelation, in this case: Phil had more than provided for us. But when would I find an even keel? A little perspective? It was all so exhausting.

Sam's voice broke into my thoughts. "He was indeed thoughtful. Temperament, of course, is key. Was he a methodical man?"

"Yes."

"Tidy?"

"Oh God, yes. Obsessive."

"Those are often the ones who squirrel money away. And if they do it early—in your husband's case, the moment you got married—it mounts up quickly." He sighed. "People who live by the seat of their pants, on the other hand, often discover there's nothing for their dependents in the kitty when they look. See my ex-wife on this one."

"Oh. I'm sorry."

"Don't be. She married my best friend, who's infinitely more solvent than I am." He grinned. "So all's well that ends well."

I was taken aback. "You don't mind?"

"That he's richer than me?"

"No, no I meant…"

"Oh, I see." He paused.

"Sorry," I said quickly, blushing. "Absolutely none of my business."

"No, but then again I brought it up." He seemed to hesitate. Then he shifted in his seat: a regrouping gesture. "Anyway, back to you." He cleared his throat. "This colossal sum of money will plop reassuringly into your bank account on an annual basis unless you leave further and better particulars to the contrary. Unless you have plans perhaps to reinvest it on the stock market, or on the roulette tables of Monte Carlo, the horses in Deauville…?"

"No, no plans. Let it plop."

"In which case I'll leave instructions with the bank for that to happen when all the paperwork's been seen to. This copy is yours," he handed me a pristine document, "to peruse at your leisure, and I'll keep this one for the files."

"Right. Thank you, Mr. Hetherington."

We looked at each other. The meeting appeared to be over.

"Sam."

"Sam."

I stood up, not without a tinge of regret. Tall. Very tall, I thought as he also got to his feet, to shake my hand. I'd forgotten that. Burly almost, with that rugby-player physique, as he came round the desk to show me out. Nice eyes that crinkled at the corners and almost disappeared when he smiled, like now, as he went to open the door for me.

As I passed under his arm, a thought occurred. I turned.

"Do you read, Sam?"

"Read?"

"Yes, books. For pleasure. Novels, that kind of thing."

He shrugged. "A bit. Biographies, mainly. Oh, and Nick Hornby, if he's got a new one out. Why?" He smiled down at me.

I smiled too, trying to replicate the crinkling-eyes effect. "Just wondered."

―――

Jennie had had the children for me, and I popped next door to collect them when I returned. As I entered her kitchen a clutch of ghosts turned to look at me. Closer inspection revealed that Hannah,

Jennie's youngest, was making cakes and that everyone, including my children, was covered in flour. Jennie looked harassed.

"You are a star, Jennie," I said, going quickly to relieve her of at least two of the young chefs. "Have they been all right? No trouble?"

"Total heaven."

Archie opened his mouth and started to wail.

"But of course they always do that when their mother appears. How did it go?"

"Really well," I said eagerly, scooping Archie up, then I became aware of Clemmie's huge eyes on me as she caught my tone. Perhaps not the moment.

"*Pas devant les enfants*," Jennie agreed quickly. "Tell me later. Are you all right?"

"Yes, why?"

"You're smiling in a funny way, like you've got a headache. Your eyes are all crinkled up."

"I thought it was attractive."

"No, it's not. Oh—here, Archie did a picture." She thrust a still-wet painting into my hand then hastened round the table to where her daughter, on a stool, was tipping an entire packet of currants into the mixing bowl.

"Not all of them, Hannah!" she cried.

I left her to it, but her phone rang as I passed it in the hall. I stopped, Archie on my hip.

"D'you want me to get it?" I called back.

"Please. And I'm not here. Hannah—darling, whoa!"

I picked up the receiver. "Oh, hi, Dan."

Jennie stopped what she was doing. Her back stiffened, hunched over the mixing bowl. She turned, in listening attitude, as I listened too.

"OK, hang on," I told him. I cleared my throat. Put the phone to my chest.

"He's at the station," I relayed calmly. "But he's had a teensy bit too much to drink, so he thinks the responsible thing might be not to drive home."

"Which station?"

"Our station."

"I thought he was staying the night in Leeds?"

I replaced the phone to my ear. "She thought you were staying in Leeds?" I listened. Turned back to her. "The meeting was canceled because the media buyer's mother was rushed to hospital. He just had lunch there and came back."

"Well, that's something, I suppose," said Jennie grimly. "Bloody man took my overnight case instead of his. I've just found his, all packed and ready in the wardrobe. Idiot."

"That'll teach you to have smart his and hers luggage," I told her.

"There's nothing smart about this marriage, Poppy. So he wants me to pick him up, does he?" She said testily, her hands covered in sticky gloopy flour.

"I'll go," I said quickly, as her nostrils began to flare ominously.

"*Bloody* man. *So* irresponsible. Why does he always have to get pissed? And then we've got another car sitting at the station—marvelous!"

"We'll both go," I placated her. "And then you can drive the other one back. Come on, Jennie, it's not the end of the world."

"It's the beginning of the end of the world," she grumbled, wiping her hands on a tea towel and grabbing her car keys. "Frankie!" she yelled upstairs as she marched down the hall toward me. "Can you come and finish Hannah's cakes? I'm going to get your father."

There was a silence. Then: "I'm busy."

Jennie looked fit to bust. "Just come down now and look after your brother and sister for me for two minutes!"

Frankie appeared at the top of the stairs. Her face was very pale.

"Of course, Jennie. Whatever you say, Jennie."

I followed Jennie down the path to my car.

"She all right?" I said lightly as I strapped the children in the back.

"Frankie? No, she's a complete and utter nightmare at the moment."

I was silent. I never found her so. "Maybe she feels she's a bit put-upon? Baby-sitting all the time? She does a lot."

"She's their *sister*, Poppy; of course she does."

"Yes, but if she's busy, you know, doing her homework or whatever…"

Jennie snorted. "Don't give me that. She's up there running up her mobile bill and gassing to her friends about how to pull a boy—or worse."

I looked at her as we pulled out.

"I don't mean that," she mumbled. "You know I don't mean that. But she's tricky, Poppy. It's a tricky age. And I lose patience sometimes."

"But you encourage her, you know, in her work, and every-thing?" I persevered.

"Well, I don't sit testing her on trigonometry, if that's what you mean. I assume she's of an age when she'll get it done and still manage to help *me* out occasionally."

I fell silent as I drove. There weren't many areas Jennie and I disagreed on, but this was one of them. I knew Frankie felt like unpaid labour and I deliberately overpaid her whenever she sat for me, which I knew she enjoyed: the peace and quiet of a house where young children were put to bed early, my kitchen table all to herself. No demands made on her, no rows, just silence. We drove on past the fields where the race horses galloped, then swung into the station forecourt, which was only a mile or so down the road, but, with Dan's track record, not to be driven from under any circumstances if he was even vaguely over the limit. Jennie's rule, obviously, which he'd sensibly adhered to, and I was about to remind her of this, but a glance at my friend's stony profile beside me dissuaded me. It was a look I'd seen on her face a lot lately, and one she'd never worn when we were younger. Now it would flit across her face regularly, and I tried to put my finger on what it was: oh yes, resentment. Something else too. A faintly hectic gleam to the eyes. Defiant, perhaps. Something Peggy said the other day almost drifted back to me, but not quite. About Jennie. Something surprising. When we were talking about forming the book club. What was it? Laying no claim to a hair-trigger memory, though, and having been recently struggling under a blanket of black cloud, I couldn't remember. I sighed. Lost forever, no doubt, beneath the fog of shock and numbness and downright crippling depression I'd been feeling at the time. I gave myself a little shake. Thank heavens that was over, anyway.

"At least it's on time," I said cheerfully, as heads began to appear up the steps from the platform and commuters dribbled out of the exit. We were a tiny station, and not many people alighted here; most got off at Milton Keynes, further down the track. We waited.

"Still no Toad," she said darkly.

"There he is!" I said, relieved, as the top of his head, hair swept back like an ocean wave from a high forehead and piercing blue eyes, came into view. He looked a little sheepish, I thought.

"What is he wearing!" gasped Jennie as the rest of him appeared.

From the waist up he was in a perfectly normal linen jacket, shirt and tie, but something strange was going on below. Instead of trousers, something pale pink with daisies clung to his legs and hung around his crotch. Woollen, like leggings.

"It's my jumper!" cried Jennie.

It was indeed. Very stretched. And Dan seemed to be sporting it upside down with his legs through the arms, as it were. Hairy shins, grey socks and brogues protruded. As he approached us, I realized that to his left, very much walking with him, escorting him, perhaps, was a policeman. Dan's habitually jaunty, devil-may-care attitude seemed to have deserted him. He looked pale; stricken, even.

"Oh dear God," Jennie breathed, as we both leaped out of the car.

"Hello, darling," said Dan, with the faintest of smiles and terrified eyes.

"Why are you wearing my jumper like that, Dan? Don't tell me you're a fucking transvestite as well?"

"There's a very simple explanation, love."

"Don't call me love. Are you a transvestite? Just tell me now, please."

"Ah, so it is your jumper, is it, madam?" interjected the policeman.

"Sadly, yes."

"And he is your husband?"

"Even more sadly."

"In that case, sir, I imagine your story holds water. Just checking," he assured Jennie, as he turned back to her. "Only, we can't be too careful. We had a couple of complaints from people on the train; they rang in, so we had to check it out. Had to meet him off the train and ensure he wasn't…well, you know. A danger."

"Oh, he's a danger all right," she said grimly.

"Thank you, officer," I said quickly. The policeman seemed to be rather enjoying this now, his mouth twitching. "I'm sure we'll be fine now. So sorry to have troubled you."

"No trouble at all," he said, giving Jennie a nod. As he turned to go he grinned and gave Dan a huge wink. "Good luck, mate!"

"Right, mate," snapped Jennie when he was out of earshot. "What exactly is your story?"

"It's very simple, love."

"*Don't*"—she shut her eyes for a long moment—"call me love."

"I had a rather hot vindaloo at lunchtime in Leeds, and perhaps a few too many beers with Ken from marketing—you know how he overdoes it—and then, on the way home, I experienced a spot of turbulence."

"Trains don't do turbulence, Dan. You're not on a bloody jumbo."

"No, I meant internally."

His wife stared, uncomprehending.

"I had an overconfident fart and soiled myself."

There was an appalled silence.

"Yes, so I went to the lavatory," Dan ploughed on heroically, "to sort myself out, and since my trousers and pants were beyond the pale, I threw them out of the window, sensibly having brought my overnight case in with me; except when I opened it, I realized I'd brought your case instead. Happily, though, you'd left an old jumper inside. Wasn't that lucky? Otherwise I'd have been in real trouble."

"There's nothing lucky about you, Dan, and trouble barely covers it." She seethed, fists clenched, simmering with rage. "You stupid, *stupid* man. Look at you, trussed up like a bloody fairy, and all because you can't be bothered to check you've got the right bloody case in the morning. Too busy lying in bed leaving everything to the last minute. Why are you such a git, Dan? Why? You're like my fourth bloody child; it's pathetic. And why d'you have to have a drink *every* lunchtime, hm? Why is that such an imperative? Why do you find it completely and utterly impossible to walk past a hostelry without—" Suddenly she froze. "Get in," she said through gritted teeth, lips frozen like a ventriloquist's. "Mrs. Mason's watching. Get in Poppy's car *now*."

Dan's head swiveled, then, needing no further prompting, he leaped in my car, where Clemmie and Archie sat in the back, mute for once, eyes like saucers. Mrs. Mason, from Apple Tree Cottage, a wizened, tortoise-like woman, here to collect Mr. Mason from the six twenty-five and ferry him back home for his liver and bacon, was indeed staring incredulously from her Polo window, her own eyes round like the children's, but more the size of dinner plates. Jennie, looking fit to be tied, gave her a tight little smile then turned on her heel and stalked, with dignity, in the opposite direction, toward the station car park, and the other car.

"Shit. Keys." Dan leaped out of my passenger seat and sprinted after her, pink sweater bunched in his hand to stop it falling. He waved the car keys. "Darling…darling, you'll be wanting these—"

Jennie turned and thrust a bunch of keys in his face. "I've got the spare keys, Dan. I thought of that before I left the house. Now stop running around the station like a girl and get back in that car, *now*."

"Righto." He sprinted back to me. By now I was choking into the steering wheel as he got in beside me.

"Thanks, Poppy." He sighed.

"My pleasure," I gurgled.

"These things happen, don't they?"

"They certainly seem to. To you, at least."

"Not my finest hour."

"Nope," I agreed cheerfully.

He leaned his head back wearily on the rest as we pulled away, pink legs akimbo. Then he cocked his head in my direction, his blue eyes resigned. "Divorce? D'you think? This time?"

"Oh, undoubtedly, Dan," I assured him with a grin as we sped off home and the sodden fields flashed past. "This time, undoubtedly."

Chapter Ten

"FORSTER," ANGIE WAS SAYING importantly, pencil poised over her notepad. Her skinny knees in black opaque tights were crossed and protruding from a very short gray skirt. She pulled her skirt down a bit.

"Who?" asked Peggy.

"You know, E. M. Forster."

"Is that Foster in a posh voice?"

"No, it's got an r in it. Something like *Howard's End*."

"Sounds promising," mused Peggy. "Who was Howard? And what was so special about his end?"

"It's a house, Peggy. That's the name of the book."

"Oh, a house. Oh no, I don't think so, do you? We might as well read *Ideal Home*. Tell me, how long have you been a farrier?" She turned and bestowed a dazzling smile on a burly and impossibly handsome flaxen-haired young man beside her, who was blushing furiously and spilling out of a tiny button-backed armchair which struggled to contain him.

We were an improbable gathering assembled in Peggy's sitting room that evening: Jennie, Angie, myself, Saintly Sue, Angus, Luke, Passion-fueled Pete and Simon Devereux, a dashing and debonair porcelain expert from Christie's, with hooded eyes and a fine line in Savile Row suits. We'd been astonished when Peggy had announced the guest list, but Peggy had remained unmoved.

"Why? What's so surprising?"

"Well, Simon Devereux, for heaven's sake. I didn't think you were serious, Peggy. And Pete! What on earth did you *say*? You don't even know him; you've never *met* him!" Angie spluttered.

"No, but his number's in the book under farrier, so I simply rang him. Explained I was a friend of yours, and asked if he'd like to join our book club. What d'you think I said?"

Angie was speechless. "But he must have thought it so odd!"

"Well, if he did, he didn't say so. And he wouldn't be coming if he did, would he? But he is. Said he'd like to read more and didn't get the chance to do much in his line of work."

"Oh, he *clearly* thinks I fancy him and put you up to it!" Angie stormed.

Peggy's eyes widened. "He's coming to read books, Angie, not have a sleepover. Do get a grip."

"And what did you say to Simon Devereux?" Jennie said, taut-faced and pale. "Did you ring him as well?"

"No." Peggy sighed patiently. "If you must know I sat next to him at dinner at the Holland-Hibberts last Saturday. Oh, he was itching to come. Couldn't say yes quickly enough. Don't forget, he's desperate to get elected as our local parliamentary candidate and at the moment he doesn't even live in the constituency. Just darts in at weekends from his pad in Chelsea. He keeps saying he wants to get more integrated in village life and he's joined the hunt and all that, but being a member of a local book club will give him huge brownie points. He's jolly nice, actually, and, to be fair, he grew up here. We had a really good chat. He's adamant he won't let the post office in the village shut if he gets in. I don't know why you're all so outraged. This was the plan, wasn't it? A bit of new blood? Some of it hot?" She lit a cigarette and blew out smoke in a thin blue line.

That had rather silenced us.

So now, here we all were, in a rather therapy-like circle in Peggy's creamy sitting room, splashes of modern art squeezed between the beams, the drizzle outside spattering the darkened window panes, while we passed a bowl of Doritos like children playing pass the parcel. I snuck a look at Simon Devereux opposite. Urbane, handsome and sophisticated in an immaculate suit with spotty silk tie, fresh from the auction rooms of South Ken, he looked faintly amused, I thought, as he passed the crisps. I wondered how long he'd last. This was manifestly parochial for him and once he'd ticked it off his list of Things to Do we surely wouldn't see him for dust. I wondered why Peggy had asked him. Beside him sat Angus, his craggy distinguished face wreathed in smiles, pleased as punch to be out and already on his second glass of Muscadet. Next to him was Angie in her very short skirt, and beside her Pete, who, as I say, looked self-conscious but gorgeous, and beside him Luke, who, with freshly washed blond hair, was looking disarmingly handsome himself, actually. Much better now than in church, I decided. Better when he wasn't shutting his eyes and making ecstatic faces at his organ, which I found faintly giggle-making. But of course it could be a piano, I realized suddenly. Surely if you played one you played the other? That could be promising. I had a quick vision of us in a pretty cottage somewhere, Luke playing Chopin, glancing over his shoulder to smile and gauge my reaction as I sat sewing by the fire. Hm. Perhaps not the sewing. And was an organist in the same league as a cyclist? A bit…nerdy? Well, presumably he didn't do it fulltime. Presumably he had a day job. What was it, I wondered. I had a feeling Angie had said, but I couldn't remember. I shook my head. So much to learn. Still, I would be careful this time.

I must curb my predilection to leap and snatch; I would be circumspect and slow. Oh yes, this time I would crawl.

"Hilary Mantel's awfully good," Saintly Sue was saying, after Angie's Forster suggestion had fallen flat.

Ah yes, Sue. Probably just as well she was here, as a matter of fact, saving us as she did, by providing an odd number, from looking too much like a dating agency. But she was so intense. Prim and straight-backed in her chair, a pile of books on her lap which she'd brought along as suggestions—we hadn't actually chosen a book yet—she was already getting shrill.

"She won the Booker Prize last year with this one," she told us importantly. "But of course, you all know that."

We all murmured appreciatively as Sue passed the book to Peggy beside her. But Peggy's appreciative murmurs were still for Pete on her other side, and she took the book distractedly. "You must be terribly strong," she purred, batting her eyelids at him. "Must do an awful lot of hammering."

This remark hung rather pregnantly in the air. Pete blushed and looked at the floor. Sue cleared her throat impatiently.

"Peggy? What d'you think?"

"Of what?" She turned.

"Of the book, of course."

Peggy glanced down at the tome she appeared to be holding. "Oh. Oh, no. Far too long. We'll never get through that. I should think Pete here's the only one who can lift it!"

She passed it to him, mock staggering under its weight, and he laughed, agreeing in flat northern tones that aye, it was terribly heavy. Angie rolled her eyes despairingly at me.

"What about something a bit lighter to kick off with?" suggested Jennie sensibly. "It does look a trifle ambitious, Sue, although I'm sure it's very good," she added in a placatory manner.

"It's first class," Sue said pompously. "You've read it, haven't you, Luke?"

"Er, started it," Luke said sheepishly.

"Well, if you've already read it, Sue, that's cheating," Angie said sharply.

Sue looked stung. "It's not a competition," she told her acidly.

"Exactly," retorted Angie. "Which means no one should have a head start."

They glared at one another.

"Anyway," interjected Angus appeasingly before things really degenerated, "something a bit lighter might be more the ticket. I agree with Jennie." He smoothed back his silvery locks and leaned forward eagerly, resting the leather elbows of his tweed jacket on his knees. "I thought Poppy here said we were going to do Robert Harris. Eh? Splendid!"

"Did you, Poppy?" Jennie turned in surprise.

"Oh, well, I just…"

"It's not a bad idea," said Simon, easing smoothly into his diplomatic, prospective MP role. "I, for one, love Harris. How about we all read his latest?"

"I've got it right here!" boomed Angus delightedly, producing it from under his chair like a magician. "Went to Waterstones specially." He passed it around, and as it progressed the rest of us looked enormously cheered. The accessible cover and the thought of a rollicking good thriller at bedtime, not some heart-sink intellectual tome, were most satisfactory. Pete, still pink from talking so much in public, agreed it looked terrific, action-packed and just the sort of thing he was dying to have a go at but never knew which one to choose; Luke said it was the only one he hadn't read and assured Pete that once he'd read one he'd read the lot; and Angie, Jennie and I agreed that whilst we read a lot of Aga sagas and chick lit, we never read the he-man stuff and were keen to have a go. Only Sue looked as if she'd sucked a lemon.

"Popular fiction," she sniffed, as the book made its way round to her. She regarded it distastefully. "I thought we were going to do something a bit more thought-provoking?"

"It's only popular because it's good," Jennie pointed out. "If it didn't work, no one would buy it."

"The Beatles were popular," Angie reminded her. "And they were completely brilliant."

"Yes, but they were easy listening," insisted Sue. "Just as this is easy reading."

We all fell silent; slightly shamed.

"Does it have to be difficult to be good?" I asked, miles away, actually. I'd been wondering if Luke had a ghastly mother and sister; I couldn't cope with that again. In-laws were so important.

"No, it has to be difficult to be exclusive," said Peggy with a small smile. There was another silence.

"So." Angus stood up, rubbing his hands. "That's all settled, then. Splendid. I'll pop into town and get another eight books and post them all through your letter boxes tomorrow. Now, Peggy, what about opening that other bottle of wine? It's like the Gobi Desert in here!"

Everyone got to their feet. Angie and I passed around smoked-salmon nibbles and the wine flowed, the noise level growing as people chatted, relieved the rather formal part of the evening was over. Indeed, before long, a veritable drinks party had ensued and even Sue looked slightly mollified, especially since Simon was chatting politely to her; but then Sue's family—aside from the Jardines—were the grandees of the village, Sue's father being a local judge, and Simon did need an awful lot of pukka support to ensure selection.

"But will you live in the village?" Sue was asking him earnestly.

"My family lives in Wessington."

"Yes, I know, but will you buy here yourself?"

"Oh, I'd love to, and fully intend to do that, just as soon as I can," he assured her.

"And just as soon as he's elected, he'll treat it as a holiday cottage," Luke told me quietly. "Where do you live, Poppy?"

"Just across the road." I pointed through the bay window. The drizzle had abated and the dark night had gathered softly outside the glass. I was feeling rather warm and happy now. The wine was flowing through my veins and I was among friends; some old, some new, hopefully, I thought, looking into Luke's greeny-blue eyes, liking the way they matched his jumper. But I wasn't too far from home: not too unsafe.

"Pretty," he said, presumably referring to my cottage, but very definitely looking at me. "Will you stay there, d'you think?"

"Oh, yes," I said, surprised. "At least, I think so. It's the children's home and we love it." It hadn't crossed my mind to move. It had always been the only thing about my marriage I'd loved. My dear little house, having my friends close by, Jennie next door. It was my compensation for Phil. But Phil wasn't here anymore, and now it occurred to me that I didn't have to cushion myself against him. It also occurred to me that with the money I was about to inherit, I could easily sell and buy somewhere bigger, even prettier. Would I want that?

"I just wondered if you'd want a new start," Luke said carefully. Kindly, though. Not artfully or nosily, I decided.

"I might," I agreed. "I hadn't thought of that. But a new start doesn't necessarily involve moving house, does it?"

"No," he concurred. "It doesn't. It can mean all sorts of things."

"And it's not as if I need to move. Not as if, geographically, I'm surrounded by too many fond memories and need to get away," I said, thinking as I spoke. "I'm sure many widows have that problem."

He regarded me carefully. "I like that about you, Poppy."

"What?"

"The way you tell it like it is. No flannel."

I thought about this. "I think that's new," I told him. "I think I've spent the last six or seven years not telling it how it is. Particularly to myself. Living a bit of a lie to accommodate others."

"You mean, to accommodate your husband?"

"Yes, Phil, but ultimately the children. Mostly the children. Who wants to rock a boat that's holding what we love most?"

"So...d'you think you'd have ever left him? If he hadn't—
you know..."

"Died?" I sighed. "Who knows? I'd certainly fantasized about
it. Fifty ways to leave your lover and all that. But I'd never actually
considered doing it." I shrugged. "The two are very different things."
I smiled. "And I've always been a bit of a wimp. What about you,
Luke? What are your family commitments?"

"Oh, I've just got a mum and a sister."

My smile froze.

"Not that I live with them, or anything. I've got a flat in town."

"Good, good," I said, horribly unsettled. "And are you...close to
them? Ring them twice a week? Sometimes more? Bring them with
you to choose soft furnishings, sofas?"

He frowned. "God, no. My sister, Nicky, is far too busy. She
works for *Vogue*, and Mum wouldn't know a soft furnishing if it hit
her. She lives in a hotel in Monaco, mostly."

"Excellent!" I breathed. I liked the sound of the Chambers women.

"My dad encouraged Mum to live in style before he died. He
had this theory that—Good heavens, what's that?"

Sadly this fascinating insight into Luke's exotic family—where
did the organ fit in?—was cut short by a rap on the window. We all
swung about to behold Sylvia, Angus's wife, glaring in furiously. Her
spectacles were glinting ominously, her steel-gray perm rigid. Angus
went pale and instinctively hid his wine glass behind his back. She
disappeared and then the doorbell rang, long and shrill. We all stood
about like naughty children as Peggy, who'd gone to get it, could be
heard placating her at the door.

"Yes, I'm sorry, Sylvia, we *are* running a bit late."

"But you're not even reading! Or even sitting in a circle! Just
standing around gossiping like you're at a cocktail party. I rang the
doorbell, twice!"

"Ah yes, first meeting, though, you see. Just swapping ideas.

Batting them about, to and fro. And we thought a relaxed environment would be more conducive."

"Hello, darling, how lovely. Did bridge finish early?" This, from Angus, in a strained voice as he hastened to greet her at the door.

"No, it did *not* finish early. Our rubber finished dead on eight as usual. It's you that's late, Angus. I thought you were going to put the baked potatoes in for me!"

Other admonishments were lost in the stiff autumn breeze. As the front door closed behind them, Sylvia's angry voice could still be heard as she frogmarched Angus down the road, past the pond, and across the street toward home. We caught her drift, but not the finer nuances.

Peggy came back and immediately crossed to draw the curtains with a flourish. "Foolish of me not to have done that before," she remarked. Then she turned to face us, hands on hips. "Now. Who's for a sticky?"

"A what?" Jennie frowned.

"A sticky. You know, Calvados, Drambuie, that sort of thing. What about you, Pete?"

"Er, well, I'm not convinced I've ever had anything like that before," Pete said, palpitating nervously. "This Muscadet's nice, though," he said, pronouncing the t.

"Ah, but then you've never joined a book club before, have you?" Peggy murmured, slipping down onto the sofa. She patted the space beside her. "Come. Sit." He obeyed, as if in a trance. "So many firsts in one evening. Oh, sorry, Angie, were you sitting here?" She moved to accommodate her irate friend, who'd clearly been usurped, having nipped to the loo to refresh her lipstick. Peggy perched on the sofa arm instead. Lit a cigarette.

"Pete here was telling me earlier that he's got a furnace in the back of his Land Rover."

"Well, of course he has; he's a mobile farrier," Angie said testily.

"Frightfully mobile, I should think." Peggy looked him up and down appreciatively.

"Was Sylvia livid, Peggy?" Angie asked nervously. Angie sat on the parish council with Sylvia; she was also very much on the same dinner-party circuit.

"A bit, but she'll live." Peggy flicked ash in the fireplace. "Must get terribly hot in there," she murmured to Pete. "In your Land Rover. Very cozy."

"Well, I'm not actually in it much, except for driving. And the furnace isn't on then, of course." Pete was looking pretty hot and flustered himself.

"No, no, of course not. And what else d'you make, Pete? Apart from shoes? With your furnace? I say, aren't your thighs enormous? It's a wonder you can squeeze them into that armchair. You were saying?"

"Um, w-was I?" Pete blotted his perspiring forehead with his cuff.

"Yes, about what else it is you make. Aside from horses' shoes."

"Oh…well, I do the odd bit of iron railings and the like. But it's not on a regular basis. More one-off commissions, that type of thing."

"Iron railings, do you really?" Peggy's eyes widened. "D'you know, I was just thinking the other day I was bored with the white picket fence outside my house and could do with some darling little railings there instead." Her smoky-gray eyes gazed innocently into his. "You couldn't pop round next week and give me a quote, could you? Gone down the wrong way, Angie?" She turned to pat her friend on the back. Angie, who appeared to be having a coughing fit, shot her a blistering look and stormed off to get a glass of water. Once she'd gone, Peggy laid a hand on my arm.

"I say," she murmured, nodding toward the other side of the room, "Jennie's having a nice time, isn't she?"

I turned to see Jennie, at the far end of the room by the French windows, talking to Simon. He was standing with one hand resting on a beam above her head, leaning in toward her as they chatted.

Jennie's cheeks were flushed, and as she threw her head back and laughed at something he said, it occurred to me that I hadn't seen her look like that for a long time. Hadn't seen her look so pretty. It also occurred to me that I'd been incredibly dim.

Chapter Eleven

"SHE'S INFURIATING!" ANGIE STORMED the next morning when she and I popped round to Jennie's for a cup of coffee and a post-match analysis. "She's like some ghastly *Carry On* character: how hot is your furnace, Pete? Do you ever take your shirt off, Pete?" she mimicked. "I mean, honestly." She sank down in a heap at Jennie's kitchen table. "I thought: any minute now she'll be feeling his biceps!"

Jennie and I exchanged a guilty glance. After Angie had left early—in a bit of a huff, it has to be said—there had been a bit of bicep comparing. Quite a few people had rolled up their sleeves in a bid to compete with Pete's monumental brawn. But, in our defence, we had all been terribly drunk, what with Peggy's Calvados slipping down a treat and not having had any supper apart from a few meager bits of smoked salmon. It had all got faintly giggly. Possibly out of hand. Angie had missed quite a party.

"Peggy just gets a bit overexcited," I assured her, trying not to recall the arm-wrestling match between Peggy and Saintly Sue, with Pete as referee, the rest of us cheering them on. Sue had turned out to have quite a wild side. Blonde hair askew, pale blue eyes on fire, a button of her already overstretched shirt popping undone, she'd slammed Peggy's arm down on the table then punched the air, roaring, "Yes!" Her halo definitely hitting the deck. Luke, hooting with laughter, had swept her into his arms where she'd clung like a slug, planting a smacker on his lips. As I say, we were all very tight.

"Yes, but if anyone's allowed to flirt with Pete, it's me; he's my farrier," Angie said petulantly. "She's supposed to fancy Angus."

"Peggy flirts with everyone," I soothed, recalling how strangely watchful Peggy had been as Angie had slammed out. "Good," she'd observed to me quietly, taking a thoughtful drag of her cigarette. "Important to save Angie from herself sometimes, don't you think? Nice to see her having a bit of fun, but we don't want her making a complete fool of herself." I'd blinked in surprise. A bit of me had even wondered if Peggy had a master plan going here; if this seemingly frivolous book club she'd organized for her friends had a deeper design. One which made us turn around and take a close look at ourselves, at our motives. Before I had time to reply, though, Peggy had disappeared down to the other end of the room, where she was busy organizing a team game which involved popping a coin down a shirt and jigging about until it appeared from trouser leg or skirt, then passing it on. Simon's coin *would* keep getting stuck on the way so Peggy was instructing him in the fine art of helping it along. The porcelain expert's face had been one of pure delight, and as Peggy threw her head back and roared, I'd thought: no, no master plan. Unless it just involved getting her friends laughing again.

"Simon was nice, wasn't he?" mused Jennie, cradling her mug and gazing out of the window, a distant smile on her face. "Remember him hopping around on the sofa, trying to dislodge the coin?"

"What coin?" said Angie grumpily.

"He really loosened up," Jennie went on distractedly. "His family home is in the next village, that's why he's standing for candidacy round here. He stayed there last night. He loves this part of the world. 'My little corner of England' he calls it." She smiled, remembering. "In fact he said he might not wait to buy a cottage, might rent and commute into town."

"Why isn't he married?" demanded Angie. "He must be over thirty. He's not gay, is he?"

"There's someone he never got over, apparently. He'd known her for ages, first girlfriend and all that, and they were going to get married a few years back; they were engaged and everything, but she kept postponing the wedding. It turned out she'd fallen for someone else. He told me all about it. I really liked that about him," Jennie observed. "His lack of guile. The way he didn't try to build himself up. Some people wouldn't have mentioned they'd been ditched but he's not like that. He's a really nice man, actually."

We digested this quietly. "Bit smooth for me," Angie sniffed eventually, disingenuously too, I thought. She'd done quite a lot of hair-flicking when she'd talked to Simon. She made a pious face and helped herself to the percolator.

"I like smooth," Jennie said with feeling. "Haven't had smooth for years. Decades. Ever. Could very easily get used to smooth."

I tried not to notice her hands were clenched; just as, last night, as I'd wandered back through the village at midnight, I'd tried not to notice that Simon, as I reached my gate, had just left Jennie's. I'd been in time to see Jennie disappear inside as Simon turned to walk the two miles up the hill to his family home in Wessington, presumably leaving his car at Peggy's. A moonlit walk. A contemplative walk, perhaps. Whilst Jennie had gone inside and up the stairs in her dark, sleep-filled house, feeling just a little bit warmer, a little bit happier. And what was wrong with that?

"You won't be getting used to anything," Angie reminded her brutally. "You're married."

"Yes, I know. To Toad." Jennie threw back her head and scratched it energetically with both hands. "Oh, I'm not about to leap into bed with the man, Angie, but surely this old heart of mine is allowed to quicken occasionally? Even skip a beat? Allow me a little extra-marital flirting, please. It's surely not a crime to have a tiny light shining in some dark corner of my life?"

There didn't seem to be much to say to that. Jennie got up to refill the kettle noisily and banged it down with a clatter on her hob. She turned and leaned on the Aga, folding her arms and staring determinedly out of the window, gimlet-eyed. Angie sat up. Cleared her throat.

"Well, if you're not going to—you know—take it any further," she said, "do you mind if I do?"

Jennie and I turned slowly to stare at her. "What, with Simon!" spluttered Jennie.

"Well, as you say, he is rather nice. Much nicer than I thought, and not at all slimy when he loosens up; and I am single, Jennie. And since Peggy's so set on Pete, who, frankly, was only a joke, some twenty-something farrier—"

"You just said he was smooth!"

"And as you so rightly say, nothing wrong with that."

"I think that's a bit rich, Angie!" Jennie snorted. "You can't just cruise in and nick my—my, you know—"

"What?" demanded Angie.

"My book-club partner," she said primly. "Just because Peggy's nicked yours!"

"Book-club *partner*?" scoffed Angie.

"We agreed to swap notes," said Jennie stiffly. "When we'd finished the book."

"I bet you did."

"Now look," I said nervously, as my two friends glared at one another across the room, "this is all getting a bit out of hand, isn't it? We've only had one meeting and we are supposed to be discussing literature here, not matchmaking. Shall we all calm down?"

Angie and Jennie looked embarrassed. "Sorry," they both muttered sheepishly.

"Totally pathetic," added Angie. "Talk about frustrated housewives. And anyway, the whole point was to get you back on track again." She looked at me. "Give you a bit of fun. What did you think of Luke?"

"Nice," I said evenly. Patiently. "Easy to talk to."

"When she could get him away from Saintly Sue," remarked Jennie. "I noticed she was *very* quick to play hide the fifty p with him."

I sighed. "I'm in no rush," I said, meaning it. "I've got the rest of my life, haven't I?"

As I said it, the enormity of that simple statement, the freedom it conveyed and the joy, threatened to explode within me. I got to my feet as Archie wailed. The feverish rage of the last few days had left me as abruptly as it had arrived. That white-hot outrage at Phil's betrayal had gone, and in its place a kind of calm acceptance together with an astonishing clarity prevailed. After a few minutes I said good-bye to my friends. Archie was getting cranky and needed his sleep, but, also, I wanted to savor that feeling on my own. Wanted to cradle my new-found freedom to myself as I cradled my son while he nodded off in my arms. How wonderful it was: I had the whole of my life to choose better, if at all. I shut Jennie's front door softly behind me and walked down the path. It hadn't escaped my notice that Sue had made a major play for Luke last night, but as the coin appeared from his trouser leg and as Sue, like a crouching tiger on the floor, had grabbed it with a shriek, I'd been happy to slip away. Been happy to go quietly. I certainly wasn't going to fight for a man I hardly knew. And anyway, aside from our earlier conversation, he hadn't exactly sought me out.

As I turned into my garden I wondered if it was true that everybody had a soulmate out there somewhere, or if most people just patched and made do? Met someone appropriate and in a fit of youthful enthusiasm turned a blind eye to any imperfections, thinking: perfect, you'll do. Just after Phil and I got engaged I found a list in the breast pocket of his jacket which he'd left behind at my flat: pros and cons, with my name at the top. That should have been my moment. To call the whole thing off. Instead, I ran a fevered eye down and realized, with relief, that there were more pros than cons. One more. "Quite tidy" had been the deal-clincher for Phil. Shaming. But don't forget I'd been feeling very desperate at the time. Very much like a stale bun on a shelf.

Well, I wouldn't be feeling that again, I determined as I went up my path and delved in my bag for my key, flushing with anger as I remembered. Wouldn't be Making Do. I'd be very happy with Clemmie and Archie; yes, thank God I had children. That, of course, was pivotal in the desperation game: wanting—needing those. That biological urge. But now that I had them, we could be on our own forever. I'd never have to panic-buy again.

"I say, Poppy!" As I turned to shut my front door, I saw Angus hurrying toward me, *Spectator* under his arm, fresh from the village shop. I went down the path to meet him, the autumn sun warm on my face, late hollyhocks brushing my arm. Angus raised his hat as he approached.

"Hello, old girl, wasn't that fun last night? And I gather I missed the best bit. Gather the party really got going!"

I smiled, shifting Archie in my arms so his head lay on my shoulder. "Well, it was eased along by almost the entire contents of Peggy's drinks cupboard, so it's hardly surprising."

I had a vague memory of her bringing out something green and vile, peering myopically at the label and saying, "I think I brought this back from Paxos in 1997." That had been my exit moment.

"Yes, well, I was just going to say that next week Sylvia is visiting her sister in Cirencester, so happily I can join in the—you know," he winked broadly and rubbed his hands together, "fun and games!"

"Oh, I'm not sure every book-club meeting will be like that, Angus. I mean, we didn't have a book to discuss, did we? Next week, when we've all done our homework, I'm sure it'll be much more cerebral."

"Euh." His rheumy old eyes looked downcast. Then brightened. "Oh yes, once we've done all that malarkey, but there'll still be lots of time for fun too." He lowered his voice. "When I was in the army we played this terrific game at an all-ranks dance where you had to guess the bare backside. Blindfold, you know? Really broke the ice."

"I'm not convinced much ice needs breaking," I said uneasily, remembering Simon and Jennie chatting very quietly in a corner, heads bent so close together they almost touched.

"Nevertheless I think I'll bring one along."

"What?"

"A blindfold. Scarf, or something. Got some marvelous Glen Morangie too that my brother-in-law gave me last Christmas; pretty sure Simon will like that. I'll bring that too. Toodle-pip!" And off he scurried, thrilled to bits, an entire screenplay playing out in his head, his Border terrier on a tartan lead trotting along beside him.

Later that morning, as I left the house to collect Clemmie from school, old Frank Warner, who'd been sitting outside the Rose and Crown across the road having a pint with Odd Bob, put his glass down on the bench and shuffled toward me.

"Hello, Poppy."

"Hello, Frank."

"Um, Poppy, I gather there's a bit of a book-club thingy occurring at Peggy's place these days. Wondered if I could join?" Frank was late sixties, an ex-squadron leader, widowed, vast moustache, excessive dandruff. He spent a lot of time outside the Rose and Crown sinking pint after pint with Odd Bob, who never said much but nodded sagely as Frank held forth about Harrier Jets. Bob, slower in every respect, had now joined us, it having taken him that much longer to circumnavigate the pond.

"Bob would like to join too," Frank assured me firmly, as Bob nodded mutely. Bob was the closest thing we had to a village idiot. He was a tenant farmer who lived in the filthiest farmhouse imaginable on the road out of the village. If, perchance, as a favor to Angie, one ever popped the parish magazine through his door, such a cacophony of dog barking and howling would start you'd hear it all the way home, and then the geese would start honking and the whole village would turn and look accusingly at you when you returned.

"Um, right. Well, I'm not quite sure, to be honest." I scratched my leg nervously. "Can I get back to you? Only—I'm not really organizing it. I'll have to ask the others."

Frank smoothed his luxuriant moustache in an alarmingly Terry Thomas manner. "If you would, my dear. And put in a good word for us, hm?"

"Of course."

He gave me a huge wink. "Ding dong," he murmured.

I hastened off up the hill with my buggy.

I told Jennie about it when I got back. She was weeding her front garden and leaned on her hoe to listen.

"Oh God, that's nothing," she told me. "When I was in the shop just now, Dickie Frowbisher sidled up to me and said he'd read a lot of John Grisham and did that count?"

"Oh dear God. What have we started?"

"A book club," she said firmly. "With an exclusive, restricted membership. No new members unless they've been thoroughly vetted and agreed on by all existing members; and, as of next week, we get down to the serious business of talking books. Angus should drop them off today and then we can get reading."

"Exactly." I agreed. My eyes roved down. "What's wrong with Leila?" The usually irrepressible Irish terrier was lying at Jennie's feet looking morose, a huge plastic collar, about a foot wide, like a halo around her neck. "Why has she got that on?"

Jennie regarded her hound speciously. "She self-harms," she told me gloomily.

"No!"

"Well, no, OK, she scratches herself. So she has to wear that stupid collar. D'you think I should blame myself? For her mental-health issues?"

"Oh, shut up, Jennie. How long has she got to wear it for?"

"Till she stops scratching, I suppose." She sighed. "Anyway, she's in therapy now."

"Leila?"

"Well, not me—yet. There's a girl in the next village offering free dog-therapy sessions because she's just starting." She made a face. "After Leila, she might be just stopping."

I giggled.

"Anyway," she grinned, "on, on." She stuck her hoe in the ground and starting digging. Humming too, quite merrily for her. And she hated gardening. As I went up my path, the window above her porch flew open. Dan appeared half dressed, hair askew.

"Can't find any ruddy socks!" he roared.

Jennie put down her hoe. "Coming, darling," she said, in an unusually mild voice. I watched her walk inside, in astonishment. Such a statement would normally be met with a sharp rebuke to bloody well find them himself, and even Dan blinked down at me in surprise, ocean wave flopping. He grinned.

"Hi, Poppy. Enjoy your evening last night?"

"Yes, thanks, Dan, it was fun."

"Good. Well, I must say I'm all for it. It's done wonders for Jennie's humor; can't think what's come over her. She really ought to get out more. Well done, you, for organizing it."

"Oh, er, it wasn't really me. It was Peggy," I said uneasily, shifting the blame.

"Well, good for Peggy. You girls need some stimulation in your lives. Can't be running round after your bloody husbands and children all the time, can you? And think of all the books you'll read. Great stuff!"

And with that he popped his head back in to greet his brand-new wife, who, perhaps not enjoying entirely the stimulation Dan had in mind, and with a different sort of fantasy fiction evolving in her head, was at least less susceptible to the irritations he provided.

Was that such a bad thing, I wondered as I went inside, lifting Archie from his buggy and refusing Clemmie's demand for a biscuit before lunch. I took their cottage pie from the oven and let it cool a moment on the side. If living in one's own head made one more amenable to others, more accepting of the real world and the people one lived with, so what? Surely that was OK? Up to a point, I decided, as I scooped out a bit of pie for Archie and broke it up with a fork to let the steam pour out. The problem came when one lived more in one's head than in the real world. It had always been a safe place for me to go, both as a child when Mum had died and later on as my marriage failed. But if we all moved around in our private worlds, we ended up living with strangers.

I sat a moment, gazing out of the window, remembering Dad and me in the early days after Mum's death; being so careful, so polite to each other.

"I thought we'd give her clothes away to one of those charity shops," he'd said one day, coming in from the fields. "You know, Save the Children or something. Too many memories."

"Sure. Whatever you think, Daddy." And he'd gone off back to the yard. Meanwhile my head had screamed: "You mean, someone else gets to smell my mother on the collar of her suede jacket? The one I sneak out of her wardrobe and inhale daily?"

And then later with Phil:

"Cycling in Majorca in August," he'd say, closing the guide book decisively. "We'll leave the children with your father."

"No. *No.* Cornwall. Rock pools, *with* the children," my head had raged, too tired to fight. All fought out. I'd heard Phil's arguments before, every year.

"When they're older, Poppy, of course we will," he'd say patiently. "But sand and nappies don't really mix, do they? Be reasonable."

We had gone to Cornwall once and he'd hated it. "I don't get it, Poppy. I'm sorry, I just don't. A ham roll on a freezing rock with a flapping *Telegraph*?"

I'd seen only my baby in the sand, little Clemmie, gazing in rapture as a minute sand crab shifted sideways down the beach at speed. Later, building a small castle; building poignant memories too. Mind you, I also remember my husband's skinny white legs protruding from a towel and his clenched expression. It was the look of a man controlling himself in impossible circumstances. So off we'd gone to Majorca the following year, and Phil had been happy and I'd once more retired to my head. So much so that once, in a restaurant in Palma, when Phil asked me what I wanted, I said I'd have a pasty.

I'd have to keep my eye on Jennie.

Chapter Twelve

THE NEXT DAY, I went to see Dad. There wasn't any real need to ring; he was always there, doing what he always did, and was always pleased to see me, but I gave him a call anyway before I pitched up. He was there. And he was pleased too.

I found him lunging a yearling in the field behind his cottage: a nervous young filly trotting round him in circles on the end of a long piece of rope. My father's face was a picture of rapt concentration, the only time it looked like that, aside from when he was picking out seedlings in what passed for his greenhouse. Yes, young things: fillies, seedlings, children. I'd been lucky. And only my gran had known that when Mum died. Most people had looked at one another in horror: Peter Mortimer, with a child of eleven! A little girl! But Gran had known about his nurturing heart and had no truck with people who'd told her she should step in and take over. She lived reasonably close by and had popped in regularly—Mum's mum, this is—and if she'd ever been appalled at the chaos, the confusion, the endless saddles and bridles slung over chairs, the hastily opened tins of beans for tea, she never said. Might have quietly cleaned up, but, looking out of the window as she washed up, would have seen me perched in front of Dad in the saddle of some huge hunter, or with him in the barn filling hay nets or water buckets, which could easily descend into a water fight in the yard, both of us running in drenched. I was always pretty grubby and oddly dressed, but I was always with him: beside him in the rattling old horse lorry off to the sales—never a seat belt and probably never a tax disc either. Dad wasn't dishonest, but if he was up against it money-wise, which he always was, he sailed fairly close to the wind. And Gran would have left us to it. Stayed for tea—more beans—and gone away knowing I'd probably be awake until Dad went to bed. Knowing too that I didn't always make it to school if we'd been up all night with a mare foaling, that I drove around the farm alone in a horse box with hardly any brakes, but also that I appeared to be thriving. That I was getting a different sort of nourishment.

Calling it a farm was pitching it high, I thought with a small smile as I stood at the edge of the flat, windy field, watching the filly, who, nostrils flaring, all her instincts telling her this was not right and she shouldn't be on the end of this rope, was nonetheless falling for the patience and kindness of the man on the other end. The field was one of six, all patchy and overgrazed, which together totalled thirty acres. A smallholding, really, with a cottage, a few tumble-down outhouses and a barn, which Dad had personally divided into stalls. All the stalls were crib-bitten and crisis-managed, held together with bits of plywood and binder twine, but they were scrupulously clean, and the occupants looked happy enough. Glossy, healthy and relaxed, rather as, years ago, the young occupant of the cottage had been: thriving on benign neglect.

"What d'you think?" Dad called softly. He'd slackened the rope and was walking toward her, stealthily winding the rope in loops around his elbow as he went until he was beside her.

"Lovely," I said quietly, walking across. I reached out a cautious hand, making sure she'd seen it first, to stroke a silky chestnut neck. "Is that the first time you've lunged her?"

"Second. Might put a blanket on her tomorrow."

I smiled. Received horsey wisdom suggested one might not do this until the age of three, but Dad had his own method of break-ing horses, which involved treating them like adults from an early age. He'd adopted the same policy with me. He'd never turned a hair at teenage indulgences, never joined the clucking mothers who endlessly dissected their children's love—or rather sex lives; indeed he had no problem with my sexuality at all. What he did mind very much, though, was whose car I got into.

"How long have you been driving?" he'd quiz some surprised seventeen-year-old boy, probably Ben, as he came to pick me up.

"Um, about three weeks, Mr. Mortimer."

"Shift across and let Poppy drive, would you?"

"OK," the boy would say, stunned. And he'd shift, because of course I'd been driving untaxed cars since I was twelve.

There again, as many of the mothers muttered, it was all very well. He was lucky with me. I hadn't rebelled. I hadn't had sex at thirteen, didn't get pissed on a regular basis, and I hated smoking. Now if Peter Mortimer had had our Chloe, for instance, they'd say, rolling their eyes…and Dad would smile, incline his head and agree. Privately, though, he'd wonder whether, if our Chloe had been around enough whisky and overflowing ashtrays in her formative years, had sipped Famous Grouse straight from the bottle and been sick, taken a puff of Capstan Full Strength and been sick again, and not had the rules and regulations about such things almost planted in her shoulder bag, she would have been in so much of a hurry. Would it have been such a thrill?

Jennie's mother, Barbara, hadn't been like that: quietly tutting and waiting in the wings for Peter and Poppy to come to grief. Barbara, like Gran, had been discreetly helpful, taking me and Jennie to Boots and letting us fill a basket each: a bit of make-up, shampoo. "You'll want some conditioner now, Poppy." Quietly popping in some sanitary towels. "For your drawer, by your bed," she'd explained. Things Dad really wouldn't have a clue about.

So yes, we'd had a bit of a support network. But so subtle and considerate you'd hardly know it was there, like a cobweb. When some busybody in the village had suggested Social Services look at the state of our bathroom, which at that point not only had a whisky optic on the wall so Dad could top up his glass in the bath, but also some guppies of mine living in the tub, Barbara and Gran had pointed out, metaphorically rolling up their sleeves, that it was summer, and Peter and Poppy swam in the river every day, so what was the problem? The busybody backed off and the fish stayed a couple more weeks until Dad, half-cut, accidentally pulled the plug out. I remember being distraught and Dad couldn't have been more sorry; but then, he was always sorry after he'd been drinking heavily. I make the distinction heavily, because Dad always drank, it was just that sometimes he drank a bit more than usual. If truth be told, he was probably always faintly sloshed after midday, but so amiable and jolly no one really minded. He never got to the abusive or slurring, embarrassing stage, because when he got too tight he simply fell asleep wherever he happened to be. He'd wake up flat on his back in the garden, or on a sofa, or beside one of his mares in a stable. Then he'd blink a bit, look faintly surprised at his surroundings and say, "Right. Must crack on."

These days I doubt I'd have been allowed to stay with him, I thought, as we walked the filly back to her stable. Yet would Dad have parked me with Gran while he went cycling in Majorca? Or, OK, hunting in Ireland? No, he would not. If he went to Ireland I went too, while the lad down the road did the horses. The one and only time I didn't accompany him was when someone tipped the school off that I was about to have my annual day's holiday at the Newmarket sales. Dad, rebuked by my teacher, had sheepishly gone alone. He'd been very late picking me up. I remember waiting on the school steps, getting nervous. Then panicky. Dusk had gathered. No mobile, of course, and my mouth had lost all its moisture. I had him dead in a ditch. I started to cry, which turned into hysterics. By the time Dad arrived, I was shaking with sobs, and even though he was beside me, holding me, I couldn't stop. Wave after wave broke over me, all to do with a terrible sense of loss. Because despite Dad being so brilliant, and despite the fantastic support of Gran and Barbara, I'd lost my mother. And I didn't have siblings. It would be too convenient to hope I'd come out of that unscathed. I was left with an impenetrable fear of being alone.

The only time I felt like that again, that terrible rising panic, just the tip of it even, was when I put down the phone to Ben on the stairs in Clapham. When he told me he'd met someone in New York. I'd recognized the signs. Felt them bubbling within me, as, with a trembling hand, I'd put the brush back in my nail varnish. And it had scared the living daylights out of me. I'd acted fast.

Gran was long dead now, though, and the support network had dwindled with her. Now it was my father who was very much alone. Not that it bothered him. Left to his own devices he went his own sweet, shambolic way. I tried not to show my despair as we left the filly in her immaculate stable, crossed the yard and went through the peeling back door, which Dad had to shoulder-barge twice, and into the kitchen.

Raddled blue lino curled on the floor, bare in patches, and the Formica surfaces—what you could see of them for empty tins, cartons of cigarettes and plastic milk bottles—were chipped and pitted. Plates on the side by the sink looked suspiciously clean but then Dad put them down to be licked by the dogs, picked them up later, and later still—I swear this is true though he pooh-poohs it—absentmindedly put them away thinking they were clean. Even if things were washed, pans and oven trays were always black and crusty. All with what my dad—who, incidentally, barely had a day's illness in his life—would call an acceptable level of filth.

Upstairs the place smelled of ripe bachelor; downstairs of stale smoke, dogs and saddle soap. The sitting room—I poked my nose in—was, as ever, a homage to the *Racing Times* and *Sporting Life*, pagodas of which tottered in every corner. I sighed and shut the door. It was probably no more chaotic than usual, but what had seemed normal when I was growing up looked abnormal the more time I spent away from it. I went to the loo, which I won't tell you about, but then, to be fair, it got a lot of use. When Dad realized pulling the chain in the upstairs bathroom caused plaster to cascade into the sitting room, he'd done the only sensible thing and put it out of action. Three years ago. I came back and put the kettle on, quietly pleased I'd put my cleaning things in the back of the car. Dad reached for his whisky.

"You look better, love," he remarked, eyeing me narrowly. "Much improved. I'm relieved." He moved *Horse and Hound* from a chair and sat down, rolling a cigarette on his knee. Mitch, his Jack Russell, jumped up on his other one, while Blanche the beagle scavenged under the table. Elvis crooned softly in the background.

"I am better. Completely."

Dad raised his eyebrows.

"Well, no, OK," I conceded. "Maybe not. It's not that simple, is it? I'm still a widow and I've still got fatherless children. But that terrible feeling of blundering around in a fog has gone." I sat down opposite him, still in my coat for warmth. "I didn't think I'd ever see my way out of that and I panicked. Then later, I think I just gave up. Like people do in the snow eventually." I wrinkled my brow. "It's weird, Dad, but when he died, I felt pretty abandoned, I can tell you, even though we didn't have the happiest of marriages. Even though I didn't really love him. I'd even gotten to the furious how-dare-he-leave-me stage; quite normal, according to my doctor. But when I heard about his bird"—Dad knew all the sordid details now—"it was like a double whammy. Like he'd left me twice. There I was, thinking at least I was coping, plodding on, when all of a sudden I was back at the starting line again. Miles behind it, in fact."

Dad stroked Mitch's coat and waited. He'd always known how to listen.

"And the odd thing was," I stared up at the ceiling for concentration, for clarity, "I somehow felt I'd let *him* down. That it was all my fault." I came back, shook my head. "Ridiculous, really."

"Guilt," he grunted quietly, making a long arm to the tap and adding some water to his whisky. "And if you felt like that with your tit of a husband, imagine how I felt that Boxing Day. When your mother was haring around trying to be all things to all people as usual."

It was said lightly but it struck me Dad's burden of guilt must have been tremendous. And he'd never shown it. Oh, we'd cried buckets together, great torrents of grief—Dad said he never trusted a man who didn't cry—but he'd never saddled me with the more complicated, adult feelings of culpability. He was made of sterner stuff than me. Suddenly I felt rather ashamed of my recent little collapse in front of my own children.

"I suppose the only good thing that's come out of it," I went on, feeling my way, "is that recently I haven't felt so bad about not grieving him enough initially. I sort of feel vindicated, if you know what I mean."

"I do," he said shortly.

We were silent a moment.

"Anyway," I swept on, taking a great gulp of my coffee, which was cold. "I'm not here to dwell on that. The thing is, he left me some money."

"Did he?" Dad said distractedly, reaching down to take something from the beagle's mouth. "Well, that's something. What have you got, you little minx?" This, not a reference to my financial gain, his commercial acumen being about as acute as mine, but to Blanche the beagle.

"What *has* she got?" I peered as he removed something cream and pearly.

"My false teeth. The little tyke gets them from by my bed. Oh, it's OK," he said, seeing my face, "they're my spare ones." He got up and rinsed them under the tap.

"Well, that's a relief. Wouldn't want those sported on the cocktail-party circuit, would we? That wouldn't impress the sexy widows." Dad and I had an ongoing joke that one day he might meet one of those.

He snorted with derision. "Chance would be a fine thing."

I watched his back at the sink. "D'you want to know how much?" I asked.

"How much what?"

"Money."

"Oh, all right. Go on, then."

I did go on, and even my father, impervious to such things, dropped his teeth in the sink. He turned.

"Good grief."

"I know."

"That's a lot of money, Pops."

"I know."

"What are you going to do with it?"

"Well, give some to you, for a start."

He stared at me. Then scoffed. "Bugger off. I don't want your money."

"To do the house up, Dad. Fix the plumbing, that type of thing. Not holidays in Mauritius or anything. I've got masses."

He fixed me with a clear blue eye. The sternest Dad ever got. "I don't want the money, love. Not yours. Certainly not Phil's. I won't take a penny. Put it in the bank. For a rainy day." He turned, retrieved his dentures, rinsed them again, and set them on the draining board.

"Perhaps I should offer some to Marjorie and Cecilia?"

"Would they offer you some? If it was the other way round?"

"No. But that's not really the point, is it?"

"No, it's not." He shrugged. "Up to you, love. Entirely up to you." My father never told me what to do. Instead he bent and rummaged in what passed for a larder: an old pine cupboard beside the sink. "Now. Lunch. There's the Full Monty but, disappointingly, no one takes their clothes off. It's a complete bacon, egg, sausage and beans affair in a can. A new one on me. What d'you think?"

He turned and brandished it, complete with full fry-up illustration, and I knew that was the end of it. The conversation. Knew, before I came, that Dad would no more take money from me than go to the dry cleaner's. But it had been worth a try.

I sighed. "Go on, then," I said, making room on the table amongst a pile of old newspapers. "Let's silt up our arteries together."

—◦◦◦—

Worth a try? Not really, I thought as I drove home later, full of beans and bacon and something indeterminable that must have been mushroom but, as Dad said, could easily have been toenail. Not worth it, because I knew Dad had been offended I'd even suggested it. He chose to live like that. He was a free spirit in the very real sense of the expression. But I'd been toeing some conventional line which dictated I make the offer to my ramshackle father; adhering to conformist nonsense that Dad never adhered to, and always turned and regarded me with surprise when I did. I squirmed behind the wheel. I wished too that I'd taken the children. Dad had been surprised not to see them. But I'd somehow imagined I'd wanted a grown-up financial conversation, complete with spreadsheets and charts and what have you, without two small children running around. Instead the conversation had taken all of two minutes and had offended my father, who'd much rather have seen his grandchildren.

I parked and smiled ruefully as I went up Jennie's path to collect my offspring. Interesting. As ever, a visit to my father had made me feel better and worse, both at the same time. Just as the superficial chaos was thrown into starker relief when I'd been away a while, so too was his refreshing alternative outlook. To sparkling effect. I sighed. I should see more of him.

Jennie was clearly bursting with some sort of news as she opened the front door. She didn't allow me to push on through as usual and was perhaps even lying in wait.

"Guess what?" she breathed with barely concealed excitement. She faced me in the hall, eyes glittering.

"What?"

"Word of the book club has spread to Potters Wood. The Americans want to join."

I'd hardly even made it across the threshold. Hardly got my foot in the door. But I have to say, her delight was instantly matched by mine, as she knew it would be.

"Oh!" I couldn't speak for a second. Stared at her bright eyes. Then cautiously: "You're kidding."

"No, I am not! They absolutely want to join our gang!" She shut the door behind me with a bang. "How about that?"

The Americans were a thrillingly exotic couple who lived in Chester Square, Belgravia, during the week and rented a cottage—more than a cottage, actually, a pretty big house—just outside the village at weekends. He was a film producer, and she, a beautiful raven-haired mother of three. The only time Jennie and I had come across them was when Leila went missing and I went to help find her. Having asked everyone in the village, in desperation we'd gone to Potters Wood, a pretty white house with tall chimneys at the end of a no-through lane. We knew it was owned by the National Trust but were unaware who was renting it. The most divine-looking man, tall, broad, bronzed, and naked to his jeans had opened the door. His hair was brown and wavy, his lips full, and he had a smile that split his face. He'd shaken our hands and introduced himself in an American accent as Chad Armitage. Then he'd offered us proper coffee and listened to our stammering story. Instantly he'd suggested he help look for Leila, at which point his beautiful dishevelled wife had appeared down the stairs, dressed only in a silk dressing gown, at eleven o'clock in the morning.

"Oh, God. Shall we help look? Shall I get the kids?" She swiftly tied her robe and reached for her mobile, looking concerned.

"No, no, she'll turn up," we said hastily, drinking in everything. The tumbled, post-coital look of this golden couple so late in the morning. The fabulous modern art on the walls. The children out BlackBerry-ing with the nanny, apparently. The way he called her "honey" and looked at her with true love. We probably had our mouths open, and certainly wouldn't presume to have them look for scruffy old Leila, who was probably shagging some terrible mongrel. Eventually we'd taken our leave, regretfully; thanking them as they assured us they'd call if they saw her.

Before we left, I said shyly, "It's a lovely place you've got here." It was. The garden was brimming with wild flowers and it was all slightly overgrown, as if they were too busy in bed to prune the roses.

She, Hope, as we now knew she was called, linked arms with Chad on the doorstep and smiled up into his eyes. Then, in a husky voice, she said, "It's paradise."

Jennie and I crept away enthralled. I just knew I'd have said, "It's heaven," and thought how much better her version sounded. How it had truly conjured up the Garden of Eden, and how the pair of them, standing on the threshold like that, had looked like Adam and Eve. Jennie had been equally overawed, and we hadn't spoken for a good few minutes.

Later that week I'd met Jennie coming up the no-through road to Potters Wood with Leila on a lead. I'd been going down it with Archie. We'd both stopped, blushed.

"It's a footpath," we both blurted in unison. Which it was, but not one we'd ever used before.

It was obvious what attracted us. Their perfect lives. Moneyed, cultured and happy, with golden children, who we later spotted around the village with the nanny, while Chad and Hope no doubt tried position number forty-six beneath a Picasso. Jennie and I, having imperfect lives, were fascinated; although, interestingly, we never really voiced this to each other. Never let on. This opportunity, however, was too good to pass up.

"Where did you see them? What did you say?" I demanded, still in her hallway.

"In the lane, in their huge Land Cruiser. Just Hope. She slowed down, stopped and said she'd heard about the book club and would we mind, only it was *just* what she and Chad were looking for, and had hoped to find here, but hadn't."

"Both of them? They both want to join?"

Clemmie and Archie had now found my legs and were clamoring for attention. Sometimes I did wish my children could go BlackBerrying with a nanny. I hoisted Archie onto my hip.

"Yes, because he's on gardening leave, apparently. In between films, so slightly at a loose end."

The idea of either part of that glamorous double act being at a loose end gave us pause for thought and almost threatened to shatter an illusion.

"Well, relatively speaking," Jennie said quickly. "I'm sure he's got something in the pipeline. Reading scripts, et cetera."

"Oh, absolutely," I agreed quickly. They certainly weren't allowed to kick their heels.

"So you said yes?"

"I said yes, and they're coming on Tuesday. Don't you think Simon will be rather impressed?" She couldn't resist adding.

Ah. That little agenda. Her own private subplot. And yes, he would. Chad and Hope were quite a feather in anyone's cap. Once they'd been outed as Exciting Newcomers everyone had tried to nab them. Their doorbell at Potters Wood had never stopped ringing. Hope had been asked to join every bell-ringing, tapestry-making group in the village, by everyone who had a little fiefdom to push. Sylvia had popped round to see if she'd like to help arrange the church flowers.

"Oh, I'm hopeless at that kind of thing," Hope had purred at the door. "I just pick them and cram them in a jar any old how, I'm afraid." She'd indicated the cow parsley tumbling sexily from a jug on the table behind her.

"Oh, don't worry," Sylvia had warbled. "I'm a plonker too!"

No wonder Hope had looked startled.

Even Simon had tried, with the local Conservative Association, and been politely—and sensibly—declined. Angie had popped round to ask if Chad would sit on the parish council, something, as chairman, she *was* allowed to ask, but everyone knew you had to schmooze for years to achieve. No one had reprimanded her, though. No one objected.

"What did he say?" we all asked Angie avidly, about six of us in the village hall at the fete flower-arranging group, when she'd bustled in late to report.

"Hope answered the door and said he wasn't there. She said he'd be thrilled to be asked, though, and she knew he'd be really sorry to turn it down, but he was just too tied up right now. She was still in her dressing gown, hair all mussed."

"Ivory silk?" breathed Jennie.

"Yes, and then *his* voice drifted downstairs, all American and husky. 'What are you doing, honey?' And she went all pink and stammered, 'Oh, I-I guess he is here, after all.'"

We all paused wistfully in our peony-trimming.

"Sex all day," pronounced Jennie at length. "Dreamy."

"And maybe he really was tied up?" mused Peggy, going back to her zinnias.

Back in Jennie's hall, though, facing my friend now, a thought occurred. "But what will we say to everyone else? You know, Frank, Odd Bob, Dickie Frowbisher and everyone else who wants to join?"

"We'll tell them to get stuffed," Jennie said firmly. She squared her shoulders. "This is an exclusive club, Poppy, not a free-for-all. We allowed Saintly Sue to join to show willing, and now Hope and Chad, but that's our limit. We won't get in anyone's sitting room otherwise, for heaven's sake."

I nodded in agreement as I left with the children, but knew this was thin. Angie had a huge drawing room. And quite a few noses would be out of joint. Ours was a small village. Oh, to hell with them, I thought, as I let myself in. Jennie was right. We had to be just a little bit selfish occasionally. And the Americans would certainly inject some glamour.

As I went into the kitchen, the answering machine was flashing. I pressed it absently as I lowered Archie from my hip, watching him toddle off to his playpen, clamoring to get in. It was pretty much his favorite place these days. Wasn't it supposed to be a prison? Would a child psychologist tell me he felt safe in there, or something heart-stopping? As I lifted him inside, a deep male voice politely asked me to make another appointment, whenever it suited. Nothing drastic, but something had cropped up and he wondered if I could pop in and talk about it. Sam, the solicitor.

Well, obviously it had been a while since a deep male voice had asked me to do anything, politely or otherwise, surrounded as I was by women and children. But had there been any need to ring back immediately? Before I'd even taken Clemmie's coat off? I got through to Janice, who made me an appointment. When I got off the phone, I moved around the house feeling lighter, brighter somehow. More energized. I went to the window to smile out at the day. Yes, that'll be the Americans, I thought. That's what's put a skip in *my* step. The irrational desire to play the message again—which I did, three times—was only to make sure I'd got it straight. About it being nothing drastic. And nothing to worry about. That was all. I turned up the radio as I passed and sang along with West Life, then I swept Clemmie into my arms to twirl about the room with me. She threw her head back and laughed with delight.

Chapter Thirteen

ON MONDAY NIGHT AT choir practice, I thought we were going to be lynched. Three people on the way to church told me it was outrageous they weren't allowed to join, particularly since we'd allowed the Armitages; and once I'd achieved the church and was in the choir stalls, Sylvia told me she'd even moved her bridge evening.

"We decided Wednesdays were much better," she told me firmly, turning round from the pew in front. "So I'll read Angus's book when he's finished and see you there. We thought one copy between the two of us would be fine." Sylvia was notoriously tight.

"No, Sylvia, I'm sorry," Jennie butted in beside me—Sylvia had pointedly addressed me, not her—"we've reached our limit. Otherwise the group is too large and people feel intimidated. They won't pipe up."

I doubt if Sylvia had ever felt intimidated in her life, particularly when it came to piping up. I also doubt whether anyone in the village had ever stood up to her. Her left eye began to twitch manically, and she looked fit to burst her tubes. Happily Saintly Sue was tapping her lectern importantly, reminding us we'd be singing at the real thing soon, therefore it had better be good, and Luke was flying through the door, so Sylvia didn't have a chance to come to the boil. But I saw Angus, who'd been studying his brogues during this little exchange, glance up to give Jennie an admiring look. Whether he'd be allowed out to play with the rest of us now was, of course, debatable. I had a feeling he'd be in his carpet slippers, toying gloomily with his cauliflower cheese in front of *Panorama*. Sylvia wouldn't want him mixing with the Americans if she wasn't allowed to; although her curiosity might get the better of her. She might want him there as a spy, taking notes, so she could quiz him later.

As Luke bounded boyishly up the steps to the organ, blond hair flopping, he flashed me a grin, and I smiled back. Smiled, though, not glowed. And as Angie and Jennie either side of me exchanged a delighted glance, like proud parents—one they clearly thought I didn't notice—I hoped I wasn't going to disappoint anyone. He was nice. Very nice. And good-looking too. So perhaps it was just the fact that he was always late and then basked self-consciously in the tiny spotlight this afforded that annoyed me? Or maybe he was genuinely busy and lost track of time? At Peggy's I'd liked him more, I decided, as he played the opening chord in a dramatic manner. We'd perhaps even had a moment as we'd chatted over a glass of wine by the darkened window—which, let's face it, was a far more conducive environment than this one. The organ didn't help, this chilly, damp church didn't help, and as we all launched into the Gloria and Molly into "Nights in White Satin," I knew that didn't help either.

After choir practice, I found myself walking out of church alone. Angie and Jennie were up ahead discussing dishes Jennie was making for Angie's freezer, when Luke materialized beside me.

"Hi." He pushed his fringe out of his eyes.

"Oh, hi, Luke."

I'd been looking in my bag for some money for Frankie. I hated rooting around for it while she stood waiting; liked to have it ready, so the transaction was swift and clean, prey as I was to the usual ridiculous middle-class hang-ups about paying anyone to work for me. As he wheeled his bike beside me, I eyed it warily. Hm. Now, it was just a common or garden pushbike, I grant you, but one thing could lead to another and before you know it he could be head to foot in blue Lycra.

"I thought we pretty much nailed it tonight."

I couldn't help smiling at his rock 'n' roll way of putting it. "I agree. We're nearly there."

Don't be mean, Poppy, he's just making conversation. And he was satisfyingly tall and slim but not skinny, I decided, as he strolled beside me in the light of a full moon.

"D'you find it hard, that he's here?" he asked, glancing around. That endeared him to me immediately. Many people would have conveniently forgotten my husband was among us.

"Not in the least. For one thing I don't believe in ghosts, and for that reason I've always found graveyards rather comforting places." I thought of the one I visited quite regularly on the other side of Aylesbury. "Quite sleepy and peaceful and not remotely spooky, even at night. I'm glad he's here and not in some urn on my mantelpiece. It means the children can come later if they want to. Have a chat."

"And even if there are ghosts, who's to say they'd be more scary than the living? I can't help thinking they'd be rather serene and calm, not having to live in the real world any more. Being well out of it."

"Exactly."

We walked on.

"I used to be fascinated by tombstones. Still am a bit," he admitted. "Imagining the people, their lives."

"Oh, me too," I said, surprised.

"I mean, look at this." We stopped at a lichen-covered stone. "Imelda Ruskin, beloved wife of Arthur Ruskin."

"Yes, I know. When equally beloved wives, Rachael and Isabella," I pointed, "are buried over there."

"And Isabella was only twenty-two when she died," he reminded me, as we paused at her grave. It was one I knew well, had often wondered about. "Childbirth, d'you think?" He nodded at the tiny grave beside her. "We know she was mother of Patrick."

"Or poison, to move Arthur on to wife number two perhaps?"

He laughed. Shrugged his shoulders. "Who knows? And was Arthur a warty old dog exercising a spot of *droit de seigneur* or a dashing young blade?"

"Oh, a young blade," I said emphatically.

Arthur had always been a bit of an attractive cad in my eyes. Cutting a swathe through the damsels in the village, who all swooned for him, before popping his clogs elsewhere, somewhere more exotic. For Arthur wasn't buried along with his wives in this churchyard. And nor would I be, I determined suddenly. Wouldn't stay here forever, to be slotted in beside Phil.

"D'you ever make it up to London, Poppy?" Luke said easily. "I thought we could have lunch."

Well, I'd pretty much known he was going to ask me something like that. But London. No, I didn't, as a rule.

"Or a pub lunch here?" He waved his hand at the Rose and Crown.

"No, I make it to London," I said, thinking of Arthur and his travels. "I'd like that. Thanks."

"Good. I'll book a table somewhere. West End? I imagine you'll be shopping."

"Oh, er, yes. I imagine."

"What about next Tuesday?"

"Perfect."

We'd reached my gate now. Stood facing each other in the Moonlight. "Goodnight, Poppy." He reached out and tucked a strand of hair back behind my ear, before lightly kissing my cheek.

Why should that small gesture disarm me?

I turned to open my gate, simultaneously swinging my bag over my shoulder, but it was a clumsy maneuver, and the strap caught on the picket fence. As I unraveled myself I turned quickly to see if he'd noticed, and just caught his eye. By the time I'd smiled nonchalantly he was well on his way.

I walked up my path thoughtfully. Well, I was out of practice. Flirting. But I'd have to do better than that. One man leaves a message on my answering machine and I'm twirling round the kitchen, another touches my hair and I'm fighting my own garden fence? I shook my head. Any woman's magazine worth its salt would point out that, recently widowed and bereft in so many other ways for years, I was vulnerable. And susceptible to any man's attention. Any man, I thought soberly, being a great deal better than Phil.

I could barely get the tenner into Frankie's hand before she'd sidled past me with the briefest of muffled thanks, and out into the night. I turned and watched her go. Toward the pub across the road. Into the pub? No. Surely not. It was full of locals; she'd never get served. She hurried past the saloon-bar door and went round to the yard where the barrels were stored. A car seemed to be waiting, engine running. She slid quickly into the passenger seat. I watched as it sped off. Oh well, it was still early, I reasoned uneasily as I went inside. And she was sixteen now. Hardly a child. I didn't want to make things hard for Frankie, and as Jennie keeping reminding me whenever I raised it, she really wasn't my problem.

—⁓—

I found myself dressing rather carefully for my meeting with my lawyer. I gave my hair two washes, wishing it was thicker but pleased it was still satisfyingly blonde from the recent highlights, and blew it dry with a round brush instead of just giving it a hasty blast of hot air. It hung in a fair sheet around my shoulders. Spun gold, Mum used to say when I was little. Then she'd brush it for me, my head in her lap. My face was a bit pale, but a spot of blusher and lipstick and a bright pink scarf improved it, although I did remove the silky skirt and replace it with a navy one. And my new boots, not bare legs. Years ago I'd still have been head to toe in black, I reminded myself, and this was a meeting, not a date. Nevertheless my heart quickened as I tripped lightly downstairs, one hand brushing the rail. I hesitated at the bottom. Ran back upstairs for some scent.

The heavy oak front door onto the high street had been varnished, I noticed, and there was a new sign on it: Sam's name in gold letters picked out just below that of the senior partner. The stairs, as I climbed the two flights, had been carpeted in something cream and expensive, with gilt stair rods. Very Harley Street, or whatever the legal equivalent was. Wigmore? No, that was teeth. Very private practice, anyway. Maybe we could share a joke about that? Except we'd already done one about makeovers. Anyway, something quick and witty would come to mind, I decided, as I bounded up with a new authority and sailed into Janice's waiting room. I was feeling decidedly sparky today.

Janice's room was more than just tidy, it was freshly painted, with flowers on the desk. After she'd greeted me with a beaming smile I admired the decor and the flora, and then we indulged in a spot of girly chat about how we both loved lilies. She ushered me on through, assuring me Sam was waiting for me, and I noticed the new carpet continued seamlessly into his room, which was also immaculate. Although the half-empty packet of Orios on the desk, I decided with a small smile as I turned to shut the door, was a nice familiar touch. I wondered what pretext he'd manufactured for this meeting?

"Poppy. Thanks for coming in again." He stood up with a smile.

"My pleasure." I gave a dazzling smile back, taking the seat he indicated. I noticed the shirt was pink today with a button-down preppy collar and a dark blue tie. A good combination. No social peck on the cheek, but perhaps later, when we said good-bye. And Poppy was a very good start, not Mrs. Shilling.

"And I'm sorry if my message alarmed you in any way."

"It didn't at all," I said, surprised.

His face, as he sat, was serious, devoid of laughter lines. I suddenly realized I should be alarmed. Very alarmed.

"Why? Is something wrong?"

"I'm afraid Emma Harding has crawled out of the woodwork. She's making a claim on your husband's estate."

My heart plummeted. All the skippy excitement of the morning went with it. It seemed to me it seeped out of my boots and right through the creamy carpet and the spongy new underlay to the floorboards below. I felt old. Tired again. And not because of the claim. Not because of the money. But because suddenly I was plunged into a world where my late husband had been sleeping with another woman for years. A world I thought I'd left behind; one I didn't want to return to. Not when I'd been happily choosing between Sam's broad shoulders and Luke's hair-tucking technique.

"I see," I said miserably. I remembered Emma Harding's scrubbed, anxious little face in my sitting room, saying she didn't want a bean. Yeah, right. I crossed my legs, noticing a tiny ladder on the inside of my knee.

"How much does she want?"

"She wants half."

"Half!"

"Well, she claims she'd been his partner—in the domestic sense—for four years, and in the professional sense for longer. Nine, in fact. Four at Lehman's, and five at the new firm. She claims they left to set it up together, albeit under his name, and that during those years any wealth he accumulated was due largely to her, because she was responsible for new investment. Apparently she gathered most of the clients. She says your husband was only a success because of their partnership, ergo she's entitled to half his estate."

"But that's outrageous. She wasn't married to him, hasn't got children by him. God—I hope not!"

"No, no children," he said quickly.

"And if she was so instrumental in the business, how come I'd never even heard of her? She certainly wasn't one of the directors. I knew them. And OK, I knew her name but, honestly, that was about it!"

"Well, that's…hardly surprising, really, is it? Under the circumstances." It was said kindly. And he was looking at me in a detached, speculative way, rather as a doctor would a patient. If he'd had half-moons he'd have been peering over them.

"No. No, I suppose not."

A silence ensued. He shuffled some papers awkwardly.

"She was only on a basic salary because she'd been promised a share in the business when it was sold later this year. If that had happened, incidentally, it would have made millions. It won't now. Not without your husband at the helm and his Midas touch. Investors have lost confidence, it seems. It won't affect your inheritance but it's not in such good shape. It's still trading, but Miss Harding has been eased out."

"She's lost her job?"

"So it seems. And of course she's lost your husband's protection. The other directors were jealous of what they felt to be her elevated position. It appears she also sailed close to the wind trading-wise, which worried them. She was bit of a chancer."

"Right. Good." I clenched my fists. That nice Robert Shaw, who Phil had also taken with him from Lehman's. Ted Barker too, with whom we'd been to dinner. Classy men; old school tie. Too right she was a chancer.

He cleared his throat. "Her claim, however, has the backing of your late husband's mother and sister. They both support it."

I stared at him. Could feel my mouth opening and hanging. "Marjorie and Cecilia?"

"Yes."

"They knew her?"

"It appears so."

"How come?" But I knew how come.

"They met her. Originally, they're keen to stress, in a business context. As a colleague of Phil's, and in order to discuss their own personal finances. But later, under more friendly circumstances. They had lunch together after various meetings in London, apparently. And she was a visitor to their house in Kent."

My heart began to hammer. Sam looked deeply uncomfortable.

"But...why? Why would they do that, support her?" The walls of my throat were closing in, but I got the words out.

"The letters I have from both parties state that Mr. Shilling was, ah, miserable at home, and only stayed for the sake of the children." He looked studiously down at the letter before him avoiding eye contact with me. "Quoting this one from Mrs. Shilling, she says, 'My son had wanted to leave his wife for years.'"

I was shocked. Profoundly shocked. Over the weeks I'd come to terms with the fact that a whole world had been continuing somewhere without me; a world of Phil and Emma, Emma and Phil, and these visits of Emma's to Phil's family home only sketched in additional appalling detail. More grotesque background. But before, it was just the two of them. More people somehow gave the whole picture a density that I knew I was going to struggle to push against. It would be like holding back the tide to suggest that all four of these people had been wrong, had judged me unfairly, and that I was a perfectly pleasant human being. A doddle to be married to. Why should they all be mistaken? And yet it wasn't true. It wasn't fair. My breathing became labored. I was a nice girl, surely? Not the girl in this picture?

I did try, though. To push. "*He* wanted out!" I said shrilly, knowing my nostrils were flaring and my knuckles white as I gripped my handbag on my lap. "*He* only stayed for the children? Oh no, that was me! I was only there because I thought they were so young, so vulnerable." My throat filled with tears. I gulped them down. "I was the one who wanted to go—always!"

Even as I was protesting, part of my mind was wondering how often he'd heard this sort of thing. Sam, the divorce lawyer. Two people slugging it out unattractively, over children, money. But once I'd started, I felt compelled to finish.

"I was the one who felt trapped. How dare he say he stayed with me for form's sake! Out of duty! Ask my friends, ask anyone; they'll all tell you. God, those bitches," I seethed. "I can't believe my own in-laws, my children's *grand*mother, their aunt, Aunt Cecilia—Christ!" I could hear hysteria rising in my voice as I tumbled over my words.

"I can see that's very hard to reconcile."

"Very hard? Very *hard*!"

I wanted a cigarette badly and I hadn't smoked for years. Instead, I twisted a strand of hair rapidly around my finger, another ancient method of restoring composure. I wondered what Phil had said to his mother and sister. Phil, who could do no wrong. Wondered if he'd told them I was a cold fish who gave him no comfort. Oh, I could picture the whole thing. Could see Phil taking Emma to Kent in her smocky white top, looking very different to the girl his mother and sister had met for lunch in London, a business lunch, to discuss their finances, in her power suit and heels.

"You remember Emma?" he'd have said, with no awkwardness. Phil didn't do awkward; he had a towering sense of his own self-importance. His own entitlement. And Emma, with a bunch of flowers perhaps, would execute her practiced, anxious smile.

"Hello. How lovely to see you again. What a pretty house."

Later, after coffee, Phil would confide in his mother, while Cecilia and Emma took a walk in the garden. This girl had brought some much-needed sunshine into his life. Much comfort. He'd never leave me, of course, never. He knew where his duty lay. But this was the real thing. True love. And Marjorie would nod, touch his hand. Her poor boy. Trapped in a loveless marriage. Of course, she'd always known it was a mistake. That dreadful father. She'd shudder. Whisky on his breath. That house, which she'd heard about from

Phil. A slum, almost. Oh no, she wouldn't condemn Phil. Instead, she'd say later to her daughter: poor boy, he deserves some happiness, and how like him to insist he can't leave Poppy and the children. So little happened in Marjorie and Cecilia's lives, I could see them thoroughly enjoying the subterfuge. Knowing something I didn't; having a secret. It would exact a certain kind of revenge, which, let's face it, was always best eaten cold. And they wanted revenge. They'd felt so robbed, you see, when we hadn't gone to Kent to live, but had settled near my father instead. My friends. Their fury at the time had been unnerving.

"But we *assumed*!" Marjorie had spat at me in her immaculate kitchen, tight-lipped, spectacles glinting. "Cecilia and I had always assumed that you'd come here, to Ashford. That you'd stay near the village!"

And look after us, was what they meant.

But I'd put my foot down. And at the time I'd thought it the greatest expression of my fiancé's love for me. The greatest capitulation, probably. One he'd immediately regretted.

"Jesus," I muttered, only half to myself.

"It certainly is a very unusual situation, I must say," Sam said uncomfortably.

I glanced up. Yes, of course it was. And as suddenly as the door to my fury had flown open, it slammed shut and another door gaped. Embarrassment. In it roared. This man, this lawyer, Sam Hetherington, didn't know me. Not really. He didn't know Marjorie or Cecilia, either. They could be quite delightful. They certainly had delightfully old-fashioned-sounding names. They could be sweet, gentle souls, sending anxious letters from Rose Cottage, the house on the letterhead. And I could be simply ghastly. With my powdered face and laddered tights. My overdone scent. My flirtatious manner. It seemed to me yet another door closed too. Softly, but firmly. Eyes glittering, I turned and stared out of the window at the day. It was still warm and clement, lovely for October, but the breeze through the open window seemed languid and heavy, whereas this morning it had been sweet with possibility.

"And I'm afraid mother and daughter are also intending to make a claim. Join the ugly rush."

I turned back to him. Nothing surprised me now. "Oh? On what basis?" My voice came from elsewhere, detached.

"On the basis that apparently your husband said he would provide for them in their dotage."

"They're not in their dotage."

"No, but neither of them works, living as they do off your late father-in-law's pension. But it wasn't index-linked and is running out. Your husband knew that, and to that end intended to make a will which would be inclusive of them. That was why he'd gathered so much life insurance before he was killed."

I regarded him steadily for a moment. This rang true. The only thing so far. Phil *had* gathered an unusual amount of life insurance. For a reason. I cleared my throat. "Do they have a case?"

"In my opinion, no. You, as the wife and mother of his children, have rightly inherited his sole estate, as, I might add, most wives do."

"But they'll fight it? I mean, if I refuse?"

"Oh, they'll fight it."

"Then we'll fight back." Yesterday I'd have willingly given them some. But not now. Not when they'd so publicly humiliated me. "Write back and tell them so immediately. Tell them I won't part with a penny."

He made a quiescent face. "Could do, but that's a fairly aggressive step. And you want to avoid slugging it out, particularly in court, which is heinously expensive. Although it might, eventually, be inevitable."

Court. A vision of me trembling in the dock of an oak-paneled Old Bailey sprang to mind. Twelve stony-faced men and women staring accusingly at me. Cecilia and Marjorie in the gallery, weirdly wearing the hats they'd worn at my wedding, complete with quivering bird on Marjorie's, except it was no longer a peacock, but a bird of prey. Their barrister, a hatchet-faced man, was cross-examining me: "*Were* you a good wife, Mrs. Shilling? Were you?" Silence. The judge reached for his black hat.

"Right," I said miserably. "So...what would you advise?"

The fight had gone out of me and I felt like writing out a check. Three, actually. One to each of them. Emma, Marjorie, and Cecilia. Oh no, four. I probably owed Sam too. Just leave me alone.

"I would advise doing nothing at this stage and see whether they proceed. They haven't actually issued proceedings, just written a couple of letters. Let's see if it's all hot air."

"Yes. Fine," I agreed.

I liked doing nothing. I was a big wait-and-see girl. My entire married life, it occurred to me, had been like that. Wait and see what happens. It might not be so bad. It was. Always. Why did divorce get such a bad name? Surely what I'd done was as bad? This ghastly acceptance? Surely it would have been braver to leave? Something small and hard and angry formed within me. I needed it to grow. I needed to take a steer on my life, that much was clear. I couldn't let these Shillings walk all over me. I had to see them off, not just pathetically scramble clear of them occasionally, as I had done for years, dodging their blows.

"Cup of tea?" Sam asked quietly. I obviously looked very shocked.

"Please."

This small kindness touched me, and as he went to the door to ask Janice if she wouldn't mind, I had to blink very hard.

He came back and sat down again; said one or two comforting things about people making threats all the time, and while it sounded dramatic, it was quite another thing to employ a solicitor, which they hadn't yet done. Hadn't put money where their mouths were. And anyway, even if lawyers were involved, it was often sorted out via correspondence.

"I won't have to see them?" I asked, my voice coming from somewhere distant as Janice came in with the tea.

"Not unless it goes to court, but we've already decided to try to avoid that at all costs."

I nodded. Sipped my tea as he chatted, leaning forward with his arms on his desk. He offered me a biscuit, which I took but couldn't eat, and even though I felt numb, a bit other-worldly, I couldn't help noticing the elbow of his suit was very worn. The right one, the telephone-propping one, and the handle of his black case beside his chair was broken and tied with binder twine. Phil wouldn't have been seen dead in a jacket like that or with a tatty briefcase, and I thought how much I liked Sam for it; and for somehow knowing I'd needed tea and a chat before I took to the high street.

Finally, when it became apparent that I couldn't decently, or even indecently, take up any more of his time, that I'd been in his office for a good forty minutes and we both knew his next appointment had been sitting outside a while because Janice had popped in and told us so, I got to my feet. I felt warmer from the tea, if a little trembly.

"You going to be all right?" It was said briskly, but there was no doubting the concern. God, he was nice. But then most people were, weren't they? I'd just been unlucky.

"Yes, I'll be fine. Thank you. And thank you for your advice."

It was a shame I saw him surreptitiously consult his watch as he walked me to the door. He smiled and we said good-bye.

Outside in the street, something made me glance back up at his building, my eyes finding his window on the second floor. But if I was expecting to see him standing there watching me go down the street, hands in pockets, a wistful expression on his face, I was disappointed.

Chapter Fourteen

"I CAN'T BELIEVE IT." Angie's mouth, painted fuchsia pink, dropped open in disbelief. She left it there for dramatic emphasis.

"I know. Neither can I. Well, no, I can, actually," I said miserably.

"But what sort of man does that?" she asked incredulously. "Ropes his entire family into his extramarital affair and asks them to conspire against his wife!"

"Phil," I said quietly. "A Phil sort of man."

"And—and what sort of family," she blinked, "agrees! Colludes with their son? And his mistress? Gives the relationship their seal of approval!"

I squirmed. "Marjorie and Cecilia," I said mechanically, noticing Jennie wasn't saying anything.

She had her back to us. Strapped into a long white pinny at her Aga, she was stirring a vast vat of boeuf bourguignon ready to be put into Tupperware dishes and thence local freezers. Angie and I were at her kitchen table. Angie had popped in to retrieve a pashmina she'd lent and wanted to wear to a charity luncheon. She'd found me, pale, hunched and in mid-flow to Jennie. Naturally the story had to be retold. And I would, of course, have told Angie eventually, but there was a definite hierarchy. I might have waited until I was more poised. No chance of that now. And Angie's incredulity was hard to bear, reflecting, as I felt it did ineluctably, on me. Jennie, too, had been shocked, but she could believe it. She knew Phil, and she knew Marjorie and Cecilia.

"Phil could do no wrong in their eyes," I explained wearily, wondering if I'd have to explain these Shillings forever. Wondering if I was going to make a career of it.

"They clearly don't know the *difference* between right and wrong!" Angie exploded. "And this—this Emma chit—I thought she came to see you? Said she didn't want anything?"

"She did. But now the will's been published she's realized Phil was probably on the verge of making provision for her, as he was for Marjorie and Cecilia." I shrugged. "I suppose she feels entitled."

"Entitled, my arse!" Angie stormed. She'd got up from the table and strutted angrily to the window, arms folded. Her eyes were bright, her face suffused with indignation. A few months ago Angie's beautiful face had been terribly drawn, terribly wretched. There was at least some light to it now. Was it a relief, I wondered, not to be quite so firmly in the eye of the storm? For the baton to have passed to me? Not to be the one everyone felt sorry for? Not that she'd relish my misfortune—Angie was a sweet girl—but nobody wanted to be the unlucky one forever. The one who had the worst time of it.

"Don't give her a penny," she warned, turning on her four-inch heel to face me abruptly. "Not a penny."

I nodded, mute.

"And what sort of a man is that bloody organized?" she asked. "Starts to tie up his estate like that, in his thirties?"

"The sort of man who has already bagged his spot in the church-yard," said Jennie without turning, still stirring. Then she did glance back. "He would have made it his business, wouldn't he, Poppy? Not to leave any loose ends."

I nodded again. It was all so embarrassing. So…demeaning. "I can't believe I made such a catastrophic mistake in marrying him," I said softly. I wanted to go on to say, "Such a lack of judgment," but knew my voice would wobble. Had I been all there, I wondered, six years ago?

Angie studied her nails, which were long and red, and Jennie kindly resumed her inspection of her casserole, which she'd done for some time.

"I was thinking that today, at the solicitor's," I said, half aloud and half to myself, when I was sure my voice wouldn't falter. "Thinking: what must he think of me, marrying a man like that?"

"Who cares what your bloody solicitor thinks!" snorted Angie. "The important thing is not to give those grasping witches a penny. It's all yours, Poppy, all of it."

"And if fighting for money goes against the grain," added Jennie, waving her wooden spoon at me, knowing I had a lot of Dad in me, "do it for Clemmie and Archie."

Yes, that helped. For them. I'd already told myself that was the way forward. That might propel me. But sustaining the momentum would be nip and tuck. I wondered what I'd think if I was Emma. If the man I'd loved for four years had provided for me, would I want it? Feel entitled? Perhaps I would.

"But she's young, for heaven's sake," pointed out Jennie, reading my thoughts. "She's earning, she has no children. You don't work."

"Don't do anything," I said, feeling slightly panicky. Except, I thought, take my late husband's money: the money of a man who didn't love me.

"None of us worked while the children were young," argued Angie. "God, I don't work *now*!"

There was an uncomfortable pause. Then: "Exactly," Jennie said quickly.

If truth be told, we'd both quietly wondered why Angie hadn't done something to contribute to the family coffers, now that she could. Jennie had once witnessed Tom coming in tired from work in his suit, standing opening bills in the kitchen and muttering about Angie's spiralling Harvey Nicols account, to which Angie had airily said, "Have you thought about getting a Saturday job?" Tom couldn't speak for a moment. When he'd found his tongue he'd acidly asked whether she'd prefer him to have a paper round or be on the till at Tesco's? Angie had angrily enjoined him to take a joke, for heaven's sake. Jennie had downed her wine and crept away.

"Having two small children is hugely labor-intensive," Angie told me hotly. "Don't you go feeling guilty about not working, Poppy. We're the unsung flaming heroes."

I sighed. I knew they were trying to make me feel better but, actually, I felt worse. Like a scrounger. Here I was, in the middle of the morning, having coffee yet again with my girlfriends, before going back to the house that Phil had paid for, and which, evidently, he'd have preferred to have lived in with Emma. Before I'd popped round here, a ridiculously simple riffle through the phone book had revealed that Emma Harding lived locally, up the road in Wessington. Meadow Bank Cottage. I can't tell you how that had shaken me. How I'd almost got under the kitchen table in fright. Somehow I'd assumed that because she worked in London she must live in London, but she didn't; she was moments away. Must have driven past my house countless times, thinking: that's where I should be, with him, where we could be together. Perhaps she should have it now? Suddenly Dad's life, held together with bits of binder twine, appealed. I wondered if he'd got a spare shed. And Clemmie and Archie could go to the local school, not the expensive village Montessori.

"Well, we'll see," I said wearily. "Sam said let's wait and see. See if they follow it up. He said they may just be full of hot air."

"Sam's the solicitor?" asked Angie, and for some reason I bent my head to pull up my sock under my jeans.

"Yup."

"Well, I hope he's good. Who's he with?"

"A small firm in town. Private practice. But he was with a big outfit in London," I added, knowing Angie would be impressed by that.

"Oh, OK. Well, listen, Poppy, April McLean at Freshfields may be expensive but she goes for the jugular. Let me know if you want to meet her. I came out of her office thinking I could rule the world."

"No, no, I'm very happy." I tried to imagine Sam going for the jugular. It was in the neck, wasn't it? Baring his fangs across the Old Bailey at Marjorie. I wondered where he went after work. Where he lived now he was divorced. A rented flat in town? Or did he stay with friends, all guys together, meeting them for a pint after work? I couldn't imagine that, somehow.

"Anyway, thanks, you two. Good to share and all that. I've got to go and get Clemmie. She finishes at lunchtime today."

When they'd murmured their good-byes, with staunch messages of support, and kissed me, Angie nearly breaking my cheekbones, I took my leave. Went slowly up the hill. Archie, who'd just learned the words to "Postman Pat," was kicking his legs in his buggy, singing his little heart out, but mine was heavy. How much was Angie asking for, I wondered. Half of Tom's wealth? More? The house? Well, why not? She'd brought the children up there; it was their home. It just didn't feel quite right. And not because Angie had never worked—oh, she pulled her weight in the community, sat on committees, chaired the council. It wasn't that. It was just…I wasn't sure I wanted to join that band of women who took their husbands for all they could. Because they'd been betrayed.

I'd overheard her talking to Tom the other day on her mobile in the street. I'd come up behind her, been about to greet her, when I realized she was on the phone: "Yes, Clarissa did meet some boy in London and she probably met him on an Internet site, probably didn't even know him, but what d'you expect with the example you set? I'm surprised she's not pregnant!" There'd been a silence, then: "Oh, piss off, Tom!"

As she realized I was there, she'd turned, a look of pure hatred disfiguring her face. "Wretched man," she said, pocketing her phone.

"Getting all parental at this late stage. It was only Hugo, incidentally," she muttered, "who Clarissa met."

Hugo was Angus and Sylvia's grandson. He was a lovely boy, who'd just left school and worked occasionally in the pub. I wondered why Angie hadn't told Tom. I didn't want to be like that. Vengeful. Spiteful. Taking my ex to the cleaners. You're not, I told myself, as Clemmie let loose her teacher's hand at the gate and ran toward me. Because for one thing he's not an ex, he's a deceased; and you're not taking him to the cleaners, you're preventing his mistress taking you. Do get a grip.

I hugged my daughter hard as she embraced my knees. But on the way home, Clemmie chattering beside me, an egg-box alligator swinging from her hand, I decided that the moment Archie was in nursery, I'd get a job. Go back to work. OK, my PR agency in London were unlikely to take me after such an absence, however sorry they'd been to see me go, and particularly for only a few mornings a week, but might they give me some freelance work? They had rung once, offered, but Archie had been only a few weeks old, and Phil so busy, I'd turned it down. So stupid, I thought angrily. Everyone knew you had to keep your hand in. But maybe it wasn't too late? And maybe I could bang on some doors locally as well? I wasn't naive enough to think it would be easy, but I'd inherited Dad's breezy optimistic gene that said anything was possible. I just had to find it.

Angie had been right about one thing, though, I thought, as I paused to let Clemmie feed the ducks by the pond with some bread I'd brought for her. Child care was hard work, and very much unsung. I remembered last Christmas, when Marjorie and Cecilia had come to stay for four days. And how, with two tiny children, I'd produced one meal after another while they barely lifted a finger. They'd sat at the table, straight-backed and prim, Cecilia wearing the blue cashmere cardigan I'd bought her, waiting for me to run in with the plates as if they were in a restaurant. Phil, carefully decanting the one and only bottle of wine we were to have. And I thought of every Christmas when they'd stayed in my spare room, in the sheets I'd changed for them, drinking the tea I'd made for them, all the time knowing about Miss Harding. The Shillings had a terrible tradition whereby we all sat on Marjorie's bed on Christmas morning to open presents, while she sat like the queen in her quilted bed jacket, in my spare room, in my house. And all the time, life was not as I imagined. Earth-shattering betrayal was being played out around me. Part of me had been eager for family traditions, I'll admit; eager for normality, a different sort of upbringing than my own for my children. I was ready to accept a great deal, not having a lot to hang my own hat on. I'd gone along with the present-opening scene with good grace. I'd even gone along with being led in a little prayer by Marjorie after the last one had been opened, bending my head and giving thanks to God. Jesus. *Fuck.*

The scale of their treachery suddenly threatened to overwhelm me. I felt so exposed. Had they all been laughing at me? I tightened my grip on the pushchair; felt my head swim. Breathe, I told myself, breathe. Because…perhaps they hadn't known for years? Sam hadn't said when. Perhaps they only became aware of Emma's existence in the last year or so? Last few months? Yes, I preferred to believe that, I decided, waiting for my heart rate to come down as Clemmie told me about Damien, Mummy, who's got a verruca. Preferred to believe no one could be quite so wicked.

―⁓―

The book club met at Angie's that evening, Angie having the most beautiful house. And Jennie did the food. Oh, yes, food, not nibbles. No bumper-sized bags of assorted crisps were to be hastily shaken into bowls this week. Instead, bite-sized blinis were piled with cream cheese and caviar, asparagus and Parmesan cheese slivers rolled in Parma ham, and tiny baked potatoes topped with sour cream and chives. And we assembled, not in the kitchen, but in the vast drawing room. A roaring fire had been lit under the marble mantle, and Angie's clever decor—heavy linen curtains, creamy sofas, antique tables topped with enormous stone lamps, fabulous oil paintings on the walls—was softly lit by scented candles everywhere. And I mean, everywhere. Angie's taste, generally impeccable, had a habit of lurching off-piste when confronted by a shop full of scented candles. Nevertheless the effect was beautiful.

"If a little sacrificial," Jennie muttered, surreptitiously blowing out one or two as she hurried in with a plate of delicate choux pastry puffs filled with salmon mousse.

Everyone was in their finery too; no jeans and sweaters this week. Indeed most people looked as if they were going to a cocktail party. The men were in jackets, the women coiffed, baubled and made-up, and a general air of skippy expectancy prevailed. Angus was dapper in a tweed jacket, MCC tie and reeking of Trumpers aftershave. He exuded boyish excitement, rocking back on his heels as he guffawed at something Luke said, thrilled to bits at having been allowed out—no doubt equipped with a notebook or perhaps even a tape recorder in his lapel. Saintly Sue was in white trousers and an extraordinary floaty top, pale blue with embroidery around the plunging neckline, which might just have been in fashion five years ago. Jennie was in very tight black trousers and had a great deal of lipstick on her teeth. Only Peggy was resolutely in jeans, an old polo neck and her trademark suede pixie boots. She was also the only one not standing up and buzzing animatedly. She glanced impatiently at her oversized man's watch.

"Come on, what are we waiting for? Let's get cracking," she said, perched as she was in the circle of chairs Angie had set out at the far end of the room, by the fire.

"Oh, I think we'll give them a few more minutes, don't you? It's only just seven-thirty." Angie patted her hair, her gaze roving out of the window which gave onto the gravel drive.

"Why? They can just join in when they arrive, surely?"

"Except that might look a bit rude, Peggy. Seeing as it's their first night."

Peggy snorted and was muttering something about the people in this village not getting out enough if they were sent into a frenzy by having a couple of Americans among them, when suddenly, headlights illuminated the room from without.

"They're here!" squeaked Angie. Jennie leaped to rearrange her asparagus rolls. "And d'you know, I think Peggy's right. Maybe we would look a bit more serious and literary if we were all sitting with our books? What d'you think?"

There was a general consensual murmur at this, and everyone dived for a seat as if the music had stopped in a game of musical chairs. Peggy rolled her eyes. By the time Chad and Hope pushed through the front door, which Angie had left conveniently ajar, we were all sitting in a circle, a bit pink and overexcited but, hopefully, with intelligent looks on our faces. Our books were open, although unfortunately on different pages. Angie's was upside down.

Chad was as handsome as I remembered: tall, slightly burly, square-jawed and wearing chinos and a shirt, no jacket. Hope, beautiful, tiny and dark, was effortlessly casual in a grey cashmere jumper, sweat pants and pumps, instantly throwing into suburban relief our ties and high heels.

"Hope! Chad!" Angie got to her feet with a bit of a swoon, manufacturing the impression she'd just come out of a literary trance, so engrossed had she been in the narrative. "How lovely to see you. Now I know you've met Jennie and Poppy before, but this is Angus, Peggy, Sue—I won't do surnames," she fluttered with a tinkly laugh. Everyone stood up: some in a rush so their books fell on the floor; some with a bit more ease, like Luke; and some, like Passion-fueled Pete, even giving a little bow as he shook Chad's hand.

Chad, looking even more Adonis-like close up, displayed

impeccable manners and some perfectly straight white teeth as he smiled. He smiled a lot and intoned "Chad Armitage" every time he was introduced, making his way around the circle and looking right into everyone's eyes. He was followed by Hope, whose tiny little hand as she extended it seemed as fragile as a bird's wing. She really was awfully pretty, I thought, as I drank in more perfect teeth and silky hair. We all beamed as she greeted everyone warmly. Only Peggy's smile was more amused, and she declined to stand, politely offering her hand and muttering to me that at her age she only stood for royalty and the over-seventies. Certainly not for a man. What did Angie think she was doing?

Angie, who'd once met Camilla Parker-Bowles and never quite got over it, was indeed becoming more and more lady-in-waiting-like as she proffered the two remaining chairs. Then she decided they were too ropey for the Armitages and made Luke and Jennie swap to give Chad and Hope more acceptable ones.

"So!" said Chad, rubbing his hands and looking huge on the chair Angie had finally deemed suitable, a tiny gilt rococo number she'd bought in Sotheby's. His voice was thrillingly transatlantic. "What are you guys reading, then? Hope and I are so excited about this, incidentally. We did a lot of reading groups back home and got so much out of it."

Angie cleared her throat. "Well, this week we're all reading *The Ghost* by Robert Harris. It's not a frightfully intellectual book," she hurried on, "and of course we will read something more challenging later on, but it's a rattling good read with a terrific plot. A good starter book, we thought."

"Oh, OK, good idea," Chad agreed. He took the book from Pete beside him, who offered it. "Hey, I like the sound of this," he said, reading the blurb on the back. "Makes a change from Philip Roth, doesn't it, Honey?"

This, to Hope, who, if she was surprised by the popular nature of the novel, was hiding it beautifully. "It certainly does. In fact it looks wonderful," she said, turning it over in her hands as he passed it to her. "And what did you all make of it?" She glanced around, smiling.

"Oh, it's tremendous!" boomed Angus. "Absolutely first class."

"Really? That's great." She smiled at Angus, perhaps waiting to be further illuminated. If she was, she was disappointed. He beamed back. "What about you, Pete?" She turned kindly to her neighbor, having remembered his name. The blood surged up Pete's neck and into his cheeks.

"Oh, um…I thought it was very good, too."

"Good, good."

This didn't give us a great deal to build on. And although Hope could have asked someone else, it would have thrust her into a dominant role, so she sensibly refrained. Instead she smiled encouragingly at Pete, hoping for more. Pete eyed the door as if he might make a run for it.

In the deafening silence that followed, Angie shot me a pleading glance. "Poppy, what about you?"

Sadly I hadn't read it. I'd had too much on my plate this week. Although, actually, come to think of it, I was pretty sure I *had* read it, years ago.

"I thought it was gripping." Angie's eyes demanded more. Much more. "And…and I particularly liked the bit where the guy hangs from the cable car, in the snow," I said wildly. "Really exciting."

"That's *Where Eagles Dare*," said Jennie, rather disloyally, I thought.

Everyone cast their eyes down to their book. "Anyone else got any thoughts?" Angie said brightly. "Who *didn't* enjoy it?"

Lots of shocked murmuring, head shaking and pursed lips at this. But no concrete ideas.

"So…everyone enjoyed it."

More enthusiastic agreement. But then something of a hiatus again. And don't forget we were all in a circle, so it was a bit like

Show and Tell at Clemmie's school. A mistake, I felt. Too intimidating. We were also missing Simon, who surely would have had some erudite, eloquent remarks on the matter. Angie, Jennie and I looked despairingly at one another. We hadn't thought this through. Did this need chairing? In which case, who was going to do it? Were there too many of us? Too few? How did it work? What *was* a book club?

"Did anyone have any thoughts on characterization?" suggested Luke, and I could have kissed him. Angie looked as if she really might clasp his head in her hands and plant a smacker on his lips. Of course. Characterization. We all glanced surreptitiously at the Americans to see if they'd clocked this bon mot. Hope was smiling, nodding. Unfortunately, though, no one did. Why were we all so tongue-tied?

"I thought the characterization was good," said Jennie desperately. "Particularly that of Adam Lang, the hero."

"I agree," said Angus staunchly. "Best character in the book."

"And I particularly liked the way he was depicted as tough, yet tender," broke in Saintly Sue. We all turned to her gratefully. She went very pink. Opened her book to where a piece of notepaper lay within. She cleared her throat and read: "It seemed to me he emphatically fulfilled the role of romantic hero in the classical sense, much as Chaucer's Troilus did in *Troilus and Criseyde*, adhering to the conventions of courtly love and the literature to which it gave rise in the Middle Ages, which emphatically supplied the first of several historical bases to underlie any adequate interpretation of the principal characters, and any situations in which Troilus—and therefore Adam Lang—emphatically coexist today." She slowly closed her book, eyes down, lips pursed.

"Well," said Jennie faintly, after a pause. "Yes. Quite. Thank you, Sue."

"More wine, anyone?" said Peggy wearily. "That is, if no one's got anything emphatic to add?"

She got to her feet, and everyone, apart from the Americans, eagerly got to theirs, agreeing that was a jolly good idea.

"Shall we pass round the food now, Angie?" someone asked. They did so, anyway.

Bemused, the Armitages stood to join us.

"A real page-turner," Angus assured Chad, pressing the book into his hands. "Go on, take mine. You'll love it. Be up all night."

"Thank you," Chad said. "Although, I should probably read next week's book, don't you think?"

"Oh, *next* week's," agreed Angie, with a note of panic, looking at me.

But I was miles away. Organizing a plumber to fix Marjorie and Cecilia's boiler, even though they lived sixty miles away in Ashford. But Phil was the man of the family, you see. Role-playing was important. Men were important. On one occasion, Marjorie had turned to me and asked: "Where are the men?" One was in his cot, six weeks old. I'd found it diverting for days. I didn't now.

"Hope?" Angie abandoned me and turned desperately to our new friends. "Any suggestions for next week? You must have been to loads of these things in New York," she gushed.

"Oh God, too many. Twice a week sometimes," said Hope. "But we tended to decide on the next book at the end of the meeting."

"This is the end," Peggy informed her.

"Oh, really?" Hope blanched. "You mean…that's it?" She waved a hand at the empty chairs.

"It's the end of the booky bit. Not the end of the evening."

"No—no, it's *not* the end of the booky bit," Angie insisted, flustered. "We're all going to sit down again and—oh, look, here's Simon. How marvelous."

It was said with feeling, and indeed it was something of a relief to have Simon breeze in amongst us. He looked urbane and expensive in his suit, bringing something of London with him, and not just the *Evening Standard*. Jennie colored up slightly, but I noticed that although he greeted her warmly, he didn't linger; he greeted everyone else then said hello to the Armitages, who he appeared to know—through mutual friends, he explained. He did some man-chat with Chad, while we women swarmed around his wife.

"You must think we're hopeless, Hope," said Angie. "Oh, that sounds dreadful—hopeless hope!" she twittered. "Being so disorganized. But we'll be much better next week."

"Oh no, not at all. I think it's all going brilliantly. And Chad and I are so thrilled to be asked, anyway. We were just saying the other day that it's high time we integrated more with the village. Really got involved in the community." We basked in her sweet smile and her wide blue eyes, feeling she really meant it. *So* lovely.

"And we really would welcome suggestions for next week," Angie told her. "We've all loved this thriller, but maybe we do need something more stimulating to get the chat going a bit more. Any ideas?"

Hope lowered her voice. "D'you know, there are huge gaps in my literary education," she confided.

"Oh, mine too!" agreed Jennie.

"So much I haven't read."

We all nodded enthusiastically. This we liked. Loved, in fact.

"D'you want to stick to this particular genre?"

We all looked at her blankly.

"I mean, the thriller?"

"Oh no, we're happy with any…genre. Tragedy, romance. I'd happily read Georgette Heyer every week!" Jennie assured her.

"I don't know her."

"You don't know Georgette Heyer?" Jennie looked genuinely shocked. She clutched her heart. "Oh my God, I've got the whole lot. I'll lend them to you. You're in for a treat. Start with *Faro's Daughter* and you'll be hooked for life!"

"Thank you, I'd appreciate that. And meantime," Hope lowered her voice again and we all had to lean in because her voice was soft. And she was tiny, so we must have looked like we were mugging her. "Well, meantime, if you're really looking for suggestions, I'm ashamed to say there's one book which I know I should have read in high school, but just never got around to. I'd love to do it now."

"Oh!" we breathed. Plenty of those. Whole libraries full. "Yes?"

"You've probably all read it."

"Noo, noo, not necessarily," Angie warbled.

"It's *Ulysses*."

"*Ulysses*!" Jennie and Angie agreed in unison. They rocked back on their heels, glancing wildly at one another. It rang a faint bell, but not a very loud one.

"Can you believe I've never read it? Must be one of the greatest novels in literary history."

"*I*'ve never read it either!" squealed Angie, hand pressed to her heart. "I've been so ashamed of that for years!"

"I've always meant to," Jennie chimed in. "Just never got round to it. Poppy, what about you?"

But I was hanging out Marjorie's washing now, because she'd asked me to. Large white pants, huge conical bras, the cups of which a puppy could have curled up and had a nap in. Hanging them on *my* line, while she watched *my* television.

"Poppy?"

"Yes, I told you. I liked the cable-car bit."

Jennie blinked. Turned her back on me pointedly. "I think that's a brilliant idea, Hope. We'll all read that for next week, then."

"And I could get a few notes from the Internet, perhaps? Circulate them, if you like, to help us along?"

"Oh, I wouldn't worry about that. As you can see, we didn't need notes for this one!" Angie trilled. She turned. "Everyone!" She clapped her jeweled hands prettily into the party atmosphere that had naturally ensued—flooded in, more like, when given the chance. Angus was already florid and booming; Luke had his hand on Sue's arm as he told an anecdote, just emphasizing a point, but still; and the volume was high. "Um, everyone! Listen up! Hope's made a marvelous suggestion for next week. We're going to read *Ulysses*, which is a lovely book, apparently. I'm sure you'll all adore it. It's by—" Angie turned to Hope expectantly.

Hope looked startled then collected herself. "Oh, OK. James Joyce."

"James Joyce, and it's about…" Angie tinkled, cocking her head to one side, liking this double act.

"Well, not so much about anything as a stream of consciousness. One day in the life of. I guess if it does has a central theme it's…well, it's—" Hope puckered her pretty brow, looked momentarily flummoxed.

"It's about death," Peggy interjected softly, from over by the window.

We all turned to look at her. Her face, in profile to us, was sad and mournful. She blew a thin blue line of cigarette smoke at the pane of glass and thence to the darkened fields beyond.

Chapter Fifteen

"Saintly Sue and Luke seemed to be getting on rather well last night, didn't they?" Jennie said casually.

I was on my way back from the shop. Jennie was on her hands and knees in her front garden, messing around with a trowel, the second time I'd found her thus in two weeks. Generally she expressed the opinion that plastic flowers were the way forward, so authentic were they nowadays, and soil-tilling was just another extension of a housewife's shackles, only we got to rattle them in the fresh air.

I paused at her gate. "Yes, they did, didn't they?"

"You don't mind?" She straightened up anxiously.

"Not in the least."

I didn't, really. Well, OK, I might have been a bit piqued that he'd spent so much time flirting and amusing her, but no more than that. "I'm seeing him on Tuesday, anyway," I assured her. I hated disappointing my friends.

"Are you?" She brightened, as I knew she would. "Oh, *good*. Oh, I *am* pleased."

"You sound like someone's mother, Jennie."

"I am someone's mother."

"Yes, but not mine." I smiled.

"Fair comment." She paused. "Probably just humoring Sue last night, then?"

"Most probably," I conceded, although privately I thought the giggling I'd heard behind the azalea bush in Angie's front garden as I'd left the party might have been more than humoring.

"Simon was on good form," I said conversationally, but not without a parrying thrust. A touch of touché.

"Yes, he was, wasn't he?" she said lightly. "Although not with me."

"He was busy catching up with the Armitages, Jennie," I said, instantly regretting the parry.

"You don't have to placate me, Poppy. I'm married, remember? I've got my Toad." She grinned. "My life is complete. You're the one that needs a man."

She knelt and resumed her digging, humming to herself, which she didn't do. I mean, years ago we all did; sing, even, but not recently. There was a strange contentment to her, too, as she chivvied those weeds, which was as alien as the horticulture. I went distractedly up my path with the children. Something about Jennie and Simon's behavior last night had alerted me; the way they rather pointedly didn't linger in each other's company. It was as if, in private time, some modus operandi had been arrived at. As if they were beyond seeking each another out at a party and having tongues wag. Had some decision been made, I wondered nervously. I wasn't sure. One thing I did know, though, was that the more I encountered Simon, the more I liked him. We'd had a good chat at Angie's, and among other things he'd said how outrageous it was that the bus route from the village was in danger, and that for some old people it was their only independent way into town; they didn't want to rely on lifts. Said it was the first thing he was going to tackle if he was elected, that and the threatened closure of the post office, which he was tackling anyway, elected or not. He was taking a petition round all the villages affected. Yes, a decent man. A sensible one, too. Which Dan wasn't always, I thought uncomfortably.

"Where are you going, anyway?" I heard her voice as I put my key in my door.

I turned. "Inside."

"No, with Luke?"

"Oh. The King's Head."

Jennie looked astonished. Then delighted. She sat back on her heels on the grass. "Oh! How lovely!"

I, too, had been surprised when Luke had rung that morning to change the venue.

"Um, I know I said lunch in London, Poppy, but I've been thinking. What about dinner instead? At the King's Head?"

The King's Head was a fearfully expensive restaurant down by the river on the other side of the vale. It was very much London prices and fancied itself hugely; in fact, it may even have been equipped with some Michelin stars. It was quite a number and not what I'd been expecting. On the other hand, I didn't have to trek to London and pretend I'd been having a lovely time in Sloane Street, shimmying in and out of outfits, which, in my present mood, I was secretly dreading. I dreaded a lot at the moment. Wasn't sure I had the heart for any of this. Luke must have felt me hesitate.

"I'd so love it if you said yes, Poppy. Please come," he said urgently.

It was a long time since anyone had insisted on a date with me, urgently or otherwise, and the King's Head was a treat. I'd only been there once, on Phil's birthday, and yes, obviously his mother and sister had come, too. I rallied and agreed.

———

Tuesday night at eight, then, with Felicity, Angie's daughter home for half term, baby-sitting, I made my way down the lanes across country, having elected to drive myself and maintain some independence. The hedgerows shivered darkly in the breeze, shaking themselves dry after the rain, the fields behind them damp and browned off for the winter. It was a beautiful soft autumn evening, and I was tempted to just drive on up to the Beacon and sit in the car, watch the stars gather over the wide flat valley floor below, such a treat it was to be out of the house at night, no children. I knew the rules, though, and dutifully turned left where the lane plunged through the wood to Cumpton, then swung round the corner and under the arch of the pretty white inn, clad in dazzling red Virginia creeper, to the car park.

Luke was already in the dining room when I arrived: a good sign, I felt. I'd relied a lot on signs recently. I crossed the room to his table in the corner, remembering to hold my tummy in.

"Poppy!" He stood up, one hand holding the bottom of his tie. "How lovely. You look amazing." We exchanged a peck.

I didn't really. I looked OK. I had on my usual Jigsaw black, which had seen better days, and a bit of makeup, but I hadn't made a huge effort. Not because I didn't like Luke, but because I was flat inside. Odd.

These last few days, instead of rallying a bit after Sam's revelation, getting angry even, I'd dipped. Dived, perhaps. Yesterday I'd even found myself mechanically going through the motions. Of living. Having been there once before, I was terrified. My hands froze on the tin of beans I was opening. Second tin that day. I ran upstairs, riffled through my drawers and found the old bottle, which was empty, of course, because I'd flushed the pills away. But then I rang the nice GP and she prescribed some more, surprised I'd stopped taking them so soon. We had a bit of a chat over the phone and I assured her I was fine really, just feeling a bit low. But I'd come off the phone exhausted. At the effort of sounding fine. Had to sit on the side of the bed for a few minutes, holding my knees.

Yet now, here I was, cranking up a smile in this softly lit, plushly carpeted dining room, taking my chair opposite Luke, who looked for all the world as if Angelina Jolie had sat down to join him.

"I thought we'd have champagne." He indicated a bottle already chilling in a bucket beside him. "Is that OK with you?"

"Perfect," I assured him.

Within moments, a suave sommelier had glided noiselessly across to pour some for me, purring, "Madame," as he did. The King's Head was a bit like that: gliding waiters, melba toast, elaborately arranged pink napkins, puddings from the trolley. Expensive, but old-fashioned and parochial. The sort of place where, if you had the right parents, you might easily have been taken as a child. All quite easy to mock these days but, having not had the parents, I rather liked it, I decided, as the waiter slid away as if on roller skates. Luke raised his glass.

"To a lovely evening," he murmured, smoldering over his glass, eyebrows waggling.

Relieved he was playing it for laughs, I raised mine back in mock salute. "A lovely evening," I agreed with a grin.

"Isn't that what we're supposed to say in this sort of joint?" Luke's eyes roved around incredulously, taking in the flickering candlelight, the napkins in the shape of swans, the throne-like chairs, the well-heeled couples chatting politely over aperitifs. He leaned in. "Then you're supposed to ask me if I had a good day at the office," he hissed, "and I ask you how your day has gone. If you got the ironing done." He grinned and popped a large chunk of bread roll in his mouth, chewing hard. "How was it, anyway?" he asked out of the side of his mouth, amidst a few crumbs.

My day was like all my days: hear Archie cry, get up, give him a bottle, get Clemmie out of my bed, where she'd been sleeping the last few nights, take her to school, put Archie down for a nap, collect Clemmie, entertain children, push push push that buggy, bed.

"Oh, you know, pretty hectic as usual. Every day is different, which is so nice." I tried to sound breezy. "How about you?" I was keen to turn the tables; didn't want to talk about myself. Didn't want to talk much at all, really. "D'you know, Luke, I'm not entirely sure I even know what you do. What exactly is re-insurance?"

"Re-insurance?" He looked surprised. "Oh God, it's bollocks.

You borrow a shed load of money, and then you lend it to someone, and then you borrow some more and lend it to someone else, and then it all comes back to you, and everyone takes a cut along the way. Pretty cynical, if you ask me, but am I bothered?" He gave a dazzling smile as he chewed hard. "Not remotely!"

I laughed despite myself. No way would Phil have described his job in such derisory terms. No way would he have not wanted to sound important, either. But then, if I compared every man I met to Phil, they'd be bound to look good, wouldn't they? I must stop using him as a sounding board.

"I'm just a little cog in the wheel," Luke went on, popping in more bread. "A minion, who's shunted from pillar to post rather like the cash. But who isn't, in a financial organization these days? Unless you're up there with the fat cats, you're bound to be taking orders. Course, come the revolution, it's guys like me who will rise up and give the management a run for their money." He tapped his chest. "The real workers."

"I thought Angie said you had your own business?" I said without thinking, then realized it sounded as if we'd been talking about him, which of course we had. I blushed.

"Did she?" He looked up from buttering his bread, surprised. "Oh, well, I suppose I did start Parkers with some other guys, but no way do we own it. That's just Chinese whispers getting out of hand. No, as ever, there's a brace of Ruperts at the top, typical old-school types, although my immediate boss, my particular cross to bear, is called Gary, who's definitely comprehensive material. In fact my mum would have him down as secondary modern. Sweet man, he's got a dotted line tattooed around his throat saying: Cut."

"You're kidding."

"I am not. He's a barrow boy made good. He had that pleasing feature adorned on his body on his eighteenth birthday. No doubt rat-arsed and with his mates giggling outside."

"God, I bet he regrets that."

"Just a bit," he said cheerfully, popping in the last of his roll. He was moving on to the bread sticks now. "You don't see it until he gets hot and bothered and loosens his collar and tie, then he suddenly remembers and does it up in a hurry. We're always turning the heating up and switching the air con off. So yeah, he's my line manager, then above him is Rebecca, a red-haired vamp who wafts down the corridors in very tight skirts, desk-perching along the way. If she asks you to step inside her cubicle you keep your hands on your belt and your wits about you. She's been known to pounce in broad daylight."

I giggled. "You wish. That's just boys fantasizing. I bet she's thoroughly professional and you're all scared stiff of her."

He grinned. "Yeah, you're probably right. Although she did snog the new trainee at the office party. Still, we've got to have something to talk about in between haircuts, haven't we? Something to brighten our day."

"Is that how you chart your life? With haircuts?" I was feeling a bit better now. Slightly warmer as I looked at the huge menu I'd been presented with.

"Well, it's not a bad staging post, is it? And it's amazing how nothing much happens in the six weeks or so in between. And don't you love the way you can tell barbers anything and it's going nowhere? Giuseppe—he's my man—asked me the other day how it was going, and I told him I'd made a million on the markets before lunch. He was hugely impressed. We had a good old chinwag about what a clever chap I was. He'd probably forgotten it by the time he moved on to the next client, but I went back to the office with a massive grin on my face, thinking I *had* made a million. It's got to be the way forward, hasn't it? Better than any therapy crap?" He took a huge gulp of champagne.

I laughed, enjoying his candor. "Perhaps you really will make a million? Then you can set up on your own without Gary and Rebecca."

"Yeah, I'd love to do that," he said wistfully. "Except it's getting harder these days. It's not like in the eighties when you could do it in your tea break and have a pile in Gloucestershire by the weekend— helipad, swimming pool, all the toys. The banks are less accommodating now. Back then you could blag your way into making anything sound like a new business venture, but they're a bit more savvy now, not so quick to hand over the loot. You need a bit of capital, too. Anyway," he said quickly, "enough of me and my crummy little life. What about you, Poppy? How are you? That's a lovely necklace you're wearing, by the way, really catches the light."

I touched the fake turquoise pendant from Accessorise around my neck, amused. I rather liked Luke's blatant attempt to charm me every so often. Any minute now he'd go down on one knee and break into "Love Me Tender," like Dad.

"Thank you, I bought it specially," I told him. "I thought it matched my eyes."

"Well, it would if they were blue. Nice try, Poppy, but I'd already spotted they were brown."

I laughed. "Just checking. Wouldn't want you to be flattering me."

"Flattery? Me?" He widened his eyes in mock protest. "Perish the thought." He cheerfully filled up our glasses. "Well?" he asked.

"Well what?" I studied the menu.

"I asked how you were. Only…" He hesitated. "You didn't seem yourself at the book club the other day." It was said kindly. I looked up, startled at the change of tone.

"Really?"

"Yeah, you were…well, distracted." He gave a small smile. "I even found myself giving Saintly Sue the eye in defense. Might even have made a prat of myself. Sorry, if I did."

I stared at him, surprised. Right. I had been distracted, but I hadn't known it had shown. And actually, I did remember Luke greeting me very enthusiastically at Angie's: bounding across the room, giving it lots of chat. But I'd been thinking about Marjorie and Cecilia at the time, had lost track of what he was saying. As he'd talked animatedly, I gazed beyond him, to Angie's horses in the field, thinking what a nice life they led: no dead husbands, no in-laws, just friends, snoozing together, nose to tail. I'd possibly even forgotten to answer. And now I came to think of it, had his face fallen? Had he looked a bit piqued? And then later, when we were leaving, had he tried to make me jealous? Perhaps he'd been deliberately flirting in the garden with Sue? Suddenly I realized this was quite an up-front admission; a genuine apology, too. I also remembered how hard it had been to get up this morning. Clemmie shaking my shoulder when Archie cried, saying it was time for school, Mummy. Quickly swallowing my pill. How I'd almost taken two. I put the menu down. Regarded my dinner companion. His eyes across the table were warm, concerned.

"Sorry, Luke. I had a lot on my mind at the book club."

"D'you want to talk about it?"

I considered this. Then shook my head miserably. "No. D'you know, if you don't mind, I don't think I do." How many more people needed to know my dead husband's family had sided with his mistress? No more, I felt. And this was supposed to be a pleasant evening out.

It helped, though, getting that out of the way, and we glided through the first two courses. There were no smoldering looks over the Dover sole, no observations about my jewelry. Just nice, general chit-chat.

"You're not supposed to know we call her Saintly Sue, by the way," I chided him as I tucked into a heavenly chocolate mousse. "That's a girly secret."

"Well, it's not a very well kept one. And I got it from one of the girlies' mouths, too. Angie told me. She's massively indiscreet, by the way, which is great," he grinned.

"I know. Peggy calls her The Only Virgin In The Village." The wine had clearly got the better of me.

"Who, Angie?" He feigned astonishment.

"No, idiot. Sue." I laughed.

"Ah yes, so I gather. Angie told me that, too. Apparently she's Keeping Herself Nice For Her Husband, which is lovely, isn't it?" he said naughtily. "So very twenty-first century. And something of a challenge, too."

I burst out laughing, a sound I hadn't heard for a while. Not a combust like that, anyway. "Fancy rising to it?" I asked.

"God, no." He shuddered. "Too pi for me. Massive knockers, of course," he added reflectively, and with mock regret.

I laughed. As I savored the last of my mousse, licking my spoon, a thought crossed my mind. "How did you start playing the organ, Luke?"

He gave a knowing twinkle across the table. "You mean, what's a likely lad like me doing with something as sensitive as a musical instrument? Tinkling the ivories?"

"Well, no, I—" I reddened.

He grinned. "It's all right, everyone's a bit fazed by it. My dad was a concert pianist. He taught me."

"Oh! How amazing."

"Yeah, amazing but not very lucrative. Only the really brilliant guys get to the Wigmore Hall. My dad was more Hackney town hall. When times got really tough he started playing in hotel foyers. South of France, mostly."

"Which is where your mum lives," I said in surprise. "Didn't you say she lived in a hotel in Monte Carlo?"

"Er, yes, although she sort of works there, too. When Dad died she got a job on reception. Been there ever since."

"Oh. Right."

As I drank my coffee it occurred to me that Luke put quite a gloss on what hadn't been the easiest of rides. Pulling the wool, some might say. I wondered if the sister at *Vogue* was on reception, too. But I decided I rather liked him for bigging it up; for not turning his life into a hard-luck story, an excuse to hang failure on.

When we said goodnight in the car park, there was just a chaste kiss on the cheek, no lingering, and no expectation of coffee back at my place either. Although he did express a desire to see me again a few days hence.

"Would you have supper with me again, Poppy? Or maybe we could go and see a film. *Aviator* is supposed to be good."

It seemed to me that twice in one week might reasonably be construed as Going Out With. Did I want that? I mean, the occasional one-off supper was nice, but did I want to go out with Luke? Fun though he was?

"That sounds lovely, but can I ring you? I haven't got my diary and obviously I need to get a sitter."

"Or I could ring you?"

"You could," I hedged, "but I'm usually so preoccupied with the kids. I'll ring you."

And there we left it. Off he went to his car, rather a smart BMW, I noticed, casting me a last smile over his shoulder, and off I went to mine.

Interesting, I thought, as I drove home. A blatant attempt, not to seduce me, but to romance me. It was rather refreshing. No pressure. It smacked of doing things by the book. Dinner, a chaste kiss, then another date, then perhaps coffee, then another date, and only then, perhaps, a grapple on the sofa. And he'd made me laugh, too. Although I hadn't been in the mood, he'd brought me out of myself. Added to which there was that rather sweet admission during supper, which had disarmed me. Why then, hadn't I agreed to another date? Thought twice?

Because you think too much, I told myself wearily as I pulled up outside my house a few minutes later. I sat there a moment. Jennie would agree. Jennie, who'd be disappointed in me, I thought guiltily, glancing at her front door. For not jumping at it, not giving him a chance.

"Just give him a chance!" I could hear her squeal, almost through the party wall. "You don't have to marry him!"

I knew myself too well, though; knew I found someone else's ardor very attractive, even if it wasn't mine. Knew I found vulnerability and little admissions like that hard to resist. So, to that end, self-protection worked best for me. In order to prevent myself falling for a charm offensive, I just wouldn't expose myself to it. Simple.

I was about to get out of the car, when I sank back in my seat. Stared ahead through the windscreen into the night. Self-protection. Was that the same as not wanting to see the truth? Not wanting to know the truth? Had there been moments in my married life when I'd been deliberately blind? It was a question I'd asked myself a lot lately. And the answer was always no. I'd never had an inkling about her. There were definitely occasions when, even in the privacy of my own head, I'd been dishonest about certain things—about loving Phil in the early days, for instance—but this was not one of them. She'd come as a bolt from the blue. Yet she'd played such a huge part in my life. Had been there for four years. I narrowed my eyes into the night.

Suddenly, on an impulse, I put the key in the ignition and started the car again. Without giving myself time to think, I drove back up the lane. It was early. Ten past eleven. And I'd told Felicity, who was baby-sitting, twelve. I had time. And no children to inconvenience me, either. I'd attempted this the other day, but Clemmie had complained, wanting to know why we were sitting in the road outside someone's house, Mummy, and Archie had started grizzling, so with a pounding heart I'd driven away. The heart was still pounding, I decided, and I knew I should probably turn around now, in that lay-by, go home, but I found myself driving through the next village. Then up the hill. I sped along the common, wide and spreading but eventually narrowing almost to a verge, where the houses set behind it were closer to the road. One of which was hers.

I'd found it the other day, a tiny flint cottage, seemingly in the grounds of a bigger one: Meadow Bank Cottage and Meadow Bank House. It did appear to have its own little walled garden, though, so it could be separate. Anyway, I wasn't interested in the set-up, more in the woman inside. Why? Why was I sitting here in the middle of the night, postdate, engine purring, heart racing, crouched at the wheel like some private detective? Because presumably she'd sat outside mine, I reasoned. And I felt that to know her was to understand her a bit better. But Phil was dead now. Surely I should move on? Not before something was silenced, I reasoned. Something inside me wanted to lie down and be quiet, and in some warped way I felt that once that had happened I could go on dates and not have a sinking feeling in the pit of my tummy, not feel detached. I wanted to be able to bang my palm on my forehead and say: ah, I *see*. Now I get it. *Now* I can toss those pills away and go out on the town. I wanted to make some sense of the last four years, and, since Phil was no use to me now, I was left with Emma.

Stupid, I thought later when I'd sat across the road and watched the dark little house for ten minutes, eyes wide like a rabbit's. What are you doing, Poppy? Go home and leave the past behind. She's nothing to you now; get going. Still I sat. It helped, somehow, that the cottage looked empty and forlorn. Perhaps she was sitting inside in the dark feeling sad, as I did sometimes? Unable to light the fire, turn on the lights. More probable, of course, was that she was out. I smiled wryly to myself in the dark. Look at you, Poppy. Look at what you've become. A stalker. And not even stalking a man.

Giving myself a little inward shake, I turned the key in the ignition and reversed with a flourish into a driveway. Then just as I was about to turn left into the road, a black Mini Cooper swung past me into the little gravel drive opposite. It disappeared around the back of the flint cottage. It all happened terribly quickly, but not so fast that I didn't make out the blonde driver and the briefest glimpse of a male passenger beside her. I sat, frozen. Turned off the engine and slid right down in my seat, pulling my scarf up over my face. A few seconds later, the downstairs front room of the cottage sprang into light. Emma came toward me across the room, laughing, head thrown back. She was wearing a tight pink cardigan with lots of silver chains around her neck, white jeans which showed off her figure, and her face was alight, blonde hair flopping over one eye. She reached for the curtain cord with one hand and flicked her fringe back in a practiced fashion with the other, before turning, no doubt to the man who'd followed her into the room, as the curtains swished shut.

I sat there as if I'd been shot. Barely breathing. I tried to marshal my thoughts, which were spinning like a kaleidoscope. So Emma had a man. And she definitely had him, there was no doubt about that: no mistaking the body language, the tight clothes, the flirtatious laugh. And she was looking good, too, which surprised me. She'd scrubbed up. Moved on. Stepped right over Phil, over his grave. For this was not a girl to let the grass grow under her feet, particularly the grass on a mound. Why was I surprised? Because I'd thought true love would last a bit longer? Because Phil was barely cold? But perhaps it hadn't been true love for her. Perhaps she hadn't been besotted with him. But if not, what had been the point? Just sex, I supposed. An affair. For four years. I took a deep breath. Exhaled shakily. You really do need to get out more, Poppy. Need to grow up.

I drove home slowly, trying to work out how I felt before I had to make small talk with my baby-sitter. It was one in the eye for Phil, surely? Emma wasn't exactly beating her breast and rending her hair, so stick that in your pipe, Mr. Shilling; nobody's mourning you now. I glanced guiltily up to the heavens, feeling bad. Guilt. Another feeling that had ambushed me lately. But why should *I* feel guilty? Emma should be the one with her life turned upside down, yet she was way ahead of me. No life on hold for her. Oh no, just the money, please, I thought suddenly. I could see her holding out her hand, clicking her fingers impatiently, nails freshly painted. Just hand it over. I gripped the steering wheel hard. Yes. Right. We'll see about that. Had it helped my resolve, I wondered, seeing that little vignette? D'you know, I believe it had. As I drove up to my house I caught sight of my reflection in the mirror, caught my own eye, as it were. For some reason it reminded me of Mum. Or… was it the woman I might have been, had Mum not died? Whoever it was seemed flintier than me. Had more of a glint to her eye. She seemed to say: find a bit of inner strength, Poppy dear. A bit of steel, hm?

Felicity was just putting my phone down hurriedly when I went into the kitchen. She went pink.

"Oh, I hope you don't mind, Poppy. I couldn't get a signal on my mobile."

"Not at all," I said, unwinding my scarf and thinking that every time Felicity baby-sat I found her on my phone, something that never happened with Frankie.

"Gosh, I love your bag," she gushed in a confident manner. "Is it new?"

"No, I've had it for years, but thanks."

Flattery to ingratiate, I thought uncharitably as I took my coat off. Understandable, of course, in a fifteen-year-old who's been found running up my phone bill. She flicked back her long tawny hair as she crossed the room to retrieve her bag from the table, just as Emma had crossed the room to the window and swept back her fringe. Some girls knew the way forward, didn't they? Had the *savoir faire*, the pretty learned manners. Did I want Clemmie to flick back her hair with a jeweled hand? I wasn't sure. I tailed Felicity thoughtfully down the hall to the door.

"Have you seen anything of Frankie, now you're back?" I asked. The girls had been at the village school together.

"Frankie?" She turned at the door. "Um, no, I haven't. I must get in touch with her."

Somehow I knew she wouldn't. Since she'd gone to boarding school, Felicity's social path had been very different to Frankie's. Not her fault, of course, but a shame, when they'd been close.

"But it's nice she's got a boyfriend, isn't it?" she said.

"Frankie? I didn't know."

"Oh. Well, I may have got that wrong. Maybe don't say anything to Jennie? Just in case?"

In case of what, I thought, nevertheless agreeing as I closed the door behind her. In case he didn't exist? Or in case he wasn't suitable? The latter, probably. I did hope Frankie hadn't been serious about flirting with the teachers at school. Don't be ridiculous, Poppy. Nevertheless I couldn't help thinking that if it was just a sixteen-year-old boy, why hide it? Why wasn't Jennie up to speed? I went back to the kitchen to turn out the lights. Perhaps she was and didn't want to share with me. Recently Jennie had become more secretive, and I respected that. We couldn't know everything about our friends, could we? If we did, where would it end? Laying bare the contents of our heads and hearts and saying: here, take a gander at that? Imagine the shock on their faces.

—∾∾—

The following morning, on my way to the village shop with the children, I felt perkier. On a scale of one to ten—always my acid test—I was five, rather than four. It was a beautiful blue-sky morning, so perhaps that helped, and being late in the year, long dramatic shadows were cast at my feet as I walked across the green. Trees mostly, but also the shadow of a man, right behind me. I glanced over my shoulder. Odd Bob, dressed uncharacteristically in a tweed jacket and tie, appeared to be tailing me. I turned. Stopped.

"Hi, Bob."

How bizarre. He appeared to have a buttonhole. A little white carnation in his lapel. He beamed. Caught up with me.

"Hello, Poppy. How are you?"

"Fine, thanks. You look very smart."

"Oh, you know. Thought it was about time."

For what, I wondered as we continued to the shop together.

"Um, Poppy. I wondered if you'd have dinner with me next week."

I stared. Couldn't believe my ears. Odd Bob? Jacket and tie? Outside the village shop?

"Sorry?"

"Yes, I thought maybe we could go to the King's Head. How about Saturday?"

I blinked rapidly. Found my voice.

"Well, that's very kind, Bob, but I'm afraid I'm busy on Saturday."

"Sunday?"

Sunday wasn't a natural night for a date, but Bob, minus a social compass, wasn't to know that. I knew if I refused he'd say, "Monday?" And so on until Christmas.

"I'm afraid I'm not really ready to go out yet," I said, more kindly.

"Really? You look fine. Just brush your hair, or something."

I swallowed. "No, I don't mean…sartorially. I mean, because my husband's just died."

Disingenuous, of course. And Bob was on it like lightning.

"So how come you were ready last night?"

None of the usual codes and conventions to let him down gently would be of any use; it was like dealing with a child. Out of the corner of my eye I noticed the usual posse of mothers who loitered outside the shop with their babies in buggies after buying milk and papers. They'd ceased their chatter and were listening avidly, amused.

"Well, I suppose that's what made me realize I'm not quite ready," I said finally. And oddly, it had a ring of truth about it. "I didn't know, until I went." This was obviously deeply unchivalrous to Luke, but it was said quietly, out of hearing of the mothers. And since Bob, like a child, only understood the truth and not coded subtlety, it was the way forward. His face cleared.

"You didn't enjoy it."

"I wouldn't say I didn't enjoy it." I felt hot. Hoped my antiperspirant wasn't going to let me down. "I wouldn't say that, but it felt a bit strange to be out." True again.

"You wouldn't with me," beamed Bob.

Wishing my own social code didn't prevent me from seizing him by the lapels and roaring, "Don't be ridiculous, Bob, stop this silly nonsense now!" I found myself inclining my head, as if conceding that this was indeed a possibility. Suddenly I wondered if, total pushover that I was, I'd find myself next Saturday night at the King's Head, opposite Bob, who might even bring his twelve dogs along; and who might, the following week, be supplanted by Frank, or Dickie Frowbisher, and all the other oddballs of the parish thereafter.

"I'm sorry," I said, quite firmly for me—remembering the inner strength, remembering Mum and the steel I was going to find—"but I simply can't make it. Good-bye, Bob."

And with that I pushed my buggy and my small child past him and headed into the shop for provisions. The eyes of the village, I felt sure, were upon me.

Chapter Sixteen

THE GLORIA WAS FINALLY given an airing the following Saturday, but not, it transpired, for the couple who had originally chosen it to be sung at their nuptials.

"Why not?" I asked Angie as we slipped into the choir stalls together.

"She dumped him, apparently," Angie told me rather too gleefully as we collected our hymn sheets. Angie was more than slightly anti-men at the moment.

"Who did? The bride?"

"Yup. Word is, she got cold feet. Called the whole thing off a week ago. The invitations had gone out, wedding presents had been opened—the whole bit. Takes some doing, don't you think? The week before?"

Blimey. It did. And I remembered how close I'd got to it with Phil during that terrible final week; the overwhelming feeling of panic as the whole thing gained momentum, like a runaway freight train, without me behind it. My mouth getting drier, not sleeping, everyone thinking it was excitement. Dad, Jennie, all looking at my wide eyes and thinking they were starry, not seeing the fear. Jennie, telling me all brides lost weight before the big day. Only my dressmaker looking concerned, because every time I had a fitting she had to take the ivory silk in a bit more. I remembered having my legs waxed the day before and the young girl asking if I was excited, and me suddenly sobbing, "No!" How it had come out in a horrible, choked voice. She'd looked terrified and ripped those strips away in silence, the fastest leg wax in the world, whilst I'd pretended the tears streaming down the side of my face were due to the pain.

I sighed, shuffling along the pew a bit as more people arrived. It did take some doing, and I hadn't had the guts. Or the neck. Or the stomach. Or whatever part of the body it took to let a hundred and fifty people down—but not yourself. I was full of admiration for Miss Anna Braithwaite, as we gathered she was called, not a spinster of this parish, but yet another Londoner who'd wangled her way into our idyllic village church by dint of having a distant relative who lived nearby, where she'd lodged her suitcase for a couple of weeks, and become a bona fide country dweller. So yes, neck had been her particular body part; the one which had enabled her first to swing the bucolic setting, and then to break a man's heart.

Would I have broken Phil's heart? I picked up the Gloria song sheet as Angus slipped in beside Angie on the end, Sylvia electing the row in front. I couldn't exactly imagine him prostrate with grief, punching walls into the night in a Heathcliff manner. More tight-lipped and furious. Livid. Nonsense, Poppy; you're rewriting history. He was actually very much in love with you. He just hid it well.

"So who's getting married, then?" I asked Angie, thinking: never again. *Never.*

"A local couple, apparently, which is much more satisfactory. They got engaged last week and wanted to get married immediately but were told they'd have to wait ages for a slot. They were about to get hitched in the registry office but then this came up, so they grabbed it."

"Good for them," I said admiringly.

"No order of service sheets, of course, because it was too late to get it all organized, but when you think about it, how much nicer to get married just like that. Next week? Good friends will always just drop everything to come, and you don't get any of the fuss. None of the usual pre-nup merry-go-round with lists at Peter Jones and brides-maids getting the hump because they're dressed as shepherdesses; just an incredibly spontaneous, romantic occasion. A really lovely joyous expression of…shit."

"What?" I frowned. She'd ducked her head down and was furi-ously pulling her fringe over her eyes.

"Bugger. It's Pete. Passion-fueled. Back row of the church. Don't look now. Don't want him to see me."

"Why not?" I said, nonetheless following her furtive glance to where Pete, blond and gorgeous in a dark suit, was indeed collecting a hymn book and joining the growing congregation.

"Made a bit of a fool of myself." Angie muttered.

"Really? When?" I was intrigued. "You never said."

I turned to stare at her in wonder. Pete was surely a harmless crush. A fantasy figure, like a member of a boy band, to pin on a bedroom wall and drool over. He was also a good ten years younger than Angie.

"What did you do, wrestle him into the back of his mobile forge?"

"Don't be silly." Angie reddened.

I blinked. "Please tell me you didn't rip off his leather apron? Have him over his anvil? Hammer hammer hammer?"

"Oh, shut up, Poppy." She swallowed. "No, he just…Well, he sussed that I was getting him out on false pretenses, that's all."

"Getting him out? What d'you mean?"

"Horses only need shoeing every six weeks or so. Pete was doing mine slightly more regularly than that," she said tightly.

"Oh."

It occurred to me that I did see Pete's van go past my house most weeks, and if I wandered past Angie's house with Archie, Pete was quite often parked in the stable yard round the side.

"Of course I always had some spurious excuse up my sleeve, about how their feet grew quickly and needed trimming, or I was worried a shoe was loose. I even wrenched a shoe off myself in the middle of the night, nearly put my bloody back out, just so I could get him round."

An image of Angie in her stables, under cover of darkness, with a startled horse and a pair of pliers, sprang to mind. My mouth twitched, but I was surprised, too. Didn't know she had it so bad.

"What happened?" I said gently.

"One day he said he thought my horse was in danger of being over-manicured, and was there any particular reason I'd got him round. He looked me right in the eye and asked if there was anything else that needed servicing?"

"No!" I breathed.

I tried to imagine the shy, taciturn Pete saying that, but was aware I'd only seen him out of his milieu, at the book club, not handling a nervous horse, a red-hot firing iron in his hand.

"Oh, Poppy, he was all strong and masterful. You should see him when he's in his own environment," she said, echoing my thoughts. "It sort of…defines him."

For some reason I thought of Sam, when I'd first met him: in his paper-strewn office, sleeves rolled up, files and books all over the floor. Not anymore, of course. Tidy now.

"So…you said?" I prompted, tremulously.

"I said yes."

"Angie, you didn't!"

"I bloody did. I looked him straight back in the eye and said yes, actually, I'd like him to do the same for me as he'd done for Mary Granger last hunting season, and gave him a terrific wink."

"He services Mary Granger?" I gasped. Mary was a rangy, scary, foxy blonde, who rode horses professionally and relentlessly. She was always trotting past, stony-faced and in a hurry, one horse under her bony bum, another on a lead rein. She probably wouldn't have time for the normal social conventions a boyfriend entailed. I could imagine her bonking a man like Pete before breakfast, as part of her horsy routine. Stable management.

And was it my imagination or was Sylvia, in front of Angie, leaning back, straining to hear?

"Why are you so horrified?" Angie looked defiant. "Not everyone wants a boyfriend, Poppy. I don't. And I certainly don't want another husband. But what I do, occasionally, feel the need for is the touch and feel of a man and some basic human comfort. Preferably without a saggy stomach, dandruff, or BO, and preferably the right side of forty." She raised her chin. "I've always liked sex, if you must know."

"Right," I said inadequately, wondering if I must know that *in church* and quite loudly, too. Sylvia's ears were as pricked as those of any horse on the hunting field.

"Well, anyway, we went upstairs—"

"Just like that?" I tried but failed to keep the squeaky excitement from my voice.

"Yes, just like that. He made the pretense of grabbing some tools, and then he asked where the bathroom was, which, frankly, I was pleased about, because don't forget he shoes horses for a living. Fairly blue collar and all that. So when we got to the top of the stairs I showed him into my en suite. Then I went into the bedroom, took all my clothes off, and got into bed."

I felt my mouth fall open.

"I had to," she confessed. "Otherwise I knew I wouldn't do it. Knew I'd lose my nerve."

I nodded dumbly, acknowledging the warped logic in this.

"Anyway, he was ages in the bathroom, and after a bit he called out, 'Mrs. Asher?', which was rather formal, I thought, and not quite what I was expecting, so I called back, 'In here!' And in he came holding my shower attachment, and saying it was rather different to Mary Granger's."

I stared at her for a long moment. Then the penny dropped.

"He does plumbing on the side," she said stiffly. "Unofficially. Just during the recession. Hasn't got a license, so it's hush-hush. He serviced Mary Granger's shower, apparently.

"Oh, Angie…"

"So there I was, in bed, stark naked, propped up on pillows and showing a great deal of cleavage. Near as damn it with a rose between my teeth."

"What did you do?" I breathed.

"Well, he went completely puce, naturally, and his jaw dropped— he nearly dropped the shower head, too—and then I had to pretend it was the most natural thing in the world to be talking to my plumber-come-farrier supine and in the buff. I said it was probably best that he took it away and sorted it out at home, where he'd got the proper tools, and he agreed. To save us, I asked conversationally in what way my shower head differed to Mary's and he said mine had bigger holes. Did I mention I'd lit a candle?"

"No."

"Yes. By the bed. And a few on the dressing table. Diptyque. And squirted Jo Malone about, too." She sighed. "Anyway, he fled. Thundered downstairs and out to his van and roared away in moments, no doubt to tell the entire village about the terrifying frustrated housewife at the manor. I should think everyone knows by now." Her face collapsed a bit. She looked older.

"They don't," I assured her quickly, but knew she was right. It was only a matter of time before it ricocheted around the village. "And anyway, you could say you always have an afternoon nap," I suggested. "Churchill used to. And a bath."

"I could," she agreed, "except it was ten o'clock in the morning and I wasn't exactly marching the troops across the Rhine. Yes, of course you can, here." This, to Angus beside her, who'd asked to borrow her hymn book.

He then engaged her in animated conversation. The overexcited gleam in his eye, and the way he was staring down her top, worried me. Oh Lord, had he overheard? Sylvia, in front, turned to me, eyes huge. Right. They both had.

As Jennie slipped in beside me from the other end, I resolved not to say a word. Not yet, anyway.

"Heard about Angie and Pete?" she muttered as she took her coat off.

"Yes!" I breathed. "But don't say a word." I swung round to glance, but Angie was still engrossed with Angus. "She's terrified it's all round the village."

"It is. Pete told his sister, who works with Yvonne in the shop, which is tantamount to putting it on the bush telegraph. Silly fool," she murmured, casting Angie a look.

"It was a misunderstanding," I said loyally. Sometimes I found myself the glue between Jennie and Angie. Jennie occasionally found Angie a bit moneyed and spoiled, whilst Angie regarded Jennie as puritanical and over-principled.

"As usual she thinks she can get what she wants simply by batting her eyelids."

This was uncalled for, even for Jennie.

"Oh, come on, she's mortified."

"Oh, really? Not so mortified that she's not throwing herself at the new master of the hunt, too, I gather."

"Really?" I was shocked. "Who told you that?"

"Mrs. Tucker at Countrywide, where I get Leila's food. The first meet of the season's next week, apparently, and Angie was in her shop yesterday, buying the tightest jodhpurs possible because some sexy new blood is leading the field. She's out of control, Poppy."

"Right," I said wearily. If anything got Jennie's blood up more than Angie at her most frivolous, it was Angie enjoying her expensive, privileged lifestyle. A wide streak of socialism shot right through Jennie, and she regarded the horsy crowd as arrogant snobs, particularly at this time of year. Personally I loved both my friends and found it all rather tiring.

"We're singing for a completely different couple today," I told her, changing the subject. "The bride got cold feet. Someone else has nabbed the spot."

"I know. It's Simon."

I stared at her. Her face was a mask. Calm; impassive.

"Simon?"

"Yes."

"Your Simon?"

"He's not my Simon, Poppy. Never was, never has been. I'm married to Dan, remember?"

I unstuck my tongue. "Yes, but…" I was flabbergasted. Totally stunned. My mind flew to him walking her home from the book club a while back; saying goodnight rather tenderly, I thought, at the gate. No more than that, but still. He hadn't looked like a betrothed man.

"All rather sudden, isn't it?" I said, when I'd finally found my voice.

"Very sudden. Last week."

"But, Jennie—it must be a hell of a shock! I mean, to you, surely?"

"Not really. He rang and told me."

"*Did* he?" I was amazed. But mostly because she hadn't told me.

"It's more complicated than it sounds," she said quietly, finally letting me in, being more charitable. "And it's not a whirlwind romance, either. He went out with this girl years ago. Remember I told you? He was engaged to her, but she got involved with someone else. Simon just trod water. He looked about but never found anyone he liked as much. Loved as much, rather. He was always, unconsciously, waiting. They got engaged for the second time last week."

"He told you all this on the phone?"

"We had a coffee, actually. He felt he sort of owed me an explanation. We had, after all, had lunch once."

I felt my eyes widen. "You had lunch with Simon?"

"Yes."

"Where?"

"In London."

I gazed at her. "Right," I said finally, faintly. Although I was staggered, I also realized that in some nebulous way I'd known. Realized at the book club there was a subplot; that they'd had private time together. Maybe even reached some sort of understanding.

"What was it like?" I was intrigued.

"What, lunch?"

"Yes."

"Dreadful."

"Oh! Why?"

"Because I felt terrible. Absolutely ghastly. Couldn't believe I was doing it. There I was, some silly, middle-aged woman, like Angie, making a fool of myself. Getting a cheap thrill out of having lunch with a man who wasn't my husband. Suppose Dan had walked in? Or some mate of his? How hideous would that have been?"

"Only lunch, Jennie," I reminded her. Jennie's rigorous principles and high moral standards didn't apply just to others, but to herself, too.

"Yes, only lunch. And a chaste peck on the cheek to say thank you, but by God I scurried home with my tail between my legs. Felt wretched picking up the children from school, listening to Hannah chatting away about her nature trip; wretched when Dan came in knackered from work and I guiltily fried him a steak. His eyes lit up pathetically when he saw it because these days he's lucky if I throw sausage and chips at him. He gave me a delighted squeeze at the Aga. That made me feel even worse, I can tell you. Lousy. I almost broke down and told him."

I hid a smile. Dan was a good man. And a worldly man. I didn't think he'd kick his wife out for having lunch with someone.

She raked a despairing hand through her dark curls and threw her head back. "How do these women do it, Poppy? Sneak around deceiving people? I felt bad enough I hadn't told *you*, let alone my husband. Oh, look—here he is."

The church was fairly bursting now—testament indeed to how one could have one's big day at a moment's notice and still fill it—and Simon, tall and striking in his morning coat, came down the aisle with his best man, an equally good-looking blade. He greeted people along the way, his face alight, looking the picture of happiness. As he came to take up his position in the front pew, his eyes found Jennie almost immediately. He gave her a lovely smile. She smiled back.

"He likes you," I said, not exactly surprised, but genuinely struck by the warmth.

"Oh yes, we like each other tremendously. He's a very nice man. Just what this constituency needs, incidentally, by way of a representative. But let me tell you, Poppy, it's one thing to have a quiet crush on someone you bump into at the village book club and quite another to invent an excuse as to why you can't take year three on the nature trail as promised, then stand on Cherton Station in a new skirt and full slap hoping to God no one sees you. I kept reciting in my head, "I'm going to the dentist," in case they did. And I can't tell you how sweaty my palms were as I went past Dan's office in the Strand by taxi. By the time I'd got to San Lorenzo's my face was shiny, my clothes, I'd decided, all wrong for London, and all the thrilling excitement had disappeared down the plug hole because I was so bloody terrified I'd be spotted."

"In San Lorenzo's?" I said doubtfully.

"Well, quite. Not exactly Odd Bob's habitual stamping ground, I agree. I didn't really expect half the village to be propping up the bar and to turn around accusingly when I came in. But you know what I mean."

"Did you tell him?" I knew Jennie well.

"Simon? Yes. Almost immediately. Explained I simply couldn't handle this and wouldn't be doing it again. He was sweet. Said he liked me all the more for it, and, actually, he wasn't convinced he could cope with the subterfuge, either.

He'd run into Dan in the local garage, apparently, as they were both putting air in their tires. Found it surprisingly hard to make small talk." She smiled. "We both agreed we could do the sex but not the deceit."

"Oh. So…you definitely knew what you were there for?"

"Well, ultimately, yes. Oh, you can kid yourself it's 'just lunch,' Poppy, but it's tantamount to sitting there in your underwear. And don't let anyone tell you any different."

The overture to *The Marriage of Figaro* was crashing in quite loudly now, presumably with Luke at the helm. Luke. Single and uncomplicated, thank God.

"The idea of running upstairs and taking my clothes off, like Angie did, is complete anathema to me," she said rather primly.

"Angie's separated, Jennie," I said quickly. "Single."

"Her husband walked out on her."

"Yes," I said, surprised and wondering what she meant by that. Surely that was morally better than the other way round? For complicated reasons, I knew Jennie was so shocked by her own behavior she was taking it out on Angie. I was pretty sure she'd normally have roared with laughter at the Pete debacle; given her friend a comforting hug.

"You've done nothing wrong," I said gently. "You had lunch with a man. Big deal. You couldn't even get as far as the starter without blurting out that it was a big mistake. Relax."

She nodded, but I saw her swallow. She was about to say something, then blinked and swallowed again.

"Should I tell Dan?" she managed eventually, in a small voice.

I was instinctively about to say: no! Then hesitated.

"Could do," I said thoughtfully. She nodded, knowing I knew what she was thinking. That it might bring them closer together. Dan was no fool. He'd realize there had to be a very good reason for a woman like Jennie to put on her best bib and tucker and shimmy off to London. With no threat intended—or even apparent now—it might give him pause for thought. Might give them both pause for thought. And marriages sometimes needed that. A moment when, as you rattle along helter-skelter, helping with the homework, arguing about who's picking up from ballet, or whether it's your turn to entertain the Jacksons, you suddenly look at each other and go—oh, OK. A half halt, Dad would call it: when a moving horse is reined in, but not entirely stopped. Just asked to take a moment. To reflect. This might be Dan and Jennie's moment.

Figaro was gaining momentum now, really building up a head of steam; then a dramatic change of key as *Lohengrin* seamlessly roared in behind it, signalling the arrival of the bride. It was prettily done, and as we all got obediently to our feet, Luke glanced over his shoulder. I gave him a smile and he grinned back, deliberately giving it some exaggerated wellie, hands raised like claws. My smile broadened. Funny. The other day I'd thought a damp church not terribly conducive to romance, but today I liked him in here. Found his particular brand of laddish humor rather infectious, probably since he'd made me laugh at the King's Head. And perhaps Angie was right: perhaps a man shone in his natural environment. He was certainly making some prodigious music, despite the intended irony, I thought, looking at his amused profile. I glanced at Simon, the very picture of radiance, beaming in the front pew, waiting for his bride.

"And Simon's happy because he got the girl he always wanted," I murmured to Jennie, straightening the back of my skirt where I'd sat on it.

"Exactly. And he doesn't have to fool around with married women like me while he waits for her to make up her mind—which he wasn't having again, incidentally. I gather there was an element of ultimatum from him about it. When she asked him to take her back, he said, 'On one condition. We get married now.'"

"Gosh, how thrilling." I shivered. "Frightfully masterful." I was intrigued. Simon was quite a catch. "So who had she been going out with all this time, then, while he waited?"

"Oh, some married man, apparently."

"Right. And what happened to him?" I asked, as the door at the far end of the church swung open with a flourish.

"He died," Jennie told me, as at that moment the gothic arched doorway filled with ivory tulle. It shimmied for an instant in the shaft of sunlight behind it, then steadied and moved toward us. Accompanied by some tiny attendants in matching ivory silk, and with lilies of the valley in a charming circlet in her blonde hair, white roses cascading like a waterfall from her bouquet, Emma Harding came gliding down the aisle.

Chapter Seventeen

IT WAS ALL I could do to stay upright and not give way to my knees, which were advising me, in the strongest possible terms, to sit down. I certainly couldn't have done without the help of the pew in front, the back of which I clutched, knuckles white. I gazed in horror and disbelief as she got ever closer, a nightmarish veiled vision, smiling coyly and acknowledging friends along the way, presumably on the arm of her father, a small, ruddy-faced man with bulbous eyes. My own eyes were giving them some competition, unable to believe what they saw.

"Pretty," commented Jennie charitably in my ear, because of course we had a bird's-eye view from the raised choir stalls.

"Pretty unbelievable!" I spat, a trifle loudly perhaps, causing even Molly, tone—if not stone—deaf, to turn.

"Shh!" Jennie hushed me, alarmed. "What d'you mean?"

"That's Emma Harding!" I hissed. "The one who was bonking Phil until he up and died a few weeks ago!"

The shock on Jennie's face gave the outrage on mine a good run for its money. The blood drained from her cheeks and the breath was seemingly sucked from her as if a high-speed vacuum had been applied to various orifices. She stared at me, dumbstruck. Then, as one, we swung back to the bride.

"I *don't* believe it," she gasped, joining me in clutching the pew in front.

"I swear to God," I sped on furiously. "She sat on my sofa in my sitting room piously explaining how she wouldn't take a penny from me, before deciding better of it. I'd know her sanctimonious little face anywhere!"

Jennie digested this in horrified silence as Emma and her father proceeded in stately fashion toward us, up to the steps where Simon and the vicar waited by the altar.

"And all the time she was busy re-bagging Simon!" Jennie said. "Little tart," she spat venomously. Sylvia, in front, turned to give her a disapproving look.

"*Schem*ing little tart," I agreed, ignoring Sylvia's furious frown.

Fortunately for Emma, Luke was still giving it whampo, and our remarks didn't drift further than our immediate neighbors. We watched, tight-lipped and incredulous. Without much fear of recognition, either, disguised as we were in unfamiliar cassock and ruff. Emma's eyes, anyway, were only for her groom, waiting straight-backed and proudly for her; she wasn't busy scanning the choir stalls for detractors. As she hove into view under our noses, I realized she was much more of a highlighted blonde than a natural one these days, and she was sporting a deep San Tropez tan, her shimmying shoulders, smooth and gleaming, rising from her strapless gown. She glided into position, and as Luke's final chord drifted away into the rafters she smiled up into her groom's eyes. Simon's face was suffused with unadulterated delight as he gazed down.

"Hussy!" hissed Jennie, and even Angie leaned around to give her a startled look.

Mike, our vicar, rocking back and forth on the soles of his shoes, said a few words of welcome—as usual mentioning the church roof—and then directed us to our first hymn. I managed to mutter a few words of it but Jennie, beside me, stood mute and pale throughout. Finally, under cover of the last verse, which was delivered at full volume by the congregation and to which we were supposed to provide the descant, she muttered in my ear, "I've a jolly good mind to say something."

My eyes widened in horror. She had a determined look on her face that I knew of old. "What—you mean at the just-cause-and-impediment stage?"

"Well, that's what it's there for, Poppy."

"Like what?" I yelped. "What would you say?"

"Something like: do you have any idea what cunning little fortune-hunter you're about to get hitched to? That's what. Oh, and incidentally, the married man she was bonking was married to my best friend and was the father of her children. That's sort of what I had in mind."

"I'd rather you didn't," I whispered nervously. "He clearly loves her cunning little heart for better or worse, and don't forget that he knew about the married man, probably the children, too. The fact that it was *my* married man, had he known Phil, would probably have been a great comfort to him."

Yes, I thought, as the hymn ended on a high note, Simon must have thought he was up against some handsome, virile love machine. Some piece of work in the sack and some insatiably smooth operator out of it. And, all the time, it had been Phil. Phil Shilling, with his thinning sandy hair, his long nose, the pointy bit of which reddened and dripped when it was cold, his thin lips, his very short temper, not to mention his very short…Well. Not that size matters. But what had *she* seen in him? This baffled me most, as we sat to watch them make their vows. It actually made me question my own recollection of Phil. Had I not spotted his startling resemblance to George Clooney? Was I perhaps jaundiced, due to a stunning lack of attention? Did he, in fact, have a scintillating wit and a charming manner, but only when I wasn't in the room? Had I sapped it out of him, squashed him? With my domineering ways, my fish-wife manner? Was it *my* fault? You don't have to know me too well to realize this line of thought was well established within my psyche; I was always ready for the finger of blame, even at my most innocent, to pivot suddenly and point inexorably at me. After all, I'd picked him, too, hadn't I? As Emma had. He must have had *some* endearing qualities.

Heroically, Jennie sat on her hands at the *moment critique* as the vicar asked the audience. I watched as Simon slipped a ring on her finger and gazed tenderly into her eyes. She could have had that look, that ring, four years ago if it hadn't been for Phil. Unbelievable. The mind didn't so much boggle as bulge pneumatically. I cast around desperately for clues.

They'd worked together, of course, which traditionally makes for a heady environment, sexual tension and all that—although Lord knows why, with the bright lights, first-thing-in-the-morning faces and unattractive gobbling of sandwiches at desks. I can't imagine it did much for Phil. But then, he was her boss, which was well documented. Yes, that must have been it: the masterful way he called her into his office to discuss new business, poking his nasal hair back with his little finger, readjusting a wedgie. That would have got the juices flowing. Or the attractive way he cleared his throat at least twice before he spoke, and then the slow, soft, ultra-patronizing tones he employed, implying he had to go at this speed and volume because the person on the receiving end was not only a moron, but capable of reacting violently if he used anything like a normal tone. It all came back in a horrific rush. The way he'd patiently take a pan off the hob and throw the water away, quietly explaining that potatoes went into cold water, not hot. How many times did he have to tell me? The way he showed me how to clean the work surfaces in the kitchen, calling it Surface Training. The way, when he came home from work, he surreptitiously ran his finger along the windowsill, still in his overcoat, checking for dust. The way, in the early days, I'd bellowed and roared, fists tight with rage, and yes, even thrown a plate. And then later, when the children were around, just buttoned it. Kept the house impeccable and got on with it. Lived life in my head; a whole different scenario, where I was married to someone else, someone lovely. Knowing, in a tiny place in my heart, as Jennie had so succinctly pointed out when he'd died, that one day I'd leave him.

Why hadn't I lived with him before I got married? OK, I had for a few months, but it should have been a few years! No child of mine, I decided vehemently, eyes blazing, would ever go up that aisle, stand at that altar, under the eyes of God, without having lived in sin first.

Emma was slipping her own ring on Simon's finger now. I looked at her in disbelief. I'd been tied to Phil. Had children by him. Without a great deal of unpleasantness to extract myself, I was lumbered with him. But this girl—I watched as she and Simon knelt together, bowing their heads to be blessed by the vicar—this girl had chosen to delay her life by four years on account of him. *What had I missed?*

The Gloria was next, while the bride and groom disappeared to the vestry to sign the register. Jennie and I belted it out furiously, one or two heads turning to marvel at our volume. Then the happy couple returned and there was another hymn: "ransomed, healed, restored, for…" No. I couldn't sing the last bit. Then a word from our vicar, Mike: his address.

I can only assume Mike had been at the sherry again, or had had a row with his wife, Veronica, seated in her usual pew, because even by his standards it was inappropriate. Mike, bearded, Welsh and thoroughly right-on, thought he'd been put on this earth to deliver challenging sermons. He felt it his duty. We, on the other hand, felt it his duty to give comforting soporific ones that we could doze off to, mentally ticking our lists of Things to Do. But Mike believed he was edgy. His theme today was love and the different forms it took. Reasonably innocuous, one might think. And so indeed it started: platonic love, then brotherly love, then paternal, and then erotic—"about which I know absolutely nothing!" he spat venomously, glaring at his wife. Naturally the entire congregation tried not to look at Veronica, who, if she had a spasm at being outmaneuvered, mastered it admirably, sitting calmly, impassive, while "No, Mike, for the last time, I am *not* doing that!" rang clearly in her neighbors' heads.

Another hymn, then Luke got very busy with a Mozart canon, and then, finally, the service was over. As the bride and groom swept back down the aisle to triumphant chords, Jennie and I, pausing only to throw our cassocks over our heads and leave them in a heap in the vestry, marched straight out of the back door. We paused neither to congratulate nor to throw confetti, but most certainly to give vent to our feelings.

"Bitch!"

"Slut!"

"I *cannot* believe it," I seethed as we hustled down the little side path together, avoiding the main entrance. Handbags were clutched fiercely to chests.

"And how could she get married here!" squealed Jennie. "In your church, where you got married, and where you've just buried your husband—her lover!"

"Quite!" I agreed, stopping still a moment as the impact of this hit me. I swung around. "She's going to have to walk straight past him," I breathed. "He's right next to the path."

We watched as the bridal procession did indeed make its way out of the main door and past Phil's very prominent, very fresh mound of earth. Emma didn't give it a second look.

"That is one very shrewd operator," observed Jennie, narrowing her eyes.

"Cool as a cucumber," I agreed, marveling at the magnitude of her gall.

"And poor Simon has no idea what he's taking on. What a piece of work he's just married."

"Will you tell him?" I asked, as we turned and hurried away. "I mean, that it was my husband whose death he was effectively waiting for?"

Jennie gave it some thought. "No," she said finally. "I won't be speaking to Simon again. Not now, not after who he's married. I had hoped we might stay friends but I doubt our paths will ever cross. I'm sure he won't come to the book club now. Odd, though, isn't it?" She wrinkled her brow as she looked into the distance. "He clearly thinks he knows her inside out. She lived next door, you know; they grew up together. Her father was their gardener. They lived in the grounds, in the cottage."

"Oh...right." I remembered sitting in my car outside Meadow Bank Cottage, in the grounds of Meadow Bank House. "So presumably they'll live in the big house soon, when Simon inherits it. Didn't you say his father had died?"

"Yes, and the mother wants to move out because she thinks it's too big for her."

"Perfect timing, then, once again, from Miss Harding," I said grimly in disbelief.

"Exactly," said Jennie as we reached the gate. "Well, good luck to them," she went on acidly. "You know what they say: if you marry money you pay for it. And she clearly *has* married him for that. If she loved him she'd have married him years ago." She shuddered. "Poor Simon. It's making my own marriage look increasingly less flawed, I must say. Comparatively speaking, of course. Dear old Dan," she said almost fondly. "At least I didn't marry him for his money. I'd have been sorely disappointed if I had. Oh, hello. Talk of the devil."

We were in the lane now, which led in one direction to the gallops where the race horses trained, and in the other, up the hill to Wessington, where no doubt the reception was being held—presumably not at the bride's house but in the zonking great grounds of the groom's, next door. Dan was standing in the middle of the road beside an old Morgan, one of his many disastrous cars. The bonnet was up, steam was billowing, and Dan was scratching his head.

"Oh, what a surprise. He's broken down," observed Jennie, but she didn't say it with quite the vehemence she was capable of. "And there I was, thinking he'd come to whisk me away. My knight in shining armor."

"Bit of a problem with the radiator valve!" Dan called to us cheerily over the raised bonnet, as clouds of steam threatened to envelop him. One or two cars had already stopped behind him in the lane.

"Is there, darling? Never mind," Jennie cooed back. "I'm sure you'll fix it." She gave me a grin. "It's my new approach. It's called Not My Problem. Can't think why I hadn't thought of it before." And off she swept, tossing her husband a dazzling smile, in the manner of a woman who was off to open a bottle of rosé.

It was, however, a problem for the wedding party. Church Lane was narrow, and with Dan blocking it there was no way the bottle-green vintage car, wide and Chitty-chitty-bang-bang in style, could get past. The happy couple had already climbed into the back, behind the elderly chauffeur, ready for the off. They looked increasingly unhappy as Dan failed to budge.

"Can't you move that thing?" Simon stood up commandingly in the back. He and his bride were being showered by just a little too much confetti. One or two of the village boys were picking it up off the road, thinking it a huge lark.

"Stop that!" Emma snapped at them as a fair amount of gravel came with it.

"Sorry, old boy. Seems to be caput." Dan grinned back pleasantly.

"Well, push it, can't you?"

Dan shrugged and looked away up the hill to Wessington. Very much uphill, so no, he couldn't, not on his own.

With a sigh, Simon vaulted smartly out of the back of the car. Following suit, one or two of the male wedding guests surged to help: young men in morning coats, testosterone-fueled, keen to show off to their girlfriends, then get to the champagne. Together they made a big show of taking off their jackets and handing them to the girls, rolling up their sleeves while Dan got in the driving seat of the Morgan amid much laughter. I, however, found my legs taking me, not across the road to my own house and my own bottle of rosé, but toward the lychgate at the bottom of the church path, where the vintage car was parked.

Emma's eyes on the debacle ahead were full of irritation. She sat on the red leather seat gripping her bouquet, tight-lipped. This was a girl who got what she wanted, all right, I thought as I approached. A girl with a huge sense of entitlement. She wouldn't see the funny side of this, her wedding car held up by a clapped-out old banger. Wouldn't throw her head back and roar with laughter at her new husband pushing it up the road, saying it would be one to tell the children. And neither would Phil, it occurred to me abruptly. He'd have been very cross. As she was. How alike they were, I realized; how similar. They'd have got on like a house on fire. My heart suddenly lurched for Simon, laughing with his mates as he pushed Dan up the road in his Morgan. Love surely was blind, and particularly when it became fueled by the lack of it. Became infatuation. Which wasn't the same thing at all. I was beside the vintage car now, where Emma sat alone, glaring.

"Congratulations," I said quietly.

Her head turned and her eyes came to rest on me. They took a moment. Then her face blanched. She looked stunned.

I smiled. "You look like you've seen a ghost. Not the one back there in the churchyard, is it?" I jerked my head.

She inhaled, sharply, between barely parted lips.

"I've just been at your wedding," I said. "Singing for you, in the choir. I live here, remember? It's my church. My village. Lovely service. Wonder if Phil enjoyed it?"

She glanced around quickly, looking for her groom, for moral support. Her eyes were panicky. And Simon was coming back, but slowly, brushing his hands on his trousers, stopping to share a joke with his ushers. She was on her own.

"And don't think you'll get a penny out of me," I said carefully. "Because you won't. Not one penny. You've got a flaming nerve, Miss Harding. Or should I say, Mrs. Devereux."

I turned and walked away, toward home, toward my well-earned drink. I felt just a little taller and a little light-headed too. It isn't often you hope to spoil a bride's day, I thought as I crossed the road to my cottage, but I sincerely hoped I'd wrecked that one.

Chapter Eighteen

As I opened my front gate it occurred to me that I could have spoiled it further for her. I could have had a coughing fit in the choir, made myself known, so that those sharp little eyes would have sought me out, irritated, wondering who was making such a racket. I could have done it during her vows. Looked her coldly in the eye, had the satisfaction of seeing her blanch at the altar, rock back beside her new husband. Yes, that would have been sweet. But would it? Might it not have left a nasty taste in my mouth? I gave a wry smile. It seemed I could spoil her day but not entirely ruin it, even though she'd had no qualms about ruining my life.

Had she, though? Ruined my life? Apart from the claim she was making now, which was decidedly unwelcome, surely I'd have welcomed her, had I known of her existence. Surely, if I'd caught them in flagrante in their love nest, or at the office, say, when on a hunch I'd stormed to London, found them locked in a passionate embrace in a stationery cupboard, surely, after the initial shock, I'd have stood back, waved a genial hand and said, "How marvelous! Do carry on. Don't mind me. Have him!" Slammed the stationery-cupboard door shut.

I went up the cobbled path, absently deadheading a faded old rose on the way. It dawned on me that my life could have been very different if only I'd discovered them earlier, when it first started, when I was pregnant with Clemmie. I'd have been frightened, sure, to be betrayed and pregnant, but calm and still within a twinkling.

So. A single mother. Just me and my baby. Yes, I could have done that. I would have gone to Dad's for a bit, been quite happy. But then I wouldn't have had Archie. I sighed. If if, maybe maybe, perhaps perhaps. So many imponderables. Maybe I just shouldn't have married the wretched man in the first place?

Archie and Clemmie were clamoring for my attention when I got inside, and Peggy, who'd held the fort, was full of praise for their achievements.

"Archie called me Piggy and then Clemmie drew me with a snout—do look." She flourished a wax-crayon picture. "Quite adorable. Don't you love the pixie boots she's put on my trotters? And the beads around my fat neck?"

Normally this would have had me purring with pride, but today I was distracted. I gave it the briefest of glances, flashed a weak smile and crossed to the sitting-room window.

"What's up?" Peggy narrowed her eyes and sat down, lighting a cigarette, watching my back. The children had run back to their crayons in the kitchen.

I turned from staring out at the road over my little hedge. "You know that woman Phil was having an affair with? Emma Harding?" Funny, I'd thought I was calm, but my breathing was erratic. "She's just married Simon Devereux."

Peggy frowned. "Simon? Are you sure? I heard he was marrying someone terribly good-looking."

"Well, she is quite good-looking."

"But Phil was..." She stopped.

"Quite." I bit my lip. "God knows why women fell for him, Peggy," I said softly. "Anyway, she's nabbed Simon now. A much better prospect."

"Fast work," she murmured. "In your church, too. Takes some doing. How did she know she wouldn't see you?"

"Well, she knew I wasn't on the guest list, so I imagine she thought there was only a slim chance I'd be bustling round the village, and even then it's only yet another bride sweeping out of our oh-so-popular church, so why would I bother to stand and stare? And it's all over bar the shouting by then, isn't it? When she's out, showered in confetti? And who cares, frankly, if a scruffy mother of two with egg down her front comes out of the village shop and does a double take?" My words were coming rapidly, like quick fire. Peggy was watching me closely.

"I see. She didn't waste much time."

"I'll say she didn't; she moved like flaming greased lightning. And the thing is, Peggy, since it *is* all so speedy, and now that she's married and everything, surely it negates her claim to Phil's will? I mean, if she's relying on another man's wealth, why should she have some of mine?"

"Yes, I imagine it might make a difference." She looked beyond me and blew a line of smoke. Then back at me, curiously. "I should think she got the shock of her life, didn't she? Not just seeing you, but knowing the financial cat was out of the bag?"

"Well, I would have found out eventually of course, but yes. I definitely found out sooner than she'd hoped. Ha!" I barked out a strange-sounding laugh. "She can put that in her pipe and smoke it."

"Sit down, Poppy," she said gently.

I crossed to the sofa and perched, still in my coat. Archie appeared again and toddled across to clamber on my lap.

"Why don't you ring your solicitor, find out where you stand?"

"Really?"

"Why not? Tell him what's happened."

It was the green light I'd been hoping for. "You mean now? On a Saturday? You don't think it could wait till Monday?" I was already on my feet, setting Archie down, looking for my mobile. Not in my pocket. In my bag? No. Down the side of the sofa, perhaps. I searched frantically, already rehearsing in my head: hello, Sam, it's Poppy. No. Too familiar. Good morning, Sam, it's Poppy Shilling here.

"Well, I suppose I did mean Monday," Peggy said slowly.

I turned, one hand between the sofa cushions. I must have looked disappointed. My face might even have collapsed.

"But why not today?" she said quickly. "Everyone keeps odd hours these days, and a lot of people work at the weekend."

"They do, don't they?" I agreed eagerly, retrieving my phone. "And he did give me his mobile number."

"Well, there you are, then." Her eyes were steady. "Have you got some lunch, Poppy?"

"Oh yes, there's some cheese in the fridge."

"No, there isn't."

"Well, there are some eggs."

"They're quite old. A couple of weeks. Why don't you come across to me and bring the children? I'll make some pasta."

"No, no, Peggy, we're fine. I'll pop to the shop."

I glanced up at her from my mobile, finger poised. Go, Peggy, go. I need to do this alone.

"And thank you so much for looking after the children," I said breathlessly, knowing better than to pay her. She got to her feet unwillingly. Slowly picked up her Marlboro Lights. I walked her to the door so she had little choice but to exit. "I'll see you later. Or tomorrow," I promised. "Soon, anyway. Thanks so much for coming."

"Look after yourself, Poppy."

The moment the front door had shut behind her, I hustled Archie down to the kitchen and settled him with his sister at the table, with juice and biscuits, making a long arm to flick on the television in the corner. Oh yes, it still came into its own in extremis. Then I slipped back into the sitting room. Adrenalin was rushing around my body like nobody's business. I liked a plan. Liked it very much. It helped enormously to see a way forward. My heart was racing as I punched out his number. It rang for a bit, then he answered.

"Hello!" Deep, but cheerful. Not low and suspicious like Phil would have been if he didn't recognize the number. No question mark stuck on the end.

"Hello, Sam, I'm so sorry to bother you on a Saturday, it's Poppy Shilling here."

"Oh, hi, Poppy." A hint of surprise there, I thought.

I hurried on, explaining the situation, tumbling over my words, getting a bit muddled occasionally—I should have sat down and thought this through, had a bit of paper in front of me with bullet points—but eventually I got my point across: that my husband's lover had, moments ago, tied the knot with a man of surely some standing. That she'd seamlessly cruised on in her scheming little way, while I groped around in mine. But surely I'd got her this time?

"And she was so shocked to see me, Sam," I rushed on. "I'm in the choir, you see, didn't stalk her or anything, wasn't lying in wait; she had no idea I'd be there. She must have thought she'd got away with it!"

There was a long silence on the other end. "Well, I'm afraid she may have done just that, Poppy," he said eventually. "You see, it makes no difference whether she marries or not. If she's entitled to anything, her claim still stands."

I stared out of my sitting-room window to the road. Felt my tummy shrivel. "But—but Simon Devereux is well off! He's a flipping Sotheby's expert or something, works in Bond Street—"

"Christie's. Yes, I know Simon."

"Do you? Oh, well then, you know! His mother practically lives in a mansion—I've seen it—and he'll inherit it, apparently. She can't take my money and live in the lap of luxury with him, surely!"

"I'm afraid she can. I'll look into it, Poppy, but his wealth has nothing whatsoever to do with hers. And marriage, however swift, is not an impediment to claiming on an ex's estate."

It was said kindly, but the wind was completely buffeted out of my sails.

"He wasn't her ex. He was mine."

"I know," he said gently. And perhaps with a hint of pity.

I wondered, suddenly, what sort of figure I cut: this wronged, cheated wife, whose husband's lover was even now greeting her guests at her wedding reception, while I was left panicking breathlessly. Rather a pathetic one, that's what. Someone Frankie might call a loser. All at once my life swam before me, I saw my younger self, charging confidently around London in the Renault Five Dad had bought me and which I'd painted pink, managing three parties a night sometimes, the object of some attention, usually with gorgeous Ben. A winner, surely. How, then, had it come to this? This breathless little widow, still in her coat, hands tightly clasping her mobile, voice getting shriller as she complained to a man she held in some esteem, a man she might even have been looking for an excuse to ring…complained that it simply wasn't fair? How had I lost so much of myself over the years? Where had it all gone? I felt detached, like a spectator, watching myself seep through holes, like sand disappearing through a clenched fist. Only a tiny bit remaining in the palm.

"It would be invidious, you see," Sam was saying as I sat very still, "to discriminate between a woman who was likely to get remarried, and one who was not. A judge can't possibly say: well, you look like the back of a bus, no one would want you, so we'll give you lots of money; and to someone like Miss Harding: you can't have much money because you have every prospect of remarrying."

"Have you seen her?"

"No, of course not."

But he was imagining her. And he was right. She was good-looking. Not beautiful, but foxy. Fit, a man would say.

"But, as I say, I'm not instantly familiar with the law on this. The fact that she and your husband made the money together makes it quite an unusual case. I'll look into it and get back to you. Steady, Tess."

"Tess?" I blinked. Who was he sharing my most shaming secrets with?

"My horse," he laughed. "Sorry, I'm in the saddle at the moment. Riding out with the Armitages. But don't worry, I hung back when you rang. They're out of earshot."

"The Armitages?"

"Yes."

"The American ones?"

"Yes, Chad and Hope. They're keen to go hunting next week, so I said I'd lend them a couple of horses from my yard. See how they get on."

My head swam in bewilderment. I shook it briefly. "You've lent them…"

"Two hunters I've got spare. They need the exercise, frankly."

I stared at a damp patch on the wall opposite.

"Where do you live?"

I couldn't help it. It just popped out.

"Mulverton Hall," he said, sounding surprised. "It's near Leighton Park; not that far from your village, actually."

I knew it. Of course I knew it. And I knew the story, too. Old, pretty, not exactly derelict, but crumbling. And tenanted, because the owner, who no one had ever met, lived in America. Except recently he'd returned, minus his beautiful American wife, who some years ago had left him. Even more recently he'd given up the London house and returned to the one he'd grown up in, in the country. Ditched his city career to work locally, have a different sort of life. He was a lawyer, Angie thought. But no one really knew, as I say, much about him. Besides the fact that he kept horses. I took a deep breath; let it out shakily. The reality that was Sam Hetherington's life paraded before me in glorious technicolor, like an Easter Parade, with decorated floats, marching girls twirling batons, whistles and drums: an American tradition, of course, but how appropriate. A glorious spectacle. This wasn't a faintly shambolic solicitor in a chaotic office at the top of some creaky stairs, one that, in a secret corner of my heart, I'd looked at, liked instantly, recognized almost, and thought: I could have a tiny chance with that. This was a very different screenplay to the one I'd dreamily created in my head. The one where he returned to his lonely rented bedsit every night, above a shop maybe, and thought wistfully of the young widow he'd advised that day. This one spelled out in bright, sparkling, neon lights: *Out of your league!*

This was a man who got on famously with Chad and Hope, the new pin-up couple in our village. Who knew Simon Devereux—no doubt they were family friends in that local, big-house sort of way—and who would soon, no doubt, be introduced to Emma, Simon's wife. Within a twinkling they'd be having dinner parties. Chad and Hope, Simon and Emma, Sam and—ooh, let's see…Emma's best friend, um, Lucinda. Worthington-Squiggle. Squiggs, for short. A leggy, horse-mad beauty, who would take one look at Sam across the dinner table, his easy smile, his relaxed manner, would glimpse his beautiful house which everyone said was heavenly but unloved and surely needed a woman's touch, and before you knew it I'd be singing the Gloria at yet another wedding. Gloria, Gloria, Gloria, me and Molly—no doubt with a carer apiece—before toddling back to my cottage to cook liver and bacon.

"Right. Well, sorry to have bothered you, Sam," I said, breathing very shallowly. Very unevenly. "I'll, um, wait to hear. Should you decide there's anything in it for the wronged wife," I couldn't resist adding.

"I'll let you know," he assured me, no doubt steadying his impatient steed, keen to catch up with the others, and not, therefore, catching my tone; which was just as well, for what was it, Poppy? Sarcastic? Bitter? But he needed to get on. The Armitages were doubtless even now galloping across his immaculate parkland, down by the lake, the grand house perched on the hill: Hope, riding side-saddle, in a full-length black habit; Chad, bareheaded in breeches; Sam, in a dripping-wet white shirt, clinging and faintly ruffled.

We said good-bye. I sat in my coat, on my goose-poo sofa, knees and hands pressed tightly together, cold and knowing. I should light the fire now, get some lunch. Go rally the troops in the kitchen. Not leave my under fives at the table, albeit safely strapped in Archie's case, but be in there making biscuits, "Nellie the Elephant" on the CD, being effortlessly cheerful. But my life didn't feel cheerful. I gazed at the damp wall. I thought I'd spotted in Sam someone a bit like me, who needed a stitch or two on his shirt sleeve, a few patches on his life where it had come unravelled. I'd been attracted by that; had perhaps looked forward to some cozy comparisons, some mutual sharing of sob stories. But his life wasn't like mine. It was in much more shape. Of course, he didn't appear to have children, which helped, but men were generally more baggage-free anyway, weren't they? Look at Angie's Tom. He had two children but was carefree—although according to Peggy that relationship wasn't without its problems. A liking for extreme sports, which Tom didn't share, had raised its head, bungee jumping, in particular. Well, Tom didn't have to bungee jump all day, did he? I hope the fucking rope breaks, Angie had hissed. And even if it did hit the rocks—the relationship, not Tom—men were still, by definition, able to pick themselves up, dust themselves off, slap on a smile and say: hi, Lucinda! Oh, Squiggs, is it? Lovely to meet you. Glass of champagne?

The doorbell went, making me jump. From the kitchen came the sound of the children's voices: less happy now, more shrill and fretful. Something I should pounce on before it went critical. Archie screamed very loudly in sudden outrage, as Clemmie no doubt pinched his last biscuit. I shut my eyes tight. One read terrible stories in the papers, ghastly ones. But who hasn't, on occasion, sympathized with the young girl in the high-rise flat, alone with three small children, driven to distraction, driven to shaking her baby? Who hasn't wanted to jump up, storm into that kitchen, pull Clemmie roughly from the table, shake her arm and shout in her face about being mean to her brother, about being a little cow, then slap her leg hard? Archie was roaring fit to bust now, giving it both barrels. There'd been one in the *Mail* just the other day, about a girl who'd simply gone away. Shut the door to her flat, two small children inside, and got on a train to Edinburgh. One was only six months old.

The doorbell rang again. A longer, more persistent summons, and this time I got stiffly to my feet. I walked slowly down the hall to the kitchen where Archie, brick-red in the face, was bawling. I calmly unclipped him from his high chair and set him on my hip, then, reaching into the biscuit tin, gave him one, wordlessly. He took it and the shrieking stopped instantly, to be replaced by silent sobs and hiccuping, his face drenched, nose snotty, boiling hot in my arms. I took another biscuit and passed it to my pale-faced daughter, sitting silent and guarded, turning her back. She took it in surprise, guilty eyes catching mine. No words were exchanged. Then, as my doorbell went for a third time, I went back down the passage with Archie in my arms, to answer it. Only the more astute observer might notice I still hadn't taken my coat off, and that most mothers would have wiped their baby's sopping face with their hand before answering the door. Other than that, it was business as usual. Oh, and I usually flicked the light on before I opened the door, the hall being so dark, but I couldn't be fagged. Couldn't be fagged to turn on a light? An alarm bell sounded somewhere dim and distant and I reached quickly for the switch. Lifted my chin, too, as I opened the front door.

"Oh. Luke. Hi."

Looking a bit temporary and as if he might well be on his way, Luke Chambers turned, halfway down my front path. He was wearing a pair of old Levis, a white T-shirt and a bright blue V-necked jumper. It wasn't a bad look. He flashed me a smile, raked his hand through his blond hair and bounced back up the path.

"Poppy, hi! What kept you? Were you enthroned or something? Compromised in the smallest room? I was about to give up on you and go and do some solitary drinking."

"Sorry. Archie was crying. Couldn't hear the bell." Couldn't raise a smile, either.

"Oh, right." He hesitated, unnerved perhaps by my deadpan expression. And I hadn't asked him in.

"Yeah, well, I might not have pressed it hard enough, one never quite knows if it rings louder inside than out." He licked his lips as I didn't reply. "Um, Poppy," he ploughed on, perhaps a mite nervously for him, "I wondered if you and the kids would like to have some lunch? Only I was going to go across to the Rose and Crown to grab a ploughman's, and they don't mind children, apparently, I've checked. As long as it's in the saloon bar and not the public one. Oh, and they do a kids menu too, if a ploughman's doesn't appeal, nuggets and chips." It was said eagerly, nicely. Albeit in something of a rush. Rather as my words had tumbled out on the phone just now: the voice of someone who gives a damn.

I considered his offer. Another reason I'd sped out of the church via the side door with Jennie was to avoid Luke, who I knew would be looking for me after the service. It was a plan I'd hatched well before I knew the identity of the bride and groom. You see, I wasn't sure I was ready for him. For the determined campaign I sensed he was about to wage on me, the steady romantic advance. I knew I was capable of falling for his ardor, should he turn up the flame, which he appeared to be doing: this nice young man with his megawatt smile, his floppy blond hair and blue eyes. Eyes, it seemed, only for me. But why was I looking so closely? So minutely? Being so forensic about this? Naturally I'd been badly bitten, but still.

All at once my cold little house, my bickering children, my aged eggs in the fridge for lunch didn't appeal. And the warmth of the cozy pub opposite, with its open fire and yes, OK, all manner of interested locals, all sorts of gossiping tongues—did. Suddenly it was no contest.

I shored up a smile on my doorstep, the most brilliant I could muster under the circumstances. Felt it wobble only slightly.

"Thank you, Luke. I'd love to."

Chapter Nineteen

OWING TO A PARISH council meeting involving both Angie and Angus, last week's book club was postponed until this week, when, to save me securing yet another baby-sitter, it was to be held at my house. One by one, though, its members called to express regrets. Jennie was first, and she came right out with it.

"I'm not coming on Tuesday, Poppy, because I haven't read the book—I can't get beyond the first chapter. Wikipedia said it was one of the most difficult books in the English language, and I can believe it. I've started it six times and each time I'm lost, confused, and asleep in moments. Sorry. It's obviously far too cerebral for me."

"But I haven't read it either, Jennie," I said nervously. "Don't leave me. What am I supposed to do? It's at my house. Won't I have to chair it, or something?"

"No, no, don't worry, someone else will do that. Ask Angie; she'll love it. Or even Angus—he'll love it even more. Make him feel important."

But Angus rang not long afterward, to confide the details of some sudden and mysterious malaise.

"Sorry, Poppy, old girl, but not sure I'm going to make it to this one. Got a bit of a jippy tummy. Oh—and this infernal tickly cough, too. Kept me up all night." He gave a shining example of it down the phone, hacking beautifully.

"OK, Angus, not to worry."

"Shame, because the book is um…terrific. You'll let me know

when you get back to the thrillers, though, won't you? What about that Danish fellow, Stig something?"

Why was I suddenly responsible for the reading list?

"Will do, Angus."

"And nice to see you enjoying a spot of lunch with young Luke the other day. He's a lovely lad, isn't he?"

I ground my teeth and said good-bye. Responsible for the reading list, and also engaged.

Saintly Sue was next, in a bit of a huff.

"It's just not my sort of book, Poppy." As if it were mine! "So I'm afraid I won't be coming. I know I suggested we read something a bit more thought-provoking, but I meant something contemporary, something Booker Prize-ish. This is like wading through quicksand. And it's all very well flinging these heavy classics at us, but some people have got full-time jobs as well. We don't want to come home to yet more work."

I held the phone from my ear. Christ alive.

"I also think if I did come, it would be rather…well, invidious."

"Would it?"

I was still recovering from the unemployed-housewife jibe. Did she mean because Luke would be there?

"Luke will obviously be there." Ah. "And he appears to have made his feelings plain to the entire village. I can't compete with you, Poppy, not in that department." She gave a little strangled sob and then the phone clicked off.

I stared at it, amazed. In what department? Instinctively I glanced at my chest. No, Sue was miles bigger than me. Did she think I'd read the book? Thought my brain was bigger? Had she got to page three and thought: blimey, if Poppy's read this I can't compete?

Luke, however, it transpired, wouldn't be there either. He rang to enthuse about our lunch the other day, saying how much he'd enjoyed it; and actually, it had been very pleasant, in the Rose and

Crown's cozy snug, around the fire with the children, Luke teaching Clemmie to balance a beer mat on her nose, all of us laughing as Archie just plonked one on his head and gazed around, beaming. Sadly, though, Luke said, he had a meeting on Tuesday evening.

"It's a shame, because the book is absolutely riveting."

"It is, isn't it, Luke?"

"You've read it?" Some surprise in his voice.

"Oh, yes. Cover to cover."

"Me too," he said quickly.

"What did you think about the protagonist having a sex change halfway through?"

A pause. "I thought it was…a good twist."

I smiled. "I haven't read it either, Luke."

"Ha ha! Nice one, Poppy." Although I could tell he wasn't that amused at being caught out. "I intend to read it, though."

"Oh, *yes*. Me too."

"And I wondered, if maybe we could do something the following night instead? See a film or something?"

"Can I let you know, Luke? Obviously the eternal childcare question looms."

"Sure, or I could come to you?"

I caught my breath. Quite familiar. In my house, a cozy supper, bottle of wine, children asleep. Coffee on the sofa by the fire later. But why not? That was surely the next stage.

"We'll see," I assured him. "I'll give you a ring."

I put the phone down and scurried away from it, to the kitchen. Apparently needing some distance. But minutes later I was back, because Peggy was next, saying she had a prior engagement and that if I asked her the book was a complete nightmare. Then Angie, who said she was hunting the next day, so not to include her, even though she'd adored the book. Yes, she thought the sex change was entirely plausible, and actually served as a fitting motif to demonstrate how transitory life could be. It was very emblematic of the ephemeral nature of things, didn't I think?

I agreed wearily. Although I wasn't convinced going hunting the following day precluded attending the book club and told her so.

"Ah, but I like to clean my tack the night before. Plait my horse, that type of thing. It's the opening meet, you see. Terribly smart."

Everyone knew Angie took hunting seriously, to the point of undergoing a personality change when thus engaged, scarily barking out orders in the field and becoming a mounted hunt-etiquette manual, so no doubt her horse would be subjected to all manner of cleansing rituals. Even though I was pretty sure she had an army of grooms to do it all for her, I didn't quibble.

"And obviously I need to look the part because the new master is divine. I told you that, didn't I, Poppy?"

"You did."

"This one's got my name on it," she told me firmly. "Plastered on his very cute, tight-jodhpured behind. Single, loaded, good-looking—hot."

"All yours, Angie." Was she warning me off?

"And the Armitages will be out, too, apparently, and they'll obviously be impeccable."

"Yes, so I heard."

"How did you hear?"

"Oh…someone told me. Have a fun day, Angie."

"I will. Oh, and *lovely* that you and Luke had lunch the other day. That's so sweet, Poppy!"

I was all packaged up, wasn't I? All sorted. People so liked to dust their hands of one, I thought rather uncharitably.

"He's just a friend," I said wearily.

"Oh, of *course*."

We left it at that.

Later, I bumped into Hope in the village shop. I'd never seen her in there before, assuming she shopped in Fortnum's before coming to the country. She looked like she was going to lunch at the Ivy, although she was, in fact, buying Rice Krispies. Her dark hair was swept back in a sleek chignon and she was wearing shiny flat black boots, a swirling grey skating skirt and a crisp white shirt. It was the sort of effortless ensemble that no one ever managed to pull off in our village.

"Oh—Poppy." She looked embarrassed. "About the book club."

"Don't worry, we've cancelled it. There didn't seem to be much enthusiasm this week, Hope, which is odd when you consider we're reading one of the greatest novels in literary history." I deliberately echoed her words.

"If not the greatest," she said quickly. "I go all tingly just picking it up!"

"Oh, me too. But I suppose you're going hunting the next day?"

"I am, as a matter of fact. Don't you just love Stephen Dedalus?" she purred, touching my arm.

"Is he the new master?"

She frowned. "No, he's a character in *Ulysses*."

"Oh." It occurred to me I might have run into the one person who had read it. "Dreamy," I agreed. "Until the sex change."

She stared at me long and hard. "Ye-es…But then, one is never encouraged to think of him as a traditional romantic hero, is one? In the mold, say, of a Mr. Rochester?"

"No, one is not," I agreed. I wrinkled my brow. "And it's emblematic, don't you feel, of the transitory nature of life? Symptomatic of how ephemeral things can be?"

"Yes!" she said eagerly. "Isn't it just?"

"Although between you and me, it hasn't quite got the page-turning appeal of a jolly good read, like Jilly Cooper."

I was losing her now. My in-depth analysis into the mores of contemporary literature was too much for her at half-past eleven in the village shop. She looked confused.

"Jilly…?"

"Never mind. Anyway, as I say, I've called the whole thing off."

"Such a shame. And a pity not to see everyone again. Chad and I so enjoyed ourselves last time. But I expect I'll see you at the meet, won't I? There are usually lots of foot followers," she added kindly.

I blinked. "Yes. Well, maybe."

She bestowed a dazzling smile on me and swept out in a cloud of Diorissimo, jangling her charm bracelet.

"You going, love?" Yvonne asked me, weighing the bananas I'd handed her.

"Where?"

"To the meet."

"I don't know. Where is it?"

"Mulverton Hall at eleven. It's old George Hetherington's place; belongs to his son now. D'you know it?"

I stared at her as she handed me back my fruit in a brown paper bag. "Well, not intimately. But I know where it is."

"'E's come back from London apparently, to take it on again. Been tenanted for years, that place, all sorts of people who didn't really look after it after the old boy died. Well, you don't if it's not your own, do you? Let the garden go to rack and ruin by all accounts. Shame. Be nice to have someone breathe a bit of life into it again, eh? Nice to have some new blood around, too." She grinned, revealing her unusual dental arrangement.

"Thanks, Yvonne," I said as she handed me my change, declining to comment. I turned to go. "Nice to see you."

"You too, Poppy. And I'm glad you're finding your feet again."

I turned back. She'd lowered her voice conspiratorially even though there was no one else in the shop. "Getting out and about," she went on softly. "And don't you pay any attention to those that think it's a bit soon. Can't be in widow's weeds forever, eh? I know after my Bill died I stayed indoors for months on end, but that's not everyone's way, is it?" And she shot me a kindly look before bustling away to attend to a consignment of lavatory paper which had just arrived and was sitting in a tousering pile by the post-office counter, ready to be stacked.

I went home, thoughtful. Stirred, but not shaken by her remark. No, I wouldn't pay any attention. Yvonne wasn't to know I hadn't had a man in my life for many years; wasn't to know that in fact, rather than it being too soon, I'd left it rather late.

Archie was sound asleep in his pushchair now, eyelashes a pair of perfect crescents, mouth open, wet thumb dropped on his chest. Once inside I lifted him out carefully and carried him upstairs to his cot, then went down and gazed out of the front window, arms folded across my chest.

A gray mist had descended like an aged duvet, the once crisp and golden leaves dank and soggy now underfoot. Of course, it was that time of year again, wasn't it? The hunting season. Other country sports too. A time when shots were fired in the air, horns were blown, bonfires crackled. The long run-up to Christmas, when people in towns hunkered down, and those in the country revved up. Polished their spurs, filled their hip flasks, had their horses clipped for action. Hunting. An ancient tradition, which, it seemed to me, still sorted the men from the boys, at least in this village. Mounted: Chad and Hope Armitage, Angie Asher, Mary Granger, Angus and Sylvia in their younger days but represented these days by their grandson Hugo, fresh out of Harrow, and, no doubt, Sam Hetherington. Foot followers: people like me, Jennie, Yvonne, Bob, Frank—oh, and Pete, who shod all the horses around here but didn't actually own one.

And Hope had automatically put me in that foot-soldier category, hadn't she? Wouldn't have given it a second thought. And she was right. I'd followed before, stood around at meets. The whole village would turn out for this one, the first of the season, unless you really didn't agree, which was unusual in the country. Yes, everyone would be there: the great and the good aloft and on high on their stamping, snorting beasts, bits jangling, and oozing…what was it, sex? Money? Status? Then down below, people like me and Jennie and Frankie, who'd help the publican pass up the port in little plastic tumblers, looking on in awe and wonder. Later, the whole ensemble, horns blowing, hounds alert, would trot smartly off up the lane. As Sam would trot, too, flanked perhaps, on either side, by Angie and Hope, sexy in their tight breeches, hairnets, lipstick, nipped-in jackets. I was pretty sure I had one of those jackets somewhere…

I gazed at the mist. An idea began to form. Consolidate and thicken, like the gray haze outside. Suddenly, on an impulse, I plucked my phone from my pocket and perched sharply on the arm of the sofa. It rang a moment, then answered.

"Hi, Dad, it's me."

"Darling. How lovely. How are you?"

"Really well," I assured him. I hadn't been, as recently as a couple of days ago, but was determined to be now. Not to go backward. Fall in any holes. I rushed on. "Um, Dad, a favor."

"Of course, my love. Fire away."

"Can I borrow a horse?"

"A horse?"

"Yes, there's a meet here the day after tomorrow. The opening meet, actually. I thought I might go out."

There was a long pause. Finally, when he spoke, incredulity and delight filled his voice. "But you haven't ridden for years, Poppy!"

"I know, but I *can* ride, can't I? One doesn't forget?"

"Oh, sure, it's like riding a bike, but—"

"But what?"

"Well, hunting is a slightly different kettle of fish, love."

"In what way?"

"Well, everything goes up a gear. Fences, ditches—the horse itself. More adrenalin. Much more speed."

I thought of Sam, galloping along on some gleaming steed, spurred and confident, the Grangers behind him.

"I can go up a gear."

"Of course you can!"

My dad had a terrific can-do attitude. All he'd felt honor-bound to do was voice some caution, which he'd surely done. Now, however, the brakes would come smartly off.

"Come over tomorrow," he said eagerly. "I'll see what I can fit you up with. Tosca, perhaps. Or even Badger? Quite a challenge. A mount for my girl! Yes, pop by tomorrow and we'll sort you out. Day after tomorrow, you say?"

"Yes."

"Well, you can take it back in my lorry. Leave your car here."

"Except…where would I put it?" I glanced wildly around my very small sitting room.

"Hasn't your friend Angie got stables? You can pop it in with hers for the night, can't you?"

"She has got stables…" I stood up from the sofa and caught a glimpse of my face in the mirror above the mantle: quite flushed for me. Some unfamiliar bright eyes looked back, too. I licked my lips. "Except, I quite wanted to keep it a secret. Just—you know. Turn up. Surprise everyone."

My father barely missed a beat. If there was one thing he liked more than a challenge, it was a surprise. "Oh yes, *much* better! That'll show them. Anyone who'd written you off as a wilting widow."

"Well, quite," I said quickly. He'd got the gist. I walked to the window, arm still clenched round my stomach. "But…where *would* I put it, Dad? Would it be all right in the field with the sheep at the back, if I cleared it with the farmer?"

"Farmers can be awfully antsy about that sort of thing. Haven't you got some sort of outbuilding at the bottom of your garden?"

"It's called a garden shed, Dad. With a lawnmower and spades inside it."

"Well, you can move the lawnmower, love. Don't get bogged down by the minutiae."

I sensed my father warming to this. He'd been known to employ some pretty eccentric dwellings for animals in the past, and we'd once had a miniature Shetland pony that wandered into the kitchen when it rained, to lie down by the stove. And of course the fish in the bath. I could sense him powering on regardless.

"Saw the door in half," he said firmly. "I can't visualize that shed off hand but I'm sure it's big enough. Anyway, don't you worry—we'll sort something out. I'm just so thrilled you're up for it, Poppy! Atta-girl! Good for you."

It occurred to me as I put the phone down, that for all his relaxed attitude, Dad might have been more worried about me than he'd let on. He was clearly thrilled to bits. I should have taken more time previously, to reassure him. Oh well, he was certainly reassured now.

As I bounded up the stairs to Archie, who I could hear crying—clearly not as sleepy as I'd thought—I realized I was humming. "Raindrops on Roses," Mum's favorite. And cheesy though it was, *The Sound of Music* always came to me in moments of elation. Elation, I thought in some surprise, as I lifted my son from his cot. I twirled him round the room in my arms and he gurgled in astonished delight. I planted a resounding kiss on his flushed cheek. No, I would not be written off. Not yet, anyway. I would not sit quietly in partial shade. I would have a stab at the sunlight. I would trot up the road alongside Sam Hetherington, cheeks pink, lipstick gleaming, I would not be sweet Poppy Shilling who was slowly finding her feet; I'd be up and running. Galloping, even. I sailed out of the room with Archie in my arms. Even if I broke my bloody neck in the process.

Chapter Twenty

I FOUND MY FATHER in front of an old Elvis DVD, slumped on the exploding beige sofa, the one where you had to know where to sit to avoid the springs. A couple of bantam hens seemed to be watching, too, from the top of the piano, where they roosted occasionally among elderly copies of the *Racing Times*. The two dogs lay across his lap. Dad was playing an acoustic air guitar, winsomely plucking at imaginary strings, crooning softly. As I came in the room, he turned, and I saw his florid cheeks were damp with tears.

"It's the bit where she tells him she can't marry him because she's dying of that dreadful disease and he sings 'This is My Heaven.' The hula-hula girls are about to come on."

"Ah."

I sank down beside him with a smile, shoving Mitch up a bit. I was still in my coat, but then coats were a necessity in Dad's house; he was still in his. I'd seen this movie a million times, had grown up on it, along with all the other black and whites in Dad's collection, but it still held a certain allure, and before long my eyes were filling, too. We even swayed a bit and waved our hands along with the hula-hula girls at the end. As more tears rolled along with the credits, I wondered if they were for Elvis and his lost love or the way this house always made me feel: its cozy shambolic familiarity, the peeling paint, the clutter of tack and books and bottles, the terrible carpet and the terrible aching feeling I got whenever I came. The temptation to stick my thumb in my mouth and stay forever, curled up with Dad watching old movies,

Mum's photo on the crowded sideboard smiling down at us. Safe. Surely most children feel like that when they're little but then can't wait to get away, achieve some distance. Most would surely hurtle from a place like this; so why, then, did I still feel some incredibly visceral, gravitational pull?

"Right. Party's over." Dad's familiar way of drawing a veil over all things emotional. He got to his feet with an almighty sniff, pulling a red and white spotty hanky from his pocket and blowing his nose hard. "Important to get it all out, though, every now and again," he observed gruffly.

Important to have a good sob was what he meant. About Mum. Which I knew we'd both been doing, the weepy movie giving us an excuse. At least I'd never have to do that to get over my more recent bereavement, I thought. In fact if I did get out a movie, it might well be *Put Out the Flags*.

"Where are the kids?" Dad asked, stuffing the hanky back in his pocket and helping himself to a tumbler of Famous Grouse to steady the nerves. Not the first of the day, I'd hazard, and it wasn't even eleven o'clock.

"With Jennie." I leaned my head back on the sofa and looked up at him. "I couldn't take them back in the lorry, Dad. No belts."

"Oh." His face fell like a child's, as I knew it would. He was disappointed. Couldn't understand why, since I'd rattled around in that lorry unfettered, my children couldn't. No matter how often I told him about laws and fines, not to mention terrible injuries, he still didn't get it.

"But you were perfectly OK," he'd say. "And I drive safely…"

"I know, Dad," I'd say sheepishly, scratching my neck, and never pointing out how irresponsible or uncaring he'd been, for Dad was neither. Although in the eyes of others he might be.

"But I thought you could take them to the meet?" I said to him now. "Maybe follow for a bit? They'd love that."

"And I'd love it, too. Good idea. I'll do that." He rubbed his hands together, pleased. "Now. Come on, let's go and see what I've got for you." Cheered immeasurably by a bloody good cry, the whisky and the prospect of a day out with his grandchildren, he made for the back door and his boots.

I got to my feet hurriedly. "You mean, you've definitely got me one?"

"Of course I've got you one. I've got two. You're spoiled for choice. Come on, they're in the yard."

I felt a flutter of excitement as I followed him outside. Dolls, ponies, boys. These apparently mark the three stages of girlhood: symbols of the definitive rites of passage. And although I would never regress to Tiny Tears (having said that, on occasion I have found myself on Clemmie's bedroom floor, brushing Barbie's hair with a gormless, faraway expression on my face), in moments of crisis, or general barrenness on the man front, I can quite easily resort to horse flesh to make my heart beat faster. Like my father before me, I find the equine world not only more reliable and dependable, but infinitely more sensitive. It was with a quickening pulse, therefore, that I swapped my shoes for one of the many pairs of boots by the back door and scurried after Dad to the yard.

At this time of year most of his horses were rugged up and grazing in the fields, having been in all night, but sure enough, in the otherwise empty row of loose boxes, occupying the nearest one was a good-looking bay, his head over the door. He watched as we approached. He had a kind, intelligent face and his ears were pricked. My rib cage hosted another little dance.

"Ooh…handsome brute."

"Isn't he just?" Dad said softly. "Dutch Warmblood. Bags of breeding."

We stopped at his stall and I stroked his velvety nose as he blew into my hand. "What's his name?"

"Well, his full title is Thundering Pennyford, but he answers to Thumper."

"Thumper," I echoed. God, he was gorgeous. Sleek, dark, and delicious. Quite big, too, I thought nervously as I looked down his arched neck to his shapely quarters. Another head appeared next door.

"And this one?" I moved on to the adjoining stable, where a smaller, scruffier piebald, with a wall eye and a back so broad you could lay it with knives and forks, had come to see what all the fuss was about.

"Agnes. The safer bet."

"Ah." I gave her nose a stroke, too. "Thumper isn't safe?"

"Oh, he's safe, but he's fast. He's a thoroughbred, Poppy. Got more temperament."

Temperament. On my first hunt. Did I need that? Or did I need Agnes? Safe and solid? Thumper was gorgeous, though. And I'd look so much better up there in skintight jodhpurs and shiny leather boots. Which was surely the point. Agnes was sweet, but nevertheless had a touch of "Where's the cart?" about her.

Dad was already putting a bridle on Thumper. "Want to try him?" he asked casually, leading him out.

"Sure. Why not." Equally casually.

Dad swiftly added a saddle.

"Just take him for a spin in the paddock over there, then, and see how you get on." In one deft movement he'd done up the girth and was holding the stirrup leather to steady the saddle.

I jumped on, pleased I could still do that without a leg up, and, as I say, Thumper wasn't small. Then I found my other stirrup and trotted off smartly. Should have walked first, obviously, and Thumper got a bit of a start at being asked to trot out of the yard from a standstill, but, apart from a slight jolt, he mastered his surprise beautifully. Terrific manners, I thought, as we glided on and he succumbed to the bit, which I was pleased to see I could still ask him to take, arching his neck accordingly. Fantastic suspension, excellent brakes, no rushing. But then Dad had only the best in his yard. In the paddock I let the throttle out and asked for a canter, which was never going to descend into a gallop, I decided, then changed the rein and did it all the other way round. I came back to the gate flushed and elated. Panting like mad, too, and sweating profusely.

"Not as fit as you used to be," my father observed with a grin, leaning on the gate.

"Nothing like! Since when did sitting on a horse take it out of you?"

"That's what they all say. But you won't need to be fit on Agnes. You really will just sit there. This one's more of a ride."

"But he is heavenly, Dad." I leaned forward and stroked his neck.

"Oh, he is," he agreed cheerfully.

Once again he'd done his bit: exercised the note of caution by proffering the Datsun, but secretly hoping I'd go for the Ferrari, which, naturally, I did.

"You don't want to try her, then?"

"Not sure I've got the energy."

"You'll need a bit more puff for a few hours' hunting."

"I know," I said breezily, "but the adrenalin will kick in."

"And I have to be honest, Poppy, I don't know if he's hunted. I bought him as an eventer. Thought he might do for the Tapner girl. No idea if he hunts."

"Don't worry; if he events, he'll hunt. It's all hedges and ditches, isn't it? It'll be meat and drink to him."

I vaulted out of the saddle. Who was this woman? Assuring her reckless dad, a man who lived by the seat of his pants and on the smell of an oily rag, that he was fussing unnecessarily? That life, in fact, was a breeze? Leaping on and off strange thoroughbreds when she hadn't ridden for ten years? Abandoning her children to her neighbor yet again, in order to do so? A woman who'd had a sniff of another life, that's who. An intoxicating whiff, from beyond the village green, of a life where women wore gray cashmere a lot, hunted weekly, shopped in Fortnum's and, more importantly, snared attractive men. Hope, Emma…I gritted my teeth. A woman who, after that phone call with Sam the other day—me in my cold little cottage, if you recall, him on his hunter in his wet shirt—had gone to bed every night since imagining galloping behind fawn and black hounds at the front of the field, tucked in behind the pink coats. Sam and I leaping a hedge side by side, grinning delightedly at one another as we landed, him admiring my seat, and then, perhaps at the next fence, Sam looking at me *so* admiringly he bogged it, misjudged the take-off, came off. Off I sped to catch his loose horse. Led it back to where he was staggering, muddy and abashed, to his feet. Held it, prancing, while he clambered on, a gash to his head, a breathless "Thanks, Poppy!" before we cantered off to join the field again: me, glancing over my shoulder to check he was OK; him, slightly dazed—could have been my beauty, could have been the bump to his head—but desperate not to let me out of his sight, not to let me get away.

I'd turned into a woman with a mission. But that, I told myself, was all I wanted. An admiring look, a sniff of another life, then I'd drop it. Because, frankly, I could take it or leave it. Could go back to my other life, my cottage, my children, their head lice, happy in the knowledge that I'd drawn admiring gasps from Sam and the rest of the village. Oh yes, naturally they'd all be watching, standing at that particular hedge as if it were Beecher's Brook. Happy they'd all seen me in a different light, in a "Wow, who's that girl?" light. That was *all* I needed. Honest.

We'll see.

My father and I shared a quick lunch, courtesy of our old friend Mr. Heinz—Dad doling it out with a spoon that had more than a sporting chance of having just doled out the cat food—and then, when I'd admired the new canary singing his little heart out in the bathroom, I made a move. Together we loaded Thumper into the lorry, and obviously he went in like a dream, no digging in of heels in a Thelwell-like manner for him. Then I mentally ticked off a list of everything I needed.

"Tack, rugs, hay nets—it's all in the cab. OK, love?"

"Thanks, Dad."

"And I've put a couple of feeds in, one for tonight and one for tomorrow."

"Brilliant."

"And you reckon your shed will be fine?"

"No, I had a look and it's tiny, and too full of rubbish, so I rang the farmer with the sheep at the back and he says I can put him in the barn he's got there, just for the night."

"Oh, ideal!"

"Exactly," I agreed, declining to add that the farmer was in fact Odd Bob and that he'd practically taken it as a marriage proposal when I'd popped round to Dog-Howling Farm to place my request. He'd beamed stupidly from ear to ear and agreed that mum was indeed the word when I'd told him it was a secret, rather as if we'd just plotted to flee to Gretna Green together, winking and tapping the side of his nose annoyingly. He'd even tried to kiss me on the cheek as I left. Bob was still behaving very strangely indeed.

"And you'll be sure to come to the meet and give me a hand?" I asked my father anxiously. While I'd rejected all Bob's offers of help, I'd be very glad of his.

"Of course I will. Although it occurs to me that if I'm coming to the meet I could take Thumper straight there for you…" He furrowed his brow and we looked thoughtfully at the horse, all ready and waiting within. "But on the other hand you'll want to get to know him, won't you? Maybe have another ride? Probably best he's with you."

"Yes," I agreed tentatively. We regarded each other uncertainly.

"Tell you what," he declared suddenly, "once my lot are fed and watered, which I'll do early, I'll come straight across to your place to get you tacked up and loaded."

"Oh, would you, Dad?"

"Course." He beamed. "I say, what fun. Good for you, Poppy. I do think you're brave."

Did he? I thought nervously, trundling home in the lorry ten minutes later with half a ton of horse flesh in the back. If my Dad thought I was brave, that was worrying. As was driving this lorry. Of course I'd driven it loads of times in my youth, but I'd forgotten how wide it was and how, obviously, one couldn't see out of the back and had to rely on wing mirrors. Surely one should have a special license? Have passed some sort of HGV test? Dad hadn't mentioned it, but then, he wouldn't.

With uncharacteristic foresight I'd radioed ahead for reinforcements, so that, as I rounded the bend into the village, it was a happy sight that greeted me. Sitting on the grass in Jennie's front garden were all the children, aka the welcoming committee. Archie was on Jamie's lap, and Hannah and Clemmie were kneeling shoulder to shoulder, intent on squeezing rose petals into water-filled jam jars to make scent, something which would have transported my daughter to big-girl heaven. At the sight of the lorry, however, they abandoned the perfumery, jumped up and poured out of the white picket gate. Simultaneously the front door flew open and Jennie hurried down the path in their wake, wiping her hands on her long white apron.

"You've got him," she breathed, gazing up at me in disbelief through the open cab window. The children were jumping up and down excitedly beside her.

"Of course I have." I hopped smartly down from the cab. "Now all we've got to do is unload him and take him round the back to the field." I gave her a huge grin as I marched to the back of the lorry, feeling like the pied piper with the children on my heels.

"Out of the way, everyone!" I called. "Stand back, folks, this comes down pretty smartly!"

They shrank back as I reached for the rope to pull down the ramp. It did indeed come down with a mighty bang in the road, all springs long gone. Jennie jumped, and the children shrieked some more. I laughed indulgently at them, realizing I was getting a bit of a thrill out of being in control here.

So much of my life was spent following bigger, bossier personalities. I must remember this. Something was definitely kicking in.

Thumper turned his head and gave me an old-fashioned look as I went inside to get him. He was slightly sweaty, I noticed, but it was warm in the box, probably nothing to worry about. As I untied his head-collar rope and made to lead him down the ramp, however, he surged ahead of me, out into the road. I hung on tight to the end of the rope. What was that about control?

"Oh my God, he's huge!" gasped Jennie, grabbing Archie, who was in danger of being trampled. "I thought you'd be on more of a pony!"

"No, no. Definitely didn't want a pony."

But she was right. He was huge. Even bigger, it seemed to me, prancing in the road outside my cottage, than at Dad's. He was snorting a lot and pawing the ground, his neck white with sweat.

"You'll need a ladder just to get on him, won't you? Oh, Poppy, I do think you're brave."

Worrying again. Jennie generally thought I was a wimp.

"Why is he stamping?" asked Hannah.

"Alarmed at being in a strange place, perhaps," I hazarded.

And without my father's soothing hand of course, and—oh Lord, he was rearing up now, pulling back on the rope. A curtain twitched opposite.

"Open the gate, for heaven's sake Jennie," I hissed. "Come on, let's at least get him out of *centre ville*."

One or two people had come into their front gardens to see

what was going on, to see what on earth Poppy Shilling was up to now, and it occurred to me that the surprise element of this plan was rapidly disappearing down the plug hole.

I'd hoped to unload him quietly and then sneak him round the back out of sight, but of course you couldn't so much as fart in this place. And Thumper was doing much more than that, lifting his tail and having a nervous evacuation, letting loose a stream of green slime. The children squealed in a mixture of glee and disgust as it bounced off the tarmac and near their shoes, their shrill voices frightening the horse even more.

"Just open the bloody gate, Jennie!" I yelled, as she finally flew to do just that, not the one into the garden, but the fivebar affair that led down the side of her house to the field.

My own armpits were a match for Thumper's now, and Mrs. Harper from next door didn't help, popping out on an urgent errand—to tighten the string around her dahlias—just as Mr. Fish from across the street was finding it terribly important to choose that precise moment to realign the milk bottles on his step.

"You ridin' that thing tomorrow, Poppy?" he called, curiosity eventually getting the better of any spurious activity.

"That's the plan," I told him nervously, hanging onto the end of the rope as Thumper, seeing the open gate and, further on, a green field, sped through.

"Blimey. Good luck."

I'd gone. Hanging onto Thumper, who was belting down the stretch of no-man's-land beside Jennie's house: the patch of scrubby ground where Dan kept his collection of clapped-out cars, some minus their wheels and on bricks, all in varying degrees of decay, his wife's chickens roosting on their back seats in true *Darling Buds of May* style. They fluttered about, squawking in alarm as our party hustled past. Another gate. This time Jennie needed no prompting and flew round me in her pinny to open it. The sheep, who'd surged across the field out of interest, now surged back, parting like the Red Sea as I came through. Jennie was busy fastening the gate behind me, but happily Frankie had appeared, hotfooting it from her bedroom, where she would have had a bird's-eye view. Sizing up the situation, she was running across to open the door to the barn in the middle of the field. In a trice I'd popped Thumper inside, slipped his head collar off and, before he knew what was happening, shut the door on him, my thoroughbred hunter thus deposited within.

"He doesn't look very happy," Frankie observed as we peered through the window. Her hair, I noticed, was a rather nice honey shade and not the usual aggressive peroxide.

"He's fine," I said confidently as Thumper twirled and snorted, pawing the sawdust I'd put down for him, nostrils flaring. What had *happened* to him? Was he on drugs? Up to his forelock on barbiturates or something? Or had it been my driving? I had, admittedly, touched the odd curb along the way. "Just settling in, that's all. It's all a bit new to him, you see."

"Still, he looks a handful," Frankie remarked. "I wouldn't want to cling onto that tomorrow. I do think you're—"

"DON'T tell me I'm brave!" I snapped.

I left her looking after me in open-mouthed astonishment as I strode back across the field, off to re-park the lorry somewhere less conspicuous than in the middle of the village, a tiny bit of me wishing I'd never, ever, started this.

That night, however, when Clemmie and Archie were safely in bed—Thumper, too, certainly to the extent that I couldn't hear him stamping and snorting from my bedroom, and last seen, when I'd snuck out to the barn in my dressing gown, quietly munching hay, albeit with a slightly wary expression on his face—yes, that night, as I stood in front of my dressing-table mirror, I felt reassured. I'd poured myself into my kit—pour being the operative word—and now felt something like courage returning. All the riding I'd ever done in my youth had been in jeans and wellies, but Dad had cajoled a neighboring teenager into lending me some clothes. The skintight jodhpurs and an ancient jacket of mine, which didn't so much nip in as charge, ensured I looked the part. I could barely breathe, of course, but surely that was the point? All accessories—long black boots, velvet cap, snowy white stock—were borrowed from Dad's same friend and completed the glamorous, sexy look, I decided, gazing delightedly at my reflection. My cheeks were flushed and my eyes very bright, which helped, but then I had drunk nearly a whole bottle of wine. For Dutch courage. So that when I slapped my whip against my boot and snarled, "Knock 'em dead, Poppy. You show that snooty lot you were practically born in the saddle," even I was pretty sure it was the drink talking. My reflection sniggered in agreement.

Later, when I'd polished off the remains of the bottle in front of the telly—madness not to—I went upstairs to bed. My equine ensemble had by now come adrift, all restraining buttons and zips undone and agape. Whip in hand and still in my boots, I swaggered across the bedroom to draw the curtains. I felt a bit like John Wayne. But before I reached the window I caught sight of my reflection in the dressing-table mirror, and halted. This, I decided, swaying slightly, was what I'd look like post-hunt, after a hard day in the saddle: windblown, unkempt, but exhilarated. All woman. Steadying myself on the back of the dressing-table chair I straddled it backward, swiveling to see what my bum looked like in the mirror. Not bad. I executed a rising trot to see how it would fare going up and down, away from the meet, as it were. Very passable. Then I hung onto the chair and leaned forward to mimic a gallop, bottom out of the saddle, bobbing slightly, whip flourished. Suddenly I froze, mid-bob. Mr. Fish, across the road, was drawing back from his bedroom window in alarm, no doubt hastening to find Mrs. Fish and tell her that the young widow opposite was not so much finding her feet as strapping them into black leather, brandishing sex toys, and heading to Sodom, Gomorrah, and beyond.

Chapter Twenty-one

As I CLAMBERED INTO the lorry the following morning, the drink was still talking but telling me something very different. Dad had come over early, as promised, and found me locked in the bathroom feeling neither sexy nor brave, courtesy of a paralyzing hangover and a very scary horse. Thumper, when I'd flapped out in dressing gown and wellies to politely suggest he might like to get up and have some brecker, had rounded on me with such indignant wild eyes and flaring nostrils that I'd turned and fled. Typical man, I thought, running back inside. He spends the night at my place then, the next morning, acts like he's never seen me before in his life.

"I'm not coming out, Dad!" I bleated through the bathroom door. "He's morphed into one of the seven horses of the Apocalypse. Thinks he's in a Schwarzenegger movie!"

"Nonsense, he's just feeling a bit displaced. I'll go and have a word, love."

Sure enough, when I peeked through the bathroom window sometime later, under my father's professional guidance, Thumper had indeed meekly succumbed. He was now washed and dressed and tied up outside the barn, his tail still a bit wet, but sleek and gleaming, mane plaited, shiny tack in place. It was inevitable, then, of course, that the white-faced daughter would be subjected to the same kind but firm hand, and soon I was being herded into my bedroom to change into clothes that didn't feel nearly so glamorous as they had the night before, and thence into the lorry, at which point I informed my father I was going to be sick.

"Drink," he ordered, handing me his hip flask as he climbed into the driver's seat of the cab from the opposite side.

"Don't be silly, Dad, it's ten-thirty and I haven't had any breakfast." I couldn't eat the toast he'd proffered earlier, nor drink the tea. Couldn't even swallow my own saliva.

"All the more reason to drink," he told me sternly. "No one does this sober, love. Your mate Angie tells me she's drunk before she gets to the first fence sometimes, and everyone has a nip at the meet. You're just having yours now. Anyway, you've got a hangover. Need the hair of the dog."

He talked me into it. And let's face it, it wasn't hard. If the smart crowd were already quaffing merrily outside Mulverton Hall, I'd definitely need a head start. I nervously snatched the hip flask and took a gigantic swig.

"See?"

I nodded, unable to speak on account of the heat radiating at the back of my throat. But, boy, it was good. I took another swig just to make sure and we rumbled off: Dad at the wheel, Thumper in the back, Clemmie and Archie following on behind with Jennie. My party, in fact. All there for me. As the whisky hit my empty tummy I began to feel a bit like Scott of the Antarctic, or the female equivalent, Amy Johnson, perhaps; at any rate, some super-cool heroine spearheading some major expedition of some sort.

After a while, having navigated a maze of lanes, we rattled over a cattle grid between some crumbling stone gateposts. A muddy field awaited us, and Jennie, behind, gestured that she'd drive on up the lane to park somewhere less sticky. As we rumbled toward the neatly parked rows of lorries and trailers, I looked around expectantly. Horses were being unloaded, all, to a fetlock, immaculate, but their riders, I noted, were in varying degrees of dress. A few, already mounted, were in full rig, but one or two were less formal. A stunning redhead, for instance, trying to do up her girth and yelling at her huge excited gray to "*keep still!*" was in a Barbour and tracky bottoms. At least I had the right kit, I thought smugly, as Dad expertly tucked the lorry alongside hers. I jumped out with new-found confidence, straight into a cow pat. It squelched up my lovely, shiny, leather-clad ankles.

"I didn't see any cows!" I cried in dismay, looking around accusingly and coming face to face with a hefty Friesian, who gazed back opaquely.

"The cattle grid was a clue," Dad remarked mildly as he went round to unload Thumper and as I tried to scrape it off on the grass. "You're better off in wellies, love, until you get on."

Beside me the stunning redhead peeled off the tracky bums and Barbour to reveal a pristine equestrian ensemble. She added immaculate boots and hopped smartly on board.

As Dad walked Thumper down the ramp he looked around speculatively at the surrounding country. "Oh, OK."

"What?" I said, squeezing myself into my very tiny jacket. "I honestly can't breathe in this, Dad." I was standing completely rigid, arms out like a scarecrow, as he brought Thumper round.

"Never mind, you won't be breathing much anyway," he muttered.

"What?"

"Come on, up you get." He gave me a leg up, at which point all my jacket buttons popped off.

"I've just realized where we are," he said, glancing about. "You kick off with about six or seven jumps round these fields followed by quite a hefty ditch. Hold onto the mane and don't worry if you pull the plaits out. No one notices once you've set off."

"What? Jumps? So soon? Do I have to? Oh, God—look at my jacket!" I wailed, but Dad had already smoothly produced a spare stock pin from his pocket and was busy pinning me back together again.

"Well, no, you don't have to jump if you don't want to, you can go with the non-jumpers. There're always a few. But that's not really why we're here, is it, Poppy?" He gave me a flinty look, which he was capable of occasionally. Fastened the pin with a sharp snap. "We're here to show some mettle, aren't we?"

"Right," I agreed faintly.

I felt a bit better, actually, now I was on board. And although most people looked sleek, effortless and born to hunt—a beautiful blonde, slim as a reed, rode past, nonchalantly rolling a cigarette on her taut thigh—I had seen one or two harassed riders struggling with recalcitrant mounts. Well, one. And she was about eight, on her own, with a shaggy Palomino. Dad popped across to hold the circling pony while she got on and I grinned chummily at the child. Perhaps we could ride together? She trotted off smartly, alone, waving to her friends further away. Happily, though, with Dad by his side, Thumper seemed to have morphed into My Little Pony again and was once more displaying those pixie-perfect manners. Could Dad run alongside me perhaps? Hold on to the reins?

"Wish I'd brought a horse myself," he remarked as we made our way across the field and through a gate toward the main body of the hunt in the distance: a swarm of sleek horses with riders in black and pink coats, the hounds circling at their feet, expertly controlled by a mustard-coated whipper-in. It was like a scene from a Cecil Aldin print. "I could have come out with you," he said wistfully.

I gazed down at him, stricken. "Why didn't you?" I wailed, casting wildly about for a stray horse as we approached. "Oh God, that would have been perfect! Why didn't we think of that? Why didn't we—No, Dad, *don't let go*!"

It perhaps wasn't the entrance I'd envisaged in the safety of my own bedroom: safety-pinned, muddy-booted, clinging pathetically to my father and humming "Raindrops on Roses" manically to myself, as I do in moments of stress. But if my own appearance was disappointing, the setting was everything I'd imagined.

This was a lawn meet, and although we weren't actually invited to trash the ancestral grass, we were bidden to gather on the drive right at the front of the house. Mulverton Hall was Georgian, treacle-colored, mellow, and all one would hope for, I thought, as I gazed up admiringly. Tall sash windows winked back at me in the sunshine from a benign, aristocratic facade, like some old boy in his dotage who knows he's still got it in him, twinkling away merrily. On closer inspection it was crumbling at the edges, but then old boys often are, and the window ledges were peeling too. It also appeared to have some alarming damp patches, but that didn't detract from the charm. At the bottom of the flight of stone steps, which culminated in an extravagant sweep on the gravel, the hunt had gathered: chatting and laughing atop their steeds, knocking back the port, horses gleaming, bits jangling, voices carrying fruitily in the crisp morning air. It was a perfect day: bright and blue with just a hint of a breeze to ruffle tails and catch lip gloss.

I spotted Chad and Hope immediately on a pair of placid-looking bays. Naturally they were immaculately turned out, although the crash hats with industrial-sized chin straps slightly detracted from the look, I decided. The old and bold, I noticed, had just rammed velvet caps on their heads and to hell with health and safety.

"I know them," I told Dad excitedly, standing up in my stirrups and waving enthusiastically.

Chad caught my eye, looked surprised then smiled delightedly. He seemed about to ride across but when he alerted Hope, she turned, gazed flatly, then gave me a thin little smile before turning back to the glamorous girl on the gray she'd been talking to. Chad looked undecided a moment, waved over-heartily and stuck by his wife.

"They're busy," I told Dad, sinking back into my saddle.

"Ah."

Luckily I'd spotted Angie, looking drop-dead gorgeous in skin-tight jodhpurs and a dark blue hunting coat, blonde chignon netted and tied with a velvet ribbon. Ah yes, hairnet, I thought, aware of my own locks tumbling rather luxuriantly down my back. If she had the sartorial upper hand, however, she nearly fell off her horse when she saw me.

"Poppy! Good God. Whatever are you doing here?" She muscled her classy chestnut through the throng toward me, open-mouthed.

"Surprise!" I grinned. I was feeling slightly pissed now, courtesy of that hip flask. "Dad lent me a horse. I thought I'd see how the other half live."

"Well, you might have told me! I could have lent you some clothes," she said gazing at my jacket, somewhat aghast.

"D'you know, I wish I had," I said, leaning forward confidential-ly, meaning it. "It's all been a bit of a nightmare. What with keeping Thumper in the back garden and—"

"You didn't!"

"No, but almost. And I could have popped him in with yours, couldn't I?"

"Of course you bloody could! Oh, honestly, you are an idiot, Poppy." Her eyes were still bulging, though, which was quite satisfac-tory. "Can you ride him?" She jerked her whip at Thumper.

"Of course I can," I said confidently, remembering now why I'd wanted the element of surprise. I'd quite forgotten. I straightened up in the saddle. "Don't forget I grew up with horses, Angie. You remember my dad, don't you?"

"Of course." She smiled down, seeing him for the first time. Dad raised his flat cap. "Hello, Mr. Mortimer. I imagine you were in on this, then?"

"Peter," he told her with a grin. "Yes, all the way. And Poppy's quite right, she did grow up with them, but very much in the proximate sense. They were in the paddock, and she was in the house doing her mascara. She took a great deal of interest from the window."

"Dad," I protested as they both roared with laughter. But worryingly, he had a point. Although I'd ridden as a child, as a teenager I'd been a bit more interested in *Cosmo* than *Horse and Hound*. Had I bitten off more than I could chew? Hands fluttering, I gratefully accepted a glass of port from a girl proffering a tray.

"Have you had one?" I asked Angie.

"Oh God, yes, three. Always do. Makes it less painful if I come off."

"We're coming off?" I said alarmed.

"Well, not necessarily, but who knows? Depends where we go. But you stick with me, Poppy. There are a lot of idiots out today, always are at the opening meet, and those are the ones who do the damage. Cut you up at fences, refuse slap bang in front of you. And hold on tight. I don't want to be playing nursemaid when I've got other fish to fry." Her eyes darted around. "Have you spotted him yet?"

"Who?"

"The new master."

"Why would I? I don't know what he looks like." She wasn't to know I had my own fish to fry.

"Well, he's obviously going to be in pink, isn't he? There—on the chestnut."

I'd been busily scanning the broad-shouldered black coats for Sam, and was unprepared, therefore, for the man in pink, the one she indicated, to lift his hat as he greeted a friend, present his chiseled profile, and for it to be one and the same.

I stared for a long moment. "Sam Hetherington's the new master?"

"Yes." Angie turned, surprised. "You know him?"

"He's my solicitor."

"*Is* he?" She looked astonished. "Oh yes, someone said he was a lawyer. Good God—you never said!" She rounded on me accusingly.

"Well, I didn't know you knew him, did I?"

She gazed at me; blinked. "I suppose I don't, yet," she admitted. "I will, though. He's gorgeous, don't you think? All mine, by the way," she added quickly and not for the first time. "I'm landing this one. He's divorced, apparently, and this is his manor house, and very soon I'll be installed within doing up the drawing room. If you're very lucky I'll ask you to dinner."

God, she had had a few drinks, but so had I, and I opened my mouth to remind her that, actually, she hadn't seen him first, I had; perhaps adding haughtily that I wouldn't dream of getting into a fight over a man. But anything I might or might not have said, was forestalled by Sam himself.

"*Can I have your attention please, ladies and gentlemen!*"

A deferential hush fell instantly. He was standing up in his stirrups, smiling around in a convivial manner. I gulped. Golly. *Quite* commanding. As he swept his hat gallantly from his head—no strap—to reveal his springy curls, he looked sensational. I'd forgotten about that heart-stopping smile, the crinkly eyes. Angie and I gazed rapturously as he went on to welcome everybody, thanking the local landowners and farmers for letting us ride across their fields— his, mostly, which with perfect manners he declined to mention— reminding us about gates and crops, cattle, oh, and the forthcoming hunt ball. He ended by adding that he hoped we all had a jolly good day. He looked like a young King Henry on St. Crispin's Day, rallying his troops, wind in his hair, hat under his arm. As he smiled, I swear a ray of sunlight glinted on a pearly tooth.

No time to bask in it, though, because suddenly I was jolted from my reverie by a loud blast on a hunting horn and Thumper and I were shoved unceremoniously out of the way by the huntsman and whipper-in, hounds at their heels, as they set off down the drive toward open country. The rest of the field bustled about importantly, waiting to be led by Sam. With fire in my heart and port in my belly, I couldn't help but leg Thumper through to the front.

"Hi, Sam!" I called, aware of shining eyes and a very broad grin. Not his.

If he was surprised, he mastered it beautifully. He touched his hat and smiled.

"Good morning, Poppy."

But rather than stopping for some golly, fancy-seeing-you-here chat, he was off in moments, at a very fast trot down the drive, after the hounds. Angie was beside me in a flash.

"Always, *always* call him master," she hissed. "Even if you privately know him as fluffy-bumkins. Even if you've shared a pillow the night before!"

Many heads nodded in severe agreement at this, faces grave. I'd obviously breached a sacred code.

"Oh, OK. It's just we did share a pillow and he said 'Sam' would be fine," I told her airily, clearly disastrously pissed.

Some people thought this was quite funny and tittered, for which I was grateful, but not Angie. She shot me a withering look and trotted off to join the thrusters at the front. Hard not to join them, actually, as Thumper surged excitedly beneath me, doing an extended trot down the drive. I managed to hold him back a bit, though, and keep some distance. As we went through a gate into pasture we all broke into a canter, and I scanned the airborne bottoms of Angie's smart crowd ahead. I recognized a local actress with pale blue eyes on an iron gray; Hugo, Angus's grandson, on an overwrought roan, one or two mates of his from Harrow ragging alongside him. Then there were the gays who ran the garden center and quarrelled incessantly—one was prodding the other spitefully with his whip even now; a judge Dad knew, whose horse was called Circuit so that, if anyone rang, his clerk could truthfully say, "He's out on circuit"; then a very attractive couple I couldn't quite place until…good God. Simon and Emma Harding. I nearly fell off my horse. Why weren't they on their honeymoon, for Christ's sake? Was she going to be *everywhere* I went?

I yanked hard on my left rein and sped toward Angie.

"Angie—Emma Harding's here!" I gasped as I galloped up beside her. It wasn't hard, Thumper was pulling like a train.

"I know, bloody cheek, isn't it?" she yelled back, instantly on my side despite my earlier jibe, bless her. We cantered along together, the wind whipping our words away. "They're having their honeymoon later, apparently," she told me. "She clearly means to stick around like a turd on a shoe—bloody nerve!"

"I'm going to out her," I seethed into the wind. "Just wait and see what everyone thinks when they know it was my husband she was...Holy shit. We're not jumping that, are we?"

Up ahead was a sizeable post and rails with quite a few foot followers gathered around it. I spotted Jennie, Dad and my children clustered excitedly. Clearly we were. Sam flew over it, followed by the gays, then Hugo et al., then Simon and Emma. Right. So this was my Beeche's Brook. But, boy, was it huge. Thumper pulled excitedly at the sight of it, and as Angie sailed confidently over ahead of me, I was right on her heels. Too close, actually, but too late to do anything about because I was already airborne. I clung on to the plaits for grim death, losing the reins as we landed, so that Thumper, given his head, let out the throttle and sped away. As we galloped toward another jump, a small hedge which he took in his stride, I realized something alarming was happening here: I was having trouble staying on board and pulling the reins at the same time. I could do one at a time, but not both together, and certainly not with jumps thrown into the equation. I plumped for staying on board and clung to his mane, which meant that Thumper—who, if he hadn't been hunting before, was loving every minute of it—had a free rein to take me wherever he wanted, at whatever speed, which was top, and straight to the front.

Spectacularly out of control, I rocketed past Angie, Simon and Emma, the actress on the gray, Hugo and his muckers. Then I cannoned past Sam in pink, who shot me a startled look, then the huntsman and the whipper-in, in mustard. Finally—trust me, it didn't take long—I shot past the hounds, who scattered like beads of mercury as I galloped through them, ensuring that in five short minutes, I'd broken every single rule in the book.

When I finally turned an enormous circle way out in the next field—the next county, probably—and headed back, Thumper galloping joyously to rejoin his new friends, Angie's face was white and horrified. "What are you doing!" she shrieked, appalled.

"Couldn't stop," I gasped, skidding up beside her and jolting to an ungainly halt, hat over my eyes. "Bolted."

I wanted to die, actually. Knew I probably would soon, too. I felt green with fear, sick as a dog and way out of my depth.

"But you're making a complete tit of yourself!" she hissed as, fortuitously, the whole field pulled up, pausing as they drew a copse.

"I know!" I wailed. "What shall I do, Angie? Shall I go home?" I couldn't look at Sam. I mean, the master.

"No, don't give up yet. Just keep at the back with the no-hopers. Come on, I'll come with you." She turned her horse's head.

"No, Angie," I said quickly, knowing this was indeed the true hand of friendship. "You stay at the front, I'll go."

"Well, look, see those stragglers?" She pointed behind us with her whip. "The alkies and the point-to-pointers, the children—you go with them. And for Christ's sake, don't come up the front again."

"Righto," I said meekly, hauling on the reins, trying to make Thumper see reason; at least for long enough to let me join the hoi polloi.

As I rode toward them scarlet-faced, I realized they were laughing at me. But not altogether unkindly, and when they'd all introduced themselves, it became abundantly clear that they were not only hugely friendly, but much more accepting than the smart crowd. They didn't mind a bit that it was my first time out and I'd broken every rule under the sun; in fact, once they'd dried their eyes and stopped holding their sides, they told me they'd all done it once, and that Angie was a complete pain in the tubes out hunting. She thought she ran the show and was only trying to get into the new master's breeches. I laughed along rather disloyally, vowing never to be that obvious.

Off we set again, this time, happily, at a more sedate pace. Thumper, his initial gallop under his belt, seemed to settle; perhaps, like me, recognizing he'd lost the Darwinian struggle and acknowledging his true place with the novices at the back. And I had a rather jolly time of it with my new friends, one of whom was the ravishing redhead who'd stripped off at the meet, a nurse called Polly. Then there was an electrician called Sparks, on an equally sparky ex-racehorse; an old rogue called Gerald with come-to-bed cataracts; Ted the local butcher, his face like one of his cheaper cuts of beef; and my very own painter and decorator, Grant, on a huge colored cob.

"Grant! I didn't recognize you in your hat! Didn't know you did this sort of thing?"

"Yeah, every week. I'd rather spend my money on this than send it down the red lane in the boozer. A farmer lends me his horse. Likes it exercised."

I felt rather shamed as we cantered on. I'd always assumed hunting was the province of the hideously wealthy, but these people were not remotely privileged. It was clearly a sport like any other, and although you obviously needed the four legs beneath you to do it, they weren't all pampered, expensive steeds like Angie's, but shaggy, workmanlike beasts pulled in from the field, begged and borrowed.

"My brother hunts in Ireland," Polly told me breathlessly when we finally drew up on the outskirts of a wood. "And over there the kids follow on bikes, donkeys, whatever. You don't have to have a horse. It isn't quite like that here, but we're certainly not the Beaufort. You don't have to join a queue to get in and you won't get ticked off for not looking the part. Although I might just lend you a hairnet next time." She grinned.

"Thanks!" I grinned back, thinking that this was more like it, and next time I really would look the part: no safety pins, no mud, but perhaps on Agnes, who'd be less scary. Yes, I could do this; but I'd take the slow route, not be in such a rush. The field was moving on again, and I gathered my reins to go with them, but at that moment a solitary fawn-colored hound bustled past me. Thumper, startled, lashed out with his left hind leg.

"Oh God, I hope he hasn't hit him," I said, turning distractedly, but my new friends had moved on, out of earshot, not at a gallop but a fast trot, in single file across a ploughed field. I was last. Thumper, aware of this, registered his displeasure by lifting his front hooves off the ground when I held him back, but still I held him, because I'd spotted something fawn and inert in the bushes.

"Shit!"

I was off in a trice, pulling the reins over Thumper's head, dragging him into the undergrowth. There in the bracken lay the hound: stretched out stiffly, a terrible gash to its head. I gazed in horror. Blood was pouring down its cheek. Oh God, was it dead? I lurched forward, touched it. Shook it. It most certainly was. Either that or unconscious. I felt for a heartbeat. Nothing. I shrank back, aghast. Oh God, I'd killed a hound. Or Thumper had, which was surely one and the same thing. My hand flew to my mouth.

"Oh God, I'm so sorry!" I wailed, crouching over it again, stroking its poor fawn coat, the reins looped over my arm as Thumper danced impatiently on the end. "You poor thing!" I whispered. There he'd been, happily running along with his mates one minute, and then, courtesy of yours truly, stone dead the next. Tears sprang to my eyes and I gulped hopelessly, wringing my hands. Thumper cavorted, but I ignored him. In fact right now I downright hated him and spun round to tell him so in no uncertain terms.

"You stupid, *stupid* horse!"

I cast about desperately for help. One by one the hunt was disappearing across the ploughed field over the brow of the hill and, horrified as I was, I couldn't help feeling relief. For something else was building in my breast. Some other, weighty emotion. Terror. I was fairly sure that up there in the litany of hunting sins, this was the most heinous. Forget not having the right kit. Forget not addressing the master correctly, overtaking him, the whipper-in, the pack; this was the black hat. Not just for the hound, but for me, too.

Dry-mouthed, I stared at the empty horizon. All gone. No one even in the distance. But if I was tempted momentarily to get back on and just turn and belt for home, for the safety of my cottage and a nice cup of tea, I resisted manfully. No. What I'd do, what I'd jolly well do, was get back on and catch up with them. Yes. Tell them exactly what had happened. Fess up.

Heart pounding and feeling very fluttery and sweaty-palmed, I somehow, with the help of a log, got back on a prancing and distressed Thumper—but not as distressed as I was, oh God no—and around we spun. We galloped off across the middle of the sticky plough, then through a gate and sharp left across a meadow. The riders in the distance were going at speed now, and I realized I'd have to leap a ditch or two along the way to catch up. But ditches were nothing to me now. Risking my own neck was a mere trifle. In fact, breaking it was hugely preferable to what was about to befall it.

In a trice I was steaming up a grassy hill beside Polly, the nurse. A good person. A nice person. Think of the hours she worked, the minimum wage, the bedpans. She'd understand. And maybe it wasn't dead, after all? Maybe she'd administer mouth to mouth?

"Polly—"

"Oh, hi, you're back! We were worried about you. Gosh, you must have jumped those ditches—well done!"

"Polly, I—"

"Holes on the right!" she shouted in warning as we careered past a badger set.

Thumper swerved violently to avoid the craters in the ground, and of course I was doing my level best to stay on, let alone speak. And with every furlong we galloped, we were getting further away from the poor dead hound. One of many, of course. So many. Look at them all streaming out ahead. Heaps of them, so of course he wasn't missed. But I must impart my intelligence. Must divulge the grave news. We were jumping now, a series of little blackthorn hedges, not very big, but as I landed beside Polly's huge gray, I screamed, "I've done something—I must tell you!"

She swung around. Only, to my horror, it wasn't Polly at all; it was Emma Harding.

She looked annoyed at being yelled at, mid-jump. "Oh, it's you." She glared. "I hope it wasn't you on the crops back there."

"What?" We'd straggled to a halt before a massive hedge that not even the thrusters could jump.

"Someone went on the crops, and you were specifically told to keep to the edge."

I gazed in wonder. She'd slept with my husband for four years, wanted my children's inheritance, and now she was telling me not to trample a few Weetabix seedlings?

"And you should have a red ribbon on that horse's tail if it kicks."

I went pale. Did she know? Had she seen?

"He doesn't kick," I heard myself splutter.

"Well, he nearly got my horse back there. I saw him lash out."

"You barged into me," I retorted. "And how dare you even begin to lecture me about how to behave when you have behaved *so* abominably, *so* despicably, you—you hussy!"

All my rage, all my pent-up emotion flooded out as I regarded her up on her gray mare with her carefully painted face. So much I wanted to say seethed and jostled within, but which words to choose? Surely I could do better than hussy? Strumpet, perhaps? As I struggled to find a twenty-first century expletive I was capable of uttering, she watched disdainfully. Her red lip curled as she looked me up and down.

"Just don't bite off more than you can chew, hm?"

And with that she was off. From a standing start to a canter, as the field circumnavigated the hedge through a series of gates, then out into open country again. I was on her heels whether she liked it or not. For Thumper had gotten his second wind and seemed determined to stick like glue to Miss Harding's mare. And of course she rode right up at the front, so that's where I ended up: with Hope and Chad; Simon, who had the grace to look abashed as I came thundering up; the terrifying Mary Granger of the stony face, who bonked blacksmiths; Angie, whose eyes were round as I yet again rocketed past her horribly out of control; and then Sam, who, with intrinsic style, was executing a stately collected canter at the head of the field. He raised an ironic, here-we-go-again eyebrow as I cannoned past, but no more than that. Pulling for all I was worth and travelling at a speed that made my eyes stream and the wind rush in my ears, I at least managed to turn a circle before I reached the hounds. I bounced inelegantly back, features jockeying for position, hat over my eyes, everyone staring in wonder, even the children having never seen the like. Suddenly I found my reins being firmly taken from me. It was Angie, and her eyes were sparkling.

"Poppy, I'm going to have to take you home," she told me. "I have *never* been so embarrassed!"

I couldn't breathe, such had been the exertion of trying to stop Thumper. Such was my terror and lack of fitness. I could only nod, trying to get some air into my lungs. I felt terribly sick. At that moment a grim-faced whipper-in swept past silently in the opposite direction.

"One of the hounds is missing," Mary Granger, a face like thunder, informed us, riding up. "We're going to have to hang around here a moment while Martin goes back to look. It's literally nowhere to be seen. Seems to have vanished into thin air."

She rode off to tell the others, to inform the rest of the field. I gazed after her, stricken.

Chapter Twenty-two

THAT SHOULD HAVE BEEN my moment. Of course that should have been my moment. All I remember, though, was turning back from staring at Mary's retreating back, and looking into Angie's glittering eyes as she held my reins. My own eyes cast wildly about: I saw Simon and Emma talking to Sam, grave and deadly serious. My throat clenched with fear, my heart with it. I wished so badly I was not with the thrusters, but with the Pollys and Grants of this world. I could see them at the tail end of the field, sharing a joke and a hip flask, laughing uproariously, Grant even lighting a cigarette. Please, God, I thought, let me go to them; I could tell them. Then they could pass it on, like Chinese whispers. But Angie still had hold of my reins and was telling me in low, measured tones, as one might a child who's run in the road and scared one enough to yell initially, that of course it wasn't my fault, because I hadn't been out before, but if only I'd gone to her *first*, she could have lent me something more *suitable*.

"If only you'd asked, you could have had Clarissa's pony. It's hunted seven seasons, knows exactly how to behave. You are a goon, Poppy."

I listened to this almost in a dream. It was said, certainly, in something more like her usual friendly voice as she relaxed her grip on my rein. And she was my friend; my good friend, who I could tell, surely? I opened my mouth to speak, but my mouth was so dry my teeth stuck to my upper lip. By the time I'd licked them free, Sam had ridden up beside her, mobile clamped to ear, and was talking to her, relaying what he was hearing to Angie. Angie, who, I suddenly noticed, had a mustard collar to her blue coat. Did that make her a hunt official? Like part of the secret police? My befuddled mind swam as she bestowed a dazzling smile on Sam, then, realizing the smile was inappropriate, adopted a grave expression as she listened to what he had to say, as indeed, I did, too.

They'd found the hound, stone dead in a copse, apparently. A nasty gash to his head. Kicked, by the looks of things. Someone had even had the gall to hide him with some bracken.

Angie's expression was no longer manufactured; there was genuine horror in her eyes as she gave a sharp intake of breath. Mary Granger, beside us, who was as tough as old rhino hide, put a hand over her mouth. Sam rode off, white-faced. And then it spread, in a rolling tide, around the field. The hound was called Peddler, it was Mark, the huntsman's, favorite. He'd bred him and walked him as puppy. Yes, definitely kicked, and then hidden with a blanket of bracken—no, actually, a shallow grave had been dug, to secrete it. Never had I felt such fear. Never had my heart beat so loudly or had I felt so surrounded by a mob. The horses stood steaming, withers heaving, glad of the respite from galloping, and as they tossed their heads and their bits jangled, it seemed to me redolent of the jangle and click of the *tricoteuse*.

In a matter of moments, anger had replaced shock around me. How *could* someone? One of the children perhaps, but no, they'd all been through the Pony Club, knew how to behave. And most children were escorted. And to dig a grave…No, no, unthinkable, it must have been an adult, they stormed. But what a craven one. Word spread to the back of the field and I saw Polly and Grant and crew stop their laughter as their jaws dropped in horror. In that moment I also saw Emma Harding's hard little gray eyes come round to seek mine. I met them, but only briefly. I turned away, trembling. Then, as I slowly raised my head, it was to see her ride across to talk to the master. To Sam.

The minutes ticked by. Angie was being sweet now, offering me her hip flask, perhaps feeling guilty at her earlier outburst, but I couldn't tell her now, could I? Because why hadn't I owned up immediately? Suddenly all the prisons in all the world sprang to mind, the convicts within staring out at me, gripping the bars, plaintive eyes saying: you see? That's why *we're* here. Because something happened and we didn't own up. But accidents *do* happen, terrible ones—hit and runs, lashing out at the wife in an argument. Of *course* we didn't mean it, but this is where we end up, this is how it happens. I nearly fell off my horse.

The whipper-in, the telephonic messenger who'd found the hound, arrived back. He ignored us and swept on, his face white, mouth set in a grim line, and headed toward the hounds, who were at a distance to the rest of the field on the brow of the hill. We saw him canter steadily up to Mark the huntsman, all alone, still working his hounds, still drawing the covert. The last to know. As the message was conveyed, I saw Mark put his hand over his eyes, and with that gesture I knew I'd hurt someone very badly. One of the terrier men, on a quad bike, we heard, had picked up the hound, Peddler, and was taking it back to the kennels. Meanwhile we carry on. The show must go on.

We set off at a lick, and since we'd pretty much exhausted this neck of the wood, were off to the next valley apparently, having ridden almost a full circle. Sure enough, from our vantage point on the hill I could see the trailers and lorries parked in a field below. One or two women with children on lead reins were peeling off, saying a cheery goodnight, and I peeled with them, earning a relieved smile from Angie and even a "Well done! Not easy, your first hunt."

Oh, she was sweet now. Felt guilty, perhaps, for briefly not being a friend. For snapping. And of course I forgave her that; we all snapped in the heat of the moment. But what about my own, much bigger moment? Would anyone forgive me that? If only I'd owned up. They would have been shocked and horrified, naturally; but would eventually have forgiven me. Not now, though. Not half an hour later, I thought, feeling sick to my stomach as I rode back down the zigzag track to the Home Farm beside Sam's house. The two chattering women I'd ridden silently back with headed for their trailer, tossing me a breezy farewell, and I managed at least to respond.

My breath was very shallow as I rode on alone. I thought I'd got to the age when I wouldn't find out any more about myself. Interesting, then, that I had, and it wasn't good.

Dad, Jennie, and the kids were huddled by the lorry, sheltering from the wind, which had picked up, together with a jolly band of foot followers. Dan was there, I noticed, on the other side of the field, talking to a couple of local farmers, Angus too, looking rather splendid in tweeds. Quite a few people had dogs on leads, including Leila in her huge plastic collar. They'd followed for quite a while, Dad and Jennie told me as I rode up. Great fun, but *exhausting*; wished they'd taken the car.

"But well done you!" they cried, as if I was the conquering hero returning, as I finally slid off the wretched, sweaty horse and handed him thankfully to Dad.

"You did brilliantly!" Jennie told me, her eyes shining, one arm circling my shoulders as she gave me a hearty squeeze. "Did you have a good day?"

"I'm *so* proud of you, love," said Dad, beaming and slapping my back. "I knew you could do it!"

"We saw you jump, Mummy!" Clemmie leaped into my arms. "You jumped a hedge and nearly came off and your face was so funny—like this." She made a terrified face, and I managed to raise a smile. "And then you jumped a ditch and said the f word, and there was a shouty man who said, 'Bloody woman!' cos you went in front of him!"

"Lots of shouty men, darling," I breathed. "Shouty ladies too."

I embraced my son, who'd toddled up for a hug, his head buried in my thighs as he gripped my knees fiercely. Visiting rights, obviously; perhaps more lenient ones for women with children. Dad would bring them. Or Jennie. In new clothes I wouldn't recognize.

The children both scampered away to join a few village kids they knew, who were also waiting for parents, kicking a ball around. Dan had joined in, big kid that he was himself. Just Dad and Jennie, then.

"Killed a hound," I gasped.

They both turned. Dad had been throwing a thin blue rug on a steaming Thumper.

"I did," I managed. "I killed it. Dead."

"How?" Dad had gone pale.

"Thumper kicked it. Left it in the bushes. No one saw. Didn't own up. Need to move. France, probably."

I'd already thought it through as I rode back. Down near Toulouse, a little village called Gaillac. I'd been there once on a school trip, years ago. Pretty. And I'd open a little shop, like that woman in *Chocolat* who had a secret. No one would know me. I'd be a mystery, an enigma, me and my two small children. Yes, a chocolate shop.

"Oh, God." Even Jennie, totally un-horsy, knew this was bad.

"The house will sell quite quickly," I gabbled on, "always getting things through the door from estate agents. And the children will be bilingual, huge advantage."

"Do shut up," she told me, taking my arm and sitting me down on the lorry ramp. Dad, who'd rugged up Thumper and tied him to the side of the lorry, came to join us. He sat down.

"Sure no one saw?" he murmured.

"No."

"Right. Then stay shtum. These things happen."

I thought this over a moment. Suddenly I was on my feet, furious. I pointed my finger at him; it waggled a bit. "You see? That's where I've got it from! My criminal tendencies! It's learned behavior! That's what you've taught me, what you'd do!" I glared at him accusingly.

"Well, no, actually. I'd have owned up at the time."

"Would you?" I crumpled instantly, aghast. "Oh, Dad, I'm so sorry, I didn't mean that. Oh, Dad, I wish I had!" I wailed. "But in the heat of the moment—so many scary people, so fierce-looking… And it's a bit late now, isn't it?"

"Exactly, after the event. Just let sleeping dogs…well." He stopped awkwardly realizing where that was going. "It's a serious occurrence, though, in the hunting world, Poppy."

"I *know*!" I quaked.

"Oh, piffle," said Jennie staunchly. "They've got hundreds of the bloody things. And let's not get too carried away here; you didn't kill him, Thumper did. At least he didn't kick a child."

"Would have been better," I said gloomily.

Dad nodded in sober agreement. "She's right, Jennie."

"Which just shows how bloody stupid the whole thing is! I mean, they're out to kill an animal anyway, aren't they? And it's only a bloody dog. Christ, I wish it had been Leila. She escaped, incidentally, joined the pack, briefly."

"Really?" I raised my head. Even in my despair this was diverting.

"Oh, yes. Was galloping joyously in the middle of all those dogs in her zany collar, looking very Vivienne Westwood, until your dad managed to persuade a guy on a quad bike to nab her. And you think you've blotted your copy book."

I knew she was trying to make me feel better but as I drove her car home later, Jennie having gone with Dan, who'd come in his Land Rover, my father returning with Thumper, I felt the world was on my shoulders.

"Chatham House rules, OK, love?" Dad had said, before he left.

"What are they?"

"Mum's the word."

"Oh. OK."

Mum's the word, I thought gloomily. Until somehow it leaked out. Which it would. And then heaven knows what the word would be. Murderess? Coward? Witch? I cringed behind the wheel. Clemmie was making Archie laugh in the back, imitating me. "Mummy riding," she was saying, holding imaginary reins right up under her chin, eyes and mouth wide with terror, bouncing in her car seat. And Archie was laughing as only a two-year-old can: as if he was going to be sick.

I tried to count my blessings, which seemed to me to be just two. Those two in the back. No chance now with Sam of course; I'd blown that entirely. In fact I couldn't quite imagine what planet I'd been on to allow it to cross my mind. He was so far out of my league, with his smart friends and his manor house, he was practically in a different stratosphere. And did I want all that, anyway? Imagine having to hunt every week. Having a near-death experience on a regular basis with all those terrifying people. No. I purred down my lane. That whole way of life was not for me: it was too fast, too glamorous, *too much*.

As I drew up outside my cottage I saw someone ringing my doorbell: a man. Oh Christ, had they come for me already? I got out warily. But as he turned around I saw it was only Luke, who smiled when he saw me. I relaxed. This man, however, with a face that lit up at the sight of me, was much more my speed. Why hadn't I spotted it before? Because he seemed reasonably keen? Because he *liked* me? What in hell's name was wrong with that, Poppy?

"Luke." I smiled, too, as I shut the car door, genuinely pleased to see him. Jeans and a navy blue jersey. Freshly washed hair. Normal. Uncomplicated. No spurs.

I lifted Archie out of his car seat and my children ran around the back of the house to get the back-door key from under the geranium pot. Clemmie could just about reach the lock to let them in.

"Christ, have you had an accident?"

My heart lurched at the thought of Peddler.

"N-no, why?" Had he heard?

"You're literally covered in mud!"

"Oh." I glanced down, relieved. "Oh no, just the detritus of the hunting field. Come in, Luke."

"Oh, you do that, do you?" he said, looking surprised, and just a little defensive. Like people do sometimes, if you mention hunting; for reasons that go beyond the prey and are more to do with class and exclusivity. I thought of Polly and Sparks and Grant but couldn't be bothered to argue.

"Not anymore," I told him. "How come you're not at work?"

"Got a day's holiday," he said, lightly touching my shoulder, and as Luke kissed me hello, Mr. Fish, deadheading roses in his front garden, nodded across at us.

"Has he tossed you off, then, love?"

It took me a moment to realize he was talking about Thumper.

"Oh, no, Mr. Fish, I just got a bit muddy," I called. Then to Luke, in an undertone: "Can't move in this place. And frankly, I've had a bit of a day of it. I could do with a very large drink. Will you join me?"

"I'd love to, but I've got to teach in five minutes." He glanced at his watch.

"Teach?"

He looked sheepish. "Oh, yeah, I got talked into it. I give a few piano lessons in the village. Sylvia and Angus's granddaughter, for one." He scratched his head bashfully, and for some reason this endeared him to me tenfold. How sweet. He didn't need the money. He was in the city, in insurance, a flourishing business, yet out of the kindness of his heart...And I liked the idea of him sitting patiently by a piano listening to scales, a small child's faltering rendition of "Fur Elise." Encouraging, enthusing. Not charging around in a pink coat on an enormous horse, glaring at people.

"I just called by to see if supper was still on. You know you said you'd ring me? I didn't want to pressurize you into having it here, though, so my sister said she'd baby-sit. We could go out if you like?"

He'd colored up by the end of this. Softened? I'd melted. He'd lined up a sitter for me. How many men would do that? And, having suggested my place, in retrospect he'd felt uneasy about compromising me in the snugness of my own home—sofas, soft lighting, double bed upstairs, albeit horribly close to the children. I looked into his anxious face, those frank blue eyes. Suddenly I stepped forward, reached up and curled my hand around the back of his neck, gently bringing his lips down to mine.

"I've got a better idea," I murmured when we'd kissed. "Yes, please, to your sister. But let's make it your place."

His eyes didn't much light up as blaze like a fruit machine that's landed a row of pears. Melons, perhaps. Because desire was there, certainly.

"Oh, Poppy," he breathed as he gazed down at me.

Oh, Poppy. You see? That was all it took.

Feeling in control for the very first time that day, I said good-bye and went up my path.

"See you then," he called.

"Yes, see you then," I assured him over my shoulder as he went off to teach, a definite spring in his step.

As I went inside it occurred to me that I'd kissed him in full view of the village. Mr. Fish was certainly standing at his gate, mouth agape, secateurs limp in his hand, as I turned to shut the front door. It was as good as putting an announcement in the local paper. But, actually, that was fine. Because Luke was a very nice man. In fact he was lovely. And with him by my side, I reckoned I could face anything. Face the music, face the terrifying women of the hunt—men, too: all those who'd gladly have my guts for tail bandages.

Italy might be better, though, I thought, as I went slowly upstairs to run a bath. I poured the bubbles in, and as they foamed the idea took shape. Yes, Luke and I doing up a crumbling house in Tuscany, at the top of a hill dotted with cypress trees. Luke and I—a paint brush apiece, me in dungarees and two plaits—pausing to kiss occasionally, or playfully blob paint on each other's noses. The children running barefoot around an olive grove. Goats. Baby ones. And let's face it, being an enigma was all very well, but it might get pretty lonely. I wouldn't have much idea how to run a chocolate shop, either. I peeled off my filthy clothes and put a weary toe in the bath.

Later that evening, when I was putting the children to bed, the telephone rang. The answering machine was on, so I carried on with their story even though my heart was beating fast. I'd rather unwisely chosen an Aesop fable about a boy who kills a calf, doesn't own up, and gets chased out of town; so when I came downstairs I didn't just have a racing heart, but was manically humming a well-known tune from a popular Julie Andrews musical, one that was getting a lot of airing. As I passed the machine on the dresser, with the red light flashing, I pressed play.

"Oh, Poppy, it's Sam here."

The empty bottle of SMA milk slipped clean out of my hand and bounced on the terra-cotta tiles. My hand froze, still in claw-like attitude.

"Um, the thing is, something's come to light that I'd like to talk to you about. In private, if you don't mind." He sounded uncomfortable. "In fact, it might even be an idea if you came into my office. Say first thing tomorrow? At nine o'clock?"

There was a pause. "If I don't hear, I'll assume that's fine." He finished more grimly.

I tottered into the sitting room holding onto the furniture. Made for the sofa and flopped, prone and face down. Then I covered my head with a cushion and moaned low.

Chapter Twenty-three

THE FOLLOWING MORNING, AFTER a terrible dream in which I was chased down the street in my bra and pants by Mary Granger shouting, "You beastly, *beastly* woman!", I dressed appropriately and headed into town. Black shirt, black jacket, black suede boots. Not exactly in mourning—although the last time I'd worn this ensemble, I realized, glancing down in the car, had indeed been to my husband's funeral—but sombre, subfusc: serious. I'd started the day in a more defiant I'm-off-to-Tuscany-with-my-lover kit—pink trousers, boho shirt, high wedges—but lost my nerve halfway down the path and hurried back to change.

Archie was with me, too. I could have left him with Jennie—should have done really, he was grotty if he didn't have his morning sleep—but somehow I wanted the protection he afforded, I realized rather guiltily. You couldn't hit a woman with a baby, surely? Not that Sam would hit, but verbally abuse? I recalled his grim face, the one beneath the riding hat, mobile clamped to ear, high up on his horse, not the smiley crinkly one of the solicitor's office, and trembled. Archie, behind me in his car seat, blinked sleepily in the rearview mirror. I wondered if I should carry him in, wrapped in a shawl? Really go for the sympathy vote? The one he was sucking now, his comfort blanket, would do. I could swaddle him in it and clutch him to my breast like a foundling, take his shoes and socks off, too, so bare toes peeked out. He was quite big for that, though; might wake up and wriggle violently, exposing jeans and a hoody. Not quite the look I was going for.

Parking in Waitrose, I lifted my by-now-sleeping son into his pushchair and hurtled down the high street. Three minutes to nine. But…why was I hurtling? In such a rush? Maybe I hadn't been able to get a parking space? Maybe Waitrose had been full? Unlikely, so early in the morning, but—OK, maybe—maybe I hadn't got his message? Hadn't actually played back the tape? Or hadn't put a new tape in, had been meaning to, for weeks? These, and other shallow yet plausible excuses spooled around in my head as I neared Sam's building. Then more punchy ones. Why on earth should I just pitch up because I'd been summoned? And why at his convenience, why not mine? Friday week would suit me much better. Next month, even. Because I was the accused, that's why, I thought, swallowing. Because this was the way the justice system worked: one attended court. The judge didn't come to yours, settle down in your front room with a cup of tea, did he?

I was climbing the stairs now, Archie asleep in my arms, the pushchair collapsed and hanging from my wrist. I reassembled it at the top and put Archie back in, but not as carefully as I might. With a fair amount of jostling so that…he might wake up? Have a tantrum and go shouty-crackers, as he often did when roused from a deep sleep, so that we could surely go home? I nudged him again. No, of course I didn't pinch him, but oh, wake up, Archie. Scream.

"What a sweet baby," someone murmured over my left shoulder.

I jumped. It was the receptionist, Janice, who'd appeared out of the ladies' at the top of the stairs, pink lipstick reapplied.

"Oh. Thank you."

"It's Mrs. Shilling, isn't it?"

"Er, well…" I eyed the stairs longingly.

"Nine o'clock with Sam? He's in there, waiting for you." She beamed at Archie. "Would you like to leave him with me?"

"No, no, I'll take him in."

"He'll be no trouble?"

"He might. He's a bit of a monster."

"He looks jolly placid to me."

"Please take your hands off my buggy."

She blanched, surprised. Then: "I quite understand," she said quickly. "You've lost your husband, and one does become terribly protective."

Casting me a sympathetic look, she ushered us through into the reception area; and then there was nothing else for it because she was bustling to open another door, into Sam's inner sanctum.

The room had remained as neat and tidy as on my last visit, which didn't bode well somehow. The man himself was installed behind his desk, suit jacket and tie in place, no causal shirt sleeves rolled up, and on the telephone, communicating by way of an elegantly raised finger that he wouldn't be a moment. His face was stern, stony even. It was with a sinking heart that I sat down opposite him, drawing Archie's buggy very close beside me. No, in front of me.

"I see," Sam was saying gravely. "Yes, I suspected as much." He massaged his brow with his fingertips, elbows on the desk, face to his blotter. "Thank you for confirming it."

His dark hair was just slightly flecked with grey at the temples, I noticed. Distinguished. Handsome. An officer's face, my father would say; he'd been one himself, many years ago, in the cavalry. How could I ever have thought him a foot soldier like me? Suddenly I felt angry. This whole set-up, the whole up-the-wiggly-backstairs-to-a-provincial-solicitor's practice, had been a front, a smokescreen, an attempt to appear a man of the people. But I'd seen him outside his manor on a horse, in a pink coat. Oh, yes. I knew better.

"Overwhelming evidence," he was saying. "I agree. Circumstantial as well as actual. And such obvious guilt at the time. Fleeing the scene of the crime, for one thing." He looked up at me. Hard. I flushed. Shit. He was talking about me. "She doesn't have a leg to stand on," he went on. My thighs felt gripped in the frozen lock of my tights, which seemed to shrink like a vise. I waited, paralyzed.

After a moment he said good-bye. His face was grave as he put down the phone. But then an odd thing happened. He got to his feet, beamed, came around his huge leather-topped desk, and bent to kiss me on both cheeks.

"Poppy. How lovely to see you. You survived, I see! I must say I thought you were tremendously brave sailing over those hedges and ditches when I gather you hadn't ever hunted before. Everyone was terribly impressed, and old Gerald Harper even went so far as to tell me in a very loud voice that he thought you had spunk!" He threw back his head and laughed.

I blinked, confused. I thought I had hours to live; a condemned woman. But apparently I had spunk? Could he have been talking about someone else on the phone? Another client?

"And let me tell you, that wasn't an easy meet. Sometimes we toddle around the woods for hours on end and bugger-all happens; but we had a five-pointer yesterday, and there you were, galloping away at the front with the best of them!"

"Yes, just…a little too much at the front sometimes," I managed to stammer, wondering what was coming next.

"Oh well, that happens to everyone. When I first went out I overtook the master, the hounds and even the bloody fox! Ended up sinking a lonely pint in a pub miles away with my heaving horse tied up outside, too bloody frit to get back on again!"

"Excellent, excellent," I croaked, baffled. His eyes seemed to be glowing at me in a rather admiring way and he was still standing quite close; he was leaning back on his desk, his crotch at eye level.

"Is this Archie?" He crouched down to the pushchair and gazed equally admiringly at my son. "Isn't he sweet?"

Now he was admiring babies? Like a politician, I thought suddenly. Is that what this was? A softener, before the killer blow? Was "bigot" privately on the tip of his tongue? Or "dog killer," with a sensational snarl and a deft spit in my eye?

"Um, Sam, why did you ask me here?"

He looked surprised. Taken aback, even, as if he'd overstepped some kind of mark.

"Oh. Yes. Sorry." He straightened up. Went back to his desk and looked serious again as he sat down. He shuffled some papers about. Then he looked up at me. "Poppy, something rather interesting has come to light."

Ah. Here we go. Here it comes. I mentally adopted the in-flight crash position. "Oh, yes?"

"It seems Emma Harding has retracted her claim on the profits from your husband's business. In other words, her claim on his estate."

I stared. "She has? Why?"

He shrugged. "I imagine because she's now married to Simon Devereux. Wouldn't surprise me if it was his influence, or his family's."

"But—why?"

"Well, aside from being a decent guy who'd probably be horrified at the very idea, he's also a budding parliamentary candidate, Poppy. Doesn't look good among all the expenses scandals, does it? MP's new wife extorts inheritance from dead lover's widow? Not something Simon would want splashed over the local papers, or even the *Daily Mail*, for that matter. I don't imagine it's the career move he's looking for."

"No—I suppose not."

"And perhaps you coming out with us yesterday scared Miss Harding a bit. Made her think. Realize you're not going to go away. Won't go quietly." The eyes began to shine unnervingly. I had a nasty feeling he was going to mention spunk again. "Anyway, for whatever reason, the upshot is she's backing out, which, aside from the Shillings—who I wouldn't mind betting will back out, too, without Miss Harding at the helm—makes you sole inheritor to your husband's will, and, incidentally, to any shares within the bank that he owns, as majority shareholder."

As we already knew, that amounted to a great deal of money. I remembered the figure on the piece of paper he'd placed in front of me. But it was a rather irrelevant amount, too, under the circumstances. Because it was, after all, only money. The poignancy of that phrase went like a dart to my heart. Only money. Not honor, or integrity, or doing the right thing, however difficult. Not owning up, or stepping up to the plate—no. Hard cash. Filthy lucre. Like filthy lies. And deceit.

I raised a smile. "Thank you. How marvelous. Yes, that'll make a tremendous difference."

He blinked. I'd just won the lottery and was calmly agreeing it would make a difference?

"I should say! It's a huge relief, surely?"

He looked delighted for me. How sweet. Yes, truly thrilled. But then it was a coup for him, too, wasn't it, to win a case for a client? Which is what I was, of course. Something to celebrate in the pub tonight with the boys. "Result! Stitched up the Harding woman and got a bung for my client, some serious cash. What are you having, Dave? These are on me." Except his life wasn't like that, was it? I kept forgetting. In the billiard room at home, then, in his smoking jacket, puffing on a cigar with another cove. "Had a bit of a coup today, Peregrine. Kept a widow out of the workhouse, I should think."

"I say, well done, old boy," growled Perry. "Noblesse oblige and all that. Your shot."

I took a deep breath.

"And thank you so much for all your advice and…valuable instruction." Was that the word? Probably not. And actually, there hadn't been much of it, in the event. It was all over now, too.

"Oh, not at all," Sam said, adopting a more serious tone, becoming more solicitor-ish. More professional. He'd had to check himself from tumbling over the friend line, and a week ago I'd have been delighted to have him tumble. Would have given him a hefty push. But not now.

"Of course there are countless hoops to jump through yet," he was saying, putting on his glasses—nice glasses—and reading from a ring-bound file. "Your late husband's business deals were profitable but intricate, to say the least; it all needs unraveling. I made a few phone calls, did a bit of initial delving, and it seems the bank is under investigation at the moment by the Financial Services Authority. Did you know that?" He looked at me over his glasses.

"I did, actually," I said mechanically. "I had a letter from one of the partners." Ted Barker had written, hot on the heels of his condolence letter, to say that if I was to read in the financial press that the bank was being investigated I wasn't to worry; it was purely routine. Financial press? I hadn't even been reading the tabloids.

"It's routine, I gather," I repeated now, for Sam's benefit.

"Yes. Although…" He hesitated.

I waited. "Yes?"

"Well, it's just there's a certain amount of discrepancy within the accounting, apparently. A complaint from a client, too."

I shrugged. "Clients often complained if they felt their investment hadn't paid off. Phil always said so." I smiled wanly. "For all my husband's faults, Sam, he was as straight as a die. They won't find anything."

"No. No, I'm sure they won't. But it'll be a while, I'm afraid, until the money comes through. Because of this intervention, everything has to be gone through with a fine-tooth comb now, so it's not entirely straightforward."

Nothing is, I thought miserably, picking up the soft toy which Archie had dropped. He'd liked my baby. Crouched in front of my baby. But everyone liked babies.

"But I think that within six months we'll have it all straightened out and, hopefully, a settlement in time for the summer."

"Marvelous." I managed a smile. Stood up.

He looked surprised. Was I ending the interview? Yes, I was. I extended my hand—no, no kisses, Sam—and he slowly got to his feet, removing his glasses.

"And once again, thank you so much for your professional counsel." I sounded like a policeman. Any minute now I'd say: and in conclusion. But hey, I'd got through it. Escaped, some might say. But it didn't feel like that. I felt I was deceiving him.

Hand shaken, I turned my sleeping child around. The interview I'd dreaded so much was over, and I was on my way. I was a wealthy woman, too. The reality of that, the difference it would make to my life, would kick in soon, I was sure. Within moments probably, out there in the high street, when I realized I could buy everything in the shop windows. And then everything else would be put in perspective. Become minutiae, forgotten. Money had a way of talking, didn't it? Quite loudly. Shouting other things down. It had a way of hushing things up—hushing people up—and shuffling assuredly to the top of the pile. And I was shuffling out. I felt rather light-headed. Was that the money, I wondered. No, I didn't think so. I hadn't had any breakfast, which didn't help, of course. Hadn't eaten anything at all yesterday, come to think of it. No breakfast before hunting—too scared. No lunch—too busy leaping ruddy great hedges. No supper—too shocked. No breakfast this morning—too scared. A bit of a pattern emerging there, then.

Aware that Sam was watching me, I called a cheery good-bye over my shoulder, but as I wheeled Archie through reception and passed a smiling Janice, I stopped. Felt a bit peculiar.

"Are you all right, dear?" She frowned up at me, concerned. "You look terribly pale."

"Yes. Fine, thanks." I took a moment. Was about to push on, then halted again. "Um, actually, d'you think you could watch him for me?"

"Of course." She looked surprised. Delighted, too, as she bustled round.

I turned and went unsteadily back into Sam's room. Shut the door behind me. Then I approached his desk. He hadn't sat down; was still standing thoughtfully, gazing down at the file, fingertips poised on the desk like those of a pianist lingering on a final chord. He glanced up. Looked pleased, if surprised, as I tottered back toward him.

"I killed your dog," I croaked, clutching the edge of his desk.

"My dog?"

"Yes. It was me. Kicked it to death."

"But…Betsy? I just left her. Asleep in her basket…"

We stared at one another. Slowly the penny dropped.

"Oh no, not that one," I said quickly. "The hunt dog. Hound, even."

He frowned. "Peddler?"

"That's it. I kicked it. Or Thumper did. Same thing. And although I didn't dig a grave, I did cover him in bracken. But it was instinctive, sort of—out of respect, like a blanket. I can see how it would look furtive, though. Like I was covering up a murder."

Murder. I shut my eyes. A mistake. The room spun and I lost my balance, stepping backward and letting go of the desk. I opened my eyes quickly and put out my hand to steady myself, but there was nothing there. Instead my hand went to my forehead, which was damp. Then I saw the floor coming up to meet me and knew, in a split second, it was too late. I was passing out.

Chapter Twenty-four

WHEN I CAME ROUND later, I was horizontal. I also appeared to be on a red chenille couch in the corner of a strange room that had a plaster rose in the middle of the ceiling and an ornate but faintly cracked cornice running around the edge. Sam and Janice were gazing down at me; Janice was hovering with a glass of water.

"Archie—" I struggled to sit up.

"He's here," said Sam quickly. He wheeled my still-sleeping child into view near my feet so I could see him. "He's fine."

I sank back. "Did I faint?"

"You did. Quite dramatically. But I suppose any faint is dramatic; I've just never seen anyone do it before."

"God, how embarrassing. I'm so sorry." My eyes roved around. "Am I supposed to say: where am I? Where am I?"

He grinned. "In the senior partner's room, the only one with a sofa."

"Christ—" I struggled to move. He put a hand on my shoulder.

"Don't panic, he's in Mauritius. You could stay there for another ten days and he wouldn't be any the wiser."

"Water?" Janice proffered the glass anxiously.

"Um, thank you." I managed to half sit, although Sam sort of helped me. This was beyond embarrassing.

"Did you eat any breakfast, dear?" Janice was asking as I sipped. "Or have you got your monthlies?"

I flushed, mortified, which was impressive given my pallor. "Um, no. I mean, I didn't have any breakfast."

"Well, there you are, then," she scolded as I sank back again. "You young girls, running around with nothing in your tummies. Oh, those wretched phones."

They were indeed jumping off the desk behind us.

"Please get it," I begged her. "I'm fine, really."

"Well, if you're sure…" She looked doubtful but then scooted off to reception, handing Sam the glass and calling over her shoulder, "Don't let her get up yet!"

"Did you have to carry me here?" I asked, appalled, as he dragged up a chair. There was something faintly psychoanalytical about our configuration now as he sat at my head. I quickly unlaced my fingers on my chest.

"Well, between us, yes. You don't weigh much, though, Poppy. Janice is right, you should eat more."

It was a long time since anyone had said anything like that to me: Phil certainly hadn't and Dad wouldn't notice. Mum. It would have been Mum, then. I looked up at him. Lovely eyes. Greeny-brown, and sort of flecked with hazel. Suddenly I remembered why I was here.

"Shit—the dog!"

"Ah yes, Peddler. But you know, these things happen, particularly in the country, Poppy. People get very worked up at the time, but he was an old hound, and he died doing what he loved most. Not such a bad way to go, surely?"

"Was he? Old? Not a puppy?"

"No, no, at least twelve. And it wasn't you who kicked him, don't forget. And anyway, it was hardly premeditated."

"Yes, but I didn't own up."

"Well, you have now. And at the time I imagine you just panicked. We all do that."

"Really?" I gazed up at the calm, kind face above me. Hard to imagine he ever did. I must get up. Must get off this sodding couch. I felt ridiculous.

"Here." He held my arm as I swung my legs around, but in my haste my skirt got hitched up along the way so that I flashed far more leg than I'd have liked and I saw him avert his eyes, embarrassed. But I felt better, actually. I'd admitted my crime. And out loud, twenty-four hours later, it didn't seem so heinous. He was right: it had been my horse, not me, and the hound had died in its natural habitat, doing its job. Although the huntsman might not see it like that, I supposed. I remembered him taking his hat off, passing a hand across his shattered face.

"I'd like to explain to the huntsman. Mark, isn't it? Apologize. Tell him what happened, face to face."

For some reason Sam looked as if I'd handed him half of my inheritance. His eyes shone. "D'you know, I think he'd like that. Thank you, Poppy. I'll give you his address."

And he did, together with his phone number, when I'd followed him back into his office, pushing Archie. As he turned and handed me the piece of paper, he held my eyes for just a moment longer than was strictly necessary.

"How's the book club?" he asked suddenly.

I blinked, wrong-footed. "Oh, pretty much disbanded, sadly. I think the party line is 'literary differences.'" I made ironic quotation marks in the air then realized I hated it when people did that. "Most of us wanted to read rollicking commercial fiction, which we knew we'd enjoy and polish off by the following week, and then gather for a chat and a bit of a party. But then we were given a really hard book to read and we all sort of gave up."

"Oh. Shame. Who suggested the hard book?"

"Hope Armitage."

"Ah."

"Clever girl." I grimaced.

He nodded. Glanced away.

"A lovely one, too," I said quickly, in case he thought I was knocking her. "She's got pretty much everything, actually. Beauty, charm, brains. Chad," I added foolishly with a laugh, then wished I hadn't. I could feel myself coloring. Why was I gabbling? "But unfortunately we couldn't match her in the 'cerebral' department." More quotation marks in the air around "cerebral." Why? "Well, not that we could match her in any department," gabble gabble, "certainly not the looks department, obviously! Not that we were trying to, or anything." Do *stop*, Poppy.

"I hadn't realized she was in your group." He'd moved to the window to look out at the street below; had his back to me. He'd gone a bit clipped and terse suddenly. Not so shiny-eyed.

"Well, as I say, it's pretty much defunct now, anyway. Although one or two people were talking about forming another one, a sort of radical offshoot, but minus the literary slant."

Peggy had indeed scurried across the road a few days ago to suggest we read the latest Sophie Kinsella and then meet at her place to discuss it. Thursday at eight, oh, and by the way, it was themed. What you were wearing when the ship went down. And bring a bottle. Angus had got his costume already, apparently.

"Oh no, we can't, Peggy," I'd said, appalled. "What will Chad and Hope think?"

"Chad and Hope won't know," she'd told me firmly, stubbing out her cigarette in my clump of asters by the front door.

I wasn't sure I could share this disreputable secret with Sam, though. The Armitages were his friends, they rode together—hacked out, I believed was the expression—and anyway, he'd moved on from holding my eyes for longer than was strictly necessary and was gazing abstractedly at the traffic. I'd lost his attention and had his back.

"Well, I'll be away," I said shortly, after a pause. I felt faintly uncomfortable. "Thank you so much for the erm…water. And the couch." And the terribly strong manly arms sprang to mind, too, but happily not to my vocal chords, although it was nip and tuck.

"Don't forget your papers." He seemed to collect himself suddenly and turned to cross to his desk, handing me a large folder, full, no doubt, of the details of my stonking great inheritance: the wherewithal to educate my children at Cheltenham Ladies' College and Eton, to put me in the Hope, Chad, Simon and Sam brigade, I thought suddenly. Yes, Henley and Harvey Nichols, here I come. Why then, was there less of a spring in my step than there should have been, as I left his office?

I carried Archie down the stairs. He'd woken up and was beaming at me, cheeks flushed with sleep, drumming his corduroy booties against my tummy. I seized one of them and kissed it hard. It was the mention of Hope, I knew, that had rendered him a bit mute; had heralded a change of mood. Was he in love with her? Wouldn't be difficult. But she was so happily married. So very unavailable. We all knew she and Chad couldn't keep their hands off each other, couldn't keep out of the bedroom. I remembered the first time Jennie and I had met them while looking for Leila, both looking very post-coital. Still, that didn't stop the old ticker disobeying orders, did it? All the evidence being against one? When had that ever stood in the way of true love, or even, I thought wryly, true infatuation? I sighed.

Out in the high street I popped Archie back in his push-chair and was about to head off down the street, when I glanced back over my shoulder. To my surprise, this time he was there, at the window. Was he watching me go, or had he returned to his reverie, the one that had so saddened him earlier? Either way, we both turned away sharpish as our eyes met and I hurried on my way to Waitrose.

When I got back to my house, I found Jennie coming away from my locked front door. She was hastening down the cobbled path, a look of utter despair on her face.

"Oh, thank God!" she cried, stopping in her tracks at the gate when she saw me approach, Archie in my arms.

"What is it?" I hurried toward her.

"Quick, get in." She seized the key from my hand, ran back to unlock my door, and hustled me inside. Then she slammed the door behind us, her eyes wild as she turned to me in the hallway.

"What?" I breathed, terrified. "What's happened?"

Clemmie was my first thought: fallen out of a tree at nursery, or an accident with the scissors. At my very first parents' evening, Miss Hawkins had told me, in a doom-laden voice, that Clemmie had a problem. Heart in mouth, I'd anticipated bullying, early anorexia. On being gravely informed her scissor control was not all it should be, I'd been unable to suppress a laugh. I wasn't laughing now. They'd tried to reach me, obviously, but my mobile was off.

"Quick, tell me quick."

"Frankie's pregnant," she gasped.

I'm ashamed to say my heart kicked in. Not me. Not Clemmie. Not my darling girl. I had to take a moment to recover. Regroup. I set Archie on his feet and he toddled off. Frankie...

"Oh my God." As I straightened, my hand went to my mouth. I stared at my friend. Her face was very pale, her lips bloodless. "How d'you know? Did she tell you?"

"No, I found this!" she hissed, producing a pregnancy-test stick from her coat pocket. "In the bathroom, in the wastepaper basket!"

"Oh." I stared. There was very much a bright blue line in the window. Very positive. Very much pregnant. My head spun. I took her arm and led her into the sitting room.

"But...is it definitely hers?"

"Well, it's not mine, and I certainly hope to God it's not Hannah's!"

"No, but...it could be a friend's?" I hazarded.

"Oh, come on, Poppy. I know which friends she's had in and out of the house and she hasn't, recently. And I emptied that bin only yesterday." Jennie paced around my sitting room, arms folded, eyes over-bright, her chin tucked in as if looking into the eye of the storm.

"That's why I was surprised to see it full again, with rather too much fresh loo paper, which had been stuffed on top to hide this. Of course it's hers, the little—" She stopped herself.

I sat her down on the sofa, perching beside her. She was hyper-ventilating a bit.

"Breathe, Jennie, and think. Don't go off the deep end. You've got to help her in this, not tar and feather her."

She nodded, compressing her lips, her face grim, staring straight ahead. She knew that; but still, it was hard.

"And if she's just done the test, she's probably only just pregnant, so all is not lost."

"Not necessarily," she muttered.

"No, not necessarily, but let's wait until we know the facts. Is she seeing someone? Has she got a boyfriend? Who could it be?"

"Well, that's just it!" she cried, turning to face me. "No! No boyfriend, not even a friend who's a boy, and trust me, I would know. I keep a very close eye on that girl. And she hasn't even mentioned anyone, ever! Not to me, anyway."

Suddenly Frankie's words came back to me in a rush. What are you going to do in the holidays? "I thought I might get pregnant." And I thought she was being droll, ironic, sardonic, as she could be: brighter than she looked.

I got up quickly from the sofa; walked to the mantle to hide my face, reached ostensibly to fiddle with the clock, wind it. Something else had occurred to me, too. Jennie knew me very well, though.

"What?" she pounced, on her feet. "What is it?"

"Nothing, I—"

"Poppy, you know something—what?" She swung me round.

"No, Jennie, honestly, I—"

"Poppy—*you have to tell me!*"

I did. I knew that. She held my arms and my eyes. Hers were blazing with emotion.

I flicked my tongue over my lips. "OK. OK, but I swear to God I'm sure it was just Frankie being flippant, you know how she is."

"Poppy…"

"Well, the other night, after baby-sitting, she dashed off across the road to get in someone's car. The engine was running and they drove off together."

"She doesn't know anyone with a car."

"And earlier, at the beginning of term, well—she told me she fancied a teacher."

Jennie stared. Then shock registered on her face. She gave a strangled cry and staggered back, subsiding into the sofa, one hand covering her mouth. Then she looked up at me in disbelief. At length she removed her hand.

"Which one?" she whispered.

"Which teacher? Um, I'm not sure." I wasn't. I wracked my brains. "Could it be maths? Or biology? Yes, biology. But, Jennie, it was probably said as a jest. I'm sure she was just winding me up."

"Hennessy!" She sat up with a sensational hiss.

"Um, I'm not sure, and as I say—Jennie, no!"

She was on her feet now, striding out of my sitting room looking very dangerous, about to leave my house, car keys in hand. Jennie's tall and strong, much bigger than me, but I sprinted past her down the passage and in one fluid movement got between her and the front door, quickly turning the Chubb key, locking her in.

"No!" I gasped, flattening myself against the door, arms out like a star fish. "You are not charging up there like this. You are not hoiking Mr. Hennessy out of his reproduction class and making an exhibition of yourself and of Frankie in front of the whole school. I will not let you!"

She glared down on me, eyes blazing, nostrils flaring. "Out of my way."

I quaked briefly. "No, Jennie!"

"*Out of my way!*"

Glaring back defiantly and fully anticipating being manhandled, I braced myself. Then, suddenly, I saw her collapse. Her eyes dulled and her mouth drooped. She almost staggered backward, to sit, as if her legs wouldn't hold her, on the tiny Victorian chair in my narrow hallway, by the table with the phone. She bent her head and clutched at the roots of her hair with her hands, pulling hard. Then she sobbed. She sobbed and sobbed, and I crouched down before her, holding her knees in her jeans, letting her cry.

"My fault!" she gasped, when she was able. "All my fault! I wasn't there for her—didn't help her enough. Wasn't a good enough mother!"

"Not true," I told her, gripping her knees, shaking them. "So not true, Jennie! It's nothing to do with you, just a stage, a rebellious teenager stage, and you've always done your best by her!"

"Yes, but if I'm honest," she gulped, raising her head and giving an almighty sniffas she pulled a tissue from her sleeve, "I'd slightly given up recently. I tried so hard when she was little, Poppy, out of love for her, of course, but out of a lot of love for Dan. But lately—oh, I don't know. She's been so tricky, and of course these days I don't look at Dan anymore and think: I worship the ground you walk on. So maybe I took my eye off the ball. Maybe I sort of thought: to hell with the lot of you, if you know what I mean." Her body shuddered.

I did. Jennie was a strong woman and kept that family firmly on track with lots of robust shouting and yelling, which I'd hear through the wall and smile at, knowing it was nothing more than hot air and knowing, as she told me, that if she didn't, they became feckless. "*Feckless!*" she'd snap. And she had her work cut out with the two boisterous younger ones, not to mention a husband who got into scrapes, and a stepdaughter who could be surly and unhelpful. But recently I hadn't heard the familiar hollering through the walls. Certainly not with Frankie. That didn't mean it was Jennie's fault she was pregnant, though, and I told her so.

She gazed glumly at her hands, clutching the tissue in her lap; a bit calmer now, but shattered, I could tell.

"Still. I could have hustled more. Probed. Questioned the interminable sulks." We were silent a moment. "Poor Frankie," she whispered at length. "Poor, poor darling. She must be so scared."

She balled the tissue hard in her hand. I knew what she was thinking: that terrible moment when the blue line had appeared, the horrific shock Frankie must have got, sitting on the side of the bath last night, perhaps, or in her school uniform this morning. Then the walk to the bus stop, sitting on the bus, blankly watching the world go by, thinking: everyone else is having a normal Thursday. White-faced; devastated.

"I'll talk to her tonight," she whispered.

"D'you want me to do it?" I ventured.

We both knew Frankie talked to me. Quite a bit. Sometimes Jennie had been jealous. I knew she wouldn't let a bit of jealousy get in the way of her daughter's welfare now, though. She thought about it.

"No," she said at length. "I think I'll do it. And I promise I won't scream and shout. No recriminations. Hopefully I've done all that in your sitting room."

I nodded. "And you'll let her choose?"

She stared down at me, appalled. "She's sixteen, Poppy! Quite possibly pregnant with a teacher's baby!"

"OK, let me rephrase that. You'll let her think she's chosen?"

She gazed opaquely at me, her pale face streaked with tears. "Oh. Yes. I see. Suggest. Point out the difficulties should she keep it. But let her know I'd nonetheless be very happy to be a grandmother." She clenched her teeth.

"Exactly, so the whole thing horrifies her and she instantly says, 'Oh God, no.' But if you bully her and tell her what's going to happen, she could go the other way, just to spite you."

Jennie blinked. "You're right. I'll paint a picture of her aged thirty, with a sixty-year-old man on her arm, his middle-aged children, plus a stroppy fourteen-year-old of her own. She'll be in Harley Street before you can say knife."

"Well, I can think of more comfortable analogies, but that's the general idea."

She swallowed hard. Leaned her head back on the wall and looked beyond me, over my head. "We had such hopes, Poppy, you and me, didn't we?" she said softly. "When we set out? You with Phil. Me with Dan."

I knew what she meant. Where she was. In our first flat, in Clapham. Which we'd painted lilac and hung with Chinese lanterns. Jennie, after a particularly barren patch socially, flying off to dinner with her handsome older man; me, well, casting around rather desperately, as we know. Settling for second best. Which Jennie hadn't done. So, in fact, sharing a flat in Clapham was where the similarity ended.

"You hang on to those hopes, Jennie. It's not over yet. I never got off the starting block."

She looked down at me, recognizing, perhaps for the first time, the brave face I'd put on my terrible mistake. "I suppose not," she said absently. "But you will now."

I had a feeling she meant with Luke. I stood up quickly. Too quickly, probably, bearing in mind I still hadn't eaten for twenty-four hours. I steadied myself. "Yes, I will now," I repeated.

Jennie got wearily to her feet, looking about a hundred years old. Her face was drawn and she was hunched in her tweed coat, the one we'd thought so edgy with its frayed collar and cuffs when she'd found it in Primark, such a clever high-street find, but which now looked like a tatty old tweed coat. Archie was wailing from the kitchen, initially delighted to have been left for so long without supervision, but indignant now at being ignored. And it was time to collect Clemmie. Jennie gave a last gigantic sigh as she turned to go, her head bent, shoulders sagging. I hugged her hard.

"Good luck," I muttered in her ear.

"Thanks. I'll need it." I held her close a long moment. Suddenly her voice came in a frantic rush in my ear. "Poppy," she gulped, "imagine if she's four months gone, imagine if it's too late, if—"

"*Don't* imagine," I said fiercely, pulling back and holding her shoulders, looking hard at her panic-stricken face "Don't. We don't know anything yet. Don't think the worst."

She nodded, frightened.

"Stay calm," I urged.

"I will," she whispered.

"And listen to her. Don't"—and this was brave—"preach." Jennie could surely preach.

For a moment she seemed about to erupt, then, recognizing another truth, she nodded wordlessly, turned my Chubb key in my door, and left.

Chapter Twenty-five

THE FOLLOWING DAY, AS I drove along the lanes to Wessington, I considered the whirlwind that had whipped through our village these past few months. First Tom had left Angie and the mini tornado had settled on her house; then Phil had died and the mistral had torn up the road to me; and now Frankie was pregnant and the twister had shot next door, spinning savagely over my friend. Was that just life, I wondered. One family lurching into crisis, then climbing out of it, only to be swiftly followed by another? Did we all take it in turns to fall into holes? It seemed to me, though, that some people never fell. They led permanently gilded lives and were immune to the slipstream of life's grimy undercurrent; never so much as felt a ripple. For some reason the Armitages sprang to mind. I sighed.

And naturally, in our close-knit little community, word spread like a bush fire. I hadn't told anyone about Frankie, of course I hadn't, but when Dan came home from work yesterday, and Jennie told him what she'd found out, calmly, reasonably, with neither blame nor censure, he'd had the reaction Jennie had had in my sitting room. Of course he had. He was shocked, distraught, horrified. His little girl. A fucking *teacher*! Fucking *hell*! And then Frankie had come in late from school, not at the usual time, and before Jennie could stop him, he'd lost his rag. I knew because I heard it in my kitchen. Even though I went into the sitting room and turned the television on. Put my fingers in my ears. And then Jennie had lost it with Dan and the whole thing, as she told me this morning when she came round, red-eyed, not having slept a wink, hair standing on end, had degenerated into the worst and most terrible scene imaginable.

"I preached, I didn't listen, I wasn't calm, I wasn't strong," she gulped, horrified. "Everything you said I shouldn't be, I was."

"But not at Frankie," I said anxiously. "You didn't lose it with her?"

"No, I suppose not. Dan, mostly." She looked gray and defeated as she slumped at my kitchen table, still with her pajamas under her coat. "Trying to fend him off Frankie. But nothing about it was very attractive, Poppy. Neither adult's behavior would stand up to too much scrutiny. You didn't hear, did you?" She passed a weary hand through her chaotic curls.

"No, no," I lied.

"Good. Only Avril Collins on the other side couldn't have looked more delighted when I saw her collect her milk from her step this morning, and I thought: oh shit."

"It hardly matters who knows," I told her gently. Again untruthfully, because of course it did. "D'you know how far…you know… she is?" I asked cautiously.

"'How far gone' is the expression on sink estates, Poppy," she said with a flash of the old Jennie, brave eyes glittering briefly in their sleep-deprived sockets. "Among the chain-smoking teenage mothers on the eighteenth floor. And you don't 'get pregnant,' you 'fall,' as in, 'When did you fall for Kylie?'" She shuddered. "The answer is I don't know," she said in a much smaller voice. "She won't tell me. Won't say a word, in fact. Which is why Dan got so angry."

"Nothing?"

"Absolutely zilch. Stared at her father's distorted faced as he ranted and raved like a madman, then ran up to her room and slammed the door. Locked it."

"Oh. So…what next?"

She shrugged. "Don't know. Let it all calm down, I suppose. Try to talk to her tonight, perhaps. One more day isn't going to make much difference, is it?"

I think we both knew what she was talking about.

"I doubt it," I agreed.

She dredged up a gigantic sigh from the soles of her feet. "Anyway. Just came to check you hadn't heard."

"Not a thing."

I walked her to the door, and since she'd caught me as I was about to go out, I picked up my bag, and Archie, too, as we left. When I'd locked the front door behind me, out of the corner of my eye, I saw a little huddle of raincoats and brollies outside the shop. Avril Collins, Yvonne and Mrs. Fish. They glanced our way, wide-eyed, then re-huddled. I quickly positioned myself between them and Jennie.

Jennie, though, was beyond either noticing or caring. Halfway down my path in the rain, she was gazing into some private world of her own, the drizzle settling like a sparkling cobweb on her wild springy curls, slippers on her feet, coat open to the elements, like Lear on the heath.

"I thought I'd meet her from school this afternoon. Take her to Topshop, then for a burger. D'you think she'd like that?" She turned to look at me anxiously.

Ordinarily, yes. But under the circumstances, Jennie waiting at the school gates…

"Maybe text her first?" I suggested. "So she can think about it?"

"Good idea." She whipped her phone out of her coat pocket. I gently put my hand on it. "And maybe go and have a think about what you're going to say first?"

Jennie's eyes widened and she gave me a messianic look, full of admiration and fervor. I wanted to say: no, Jennie, I'm no guru, but I do know about this. About running around like a headless chicken, charging down the church path and forgetting to bury my husband, rushing around on adrenalin following shock. Doing the first thing that came into one's head, acting on impulse. I knew about the next bit, too, the terrible depression that followed: forgetting to feed my kids, to dress them, love them. I shuddered as I pocketed my key. Almost couldn't admit it to myself and knew I'd regret it for the rest of my life. I knew about doing all the wrong things, and later on wishing so much I'd done otherwise; I knew how guilt—or rather a sense of it, misplaced perhaps—can make us behave illogically, like people we don't recognize, never thought we'd be.

I didn't say all that to my friend, though. What I actually said was: "Go and have a cup of coffee, get your head together, and then text her, OK?"

She nodded obediently. Ran down my path and up hers, and it occurred to me that we were like a couple of little weather people, popping in and out of each other's houses, broadcasting rain or shine, depending on our day, depending on the current crisis, telling the village our business. Oh, sod it, I thought, shifting Archie onto my hip as I went down the path. Who cares?

"Morning, Avril," I couldn't help calling across Jennie's garden as her other neighbor returned from the shop, eyes darting like a magpie's. "Yes, that's right, trouble at Apple Tree Cottage." I glared at her and marched off to my car, thrusting a surprised Archie into his seat. Regretted it, of course. And if I could come to the boil like that, what hope for Jennie?

Now, however, as I drove along the edge of the common in Wessington, I considered it rationally, wondered if Frankie really would be stupid enough to be seduced by a teacher. I'd thought about it overnight and decided, on balance, it was unlikely. In which case, who was the boy? Some family was going to be equally shattered, surely? And for some reason hard to fathom, stemming as it did from time immemorial, and belying what had happened in the Garden of Eden when God had firmly pointed the finger at Eve as she tucked into the apple, the fault always lay with the boy. "He got her into trouble," the Avril Collins of this world would say, not "she got him." I glanced at my twenty-month-old son in the rearview mirror as we sped along in the weak, milky sunshine, which was struggling to make an appearance now the rain had ceased. "You be careful, my boy," I whispered. "You steer clear of those pretty girls."

He grinned toothily back.

The kennels were at the far end of the common, down a bumpy little track that terminated in a farmyard. Two functional, breeze-block enclosures for the hounds ran in parallel lines down either side of a pristine yard, and a white Victorian cottage crouched at the far end. One or two dogs bayed a welcome as I arrived, but most were sleepy and silent. I drove through the yard and parked right outside the house, where I would be able to see Archie, who was now asleep. But as I got out I realized it looked a bit arrogant, parking so close to the windows. I was about to go and move the car, when I saw Mark himself was sitting on the front doorstep watching me, so it was too late. One of the hounds was upside down between his legs, and he appeared to be doing something to its paw. I approached nervously as he regarded me, tweezers poised. The hound wriggled briefly, but was instantly limp and submissive after a curt word from Mark. I stood before him.

"I've come to apologize. My horse kicked Peddler and I panicked and didn't tell anyone. I meant to, really I did, but everything happened so quickly and I realized I'd committed the worst sin and I lost my bottle. I'm so ashamed and so sorry I killed your hound."

He continued his steady gaze, his dark eyes in his smooth brown face like two bright pieces of coal.

"You're Peter Mortimer's daughter, aren't you?" he said eventually in his slow, country brogue.

"That's right. D'you know Dad?"

"Everyone knows your dad. Where d'you think we get our horses from? That bay of yours could make a decent enough hunter, but he should have told you it kicks."

"Perhaps he didn't know."

"It's his job to know. I'll take it off the price of the next one I buy from him. I've told him as much. It's all right, he's already rung."

"Dad has?"

He nodded. Resumed his inspection of the paw, which I could see, close up, had a huge thorn in it. He removed it carefully with the tweezers and glanced back at me.

"I appreciate your coming, love. And your dad ringing. There's many that wouldn't."

"Oh." I felt a wave of a relief. A slight easing from the hook. "But you were very fond of him," I said anxiously. "Peddler. I was told he was your favorite."

"Doesn't do to have favorites. But he'd been with me the longest. Was the oldest and boldest, certainly. The most disobedient, too." He grinned, briefly revealing very yellow teeth.

"Oh, really?"

"Why d'you think he was on his own? Little bugger, sloping off like that, away from the pack. Couple of weeks ago, out cubbing, we was drawing your woods near Massingham, and we lost him. Eventually found him with some scruffy mongrel with a huge plastic collar, giving her a good seeing-to."

Blimey. Leila.

"He was an old rogue and make no mistake," he told me. "And no doubt he'd been somewhere else he shouldn't when he slunk back and your horse kicked him. Wouldn't surprise me if he died with a smile on his face. Perhaps that's why I liked him so much, the scoundrel." He got to his feet, releasing the hound who twisted himself the right way up and leaped instantly to put his paws on Mark's shoulders and lick his face frantically.

"Things die in the country, love," he said, pushing the hound down. "Badgers on the road, deer caught in wire. There's carrion and carnage wherever you look. Don't fret about it."

I sighed gratefully. Didn't speak, but felt lighter, less hunched.

"And as I say, I've told your dad I'll be having a discount next time." He was clearly very pleased with this. "And he wasn't snitching on you, neither. As a matter of fact I already knew it was you, and he knew I knew, which was why he rang."

I nodded, the Chinese whispers of the horsy world anathema to me; irrelevant, too, so long as all was well.

"Cup of tea?" he asked as he turned to go inside. I glanced back at the car. "He's asleep," he assured me, "and you'll see him from the window."

"Thanks." I followed him in, surprised and pleased. I only knew Mark Harrison by repute, but knew enough to know he didn't suffer fools, or even court much human company. And that he commanded huge respect. He was of indeterminate age, anywhere from a raddled thirty to a sprightly fifty, and a countryman like my dad; the type of man who, despite loving animals passionately, was no-nonsense and unsentimental about them—in my father's case reserving his sentimentality for other things. But if I'd been expecting a carbon copy of my father's living arrangements inside, I was surprised. Mark's house was as neat as a pin. No saddles, bridles and whisky bottles littered proceedings here, just an immaculate three-piece suite with plumped-up cushions, a well-vacuumed carpet, and a row of gleaming glasses on the sideboard. The only hint that this was a horsy household were the banks of framed photographs on one wall: hounds, horses, puppy shows—some accompanied by rosettes, and very occasionally, people.

As he disappeared to boil the kettle, I crossed the room to study them. Beautiful hunters with hounds at their feet, puppies with raised tails and keen eyes; Mark as a young man, looking almost exactly the same as he did now, those sharp bright eyes in the smooth face, the clothes and the quality of the print the only hint the snap was taken some time ago. Some of the smaller ones were black and white, presumably from his father's era: men in Harris tweeds and voluminous breeches. One photo, small and in color, albeit faded by the sun, caught my eye. It was of a group of young people in their late teens or early twenties: a very pretty girl in dark glasses, two young men, one on either side of her, one of whom was Mark, and one…

"Is that Sam Hetherington?" I pointed in surprise at the boy with long hair, in jeans and a T-shirt, as Mark came back with a couple of mugs. He handed one to me and followed my gaze.

"Day after his twenty-first birthday, aye. We'd tied one on the night before, make no mistake. Look at our eyes—like piss holes in the snow." He gave a quick bark of a laugh. "We had a lot of fun together, Sam and me." He sipped his tea thoughtfully. "His father was the master, just as Sam is now, and my dad the huntsman." He pointed to a black and white photo of two men in hunting coats, taken outside a manor house years ago. "This cottage was part of the Mulverton estate then. Not now, though." He smiled. "I bought it off him, didn't I? Sam was grateful, too, he's that strapped for cash. Death duties hit that family hard," he said grimly.

"Oh. I didn't know."

"That's why he went back to America, to make some dosh."

I held my breath. Somehow I felt if I was quiet, I might hear more. I was aware there was a lot I didn't know and wanted to. But Mark was a taciturn man, and eventually I had to prod.

"You knew him when you were little?"

"Oh yeah, Sam and I grew up together. Played every single day as kids, and then he went away to school. Boarding, you know. But we rode and drank in the pubs all holidays long when he was back, until he went to New York, that is. It was one of them relationships the liberal luvvies wouldn't understand; too feudal for them. They wouldn't get their anxious little brains round me being in hunt service and him being lord of the manor. But it worked. Still does. He's a good man, Sam. One of the best. Too bad his wife pissed off with that Chad Armitage."

I turned. Stared at him. "What?"

"I said too bad his wife did a runner with his best friend. There, that's her, see?" He jabbed a finger at a photo, and I turned back as if in a trance. He pointed out the pretty girl in the dark glasses. Very short hair, an elfin cut. Of course, it was Hope. Smiling coolly, confidently at the camera, two hungover lads beside her grinning sheepishly. Her chin was raised, her weight on the back foot. I turned back to Mark.

"Hope was Sam's wife?"

"Briefly, yes. They were all at Harvard together. Sam and Hope got married very young, not long after that photo was taken, in fact, then she fell for his best friend, Chad. He took that picture. Anyway, she divorced Sam and married him instead."

"But…" I was flabbergasted. Tried to marshal my thoughts. "But they're all such friends. They all live near each other, ride out together, hunt—"

"Oh, it all happened years ago. Chad and Hope have been together for ages now, got two kids, and Sam didn't want to lose Chad's friendship. When he was in the States, Chad's family was like his own. He stayed with them in the holidays—the Hamptons and all that. And he's a nice guy, Chad. But that Hope. She reels him in occasionally, you know?"

"Who—Sam?"

"That's it."

My mind raced. "But—why come back here, then? Why be near her?"

"Perhaps he needs to be." He gave me that steady look again. "The Armitages came over here first because of Chad's work. Bought a house in London, then a weekend cottage out here, because of course Hope knew the area from her days with Sam; it was only natural. Then Sam announces he's leaving London, too, dismisses the tenants, and takes over the reins at the Hall again, something he said he'd never do. Funny that."

"Because he can't bear to be away from her?" I breathed. "In another country?"

Mark shrugged. "Who knows? Not my business." He winked. "You learn a lot on the hunting field, though. Surprised your mate Angie hasn't told you all this, but then again, she probably doesn't know. She wasn't about in the old days, although she acts like she was born and bred in the saddle."

I licked my lips. "How long were they married for?"

"Only a couple of years."

"So…a bit like going out with someone, really?"

"Except he loved her enough to put a ring on her finger. Commit the rest of his life to her. And Sam's not a man to do anything lightly."

"No."

I returned my gaze to the photo again. God, poor Sam. That laughing, carefree young man, with his childhood friend, Mark, and his American girlfriend, who he'd brought home, soon to be his wife, looking about sixteen. Who he still loved? And who, as Mark had so eloquently put it, reeled him in occasionally. No wonder he'd looked haunted when her name was mentioned.

"Was it Sam who told you about Peddler?" I asked suddenly. He'd said Dad had rung to tell him, but that he already knew. "That it was my horse who kicked?"

"No, Emma Harding did."

"Emma Harding!"

"The one that was shacked up with your husband, love."

I caught my breath. Who was this Mark Harrison? This country-man in his isolated cottage with his hounds, who seemed to have no domestic life of his own, but knew everything about everyone?

"You knew my husband?"

"Couldn't miss him. They were down the road. Across that field over there, in the flint cottage." He jerked his head out of the window across the meadows, and I realized that, as the crow flew,

Emma's cottage, which I'd passed on the road, was surely not far. "I'd exercise my hounds in the summer past her back garden—how could I not know? Many an evening I'd go past with twelve couple and see him arrive at her back door on his bike, six o'clock, head to toe in blue nylon. Nothing subtle about his entrances."

Six o'clock. The children's bath time. Which Phil never made it home in time for. "It seems the whole world knew," I said, swallowing. "Except the wife, of course. Always the last."

"Ah, but you're well shot of him now, aren't you?" he said gently, with a small smile. "And he surely got his comeuppance."

"He did," I agreed, and couldn't help but smile back. I'd forgotten this man had a philosophical take on death.

"She said she saw you look guilty as sin when Peddler was mentioned, and that she knew your horse kicked. Couldn't come running across the field quick enough that evening to tell me, still in her hunting coat, she was. But when she bustled back to her own house, she got a nasty surprise herself. The police were on her doorstep."

"The police? Why?"

He shrugged. "Dunno. Thought you'd know, love. Apparently it's all over the village. Fraud of some sort. White collar. The kennel girl's brother is a cop down at the station and says it's something to do with business. Where she worked."

"Where she worked? You mean, at the bank?" I said, astonished.

He made a non-committal faced again. "No idea."

I sat down slowly on the sofa behind me, bewildered, dimly aware of a very plump cushion in my back. But even more aware of something else. The investigation into the bank by the FSA. I'd thought it purely routine. Had told Sam as much. Ted Barker had assured me so. Although…he'd been worried enough to write to me about it, I realized suddenly. To alert me. Something Ted said months ago, at a dinner party at his house in Esher, came winging back; something about how the female high-flyer in the office sailed close to the wind. He'd said it with a smile as he'd mixed me a gin and tonic, but I'd detected a worried tone. It hadn't meant much at the time. I'd never met the high-flyer. But they'd dropped her pretty smartly, hadn't they? The bank? The moment Phil had died? I was aware of Mark looking at me.

"She was dishonest," I whispered.

"That's what they say. And whatever it is she's done, I can believe it. She's a wrong 'un, that one. Anyway, she's in police custody now."

I stared up at him. "Emma Harding is in *custody*?" I said incredulously.

"I just said so, didn't I?"

"Yes, but…" I struggled with the concept. "She can't be in *custody*, not actually being *held*. She's a successful businesswoman!"

He shrugged. "Thieving's thieving, whoever you are."

"They took her in that night?"

"No, just questioned her. Came back for her this morning. Seven o'clock they was on her doorstep. If you don't believe me, love, ask Rob, the kennel boy. We was out back with the bitch pack, at the far end of the meadow. Watched as she answered the door in her dressing gown, then disappeared, white-faced, to get dressed. When she came back down the path to the police car she looked like she'd been shot."

"I bet she did."

"Her husband looked pretty grim, too. He was in the hall, behind her. Rob said if ever a man needed a drink it was him."

"Oh, God." I inhaled sharply. "Simon. He must be devastated!"

"I'd say so."

My mind whirred as I tried to assimilate all this. Emma Harding, arrested. "He's a good man, you know."

"Aye, but a foolish one. Not the first to fall for a pretty face, though, I'll grant you."

"He fell years ago," I muttered.

"I know he did. Thinks he's getting the same girl. And in a way he is. She was a bitch then and she's a bitch now."

I looked at him, surprised. "You knew her then?"

"I went to school with Emma Harding. The local village one, for all her airs and graces. She'd take the sweets from your desk and the rubbers from your pencil case. She was on the make then and she's still on it now."

We were silent a moment. I thought of her down at the police station. In a bare interrogation room, perhaps; a plainclothes officer questioning her, a solicitor beside her. Or perhaps parochial stations like ours didn't deal with fraud? Elsewhere, maybe. Somewhere distant. Was she frightened? No, defiant, I imagined. Ice cool. Head high, lips pursed. My heart began to beat. It certainly didn't bleed for her, though.

"Will he stand by her, d'you think?"

"Simon Devereux? No idea. But as you say, he's all right, so I imagine he might. Perhaps not the publicity he was looking for, though, eh?" He picked up the empty mugs and made for the kitchen. "MP's wife in police custody?"

"No. No, I'm sure it wasn't."

As I pulled out of the farmyard, my mind was churning. Emma Harding, the career woman, the one who rode to hounds, and who I now knew to have a painted face, a sharp manner, and a way with men, was in police custody. But why? What had she done? Taken a quick backhander? Made a bit on the side? Got greedy? Except...she was well off, doing well, why take the risk? I couldn't believe it was worth it. But perhaps she got her kicks from not getting caught? Like she did with my husband. He hadn't been worth it, either. I purred down the lane, hands gripping the wheel. And was that why she'd dropped her claim on Phil's will, I wondered suddenly. Because she knew she was about to be investigated? She wouldn't want to attract even more attention, would she? Oh no, she'd drop that like a hot potato.

Shaken, I turned onto the road that ran alongside the common. I paused briefly, engine running, outside the brick and flint cottage where Emma and my husband had shacked up for years. Where she'd cavorted with him under the eves in that bedroom, perhaps. I glanced up at the window. Sashayed downstairs in a dressing gown— silk, no doubt. And on occasion—when he'd come home from work and told me he wasn't hungry—had made him supper, wine glass in hand, humming along to a mellow CD, no fractious children to put to bed. The house where she'd not only cooked his supper, but his books, too. And from whence she'd finally been led away. In hand- cuffs? No, unlikely. Should have asked Mark. And I'd been married to a man who loved her. How bad a decision maker did that make me? Just as Sam had been married to a woman who went off with his best friend, I thought suddenly, which didn't make him much of a decision maker either. Safety in numbers, perhaps.

I drove on, my gaze fixed steadily on the road ahead; behind me, it seemed, was a shattered landscape. My past. Which I was finally taking leave of. No Radio Two broadcasting cheerily as usual; instead I hunched over my wheel, pensive. But I was moving on. I was pretty sure, for instance, that the pill I'd taken yesterday had been the last one. I'd felt it with a quiet certainty as I'd swallowed; had known there was nothing premature about it this time. And somehow, everything Mark Harrison had just told me confirmed it. There was a lot to digest, though; he'd divulged a great deal in the space of half an hour, and not just about Emma, about Sam, too. My brain was still filtering it, wondering where it left me, when my phone rang.

"Hello?" I whispered into my hands-free on the dashboard, not too loudly so as not to disturb Archie, who was still sleeping soundly in the back.

"Hi, Poppy, it's Luke."

"Oh—hi, Luke." For some reason I started guiltily.

"Why are you whispering?"

"Because Archie's asleep in the back. I'm in the car."

"Oh, OK, I'll whisper, too," he lowered his voice. I smiled, liking that. "Have you heard the news about Emma Harding?"

"I have, actually. Mark the huntsman told me. Apparently it's all over the village."

"Forget the village, it's all over the city!"

"Really?"

"The Internet is positively buzzing!" He sounded thrilled, but then weren't we all? "False accounting, they say. Plus a bit of fictitious trading thrown in for good measure, oh—and theft from a client's account, too. Well, why wouldn't you? Word is she was even brazen enough to take a few secret commissions on share deals while she was at it—un-bloody-believable! Massively risky, too. There's talk of her doing unauthorized trading in her own name. I mean, bugger me!"

"But how do they know all this?" I whispered, glancing at Archie in the mirror.

"They don't; it's pure speculation, pure swinging-dick talk. But there's never smoke without fire in the square mile, Poppy; some of it will be true, I promise you. And the thing is, once you've got away with something, you get bolder and go for the next trick, so it's all very plausible. I'll say this for her, she's got nerve. Particularly when you think she was sleeping with one of the partners."

"Quite," I said grimly. My partner. Did I detect a touch of awe in his voice?

"Anyway, she's been comprehensively caught with her fingers in the till now."

"She'd have had them snapped off if Phil had had anything to do with it. Knuckle by knuckle, probably." Or would she? I wondered how blind love would have been. Not as blind as that, I felt. Phil had been scrupulously honest where money was concerned.

"She's been taken to London for questioning by the Serious Fraud Squad; they've seized her files, her computer—the lot. They were in your old man's office at seven o'clock this morning, going through her old desk—a mate of mine works next door. These guys are so thorough, they'd X-ray your grandmother. Trust me, Poppy, her life will be trawled through like you wouldn't believe. It'll keep her thieving hands away from your inheritance, at any rate."

"Well, quite, although actually she'd already her dropped her claim."

"Oh, had she? I didn't know that."

Archie stirred behind me, eyelids flickering ominously.

"Listen, I'd better go, Luke," I whispered. "I need to get another half-hour out of Archie or he'll go grumpy on me."

"OK, my love," he said chirpily. "See you this evening. Can't wait."

"Me neither," I agreed as I clicked the phone off.

But I was pensive again as I replaced my hand on the wheel and narrowed my eyes to the hills that rose up beyond, framing my village. If it were possible, even more pensive than the last half-hour in Mark's cottage had rendered me. Because...had I told Luke about Phil's will? Or about Emma Harding's claim on it? Indeed, had I so much as mentioned my inheritance? I was almost certain I hadn't. In which case...what on earth did he know about all that?

Chapter Twenty-six

WHEN I GOT HOME, having collected Clemmie from nursery, Jennie was at her sitting-room window, arms folded, scanning the road, waiting for me.

"So that's wot I've decided," Clemmie was telling me firmly as I helped her out of the car.

"But Miss Hawkins isn't very happy about it, darling."

"I don't care. It's my life."

Blimey. "Where did you hear that?"

"Wot?"

"'It's my life'?"

"Peggy says it when she lights a cigarette."

"Oh. Right."

Jennie, meanwhile, had exited her house and bustled down the path in her long white apron to hover by my side. Horrors on her plate, her stepdaughter pregnant, news flashes coming in by the moment, she needed to share, but even in her highly fraught state she knew, too, that I had two tired and fractious children who needed to be bundled out of the car, got inside, and fed. She lifted Archie out of his car seat for me and we headed on in.

"So that is wot I'M DOING!" Clemmie shouted, stamping her feet for emphasis in her pink wellies as she ran to the front door and turned, glaring at me.

Jennie raised inquiring eyebrows.

"Clemmie's teacher's just told me Clemmie only works a three-day week," I muttered as we went up the path.

"Oh, how killing. Which ones?"

"Tuesday, Wednesday, Thursday. She has Monday and Friday off. Lays down her crayons and sometimes even takes a nap in the Wendy House. Likes a long weekend, apparently."

"Good for her."

"Well, I'm not sure Miss Hawkins sees it like that. She's keen to instill something of a work ethic."

Jennie made a face. "She's only four, Poppy. The work ethic can wait." She ruffled Clemmie's curls, and as I opened the door Clemmie ran off down to the kitchen, Archie toddling in her wake. I turned to my friend. Her eyes were shining, I noticed.

"Well? Any news?" I asked, aware I had quite a bit myself.

"Well, I texted her like you said," she told me breathlessly, following me down the hall, "and she said she'd meet me at break time so long as I didn't bring Dan."

"Oh! So you've seen her?"

"Yes, we went to Starbucks opposite the school."

"And?"

I was hastening round the kitchen now, taking sausages from the fridge, putting them under the grill, grabbing a tin of sweet corn. Jennie positioned herself against the sink.

"And…I'm convinced she's not pregnant."

I turned, tin opener poised. "Oh, thank God! She told you that?"

"No, she barely told me anything. Just sat there stirring her hot chocolate, glaring at me. But she was so angry, Poppy. And something told me her anger stemmed from being wrongly accused; it was a sort of self-righteous rage which could only come from a position of power. She said things like—" Jennie adopted a sneering expression—"So, you find a positive pregnancy test and instantly assume it's mine, eh, Jennie? Is that how your mind works? Wouldn't

that be neat? Confirm all your worst fears about me? Something to
tell your friends?"

"Oh! How hurtful."

"I know, horrid. But oh, Poppy, I was so pleased. I love her so
much, and I just don't want her to be pregnant. I don't care how
much she lashes out at me. I went to tell her that it was absolutely
her decision if she wanted to keep it and all that bollocks, like we
said—but ended up not saying any of it, didn't even embark on
the little speech I'd rehearsed. I just kept staring at her furious little
white face and thinking: wasn't it yours, Frankie? The test? Was it
really not yours?"

"Did you say that to her?"

"Of course I did, but she didn't answer. There's a certain satisfaction, I'd imagine, in my not knowing, from her point of view. She
just gave me that withering look of hers and said surely it was time
I marched down to the biology lab, grabbed Mr. Hennessy by the
lapels and slugged it out over the Bunsen burners?"

"Oh God, that's all my fault." I put a hand to my mouth. "I told
you that."

"Of course you did; you had to tell me what you knew. And I
told Dan, who blabbed last night. But you know, she was so scathing
that I thought—no. Not Hennessy. And then she suggested I lined
up all the boys in her class and questioned them one by one, and
I thought—no again. She's only sixteen, she thinks she's being so
clever, but I'm pretty sure I saw through her. I got the impression she
was paying me back big time for thinking the worst of her—please
God, that's the case." She pressed her hands together and shut her
eyes fervently, face lifted to the heavens.

"But then…who could it be? Who on earth could have used that
test? Not Mrs. Briggs, that's for sure."

"Not unless she's been at the radiance pills." Mrs. Briggs helped
Jennie with the ironing and was a good sixty-five. Jennie plucked a

bit of sweet corn between forefinger and thumb from the pan and popped it in her mouth, much brighter now.

"So who's been in your house recently, then? Apart from family?"

"No one very much. Don't you think I've already wracked my brains? That bin gets emptied only once a week, slut that I am, and I've been through everyone I can possibly think of who might have been upstairs. You're obviously in and out—"

I snorted. "Chance would be a fine thing."

"Well, quite, and Angie and Peggy—"

I turned. Raised quizzical eyebrows.

"Oh, don't be silly, Poppy. Peggy's far too old."

"No, but you've got to ask them, consider them," I told her. "I know it's far-fetched, but if they've been in the house they're in the frame, so to speak, and you've got to eliminate them from your inquiries. Even if it wasn't them, they might know something about it. Oh, and speaking of eliminating from inquiries, I must just quickly tell you—" And so I did. About Emma Harding. Sketchily, because I knew she had other things on her mind, but Jennie's load had been considerably lightened in the last half-hour. Her internal swing-o-meter had lurched in a positive direction and, rightly or wrongly, the conviction that her stepdaughter was not indeed pregnant had firmly taken root; she was much more receptive to the outside world and, as such, suitably enthralled. When I got to the end, she whistled.

"Well. She certainly got her comeuppance, didn't she? Got her thieving little fingers rapped. Shall we do a spot of prison visiting? Take her a photo of Phil?"

"I'd rather not," I said hastily.

"She could, though, couldn't she?"

"Go to prison? I've no idea."

"She bloody should," Jennie said with feeling. "Or at least community service. God, I'd love to see her sweeping the streets in a fluorescent yellow jacket. She probably thought she was invincible.

People do, you know, when they've got away with something for ages, whether it's nicking people's husbands or nicking money— probably thought she'd never get caught." Her face fell suddenly. "Oh. Poor Simon."

"I know."

She picked up a wooden spoon and stirred the yellow corn, reflective. "Funny. A couple of months ago he was all I could think about. Every waking moment. I used to drive past his house at night, take Leila to his bit of the common for a walk, Google him constantly—I could practically recite his website. I had the most almighty crush, Poppy. But now, especially with all this Frankie business, I look back in wonder. Think: who was that woman checking her phone for texts every five minutes, going dog-walking in full slap in case she should bump into him, who was she? I don't recognize her at all. And after what you've told me I certainly don't think: oh, good, he might be free again."

"Don't you?" I was intrigued. "Not even a bit?"

She regarded me, astonished. "Not even a tiny bit. Not for one fraction of a second. Honest to God, Poppy, I'm embarrassed by her. Constantly licking lipstick off her teeth, buying new bras and pretending it was time to ditch the old M&S ones—I was in danger of making a fool of myself. And I'm genuinely sad for Simon. Wish his life wasn't like it is right now. But in the long run, he's better off without her. Perhaps it's as well it happened now?"

"You mean, rather than further down the line with children." Like me, I thought.

"Exactly." She sighed, and we were silent a moment, Jennie watching opaquely as I shared out the sausages between two plates, spooned the veg. Suddenly she came to. "Anyway, I've got other things to worry about without wondering if Simon will be waiting at the prison gates for her. Here, darling." She seized the ketchup bottle and shook some out for Clemmie, who, hungry and fit to combust, was climbing into her chair. "Yes, I've got other fish to fry," Jennie said with a sudden grin. "I'm off to inquire of my hardly-spring-chicken friends whether, when they popped in for coffee the other day, either of them also popped upstairs to use a pregnancy test that was sitting in the bathroom cabinet." She snorted with derision. "As if."

I shrugged. "I agree, it's a long shot." I frowned as I helped Archie into his highchair and sat beside him. "Sitting in your cabinet?"

"What?"

"The test?"

"Oh. Yes, it was mine. You get two in a pack these days and I'd used the other one ages ago when I'd had a nasty shock and was late. Why?"

"I dunno. I just didn't know that."

She made to leave and it occurred to me, as I blew on the bit of sausage I'd speared for Archie, that I hadn't told her about Sam. Being married to Hope. Well, there'd been so much else to divulge. But I could have slipped it in, couldn't I? She'd have been intrigued. Why hadn't I? I wondered if I was being protective. After all, Sam hadn't broadcast it around the village—nor had Hope for that matter, although perhaps for more obvious reasons—so neither would I. But neither had I told her something else that was bothering me. About Luke.

Archie gave an impatient squawk, mouth wide, and I hurriedly shoveled in the sausage.

Coincidentally I ran into both of my friends later on. First Peggy, as the children and I sat on the bench by the pond feeding the ducks, and she passed on her way to the shop. She was looking pleased as punch and rather exotic, too, a purple beaded velvet coat over her jeans and pixie boots, dangly silver earrings swinging.

"I say, guess what, darling," she drawled, perching beside me on the bench and lighting a cigarette. She crossed her skinny legs. "Jennie came to ask me if I was preggers. Do admit." She flashed amused, sparkling eyes and puffed hard. "Wish I'd said yes. Wish I'd said: yes, and the father of my unborn child is Charles Dance and we're going to keep it. Charles and I are thrilled. We just popped into your house to do the test—he kept KV downstairs—and when I shrieked down the good news, he ran up two at a time and we couldn't resist nipping into your bedroom for another frenzied bout of love-making to celebrate. Had the most spine-shattering sex in your bed, hope you don't mind?"

I giggled as she rolled her eyes expressively.

"What planet is she on?" she said incredulously.

"She's just being thorough, Peggy. It was my idea, anyway, to ask whoever had been in the house. She thought it was Frankie's."

"Course it's not Frankie's; what teenage girl would do a preggy test and drop it in her mother's waste-paper basket? Even if it is wrapped in loo paper? Do me a favor."

"I suppose not," I said, feeling rather stupid. And guilty, too. I'd been quick to point the finger. Poor Frankie.

"Anyway, I'm thrilled to bits she thought it was me. That's really put a spring in my step. Thank goodness the book club's up and running again. You missed the last one, of course; it was quite a laugh. Although I have to say, Angus abandoning ship in a vest and braces did precisely nothing for me." She shuddered. "Perhaps we'll drop the theme element," she mused. "Why is it the thought of these men is always so much nicer than the reality?" She narrowed her eyes into the distance and inhaled pensively on her Marlboro Light. Clemmie was staring up at her, intrigued.

"How many do you smoke a day, Peggy?" she asked.

"As many as possible, darling," Peggy replied, smiling down. She took a bit of bread from Clemmie's bag and tossed it to a duck.

"I say, what about adding a bit of new blood?" she said abruptly.

"To the book club? There's a rather attractive widower just moved into the rectory in the next village and I saw him browsing in Waterstones the other day. D'you think he might be up for a bit of Jodi Picault of a Tuesday?"

"I've no idea. You're still going ahead with it, then, are you? Without the Armitages?" I said nervously.

"Well, they can come if they like, but they need to know we won't be reading Chekhov," Peggy said archly. Suddenly she stiffened, her face alert. "Ten to ten," she hissed.

I frowned. "For the book club? Isn't that rather late?"

"No, attractive widower, ten to ten." Peggy's late husband had been in the Royal Air Force. "Covert, Poppy, covert," she muttered as I turned to stare at a rather donnish-looking gent in a worn corduroy jacket, who'd come into view down the hill, a Jack Russell on a lead trotting beside him. They made for the shop. "With his dog again," Peggy observed, as he tied the terrier up outside, "which he'll take back via the woods for a run. See you later, Poppy." She stubbed out her cigarette in the little ashtray she kept in her bag and snapped it shut. Her mouth twitched. "I'm off to borrow Leila." And with that she sauntered across the road in the direction of Jennie's house, velvet coat floating behind her.

Angie, however, wasn't so thrilled when she banged on my door that evening. I'd been taking things at something of a canter, keen as I was to get the children bathed and into bed, thereby giving myself plenty of time to sink into my own bath and prepare for my date tonight. My date. My heart lurched and fingers fluttered as I cut up the soldiers for the boiled eggs, but not in the right way, I realized. Not in a pitter-patter nervous-excitement way, in more of a...well, plain nervous way, actually. But perhaps that was normal? After all, it was years since I'd been out with anyone, and I had rather set the tone for this one by kissing Luke firmly on the lips and telling him I'd be happy to come to his place. Had rather shown my hand. Still. That didn't necessarily mean tonight had to be anything other than a very pleasant meal, did it? Of course not. And Luke was a nice guy; there was no way he'd be expecting anything else, surely? I recalled Luke's eyes, bright with possibility at what he'd perceived to be very much the green light from me, and promptly dropped Archie's egg cup. As I picked up the shattered pieces of china, I decided I needed to calm down. I also decided that I wouldn't drink too much, but that I would, after all, shave my legs.

Which was why it was not terribly convenient when Angie banged on my door at about seven o'clock. So hard I jumped out of the bath and ran downstairs to answer it with wet hair and bleach cream on my upper lip.

"Clearly you both think I'm a complete tart!" she stormed, pushing past me in the doorway, not even commenting on my moustache, and making for the kitchen.

She opened the fridge door and seized a bottle of white wine, although she'd patently had most of one already; her eyes were pink and glassy, always Angie's giveaway. I hastened after her in my dressing gown, wiping off the bleach as I went, knowing instantly what she meant.

"No, of *course* we don't, Angie," I urged, thinking this really couldn't be more inconvenient as she hunted down a couple of glasses in my cupboard and poured two hefty slugs of Chardonnay.

"You obviously think that just because I had a teensy crush on Pete, I'm hopping into bed with all and sundry and getting knocked up in the process. Flinging pregnancy tests over my shoulder as I go!"

Oh, Lord. Furious. Livid, in fact. All my fault. "No one's saying that, Angie. It's just that for Frankie's sake we thought—"

"I mean, who did you think it was, hm?" Her eyes blazed at me as she sank a good two inches of wine in one gulp. "Bonkers Bob, perhaps? Did you think I'd wrestled him out of his raincoat and got down to it in his revolting farmhouse? Or maybe his sidekick, Frank? Perhaps you thought I couldn't resist the twirling moustache and had a burning desire to see him naked but for his dandruff?"

"Don't be silly. It's just we had to discount anyone who'd been in Jennie's house, that's all. And who was young enough"—I added toadily, hoping she didn't know Peggy had also been accused—"to, you know, get pregnant."

This mollified her slightly. She pulled out a chair at my table and slumped into it, looking alarmingly permanent. "Hm, well," she grunted, knocking back another hefty slug and refilling her glass. "Yes, of course I could still get pregnant, I'm not that ancient. But I'm not seeing anyone, you know."

She looked more shattered than angry now. Her face soft and vulnerable beneath her make-up.

"I know, I know," I said soothingly, sitting down beside her.

"It's not even as if I'm dating."

"Well, quite. Stupid of us."

"And anyway, I still love Tom."

I didn't say anything; sat very still. This was quite an admission. Usually she hated Tom. She seemed unaware of me, though. Stared into space.

"You know he's on his own again?" she said at length, more to the wall than to me.

"No, I didn't know that. Since when?"

"Since Tatiana went back to New Zealand. Wants to pursue her dangerous sports, apparently. As if nicking my husband wasn't enough of one."

"So…is there hope?"

"That's exactly what I wondered," she said sadly, "when Clarissa told me. Said Daddy was on his own. I thought: perhaps there's hope? And then I ran into Bella Stewart, who'd sat next to him at a dinner party last week, and in his cups he'd told her he'd been a stupid arse. So, silly tart that I am, d'you know what I did?"

"What," I said, guessing.

"I rang him. And left a message on his answering machine which I hadn't thought out beforehand. A long, breathless one about how maybe we could be civilized for the children and maybe he could pop round for supper sometime. And then right at the end—" she gulped and her eyes filled—"I—said I missed him."

I reached out. Covered her hand with mine and squeezed it. "That's not so terrible, Angie."

She glanced down, and a tear escaped. Fled down her face and dropped on her lap. She wiped it away savagely. "Except that that was two days ago and I haven't heard a dicky bird since. And no, he's not away. Clarissa said she spoke to him at the cottage yesterday. You see, I just thought—if he came for supper, in the lovely home we'd created together over the years, he wouldn't be able to resist it—me. And of course the girls go and meet him so I don't have that. If they were younger he'd have to pick them up from home. Realize what he'd given up. I could be on the doorstep looking radiant, dressed up, a spot of scent. Roses on the hall table."

"Yes, yes, I see," I said gently.

She swallowed. Attempted a brave smile but it wobbled. "You know, it's insulting enough to be left for another woman, Poppy, but to be left for no one, for a vacuum to be preferable…" She fell silent. Ran a fingertip around the rim of her wine glass. Round and round it went.

"I can't stop making a fool of myself," she whispered.

"That's not true."

"It is. It is true. Pete. Tom." She paused. "I made a fool of myself with Sam Hetherington, too," she said quietly. "After the hunt. Not that I care now."

"Did you?" I felt all my sinews stiffen.

"We all went back to his place for tea. It's a bit of a tradition at the end of a day's hunting, for anyone left in the saddle to wind up where you started, where the meet was, except it's hardly tea. Bottles of whisky come out and everyone drinks jolly hard, I can tell you. Well, as you know, I'd already had a few pre-match tinctures at the meet, so by about six o'clock I was flying. Particularly since I had to wait until everyone had gone before I could—you know." She fell silent.

"Proposition him?" I prompted breathlessly, unable to resist.

"Oh, I didn't jump him or anything," she said hastily. "Just asked him if he was taking anyone to the hunt ball on Saturday, and if not, since we both seemed to be on our tod, whether we shouldn't team up together. In the nicest possible way, of course."

"Of course." I was rapt. "And?"

"He sort of laughed and said he wasn't sure what his plans were. So I persisted. Will I ever learn? I said, 'Come on, Prince Charming, how about taking Cinders to the ball?' Even plucked a rose from a vase and put it between my teeth, perched coquettishly on his kitchen table in my jodhpurs. I was well and truly smashed, obviously."

"Obviously." I was trying hard to hide my agogness.

"And he was terribly charming. Removed the rose and escorted me to my horse box where Libby, my groom, was waiting to drive me home. Said he was really sorry, but since he was hosting the thing, he thought he'd be pretty busy. It was only when I threw my arms round his neck—all in front of Libby, incidentally, who didn't know where to look—that he disentangled me and told me there was someone he couldn't get over. That he wasn't quite ready for "teaming up" with anyone. His ex, I suppose."

"Yes. I suppose." Suddenly I felt the need to hide my face. I got to my feet and went to the sink, busying myself on a spurious errand of hanging out a dishcloth, hoping she'd go. I wanted my heart to sink alone, not in company. Angie didn't seem inclined to move, though.

She sighed. "So there we have it." She gave an ironic little laugh. "Two unattached men, one of whom I have children by, both of whom would rather be alone than with me. Marvelous, isn't it? And d'you know, Poppy, at my age, and at my stage in life, I really didn't think I'd be worrying about this sort of thing. Thought I'd be planning little dinner parties, titivating the garden. Didn't think I'd be working the singles market. There's Clarissa at school with boyfriend trouble, crying down the phone about some boy she likes who's gone off with a friend of hers, and I'm too busy with my own disastrous love life to even sympathize. Too busy being rebuffed myself. Pitiful, isn't it?"

This didn't seem to demand an answer. But it occurred to me that I, too, had been rebuffed by Sam, when I'd invited him to the book club. Charmingly brushed aside. So charmingly I might even have been in danger of not noticing: of repeating the error, going back for more, if the hunt had gone otherwise. If, say, Thumper had behaved perfectly, might I not have found myself back at Sam's place with Angie for tea, outstaying all the other riders, elbowing her out of the way over the whisky bottle, nicking the rose from her teeth, asking him to accompany *me*, not her, to the hunt ball, while she staggered to the loo to reapply her lippy? One of two very pissed and very desperate women? I shuddered. Glanced furtively at the clock. Thank God I had a date tonight. A proper one. If only I was allowed to go on the bloody thing. I had a feeling it might not be tactful to mention it under the circumstances, but the fact remained that Luke was probably even now laying the table and polishing the glasses. Meanwhile my fringe was curling horribly, and in precisely ten minutes Peggy would be here, and I wasn't even dressed. The laundry basket was under the table and I riffled in it. Grabbed some pants and pulled them on surreptitiously under my dressing gown.

Angie narrowed her eyes, suspicious. "Where are you going?"

"Nowhere, why?"

"You've just put frilly pants on."

"Oh. I'm...just having supper with Luke, that's all."

"Ooh," she said archly, and I had a nasty feeling the combination of baring her soul and a bottle of wine might drive her to lash out.

I braced myself, but we do, after all, choose our friends wisely, and Angie had a kind heart. Her face softened.

"Good. I'm really pleased. He's a sweet boy."

I relaxed, although rather wished she hadn't added the last bit.

"Excellent. Well, I'm glad you approve," I said, rallying. Wishing, too, for just a spot of privacy, for not living in a village where everyone knew my business. "And now if you wouldn't mind buggering off, Angie," I said pleasantly, "perhaps I could get dressed as well? Not just leave it at knickers?"

She raised a smile and got to her feet, swinging her Chanel bag over her shoulder, simultaneously draining her glass.

"Where's he taking you?"

"He's, um...cooking me supper."

Her eyes came round from her empty glass, wide and delighted. "Is he now? Ooh, Poppy, how exciting! No wonder you've got your frillies on. Are you sure you'll need them at all?" She threw back her head and cackled loudly.

I regarded her narrowly. "Thanks for that, Angie."

"My pleasure," she grinned, clearly enjoying herself now, morale somewhat restored. "Well, I hope it goes well. You're so suited to each other, everyone says so. You should have got it together from the word go, which is exactly what I told him after I found him in the garden with Saintly Sue, that night at the book club."

"Did you," I muttered. How pissed was she? Did she have to bring that up? "What else did you tell him?" I asked as I hustled her toward the front door. Damn. I could hear Archie crying upstairs. I'd have to give him a bottle, and Peggy would be here to sit soon. I hadn't even dried my hair.

"Oh, nothing else," she twinkled merrily, jingling her car keys—Angie lived five minutes' walk away but always drove. "Although he was so sweetly concerned about how you were going to manage on your own as an impoverished widow, et cetera, that I did set his mind at rest on that score. Toodle-oo, Poppy! Have a lovely evening."

And with that she sashayed out of the front door, hips swaying, and down the path to her car.

Chapter Twenty-seven

I STARED AT THE door as it shut behind her. Remained motionless a moment, engrossed, it seemed, in the paintwork. Then I went
into the sitting room, crossing to the window to watch as her car
drew away from the curb, headlights going on against the heavily
gathering darkness, faint drizzle sparkling in their beam. Across the
road the Fishes' light went on, too, briefly illuminating their front
room, before their curtain swished shut. Archie was still crying, his
wails gaining momentum upstairs, but I seemed transfixed by the
spot Angie's car had just vacated in the road. Eventually I turned
and went mechanically to the fridge for a bottle of milk; warmed it
in the microwave. Well, it had probably been a slip of the tongue.
And taken out of context, too. I didn't know the full extent of the
conversation. I'd give her a ring in a moment, when I'd given Archie
his bottle. When she'd had time to get home and put the car away. I
could hear her voice on the phone now: "Oh *no*, Poppy, he was just
genuinely concerned about *you*, about how you were going to cope,
that's all! After all, he is in finance and he probably wondered if you
needed advice." Yes, that would be it. When Archie's eyes closed I
lay him down; went back downstairs to the kitchen and rang Angie's
land line. But as it rang and rang, and just as I was about to try her
mobile, a funny thing happened. Suddenly I wasn't sure I wanted
her reassurances, didn't want to hear her falling over herself to assure
me that I'd taken it the wrong way. I didn't want any damage limita-
tion, because, it occurred to me, I didn't particularly want a reason

to believe. Would be very happy without one. In fact it seemed to me it might even be a relief. It was quite an epiphany.

I quietly replaced the receiver. The phone sat on the dresser, which was antique pine and rather old hat in these days of space-age designer kitchens, but I still liked it. Still liked the blue and white Asiatic Pheasant plates that ranged across it, a collection I'd made over the years, piece by piece. What I didn't like, I realized, was the toby jug that sat in the middle of the top shelf. Phil had bought it on a trip to Yorkshire years ago: an ugly old man, his belly the swell of the jug. He'd placed it there, in pole position, and since everything else on the dresser had been chosen by me, I hadn't had the heart to protest; so it had stayed. It had been there so long I'd almost forgotten it was there, or that I disliked it. Which was how things took root, wasn't it? Accommodated out of a sense of duty, one then becomes accustomed to them, and thus a permanence is achieved. I reached up for the jug, took it to the kitchen bin and dropped it in. The bin was empty, so it smashed, rather satisfyingly, on the bottom. Then I went back to the dresser and picked up the phone.

He'd have gone to some trouble, I knew: buying ingredients, concocting something really rather delicious, poring over cookery books—perhaps casting around for advice, ringing his sister even. Still, it couldn't be helped. And better now than later. Because later, who's to say I'd have the nerve? Who's to say I wouldn't paper over this crack, as I'd papered over many others in my time? Have it explained away as a nothing, when I knew, in my heart, it was a something?

He answered breezily; a little harassed, perhaps, not relishing the phone ringing in the middle of his culinary devotions.

"Hello?"

The walls of my throat had closed up a little. "Hi, Luke, it's Poppy."

"Poppy, hi! You just caught me shelling the prawns. To tell you the truth I had no idea they came with their coats on; had to consult Delia on how to disrobe them. Slippery little devils, aren't they?"

"Yes, I suppose. Although, actually, you can buy them already shelled. Um, Luke, I'm terribly sorry, but I'm not going to be able to make it tonight."

There was a silence. When his voice came, he sounded crestfallen. "Oh no, what a shame. Why not?"

"I'm afraid I'm not feeling too good."

"Really? Oh dear, what's wrong?" He was doing his best to hide his disappointment and sound concerned, but his voice had an edge to it.

"I'm not sure. Sorry, Luke."

My brevity wrong-footed him. There was a silence. Then he rallied. "Oh well, never mind. I expect I can freeze it. Sure you won't change your mind?"

"Quite sure, thanks." I realized I needed to get off the phone now. Before I said something I regretted. I realized I was furious.

"Let's get together soon, eh? I'll ring you when you're feeling better."

"I'm sure I'll see you around."

Luke wasn't stupid. Far from it. Very astute, in fact, and he recognized the finality in that. Recognized, too, that I wasn't even inventing a malaise—complaining of a tummy upset, a headache, saying a child was ill—and I wondered, for a brief moment, if he knew the real reason I was canceling. No. How could he? But as we said good-bye, he did sound slightly shaken.

I, however, felt completely bloody marvelous. I was fizzing with fury but, boy, it felt terrific. I bustled around my kitchen like a whirling dervish, sweeping toys from the floor in armfuls, rescuing a Lego man from the vegetable basket, flinging yesterday's paper in the recycling bin, wiping down surfaces, getting behind things I'd never got behind before. Then I seized the mop and gave my terracotta tiles the sloshing of their life. And once the superficiality had been achieved, I went for the profound. Thus Peggy found me, five minutes later, on my hands and knees, giving my Aga a jolly good seeing-to, wiping down the front of it for all I was worth: Jil in one hand, a new and very brutal Brillo Pad in the other.

"Oh, hi, Peggy." I sat back on my heels. Gave her a dazzling smile.

"Oh—I thought I was late," she said breathlessly, coming in on a blast of cold air in her mauve velvet coat. She shut the back door behind her. "How come you're not dressed?"

"I'm not going," I told her, opening the door of the cooler oven and disappearing with a wire brush. "Decided against it."

"Right," she said faintly. She was still out of breath and took a moment to watch me, bewildered. "Any particular reason?"

"My oven needs cleaning," I told her, brushing furiously.

"Oh."

After a second I sensed her sitting down at the table behind me. Heard the click of a lighter. Smelled smoke.

"And that's reasonably crucial, is it? On a Friday night? A clean oven?"

"Reasonably."

"Nothing else detaining you?"

I sat back again. Turned. "Oh well, since you ask, there's also the very real prospect that Angie told Luke that Phil had left me a lot of money. I have an idea he wasn't that interested in me per se, but rather in my inheritance. In fact I believe he was initially keen on Saintly Sue, but changed his tune when he heard I was an heiress. Or as good as it gets in these parts. The Jackie Onassis of the Chilterns," I snorted. "I've put him off. I'm not going, Peggy. I can't afford to make another mistake, you see."

I felt her thoughtful presence behind me as I resumed my scrubbing. She didn't gainsay what I'd just told her, didn't rush to pour scorn: for Peggy was a proper person. A grown-up. I went for the really caked-on bits on the oven floor, which ordinarily I didn't attempt, just left to carbonize or whatever they eventually did. I'd pull the fridge out in a moment, I decided, clean behind it, which I hadn't done for months. Years, even. Defrost the freezer. Oh yes, it was the day of reckoning.

After a moment, Peggy spoke.

"Perhaps Angie thought by giving him a little nudge, it would help you both on your way? You know what she's like. Very well meaning, if a little misguided. I do know she told him you were gorgeous, and he made a face and said, 'Two kids.' Maybe that's when she mentioned the money."

I crouched back on my heels. Stared into the stainless-steel cavern. I knew Peggy was deliberately enlightening me. Giving it to me straight. Not allowing me to be under any illusions. I could visualize the sort of face he would have pulled, too. A couple weeks ago, I realized, this might have brought tears of self-pity to my eyes; might have had me reaching for some pills. It was nice to know I was better. Nevertheless, I kept my eyes firmly on the pilot light at the back. After a bit, I turned.

"Something wasn't right, Peggy. The rather abrupt change of gear. I was supposed to trek to London to meet him for lunch, then all at once he changed it to dinner at the King's Head. I thought: why so ritzy? And at my convenience? I had the feeling there was something strategic about the whole thing. And he was great fun and everything, we had a laugh, but when we got onto the subject of him starting his own business, he suddenly clammed up. Changed the subject when I asked about capital. He kept complimenting me, too, really randomly, like he was ticking boxes. I couldn't work out why, from being rather blasé, he'd suddenly got so terribly keen. I should have smelled a rat. Knocked it on the head much earlier." I regarded her squarely. "Why do I attract them, Peggy? Rats? Is there something wrong with me? Why do I pick men like Phil and Luke? Or are they not rats at all? Is that actually what men are like? Is there, in fact, nothing wrong with Phil having a mistress for years as long as no one finds out and no one gets hurt, or with Luke cozying up to me because I might be just what he needs to start a new business? Is that the way of the world? Am I being difficult? You said earlier the thought of these men is always much nicer than the reality. D'you really believe that's true?"

Peggy tipped ash into the palm of her hand, considering. "No, I don't," she said carefully. "I was being flippant. And neither are you being difficult. The fact is you picked a couple of duds."

"Or they picked me. Saw me coming. Thought: ah yes, Poppy, she'll do. She's malleable, biddable—rich even, now. If only I were lovable."

"Poppy," she admonished gently.

I grinned. "Don't worry, I'm in no danger of breaking down about it. Luckily I'm livid and, actually, very calm. I shall never marry again, Peggy, never." I said it dispassionately. Knew it to be true. I got to my feet and I threw my Brillo Pad in the sink. Then I turned back to her. "Why is it I'm surrounded by lovely women, fabulous girlfriends, have never had such terrific luck in that department, but never, ever with a man? Why is that, Peggy?"

"Because you're not looking in the right places," she said briskly. She poured herself a glass of wine from the bottle Angie had left on the table, and one for me, too. I sat down beside her and gratefully took the glass she offered. "You go around looking in bargain basements and then you panic-buy. You riffled around in the sales and found Phil, and then when he'd gone, you went as far as the church across the road, found a thirty-five-year-old organist with a failing business lurking in the shadows and thought: he'll do. Literally the first single man you met. And why is he single? At thirty-five? Why isn't he married?"

"I don't know."

"You let all your friends tell you he's perfect because they want you packaged off and happy, and you don't stop to wonder if *you* think he's perfect. You wouldn't buy a new winter coat like that, Poppy; why on earth a man? The trouble is, you aim too low. You've no confidence. And if you aim low, you get low. You get a loser. And you are more than worthy of a winner. There are plenty of them out there too. I should know, I married one."

"Roger."

She didn't talk about him much. Barely at all, so I never did, either. Angie probed occasionally, but got nowhere. But she did once say that the fifteen years she'd been married to him had been the happiest of her life. He'd died of testicular cancer at forty-five; no children.

"Yes, Roger. And because of him, because he was such a find—" Her eyes shone suddenly. "Oh, Poppy, if only you'd met him. Such fun. So alive. And such a safe pair of hands, too. Because of him, I won't marry again. No one will ever match up. Oh, I know I play it for laughs and flirt with all the eligible old bachelors, but that's all it is. A laugh. I haven't been with another man since Roger died."

I tried to hide my surprise. He'd been dead a long time.

"But you'll meet someone," she urged. "You're young, you may even marry again, but, Poppy, never, ever settle for anything less than perfect." She eyed me steadily over the rim of her glass. "A good marriage is the best thing in the world, but a bad one is the very worst. If a racing certainty doesn't come along—and it might not—stick to your own company." She smiled. Touched my glass with hers. "We'll be merry widows together. Deal?"

I smiled. "Deal." I felt my anger subside and something like relief flood through my veins. To be like Peggy. To end up like Peggy, who I'd always admired, would not be so bad. Would be pretty terrific, actually.

"And there are some nice men out there," she mused. "Jennie's Dan, for instance, albeit in short pants."

"Yes, Dan's lovely," I agreed.

"Angie's Tom, too."

We regarded each other guiltily. We both liked Tom, even though he had behaved very badly. But then, Angie probably wasn't the easiest woman to live with. There were two sides to that story, as there often are.

"Did I tell you I saw him the other day?" she said casually.

"No, you didn't. Where?"

"I ran into him in town. Had a drink with him."

"Really?" I was intrigued. "Does Angie know?"

"No, she doesn't, and don't tell her." She sipped her wine. "Apparently she rang him."

"Yes, she did, and he didn't return her call. She's devastated."

Peggy didn't say anything for a moment, then: "Angie's either devastated or thrilled to bits. Cast down or euphoric. Never anything in between. That can be quite exhausting. Tom knows he behaved like an arse but sometimes…" she hesitated. "Well, sometimes we all need some space. Just to get things into perspective."

I snorted with derision. "Space. That sounds horribly like psycho-twaddle to me, like some garbage some counselor's told him. And I wouldn't call a middle-aged man running off with a twenty-six-year-old groom and leaving his wife and children perspective. Last drop?"

"Why not," she said, looking at me with interest as I poured. Normally I agreed with most things she said. Was easily persuaded. But my nerve endings were still quite exposed from the last ten minutes, and much as I liked charming, good-looking Tom and had had some riotous evenings in his company, I wasn't prepared to make too many excuses for him.

"Are you going to that?" Peggy asked, changing the subject. She nodded across at the dresser where, among the blue and white plates, I propped the occasional invitation. I followed her eyes to a stiff white card embossed with an elaborate italic script.

"Oh. No, I doubt it."

It was a ticket to the hunt ball, which had been dropped through my door. By Mark, I assumed. "Compliments of the hunt" had been scrawled on a slip of paper inside the envelope. But then, I had made quite a large donation to the hunt. A handsome check, which I'd popped through his door earlier. And Mark had rung me, overwhelmed.

"We can refurbish the kennels, Poppy, keep all the staff. I was going to have to let the kennel girl go. It's so generous. I don't know what to say."

"Don't say anything."

And then the ticket had arrived pronto, by hand through my door. And, actually, my plan had been to ask Luke, tonight. See if he'd come with me. Waltz in with my new boyfriend. But that would have sealed the deal, wouldn't it? And my fate along with it. Knowing myself as I did, it would have been hard to stop that stone rolling into a relationship.

"In fact not, I'm definitely not," I said with some relief, and only a little regret at the thought of the glittering occasion I knew I would be missing. It was being held at Mulverton Hall, Sam's place. Even more reason to waltz in with Luke, a bit of me had thought. I realized I'd felt ridiculously betrayed on discovering he'd been married to Hope. Had wanted to trump him. Why was that? And naturally everyone in the area was keen to go to the ball this year, being held as it was, not in the usual soggy marquee in a field at the kennels with a sticky dance floor and overflowing portaloos, but at the local manor, which no one had been inside for years. Oh yes, even the most fervent anti-blood-sport types would be there: never underestimate the snoop factor. There was talk of a vast black and white hall with a gallery and sweeping staircase—Mrs. Briggs knew someone who cleaned—and there Sam would be, at the foot of it, handsome in black tie, with Chad and Hope, too. The three of them in an eternal triangle. I wondered how much Hope enjoyed that. Sam shooting her haunted looks? No, that was uncharitable. I didn't know the woman. It probably tore her apart. Not as much as it did Sam, though. I gave myself a little inward shake. Other people's lives. Get on with your own, Poppy.

"I take it you're not going, either?" I asked Peggy, wrapping my dressing gown firmly round my legs. It wasn't really her thing. Peggy had an aversion to establishment socials, preferring instead her usual corner at the Rose and Crown, where she played backgammon with her cronies.

"Yes, I thought I would, actually. Tom was sent a double ticket. I might go with him."

I was astonished. "Really? Golly. Square it with Angie first, don't you think?"

"No, I didn't think I would," she said calmly, draining her glass. "Tom quite wants the surprise element."

"Right," I said, boggling. Quite bold of Tom to show his face, and even more bold of Peggy to accompany him. "That's very much Angie's fiefdom," I told her nervously. "She'll be queen bee, top table."

Peggy shrugged. "As Tom was for years. And all his friends will be there, and he hasn't seen them for ages. His girls will be going, too, don't forget. They'd love to see him. I've talked to Clarissa about it."

"Have you? Isn't she away at school?"

"Yes, but I've got her mobile number. She thinks it's a good idea." She gave me a steady, impenetrable look I couldn't fathom. "Anyway, we'll see. Haven't decided yet. Night, Poppy." She got briskly to her feet and blew me a kiss. Peggy didn't do embraces. Didn't go in for much bodily contact at all, come to think of it. "And well done you." She smiled down at me. "Good decision. Cleaning that oven."

I smiled. "Thanks."

Peggy left the same way she'd arrived, via the back door. I got to my feet and stood in the open doorway, watching her go down the garden path, from where she'd disappear through the gate, then into the field and around to the front. Suddenly it occurred to me that she might not have run into Tom in town. She might have arranged to meet him, to talk to him. Persuade him to come to the ball, knowing he'd been sent a ticket. For Angie's sake. She might, in fact, be working some sort of magic. Now that Tatiana had gone, and now that Angie appeared to be softening slightly, was less bitter. Now that both husband and wife had had time apart to think, she might be judging the time was right. Because Peggy was like that. A good judge. Or…was I endowing her with powers she didn't have? Perceptions that were beyond her? I didn't think so somehow. Odd, wasn't it, how some people had that sage-like quality. Did it come with age, I wondered? Or had it always been there? As Peggy's mauve velvet coat disappeared in a flurry through the garden gate it reminded me of something. I couldn't think what. Ah yes, an illustration in one of Clemmie's books. Merlin.

I stood in the open doorway a long time after she'd gone. The ewes grazed quietly now without Shameless, and I loved the way the enormous chestnut tree spread its boughs over them. In summer the huge dark leaves hung like a protective swirling skirt, and although they were almost bare now, the branches still seemed to offer shelter. The late climbing rose by the door brushed my cheek, its scent redolent of warmer days, and drizzle dampened my face. In the certain knowledge that my fringe was beyond redemption, I let it fall: let it frizz. I realized, with a start, that I was quite content. Was, in fact, relishing being alone. I smiled up at the chestnut tree and was about to go inside when, suddenly, the French windows next door flew open. Frankie shot her head round.

"Oh, thank God you're there. I thought I heard you. We need you right now, Poppy. Jennie has gone completely mental. Can I come in?"

Before I could reply she'd leaped the little wall that divided our gardens and nipped inside my kitchen anyway. From her own house I could hear the sound of voices raised in anger. Then an outraged scream, shouting, and the sound of things being thrown. Something smashed against our party wall. I jumped, clutching Frankie's wrist.

"Jesus. What's going on?"

"Jennie, right, has completely lost it," she told me breathlessly as we listened. "She's convinced it's not my test, which it bloody isn't, and she knows it's not yours or Peggy's or Angie's, or even by immaculate conception Mrs. B.'s, so she's decided the only logical conclusion is it's Dad's. That he's having an affair, brought someone back here, and she dropped it in the basket."

"Oh, for God's sake!" I gasped, incredulous.

"I know, bonkers; but I told you, she's lost the plot."

We listened, clutching each other, as Jennie, at full volume, which we knew to be loud enough to penetrate ancient walls, told Dan exactly what she thought of him, followed by what sounded like the toaster being flung across the room. Dan yelped in pain.

"Shit—*you bitch*—my ankle!"

"Shall I go in?" I breathed.

"Oh yes, please," begged Frankie tearfully. "She's going to kill him, I know she is. I honestly think she might—Oh!"

No doubt also believing this to be true, Dan was even now leaping the garden wall. The next thing we knew, he was in my kitchen, cowering shamelessly behind his neighbor and his daughter, even going so far as to clutch my dressing-gown cord. His wife, however, was only moments behind him, in very hot pursuit, leaping the wall and brandishing a golf club.

"Jennie, *no!*" I screamed, springing forward to seize her wrist as she charged in brandishing the club. As the five iron flailed in the air Mrs. Tiger Woods sprang to mind.

"Let go of me! LET GO OF ME!" she roared.

"No, Jennie!" I flung her arm to the left with a monumental effort, so much so that the club flew from her hand. She cast mad, wistful eyes after it as it hit a framed poster from the Royal Academy on the wall, smashing it. The sound of breaking glass did nothing to deter her, though; in fact, it seemed to galvanize her. Her eyes came back to her prey, who was shrinking back down the kitchen, white-faced.

"BASTARD!" she screamed. As Dan turned and fled she pushed me out of the way, but as she ran past I managed to swing and grab her jumper. I held on tight as Frankie, with great resourcefulness, rugby-tackled her ankles and brought her down. A terrific struggle ensued, with Dan, I noticed, not helping in the least; he watched, petrified, peeping out from behind the doorway into the hall, as Frankie and I pinned his wife to the floor.

"Let me up! LET ME UP!" she insisted hotly.

Relenting only a fraction, we tentatively allowed her to at least struggle to a sitting position against the wall, where we crouched beside her like jailers, Frankie holding tight to one arm, me to the other.

"In my bed," she was spluttering, "some tart, while my children slept!"

"Jennie, *don't* be ridiculous!" I yelled. "You're out of your mind!"

"You've gone properly weird," gasped Frankie.

"He wouldn't, Jennie, he just wouldn't!" I urged. Dan shook his head vehemently, in helpless agreement, but knowing better, perhaps, than to utter. Out of the corner of my eye I could see my other neighbor, Mrs. Harper, at the far end of her back garden, peering around the pyracantha on the party wall, possibly even standing on a flower pot.

"Oh yes, he *would*!" Jennie seethed, mad eyes leaping out of their sockets, her face crimson with rage. "That's just it, he bloody *would*! He is not the man you think he is, Poppy, not harmless lovable Dan, can't help getting into scrapes, poor lamb. He *would* do that and I *know* he did it because I found a black lacy bra UNDER MY BED!"

"It's mine!" wailed Frankie, distressed. "I told you it's new. I tried it on in your room because you've got the best mirror—I must have left it there!"

"You lie!" she spat, her head spinning round to her daughter like something out of *The Exorcist*. "I wash your underwear constantly, young lady, and you possess nothing of that nature. You lie to protect him! You both lie!"

"No!" Frankie cried, tears springing to her eyes as, at that moment, her younger brother and sister materialized in their back garden. Jamie and Hannah were even now climbing over the garden wall in their pajamas. Jamie helped Hannah down. They crept, terrified, into my kitchen. If anything would stop my hugely maternal friend in her tracks, it was this: the sight of her two frightened, vulnerable children, little faces bewildered, Hannah still clutching her teddy, dragged from their beds by the screaming. But Jennie was too far gone. Her tether, which, as we know, some would dispute her ever having been in possession of, had well and truly snapped. Despite her jailers, she struggled to her feet and balled her fists.

"WELL, WHOSE IS IT, THEN?" she bellowed as we held her arms tight, her face a strange purple color. "The sodding test? If it's not yours, and it's not your father's and it's not Poppy's or Peggy's or Angie's, WHO THE HELL DOES IT BELONG TO?" she screamed.

There was a silence. It seemed to me the entire village held its collective breath.

"It's mine," came a voice to our left.

We swung around as one. Twelve-year-old Jamie, not thirteen until the winter, in his M&S jim-jams, getting taller by the minute but still very much snub-nosed and freckled, still very much a child, gazed back at us. Two spots of color were high in his cheeks and I saw him swallow. A gasp went up from the assembled company. Jennie, still in a half nelson of sorts, still in some sort of custody, went limp in our hands. She let out an anguished cry, the sound of an animal in pain. Then she bowed her head and slipped slowly down the wall on her bottom, to the floor.

Chapter Twenty-eight

"YOURS?" SPLUTTERED FRANKIE, SINCE their mother seemed incapable of speech.

"Yes, it's mine. OK?"

Jennie moaned in agony again, but not so piercingly this time: it was more the cry of a defeated fighter at the very end of her strength, very much on the ropes. Dan, however, seemed imbued with a new kind of strength. He hot-footed it from one end of the kitchen to the other, and since he was no longer in imminent danger of losing his own life, he stepped over his prostrate wife to endanger his son's. He towered over Jamie.

"You got someone pregnant?" he hissed, aghast.

"No, of course not. I was testing Leila, cos I thought she might be. I think she is."

A profound silence followed this announcement. No eyes strayed from the small boy in checked pajamas.

"Leila?" his mother finally whispered, dumbfounded.

"Yes. She was getting all fat and bosomy, like you did with Hannah, and anyway I saw her doing it with another dog. So when I saw her having a wee in the garden, I took your test and stuck it in the puddle. I had to run back upstairs to check the instructions on the packet, and then I just chucked it in the bin. I was going to tell you, only I knew how cross you'd be with her." His face was very pale now under his freckles.

His mother shut her eyes. "Oh, thank the Lord," she breathed. "Thank the Lord."

"You're pleased?" Jamie blinked. "I thought you'd be, like, mental. Get her to have an abortion or something."

"Oh, I might still do that, but—Oh no, I am *so* pleased, darling!" Jennie struggled to her feet and staggered across the kitchen to take her astonished son's face in both hands. She kissed his forehead with a resounding smack, then both his cheeks equally roundly. "So, so pleased it's not your father, but even more relieved it's not you!"

"Me!" he gasped, but she'd already squashed him in a face-altering embrace to her breast; so much so that his mouth became a figure of eight, denying speech.

Dan, meanwhile, once his initial relief had passed, was rapidly engaged in regarding his wife with contempt. He folded his arms in an attitude of haughty distain. His lip curled. He hadn't stalked off, mind, as some husbands might, in high dudgeon; had remained stoically by his wife's side. Whatever else one said about Dan, he saw these things through. But then again, such moments of lofty moral altitude were few and far between in his married life; he wouldn't want to miss out on them, would he? Who knows how long it might be until another came along?

"Sorry," Jennie muttered to him now, over her son's head.

Dan regarded her frostily for a moment, but then his lip un-curled. He had the grace to accept this apology for what it was: a genuine one, from a woman driven to distraction by unexplained circumstances, whose imagination had galloped from a teenage preg-nancy, to her husband's love child, to underage sex, all in the space of a few hours. He inclined his head in acceptance, and although he was unable to resist a faint gleam to the eye, she stood forgiven. And Dan forgave Jennie a lot, it occurred to me; almost as much as she forgave him. Albeit for different reasons.

"Puppies!" breathed Hannah blissfully into the silence. She beamed up at her mother. "Will Leila have puppies, Mum?"

"No doubt," said Jennie darkly, resting her chin squarely on

Jamie's head; he was still squirming in her tight embrace. Suddenly her face became wreathed in smiles. "And there'll be no half measures for our Leila, either. She won't pop out a modest set of twins. Oh no, it'll be a hundred and one Dalmatians for her!" She gave a sharp laugh.

"And can we keep one?" implored Hannah, her eyes huge.

"No, darling, we can't," Jennie told her firmly: overjoyed, it seemed, but not completely overwhelmed by the situation before her.

Hannah's face fell, as did Jamie's when he was finally released.

"Oh, Mum?" he implored.

Dan raised inquiring eyebrows at his wife. Still in a position of power, he was keen to push home the advantage, and Jennie caught the look and hesitated, which was fatal. It was pounced on immediately.

"Go on, Mum!" they chorused.

She vacillated. "Oh God, we'll see," she said finally, at which massive capitulation a whoop went up from her offspring, including Frankie. "I said, we'll see!" she cried, but everyone knew she was shot to bits.

"Come on, you lot." Dan took Hannah's shoulders and turned her about, grinning widely and propelling his family out through the open back door. "Back to bed for you. Sorry, Poppy." He turned back to me as his offspring scampered excitedly away. "I do apologize for intruding so brutishly on your evening, but thank God we got that one sorted out. It was only a matter of time before she accused me of harbouring a love child somewhere in the village, of leading a completely double life." This time he couldn't resist a withering look at his increasingly shamefaced wife. "An affair," he said incredulously. "As if. Who with? And when would I have the time, or the opportunity?" This, when his younger children were safely over the wall, Frankie in their wake.

"Well, quite," muttered Jennie, looking exhausted suddenly. She ran a weary hand through her hair. "Or the bloody energy," she added ruefully.

"And in the marital bed, too. What kind of a man d'you take me for?" He shook his head, lips pursed. "I worry about the way your mind works sometimes, Jennie, I really do. In fact I'm increasingly concerned for your moral compass." He was enjoying himself now.

"I was severely provoked," replied his wife testily, not one to be contrite for long. "And since I'd exhausted all other possibilities—or thought I had...Of course, foolishly, it didn't occur to me it was your bloody dog shagging around, weeing on sticks—"

"That's...my canine dog, I take it," put in Dan. "Only, just now you accused me of having some dog in bed with me, and I can assure you that while Leila and I are very fond of each other we have never crossed that—"

"Oh, shut up, Dan," Jennie interrupted, irritated. "You might have the high ground for one split second but we all know it won't last long. It'll be shifting under your feet before you can say 'caught with your trousers down again.'"

"Which is why I'm making the most of it!" he cried in mock outrage as they trooped off down the lawn together, taking a more conventional route than their children, via my garden gate at the end, then back through theirs. He flung his arm around her shoulders as they went. "Why d'you think I'm milking it for all it's worth? Oh, good evening, Mrs. Harper! Yes, the bitch *is* pregnant, isn't that joyous? Doesn't she look well?" A gray perm scuttled inside in terror. "Oh, don't go," Dan cried. "Let's make an evening of it! Why make haste when there's so much to celebrate? When the night is still young?" We heard a kitchen door slam firmly. Dan grinned back at me over his shoulder. "Night, Poppy."

"Night." I smiled and went inside.

—⁓—

Jennie, however, not one to leave a drama alone for long, was through that same back door the following morning, as I was bundling my sheets into the washing machine. Clemmie, who had a cold, was playing quietly in the sitting room, and once Jennie had popped in to say hello to her, she installed herself at my kitchen table with a mug of coffee.

"Puppies!" she groaned.

"Now, Jennie," I warned, turning round from my machine, "I'm not having that. It's bloody marvelous news. You were euphoric last night. It's yippee, puppies, remember?"

"Oh, I know," she agreed. "And I was still in a good mood when we got in, I promise. I had a lovely hug from Frankie and we even shed a few tears together."

"Did you? Oh, *good*."

"Stayed up chatting for ages. She was horrified that we thought she was pregnant but understood why. She also said I'd behaved slightly better than her father, which cheered me. Said she'd had no idea her dad could go off the deep end like that. I told her it was only because he loved her so much and she agreed, grudgingly, then, being Frankie, said, "Oh, so you didn't, because you don't?" "

I laughed. "Typical."

"I know, and she didn't mean it. She was only being clever, so I didn't react. She does that too much, of course. The clever, cynical bit."

I shrugged. "It's just a defense mechanism. She'll grow out of it. And she is clever, Jennie. Far too clever to get herself pregnant. She'll go far, that girl."

"I know she will. We talked about all that, too—A levels, university. She'd like to go to Frazer House for sixth form."

"Oh. Can you afford it?" Frazer House was private.

"No. But I think we should try. She'd do so well there. I'm going to persuade Dan that we should borrow it, crawl to the bank manager."

I was silenced. Jennie didn't believe in borrowing, it was against all her instincts. She kept a very tight hold on the purse strings, but then again, as she always said, she had to. Dan would blow it all on the three-thirty at Kempton if he could.

"Don't think you'll have any difficulty there, then," I grinned.

She smiled. "No, I know. And I do also know," she eyed me sheepishly, "that I am a controlling old bag at times, but trust me, you'd be the same with my family."

I wouldn't, I knew. I'd be more like Dan; but that would be hopeless, wouldn't it? People like Dan and me frittered money until there was nothing left—like Dad, I realized, remembering, too, my hefty check to the hunt. Because it didn't really interest me. Careful people like Jennie were crucial. But then, that's what I'd thought I had with Phil. And look how careless he'd turned out to be? With feelings, rather than money.

"And there is a boy," went on Jennie, still with Frankie. She sipped her coffee. "The only problem is, it's Hugo."

"Hugo!" I turned back from stuffing my sheets in. I was astonished. Hugo. Angus and Sylvia's rather gorgeous grandson, who hunted to hounds in the holidays and was currently on his gap year before going to Cambridge. He was very much not what I'd expected, and very much the property of one of Angie's girls, surely?

"I thought he was joined at the hip with Clarissa?"

"That's what Clarissa thought, too, and is mighty upset about it. She considers him to be her property—even though he's never been out with her. She knows he's with a friend of hers but she doesn't know who. He wants to break it to her gently, which is why it's a secret."

I remembered Frankie running under cover of darkness to a car outside the pub, which of course was where he worked. Remembered, too, Angie telling me Clarissa was upset about a boy.

"Oh. Good for Frankie." I couldn't help it.

She grinned. "I know. He's a lovely boy." Suddenly she looked defiant. "But then she's a lovely girl. Interesting, too. Not your run-of-the-mill, giggle at everything, flicky-haired type."

"Quite."

"She wants to grow it," she said absently. "Take it back a shade or two. More tawny."

"Good idea."

We were silent a moment. My mind flew back to Jennie, years ago, struggling with this defiant, wilful child, whose alcoholic mother had become more and more disinterested. There'd been some good years after that, between the ages of about nine and twelve, when all that mattered had been getting in the netball team in the winter and the rounders team in the summer—Jennie had even bribed the teacher with chocolate brownies once—but then some tricky ones. Could it be that she and Frankie were entering a good phase again? And could it last, this time? Jennie had certainly put her back into it, even if at times she felt she hadn't.

"Dan must be pleased? That you two are back on track?" I hazarded, closing the machine door with an effort. Too full.

"Yes, even though it's slightly at his expense and he's been cast as the tyrannical Dickensian father."

"That was just shock talking."

"I know, and Frankie knows it, too. Yes, Dan's pleased. In fact I'd go so far as to say he was positively smug last night. I assumed he'd be asleep when I finally crawled upstairs after my session with Frankie, but there he was, propped up on pillows, bright-eyed and banking on me being extremely grateful."

"Ah." I laughed. "Bad luck."

"Actually I rather enjoyed it. Didn't seem like the onerous duty it sometimes does. I joined in for a change, rather than viewing it entirely as a spectator sport."

"Slightly too much information, Jennie."

"Sorry. Just explaining the baggy eyes this morning." She grinned sheepishly and hid them in her coffee. They twinkled a bit. "Anyway, we made a sort of pact to go away on our own for a few days after

Christmas. Get to know each other again, as they're so fond of telling us to do in women's magazines."

"Good idea. I'll have the kids."

"Thanks, but I think Frankie will be fine if you'd just keep a weather eye. Lob some fresh fruit over the fence every now and then."

It occurred to me that a few weeks ago Jennie would never have trusted Frankie to look after the younger ones. They must have had a very good chat.

"And what about you?" She eyed me speculatively. I flinched. I knew that look. Once Jennie had sorted out her own life there was nothing she liked more than getting to grips with someone else's. I wriggled under her laser beam but was trapped, like a moth on a microscope slide. "I thought you were going out last night? How come you were still skulking in your dressing gown when we burst in like the Addams Family?"

"Ah. Well." I told her about Luke. About Angie. Then about Peggy.

She looked thoughtful a moment. Compressed her lips. "Bit of a knee-jerk reaction?"

"What, mine?"

"Well, yes. Angie casually mentions you haven't exactly been left destitute, and suddenly his motives are all wrong and he's a gold-digging fortune hunter and you drop him like a hot coal."

"Well—"

"You're not exactly Jackie Onassis, Poppy."

I flushed, remembering I'd compared myself to the very same woman last night. "No, of course not."

"You've just been left enough to buy a decent house and educate your kids, which the widow of any professional man who's built up a business might expect. Luke could have worked that out for himself. And you've still got two children, as he rightly observed to Angie. Still come with baggage."

I stared at her. "What are you saying?"

"I'm saying you're leaping to conclusions, courtesy of Peggy, who only thinks in black and white. Roger was the love of her life, ergo there will never be another. End of story. So she gads about teasing the elderly bachelors but will never bring herself to land one. Is that what you want?"

I sat down slowly. "Well, put like that…"

"Life is not black and white, Poppy; it's very gray, to the point of being grimy. There's a great deal of compromise and shading of areas—ask me and Dan. Just because you went so wildly wrong with Phil doesn't mean all men are shits and you're going to go disastrously wrong again."

I gasped. "Did you have a glass to the wall?"

"What d'you mean?"

"Well, that's what I think! What I told Peggy—that I will go wrong!"

"I know, I can tell. And Peggy's encouraging you to be forensic, to settle for nothing but perfection. She would. She's all or nothing. Which is fine if you're happy with nothing. Personally I like a little something." She crossed her legs.

I gulped, horribly confused. "Oh God. Oh God, I don't know, Jennie!" I wailed, shooting anguished fingers through my hair. I clutched at the roots. "When I talk to Peggy, I think—yes yes yes; and when I talk to you, I think—yes yes yes, too! Why is that?"

"Because you're suggestible, like my husband," she said calmly. "Not a sheep, exactly—"

"Oh, thanks!"

"But very persuadable." She brushed an imaginary bit of fluff from her knee, warming up nicely. "It's terribly simple really. Do you like him?"

"Who, Luke?"

"Yes, of course Luke, not Dan. Although you're more than welcome to him."

"Um, yes." I bit my thumbnail.

"Enjoy his company? Enjoy spending time with him?"

I thought back to the pub lunch we'd shared: how he'd flipped beer mats to amuse Clemmie. Made me burst out laughing at the King's Head.

"Yes, I enjoy his company."

"Enjoyed kissing him outside your house the other day?"

I stared. "Bog off, Jennie." I muttered, blushing.

"Do you love him?"

"No. I mean...I don't know."

"Exactly, of course you don't! And why should you? You've only known him a few weeks. But give it a chance, Poppy," she urged. "You don't have to decide tomorrow, or next week, or even next year, but how will you know if you don't at least give it a chance? And if you're worried about the money thing, just ask him."

"Oh, right, like—Luke, are you after my dosh?"

"No, but you could happen to mention how Angie exaggerates like crazy—which she does—and has told half the village you're rich as Croesus. Laugh it off."

Half the village. I thought of Odd Bob propositioning me. Stalking me, even. Saintly Sue telling me she couldn't compete with me in "that department."

"Oh, Christ. Thanks, Angie," I muttered.

"He'll know that's true, about Angie exaggerating, and you can even say she got it wrong and it couldn't be further from the truth—he'll be so confused he won't know what to believe. Then see if he sticks around. Personally, I bet he will. I'll bet the money's got nothing to do with it. He's a nice guy, Poppy. Don't write him off entirely."

"Really?" I asked anxiously. "You really like him, Jennie?"

"Yes, I do, but it's what *you* think that matters."

"But that's just it, I don't know!" I yelped. "Don't know my own mind any more. Not sure I *have* one, as a matter of fact."

"Course you do." But it wasn't said with much conviction, and I slumped miserably at the table, holding my head theatrically in my hands. I knew she was being extra punchy because she'd made a fool of herself last night and was roaring back from the dog house, but still.

"When's Leila due?" I asked, jerking upright, keen to plunge her back into her own domestic crisis.

"Leila," she spat. "Who knows. Dogs are supposed to have a fourteen-week gestation period, but since she's half devil it could be any time. She's not fit to be a mother, Poppy. Quite aside from her mental health issues, she's a serial shagger, and that's not nice, is it? I'd ask the vet to terminate her but the children would never forgive me. And anyway, how d'you stop a she-devil whelping? She'd find a way to squeeze them out, just to spite me."

I grinned. Jennie huffed and puffed a lot of hot air, but I knew very well that cometh the hour, cometh the midwife. She'd be up all night, installed in Leila's whelping box, coaxing her along, holding her paw during contractions, and then be besotted by the litter, never leaving the house, so busy would she be mashing Weetabix and scrambling eggs. In fact there was every possibility she'd keep the lot. A rather satisfactory vision of eight fully grown Leilas on the end of eight leads, propelling Jennie at speed through the village, sprang to mind.

"You know, it might be the making of her," I mused.

"Leila? I doubt it. She'll probably give birth in a nasty wet bush and be off in moments, sniffing for trouser again. Looking for another Peddler to do some brisk fornicating with. Wasn't that the name of the dog?"

"Peddler? Oh God, of course. Mark said she'd been seen with him. They might be Peddler's puppies! Oh, Jennie, I'd really like one if they are."

"Would you?" She looked surprised. Then she brightened.

"Okeydoke. But there might be some demand, you know." She squared her shoulders. "Despite my own misgivings, Leila is well liked around here. Might be expensive, too. But I'll put you on my list."

Typical. Really typical. She was back in control again. Imagining herself saying, "No, Mrs. Fish, I'm not convinced your garden is big enough."

"She's definitely pregnant, is she?" I warned. "That test might not be accurate on a dog."

"My thoughts entirely, so I rang the vet. He said it'll be pretty conclusive, the hormones are much the same. And as Dan tastefully pointed out, she's dugging up a treat."

"Right. Bugger. Why isn't it starting?" I gazed at my unlit washing machine.

"Because you've put too much in."

Annoyingly I knew she was right and I stalked to open it and pull out a sheet. It had got caught somehow and I tugged at the clod of linen but it was stuck fast, so that when I pulled really hard, the whole contents of the drum came out in rush, which had me falling on my bottom. At which point the doorbell went.

"D'you want me to get that?"

"Please."

"And then I'm going to have her spayed," Jennie told me decisively as she marched to the front door. "That'll take the wind out of her sails."

"They get fat and bad-tempered," I warned.

"Who doesn't?" she snorted. "Spayed or not."

I separated a double duvet cover from the herd and stuffed the rest back in, resetting the dial. Away it went.

"Thank you," I heard Jennie say to someone at the door. She came back down the hall. "Hey, look at this."

I turned to see her bearing a bunch of white roses with pretty blue cornflowers tucked in between. She handed them to me. "For you, apparently."

Astonished, I took the paper-wrapped bouquet. Then sat down and opened the note. It was a long time since anyone had sent me flowers. In fact…no. No one at all.

"They're from Luke," I said slowly, reading. "'Hope you're feeling better, lots of love.'"

Jennie peered over my shoulder. "Oh, what a *shitty* thing to do," she said vehemently. "Gets stood up at a moment's notice and then sends flowers. I ask you." She folded her arms.

After a moment I glanced up guiltily. "I've misjudged him, haven't I?"

She shrugged. "I dunno. It depends on who you last spoke to."

It was supposed to be a joke, but it was a bit sharp and she knew it.

"Sorry," she said quickly. "Didn't mean that. Tell me to mind my own business, Poppy. It's just…I really want some happiness for you." She swooped to give me a quick hug. "And thanks for everything yesterday," she said gruffly in my ear. "I couldn't do without you, you know."

I nodded dumbly; touched. But no wiser. As she went to the back door, she turned.

"Oh, you'll never guess what Angie told me."

"What?"

"About your solicitor chappie, Sam Hetherington. The one in the splendid red hunting coat."

I felt my heart thump. I already knew.

"He was once married to Hope Armitage. Years ago, apparently, but still."

"Really?"

"I know, can you believe it? Why on earth did they come here in the first place, one wonders. If he was living here?"

"Sam wasn't here when they came," I said mechanically. "He was still in London. The Hall was rented then. Had tenants."

"Yes, but you don't relocate with your new husband to your ex's patch unless there's some pull in that direction, surely? Why are you looking so stricken, Poppy? And when are you ever going to oil this door?" She was struggling with my back-door latch, as everyone did.

"Hang on," I said suddenly. I got up quickly and went to the dresser. Seizing the invitation, I thrust it into her hands. All at once everything was as clear as day. I definitely wasn't going now. "Mark at the kennels sent me these. Why don't you and Dan go? Half the county's going; you'll have fun."

She looked at them doubtfully. "Are you sure? Don't you want to go? Couldn't you ask Luke?"

"I could, and I was going to, actually. I just think that's possibly not the right venue. I won't write him off," I promised quickly, "but I don't think I want to go public, as it were."

"OK," she said slowly, understanding. She nodded. Then her eyes came up from the invitation. They sparkled. "Well, if you're sure…we'd love to. D'you know, this is just what Dan and I need. A bloody good knees-up. Thank you." She smacked the card into the palm of her hand and went off beaming, giving the back-door latch a monumental twist; never giving it a second chance.

Archie was gurgling on the baby alarm, and I slowly climbed the stairs to get him, dragging my hand along the polished rail. As I came down with him in my arms, he flicked my lower lip, which ordinarily would make me smile. Odd, then, that I couldn't raise one for him.

Chapter Twenty-nine

WHEN I'D SETTLED ARCHIE with juice and a biscuit, I arranged the flowers and sat looking at them. Clemmie wandered through from the sitting room where she'd been involved with her Sylvanian Family dolls all the time Jennie had been here. She could play quietly with her toys for hours, something which hitherto had been a great source of pride but, more latterly, bothered me slightly. Clutching the tiny parents in her hands, she gazed at the flowers in wonder.

"Did they grow in the garden?"

"No, darling," I laughed as she clambered onto my lap and reached out to touch. "Someone sent them."

"Why?"

I hesitated. "As a present."

"Who?"

I took a breath. "D'you remember that man who came to the pub with us? Luke? He sent them."

"The one who could make an eyebrow wiggle?"

"That's the one."

"Is it your birthday?"

"No, he just sent them."

"There's a card." She seized it. Stared. "It...oh. What does it say?"

I swallowed, wishing I'd thought this through a bit. "It says, 'Hope you're feeling better, lots of love.' I...had a bit of a cold."

"When?" She twisted on my lap. Brown eyes huge. I flushed.

"Um, a few days ago."

"Oh."

As she gazed at me the whole chasm between the grown-up world and childhood seemed to yawn at me. The prospect of her being grown up one day hit me; a time when her own innocent little world of Sylvanian families and truth would be over. When she'd be quicker at spotting lies like the one I'd just told her. Oh, I told her plenty: put your coat on, it's cold out there—it wasn't, but it might be later; teddy wants you to eat your carrots—who was I to know the workings of a stuffed bear's mind? We definitely started them early on, the small white ones. Introduced them gradually, like solid food. But this was a proper one. I wondered if she'd spot it. How grown-up was she? Was I training her well? But a few days ago was an eternity for a four-year-old.

"Are you going to marry him?"

No flies on Clemmie. Forget the cold, spurious or not; cut to the chase. After a sharp intake of breath, I laughed nervously.

"No, of course not!"

"Oh." Her gaze went back to the flowers. "Becky's mummy got married and she woz a bridesmaid."

My heart gave a jolt. "Did Becky like that?"

"Yes, she had a pink dress and a bogey."

"A bouquet."

"Yes."

"And does Becky like her new daddy?"

She shrugged, bored with the finer nuances of her story. "We saw pictures at Circle Time. It was long, like a princess dress."

"Ah. Lovely."

"Can I have one like that?"

"Well, darling, I'm not sure I'm going to get married. That would mean you would have a new daddy, you see."

"We could ask him?"

"Um, well, no." I scratched my neck. "I don't think we'll do that."

"If you do, can I have the dress?" She slid off my knee, uninterested now that there seemed only a slim chance of sartorial splendor amongst her classmates.

"Clemmie, do you ever think about Daddy?"

The health visitor had said I should ask things like this. I didn't. Ever. It wasn't my instinct. My instinct screamed: protect! Don't mention it! So I hadn't. Clemmie was on the floor with her tiny parents. The irony didn't escape me.

"I don't know," she said slowly. Carefully, almost. Too careful, for a four-year-old.

"Do you remember what he looked like?"

"He was a bit grumpy," she said eventually. To the floor.

And Phil was; had been. Had increasingly regarded the children as an irritant, particularly when he was trying to work. But I didn't like the way she'd had to search her memory bank to come up with even *this* picture. Then again, I hadn't provided her with one.

Clemmie sat back on her heels and looked triumphant. "And he had a pink shirt."

I smiled. "He did, didn't he, Clem."

Later, when she was watching CBeebies with Archie after lunch, I went through the drawers in the bureau. Eventually I found what I was looking for, but it had been a search; I'd hidden them well. I found a couple of frames and popped one in each of their bedrooms. Photos of Phil, smiling. Yes, of course he smiled occasionally. Archie's was taken on holiday in Majorca, and Clemmie's on our wedding day. He may not have been perfect, but he was their father, and you only get one. Clemmie could only remember him grumpy, but that would surely fade, and then she'd have this smiley photo to take its place. I didn't put them in obvious positions, by their beds or on their walls, but on top of their chests of drawers, so that they'd come across them later, by accident maybe, when they were a bit older, then assume they'd always been there. I didn't want Clemmie remembering a cross father. I wanted her life to be perfect, to the extent that I would erase those memories and replace them with nice ones, just as I took her dirty clothes and replaced them with clean ones. And I'd talk about him more, I determined, as I went downstairs. Remember happy times; make them up. Lovely picnics, bluebell walks. I could do that for them, my children. Lie. Let's face it, I did it already. As I filled the dishwasher I wondered if he could become a bit of a hero, secretly in the SAS, trouble-shooting in Afghanistan, which would explain why he hadn't been here much? But then one day, when she was a famous actress and on *Who Do You Think You Are*, she might discover he'd been a cycling nerd with a mistress in the next village. Perhaps not. Stick to the smiling photos and the bluebell woods.

So that was her memory sorted out. But what about her life? What about replacing Phil with something better, so that, blink, and she and Archie wouldn't know any different? They were so young, any stepfather would soon be like a real father. Like Becky. She called her new daddy Papa. He was a farmer, and Linda, her mum, had never been happier. I knew Linda. Knew the family Clemmie had been talking about. Linda wasn't automatically my type at the school gates—bottle blonde, very short skirts, chewed gum constantly—but I liked her. Her husband had walked out on her one Easter Sunday and taken up with a younger model. He'd bought a motorbike too; leathers, the whole bit. Two months later he'd been killed on the A41 when his bike hit black ice. Linda now lived on a dairy farm with her little girl, Becky, and Becky's papa. The manic gum-chewing had stopped, I noticed. Jeans instead of micro minis. Hair slightly darker. Because perhaps Becky's papa didn't need the peroxide? Happy endings. Don't knock them. And don't pass them up, either.

———

The rest of the week was taken up with calming my best friend's sartorial nerves. As Jennie frenziedly pointed out, she hadn't been to a ball for years, had nothing to wear and anyway, what *did* one wear to balls these days? Was it long and slinky, or short and cocktaily? These, and other such burning issues, mostly to do with shoes and accessories, consumed us. For just as I couldn't think for myself, Jennie couldn't dress herself—something I found as easy as falling off a confidence log. Her lack of taste baffled me.

"How about this with these?" she'd say as she ran through my back door wearing yet another heinous combination, this time bursting out of a black dress of such sequined monstrosity, together with high red shoes, it fairly took my breath away.

"No to both," I said firmly. "And certainly not together. The only thing black goes with is black, Jennie. Take the shoes back to Angie and the dress to Peggy. She'd get away with that because she's eccentric and it would hang off her."

"Whereas I'd just look like a tart?"

I shrugged, slightly pleased to have the upper hand occasionally with my bossy friend. But then I took pity, and piling the children in the car, I took her shopping.

She ended up looking terrific in a gray slinky number I'd found in Coast: to the floor, high at the front, but low at the back. As did Angie in her black velvet, which she shook from a Selfridges bag and slipped into in the middle of my kitchen; and Peggy in the sequins which she'd generously offered Jennie, but which, with black pumps and on her rangy frame, looked stunning.

"If only you were coming," they all said, and Jennie looked a bit guilty, feeling perhaps she should have refused the tickets and insisted I go.

"Oh, I really don't want to," I said, meaning it. "It's not the sort of thing you go to alone, is it?"

"No, no," they chorused, as it occurred to us that Angie, and ostensibly Peggy, were doing just that.

"It's not really your sort of thing, is it?" consoled Angie.

"Absolutely not," I agreed, stung. Why wasn't it? Why? "Anyway, I'm going to Dad's," I said quickly, to save them. "Haven't seen him for ages. I'm going to cook him supper."

"Oh, *good*," they all said, relieved, feeling much better. They bustled away content.

Dad, however, wasn't much help when I decided to follow through. "Steak and chips," I told him cheerfully, "in front of *Viva Las Vegas*. I'll bring the steak."

"Oh, sorry, Poppy, I'm going to the hunt ball."

"Are you?" I was astonished.

"Yes, Mark sent me a ticket, wasn't that kind? Just a single, but they're a hundred quid a pop, so terribly generous. Especially after all that business with the hound. Aren't you going, love? Half the county's going to be there."

"Well, I was going to—he sent me some, too—but I gave mine to Jennie."

"Ah, right. Not really your sort of thing, is it? Anyway, must go, love; I've got to feed the horses before I shimmy into my glad rags."

And he was gone. Leaving me irritated. And then I found myself growing more irritated as I put the children to bed. Not my sort of thing? Why not? Christ, I could party with the best of them! Just because Phil and I didn't much—he was teetotal and liked an early night—didn't mean *I* couldn't. Bloody hell, you should have seen me in the old Clapham days, beetling back at three in the morning, bare feet on the pedals, high heels tossed on the back seat. When I was young. But I was still young, surely? I swept Archie's curtain shut with a vengeance. Through the crack I could see the bedroom lights across the road at the Old Rectory, where Sylvia and Angus would be getting ready: Angus stooping to adjust his bow tie in the mirror, Sylvia popping diamonds in her ears at her dressing table. Marvelous. How lovely for them. I seized the groaning nappy bucket and marched downstairs. Cinders by the fire, then. I shook the nappies viciously in the bin. With her solitary boiled egg, in her dressing gown and her ancient Ugg boots. Splendid.

I told myself I'd be the smug one in the morning, though, when everyone else was nursing hangovers. Oh yes. In the pub. Laughing and reminiscing over bloody Marys. Hm. They'd all be there tonight, of course. Sam—no, don't think about Sam. I'd successfully blocked him for days; resisted imagining him in his black tie, even while helping Jennie buy a new white shirt for Dan. I wasn't going to give in now. Instead I helped myself to a large gin and tonic and told myself there was a good film on at nine and that I might even stay up till it finished. Live a little.

It was a surprise, therefore, when my doorbell rang much earlier, at eight, and I opened it to find my father on my front step, an overcoat over his dinner jacket. He seemed mildly taken aback to see me in my dressing gown. Looked me up and down, eyebrows raised.

"Didn't you get my message?"

"What message?"

"I left one on your mobile. About tonight. Mark rang to say Mary Granger was throwing up and would I like to bring anyone. Didn't you get it?"

"No!" I could have kissed him. And hit him. So like Dad not to try again. Not to persevere. Just turn up and assume.

"Well, I can't come now," I said testily. "I've got the children."

"Can't you get a baby-sitter?"

"Of course not, it's far too late."

"What about Jennie's daughter, next door?"

"She's out with her boyfriend. And the little ones are at a sleepover."

"Oh." He looked vaguely stumped. Then: "Bring them with us?"

Ordinarily a suggestion like this from my father would be greeted with scathing derision from me. But genes will out, and in many respects I am my father's daughter. Can, at the drop of a hat, revert to type. I stared at him.

"OK."

In my heart, I was far from sure I was going to run with this; but in the spirit of living dangerously was nonetheless interested to see how he'd execute it: keen to give him his head.

"Right. You get changed, brush your hair and whatnot, and I'll carry them into the lorry."

"The lorry?"

"Well, the car hasn't worked for weeks, Poppy."

So my father drove his horse lorry. Blithely parked it in Tesco's car park, no doubt, as if it were a Vauxhall Cresta.

"So…we're piling the children into a dark lorry, and what, leaving it in a muddy field? Where they'll wake up cold and frightened?"

"No, no, we'll take them in the house, find a bed for them."

"Arrive at a black-tie ball with two sleepy children? Forget it, Dad. Have fun." I went to shut the door, but he was already in.

"Don't be wet, Poppy, how d'you think your mum and I ever went to parties? We were never organized enough for a sitter. You were always under one arm. Now go and put your frock on, and I'll sort the kids out. It's only one night, for God's sake, it won't kill them, and they'll love it. Everyone's going, d'you want to be the only one who isn't?"

He knew which buttons to press. He was also halfway up the stairs.

Twenty minutes later, we were in the lorry—the one with no seat belts, remember—rattling over a cattle grid at the entrance to Mulverton Hall, only this time we took the fork in the drive that led not to the home farm and a muddy field of cows, but to the main house. A sweep of dark green lawn swam like a lake in front of us. Dad, at the wheel, skirted it carefully, then followed signs to parking in the paddock alongside, behind the park railings. I had on my old black dress, and my hastily washed hair was still wet down my back; between us on the front seat, sitting bolt upright and wide awake, were two overexcited and highly delighted children.

I-can't-believe-I'm-doing-this-I-can't-believe-I'm-doing-this, was my overriding thought as a surprised car park attendant in a long white coat—surprised at the lorry initially, then the children—beckoned us into the field. Dad gave him a cheery wave and wound down the window.

"Hi, Roy."

"Oh, hello, Peter!" He peered in. "Brought the whole family, I see!"

"Well, it's a night out, isn't it?" said Dad smoothly.

He trundled away from Roy and through the gate. At the end of a line of parked cars, he expertly swung two tons of juggernaut into position. A Mercedes drew up beside us, and a woman in a fox-fur coat and a smattering of diamonds stared up in wonder from the passenger seat. I found my nerve rapidly disappearing down the drain.

"Dad…" I swallowed.

"Come on, Clemmie, look lively, love." He'd hopped out of the cab already, and as Clemmie scrambled across the seat to his open arms, he crouched and hoisted her up onto his shoulders. "Up you go!"

She wrapped her arms excitedly around her grandpa's neck, squealing with delight. Then he slammed the cab door, and was off. Naturally I had no choice but to follow. With Archie in my arms, I picked my way through the field, following the phalanx of flaming torches that lined the drive ahead and floodlit the expansive grounds. My heart was fluttering with panic, but as we crunched across the gravel sweep, I knew I was in too deep. The honey-colored walls rose up before us; ranks of windows blazed down. Dad pranced ahead, hopping about jauntily now from foot to foot, playing the fool, Clemmie, in her pink dressing gown bouncing and laughing on his shoulders. How many parties had I been to like that, I wondered. Had it done me any harm? Doing a Mortimer, Mum used to call it, when Dad veered off the beaten track, took his own route, which was more than occasionally. But this was a very grand party. People were silhouetted at the windows in their finery: bare shoulders, sparkling jewels, one or two turning to stare. And please don't tell me he was going to leap up those grand portal steps guarded by stone griffins? Breeze through the open front door where waiters stood poised with trays of champagne? Babes in arms?

My father, however, was far from stupid, and within a twinkling was nipping round the back. I scuttled sheepishly after him, feeling like a burglar, but Dad, knowing his way round old country houses—or at least his way to the stables and a cup of tea—didn't falter. In a jiggy he'd found a back door, which opened to his touch, and was striding right on through. He was deliberately going too fast for me to catch him, to dither, discuss, deliberate—chicken out—and as I followed breathlessly with Archie in my arms, he was already halfway down the passageway. Framed Spy cartoons from old copies of *Punch* lined the walls, and just before a green baize door Dad made a left turn into a well-lit room. Whistling, no less.

I followed in trepidation and found myself in a large, rather tired-looking kitchen with a very high ceiling. Cream Formica cupboards with glazed doors lined one wall, the floor was lino, rather like Dad's, and the only nod to the status of this house was a huge oak table which sailed down the middle. A well-upholstered blonde woman in a white apron had her back to us at the kitchen sink under the window. She turned in surprise. I recognized her immediately. It was Janice, the receptionist, but perhaps she didn't instantly place me out of context, and anyway she wasn't given a chance. Dad was already commanding her full attention: charming her, flirting, even, explaining about the baby-sitter letting us down, jiggling Clemmie, so that by the end of it, as she listened wide-eyed to the tale, wiping wet hands on a tea towel, she was wreathed in smiles, assuring him it was no trouble at all, and that she loved looking after little-uns. She'd pop them in the old nursery, she said, and yes, plug the alarm in, when I proffered it anxiously.

"Oh, *hello*, love, thought I recognized you." She beamed.

No, we weren't to worry a jot, she carried on. We were to run along and have a jolly good time. It seemed she remembered Dad from the races—who didn't? Warwick, was it? Or Windsor? No. No, Mr. Hetherington wouldn't mind a bit, she assured me as I interrupted their racing chat. I would turn the conversation back to more mundane matters. On they gossiped, and then, just as they were reminiscing about that epic race, the five-thirty from Heydock one summer's evening last year, when Ransom Boy, a rank outsider at 100 to one, had won by a head, just at that moment Mr. Hetherington himself swept into the kitchen.

Far from looking as if he couldn't be more thrilled, as Janice had intimated, he couldn't have looked more thunderous. But it wasn't just that: it wasn't the heavily knitted brow as he stood there glowering, dressed in what I can only assume was some sort of hunting livery—frightfully dashing and involving a mulberry velvet coat with his bow tie—no, it wasn't that. It was the churning of my own stomach that disquieted me. The pulverizing of my ribcage by what felt like needles. It was the terrible dawning sensation, as he stood before us in all his glory, that this wasn't just an unsuitable crush. This was something a lot more serious.

Chapter Thirty

THERE WAS A BRIEF and startled silence.

"Hello, Sam," I managed, cranking up a smile, as he stared. Took in this eccentric little party: this gatecrasher with her older man, her wet hair, children in pajamas. I faltered on. "Um, my f-father invited me, and—"

"And the baby-sitter let her down," schmoozed Dad, stepping forward, hand extended, beaming. "Can you believe it? Right at the last moment. Cystitis, apparently. A thousand apologies for bursting in like this with the entire family, but we were so looking forward to it. Peter Mortimer, Poppy's dad."

"Sam Hetherington," said Sam, still looking dazed, and still, for some reason, even as he shook Dad's hand, looking at me.

"Janice here assures us the children will be no trouble. They're terribly good, you know, never cry," went on Dad. "But I do apologize nonetheless, quite an invasion."

Sam's eyes came back to my father. "Sorry, you mean—?"

"Pop them upstairs? If that's all right? Quite an imposition, I know, but we couldn't think of any way round it."

Sam collected himself. "Oh, I see. Absolutely. No, not at all. Couldn't matter less. Right, well, Janice, what d'you suggest?" He turned swiftly on his heel to face her, raking a hand through his hair. "Could the children go in the blue spare room, d'you think?"

"I thought the old nursery. It's closer to the back stairs, and I'll hear them better. All right, love?" Dad had set Clemmie down from his shoulders, and Janice went to take her hand.

"My grandchildren," said my father proudly, a hand on each of their shoulders as if they were the guests of honour. I cringed. Don't overdo it, Dad. But Sam rose to the occasion.

"A pleasure to have you both here," he told Clemmie with a smile.

My daughter, a Mortimer through and through, extended her hand as she'd seen her grandfather do and said solemnly, "Clementine Shilling."

Sam took her hand, delighted, and we all laughed. I could have kissed her. "Good evening, Clementine. I hope you enjoy your stay."

"You can call me Clemmie."

After that it was easy, because, as Dad says, it always is if you oil the wheels with a sprinkle of humor and a dash of charm, or lashings of it, in his case. He and Sam spoke of point-to-points and hunter trials, as Sam got some more ice—what he'd come in for, he explained, the caterers having stupidly not brought enough—which perhaps explained his thunderous face earlier, but perhaps not. It had certainly cleared, though. And as he discovered he'd once bought a horse from Dad—years ago, as most people had, a good one, thank the Lord—it cleared even more.

"So, Poppy, how lovely," he turned to me, all smiles now. But I wondered whether an expensive education had cultivated the sort of manners that can be terribly useful on occasion. "And see you in due course, I hope. It's heaving out there, incidentally, hope you don't mind a crush, although I'm reliably informed it's atmosphere." He gave me another brilliant beam. "Anyway, must dash, people are standing around with warm drinks." And dash he did, with his industrial-sized bag of ice. Looking divine, I thought, as I watched his broad velvet back disappear.

I followed Janice down the passage and up the uncarpeted back stairs with the children. Our feet clattered up the bare wood. Clemmie was wide awake and chatting animatedly, thoroughly enjoying her role as house guest. Her brother was also warming to the task, singing, literally, for his supper, bellowing "Baa-baa Black

Sheep" at the top of his voice, swaying to the rhythm in my arms. The party was on as far as they were concerned, and I realized, with a sinking heart, that I'd never get them to sleep now. I might just as well not have come. Janice, though, was a hit, even with Archie, who's very fussy. When we got to the bedroom she sat on the bed and pointed to the faded frieze of farmyard animals around the walls, asking Archie what they said. It occurred to me that this really was a nursery, albeit an old one.

"Was this Sam's?" I asked, surprised, over Archie's deafening "MOO!"

"Good boy!" she told him. She turned to me. "It was once, and the tenants didn't use this room, so they didn't bother decorating. Didn't decorate much at all, in fact, as you'll see. Well, it wasn't theirs, was it? Not worth the investment. And Sam won't get round to it, what with the roof falling in and other things to worry about. Now then, young man," she fussed over Archie, popping him in between sheets. He instantly popped out of them, roaring with laughter. My son was having the time of his life.

"And have you worked here for years?" I persisted. Shut up a minute, Archie. I sat beside Janice on the bed. "Did you work for Sam's parents, too?" Any detail, however small, would help.

"Thirty years in all," she said, tickling Archie's neck. He squealed like a piglet, tucking his chin in. "And when my Stan was alive we were housekeeper and gardener for his folks. Lovely, they were. Well, she died young, didn't she? Cancer, it was. And he didn't make old bones; died of a broken heart, I always said. We lived in the cottage, Stan and me. But that's long been sold, what with death duties and that. I live in the village now. I worked for the tenants, too, nice people they were. Just cleaning and a bit of silver; well, they had au pairs, didn't they? And they were in London, mostly. That's all I do for Sam now, a bit of cleaning, because of course I'm in his office by day, doing the typing. Taught myself, I did, a few years back, when he needed more help there than he did here. Only four days, mind. Fridays I'm here to keep on top of things. Can't be everywhere at once, can I? But I keep the place nice. General dogsbody, that's me." She grinned as Archie embraced her neck warmly. "Well, he'd be lost otherwise, and there's no one else. Time was, we had gardeners and grooms and a girl from the village and what have you, but not anymore." I noticed the wall behind her head was riddled with cracks, the carpet, worn beneath our feet. Times were clearly tougher.

"And he's easy to work for?"

She broke off from blowing in Archie's ear to turn. She raised her chin and gave me a level stare. "There isn't a better man."

There was something decidedly eighteenth-century about this remark, and since I'd just seen him looking impossibly handsome downstairs in something resembling a doublet and hose, it didn't help my equilibrium. Why couldn't she have kept to the Regency rhetoric but said he was a cad? A bounder? I felt something I'd been determinedly stiffening inside collapse a bit.

"So, were you here when he got married?" I persisted nosily. "To Hope?"

"I was." This, more shortly.

"And—and so it must be odd for him, don't you think? Having her back here, with her new husband?" I blushed at my inquisitiveness.

She looked at me appraisingly. "I don't know how he does it. But he's that fond of Chad, who's a nice boy, and that upset for him, too. That's why they're here, I'm sure."

This didn't make much sense to me, but as I was trying to figure it out and formulate another question, which obviously couldn't quite take the form of "And is he still in love with her?" Janice got to her feet. She was leading me to the door, too. Quite forcefully, really; taking me by the arm and telling me to go off and have a good time and she'd sort out the kiddies. She thought a game of I Spy and then a story? And perhaps some hot milk? Clemmie and Archie, looking as if it was Christmas and not at all sorry to see the back of their mother, who would have put the lights out instantly, agreed, bouncing in their beds, shiny-eyed.

Down the stairs I went in my old black, thoughtful; then along the passage, following the noise to the front of the house. The front hall, of course, was the entrance we should have arrived at, and as I turned the corner under an arch, it was everything I'd imagined.

A grand sweeping staircase curled majestically down to a black and white limestone hall, two marble pillars supported a gallery at one end, and haughty-looking ancestors frowned darkly from the walls. It was heaving with people, so much so that some of them were halfway up the stairs. All seemed to be having a thoroughly good time, talking at the tops of their voices, shrieking to one another as they knocked back the champagne. Many I knew, but so deceptively attractive were they looking, in silks, velvets and sparkling jewels, the men dapper in black tie, that now and again I had to take a second look just to confirm. I took it all in for a moment, ridiculously pleased to be here. Then I cast around for Dad. We were obviously late, and there seemed to be a general move toward the dining room for supper. I wasn't entirely sure I wanted to drift in there alone. My eyes darted about. Instead of my father, though, I found Jennie, who, shimmering in her grey silk, dark curls professionally swept back in soft waves from her face, was hastening toward me from the foot of the stairs. As she muscled through the scrum, her eyes were wide in consternation.

"I thought you weren't coming!"

"No, I wasn't, but then Dad had a spare ticket and I thought: oh, what the heck. You'll never believe it, Jennie, the children are upstairs with the housekeeper. Dad swung it, naturally. How Mortimer is that!"

Ordinarily this would amuse her hugely, but it didn't for some reason. Her eyes flitted nervously about. "There's Angie. Come on, let's go and say hi."

Rather purposefully and with quite a grip on my arm, she turned me about and made to lead me across the crowded room. Indeed, so forcefully and with so much steel, something made me turn and glance over my shoulder: my left one.

Luke was in the stairwell, with his back to me. One hand above his head was hanging on to the banisters, the other was on his hip. He was leaning in, talking confidentially to someone. I craned my neck. To Saintly Sue. I shook Jennie off. Watched. Body language is fascinating, and this was compelling. The way he was arched over her, whispering in her ear: the way she threw back her head and laughed, cheeks flushed. She was in a midnight-blue off-the-shoulder dress, showing a great deal of bosom and looking far from saintly. Suddenly, over his shoulder, she saw me. She looked surprised, but then a triumphant look flitted across her face. A moment later, Luke turned to follow her eyes. He startled visibly. I walked across.

"Hi, Luke. Hello, Sue."

"Oh, um, hi, Poppy." Luke nervously smoothed back his mop of blond hair and straightened up. "Didn't expect to see you here."

"Oh, really? Why not?"

"Well, I—didn't think it was…"

"Oh, it's very much my thing. Thank you for the flowers, by the way. Sorry I couldn't make supper at your place the other night. I hope you found someone to take my place? Eat all those delicious prawns?"

Sue looked taken aback. Ah, spot on. How interesting. And I'm not normally a bitch, but it felt surprisingly good. Then she looked thunderous. Just so you know, Sue, I thought, bestowing a sweet smile on her. Then you can make your own mind up, can't you? But best to be informed, hm? I turned to Luke, who looked like a small boy caught with his hand in the cookie jar—either that or with his trousers down. Oddly enough, though, as I regarded him gazing sheepishly at the floor, I realized I wasn't about to follow through with another waspish remark. Wasn't going to tear him off a strip. Principally because—and this was quite comforting—I wasn't inordinately distressed. In fact, I decided, there was something about his chutzpah I rather admired. Perhaps because I wasn't going to have to be too closely acquainted with it? Could view it from a distance? It wasn't going to be my problem?

I let him sweat a moment, then gave a wry smile. "*Bon chance*, Luke," I said quietly, realizing, surprisingly, I meant it. His eyes came up immediately to meet mine: we communed silently a moment.

He grinned. "Yeah, you too, Poppy."

I turned and walked away, heart pounding a bit, but not too out of sorts. Although, I thought, I wouldn't mind finding someone to talk to pretty quickly. Jennie seemed to have disappeared, but—oh good, Peggy was standing by the fireplace in her black sequins. She was ostensibly talking to Sylvia, but actually watching this little scene unfold.

"Sylvia was just telling me," she told me softly as I approached, "that the piano teacher is perhaps not all he appears."

"He said he'd teach my granddaughter, Araminta," Sylvia said heatedly. "It was my birthday present to her, and of course I didn't think to pin him down on a price. Well, my dear, I've just received a bill for a hundred and fifty pounds for three lessons! Can you believe it!"

"Yes, I can, actually," I murmured.

"But fifty pounds a lesson! Who does he think he is, Elton John?"

"Different sexual inclination," observed Peggy as Jennie approached, flustered. "And nowhere near as talented."

"Sorry, Poppy. Got that wrong," Jennie muttered.

"Not to worry," I soothed. "Just a bit too much gray for my liking."

"Gray?" Sylvia peered over her spectacles. "No, he doesn't look gray. But he's clearly a bit of a spiv. You stay away from that one, Poppy. We don't want you getting it disastrously wrong again, do we?"

I was left rather speechless at this. Was I so much public property?

My affairs, my life, discussed so minutely, even at the Old Rectory? Over breakfast and the Frank Coopers? Suddenly London and all its anonymity appealed. Clapham, perhaps, where I'd spent many happy years. And surely the schools weren't all a hotbed of underage sex with crack cocaine on every street corner? As I sank into my champagne I found Dad at my elbow.

"All right, love? Children settled?"

"Yes, thanks, Dad."

"Glad you came, then?" He puffed out his chest, pleased with himself. "And wasn't our host big about it? Nice man, just had a long chat," he turned to nod in Sam's direction.

The hall was thinning out now as people filed into dinner, and I saw him over by a tall window framed by ancient tapestry drapes, talking to Hope. In much the same way as Luke had been talking to Saintly Sue: intently, leaning over her, but not flirtatiously, protectively. She was looking through her lashes at the floor, beautiful in a long white Grecian dress. She was blushing a bit. He pressed his case gently. The body language of men in love. Which I'd now seen in stereo.

The wave of jealousy that surged through me rocked me. All at once I knew why I'd been so desperate to come here, what clambering into a filthy lorry with wet hair and odd-colored pop socks under my old dress had been about. Seeing Luke with Sue had made me feel irritated. Seeing Sam with Hope made me feel desolate. And very, very alone. I'd kept Sam Hetherington at bay in my mind; kept him in a little box that I opened only occasionally, when I knew I was in a strong frame of mind. I'd protected myself from falling in love with him. Now he was bursting out like a jack-in-the-box, making himself even more lovable as he exposed his vulnerability, laid bare his soul across the room. Hope looked away as he spoke. I saw her swallow, her white neck lovely. Over by the door into the dining room, I saw Chad, watching the scene. His eyes were haunted, terrible. My breath seemed labored, but I turned to my father.

"Really glad, Dad."

"What, love?"

He'd forgotten his original question, so long had I been in answering.

"I'm really glad I came. It's about time I got a few things sorted out in my head."

And with that, leaving my father looking slightly bemused, I took his arm, and swept him into the dining room for dinner.

A sea of round tables covered in white cloths and flower arrangements and surrounded by little gilt chairs had been squeezed into the room, which, although large, was not built for feeding two hundred. A seating plan was pinned to a board at the door. With the noise level rising dramatically, I scanned it and found my place. Naturally I was Mary Granger for the night, and naturally I had a deaf octogenarian on one side, and Odd Bob on the other. He looked pleased as punch with his draw, while I thought: beam me up, Scotty.

Bob spent the first course telling me how handy he was around the house: how he could put up shelves, fix the plumbing, cook, too. How, last year, he'd done the whole of Christmas lunch for him and his aunt. I nodded and smiled politely, feeling all the time as if I were pushing torrents of dam water away from my flooding heart. I escaped him for the main course and had a shouting match with the old man on my left, one hand cupped to his ear as he yelled, "What? *What?*" Then I turned back, and Bob proposed. Asked if I'd marry him on Valentine's Day, which was a Saturday, he'd checked. Said we could live at his place while we looked for somewhere bigger. Told me he liked children. He squeezed my thigh and I slapped his hand. During pudding he squeezed my thigh again, and I pushed my chair back. Quite loudly. A few people turned to look. I pulled it in, knowing my face was flaming. Then I warned him, in no uncertain terms, that if he tried that again, I'd deck him. Bob looked astonished. Why, I could see him wondering, would I hit a man who really was my last and only hope? All there was left for Poppy Shilling in the man pool?

I'd shifted quite a lot of wine during dinner for obvious reasons, but even I knew I was more than well-oiled when I swayed into the disco sometime later. I'd bided my time, waited at my table until most people had gone through, Sam and Hope included, I noticed. Finally I followed the throng, yet another drink in hand for courage. The dark little room, lined with tatty, leather-bound books, so presumably a library, was throbbing with drum and bass and strobe light, packed to the gunnels with gyrating bodies. In the flashing light, I saw Chad standing on the edge of the dance floor. He still looked haunted. I glanced across, expecting to see Hope dancing with Sam. She was certainly dancing with someone, a blond chap, though; I could only see the back of him, couldn't see his face. And not a clinchy number, more throwing herself around the floor in a sexy manner, lots of hip action. I was just wondering whether to go and talk to Chad when there was a voice in my ear.

"Hello, Poppy."

I turned too quickly and nearly toppled. A terribly attractive older man with silvery hair swept off a high forehead and twinkly blue eyes smiled down at me. He held my arm as I lurched toward him. "Oh—Tom! Hi, there!"

"You all right?"

"Yes, thanks." I grinned as he steadied me, inordinately pleased to see him. "I heard you were coming. Quite bold on Angie's patch, don't you think?" Drink surely did loosen the tongue.

He laughed. "Possibly, but someone sent me a ticket, and Peggy and the girls told me to go for it."

"The girls?"

"Clarissa and Felicity."

His daughters. I saw them on the other side of the room making furious signals at him.

"I think you're supposed to ask their mum for a dance."

"I know," he said nervously, and I'd never seen the charming

Tom nervous. He passed a hand through his still abundant hair. "Will she laugh in my face, though? She left an encouraging message on my answering machine a few days ago, but I'm fairly sure she was in her cups and regretted it later, so I didn't ring back. Is she still furious with me? Will I get a black eye, d'you think?"

"Only one way to find out."

Angie was looking very beautiful tonight. Diamonds sparkled around her neck and down onto her black velvet dress like a sprinkling of stars on a night sky; her red-gold hair was piled in loose curls on her head. She was across the room talking to Jennie and... oh, good heavens, Simon. Here without Emma, of course, who, if she wasn't being detained at Her Majesty's pleasure, soon would be, rumor had it. I saw Tom straighten his bow tie and approach. Angie smiled and said yes, as I knew she would, and as her daughters had told her to. I caught Clarissa's eye; she smiled with relief. Which of course left Jennie and Simon together. But before Simon could even give it a thought for old times' sake, Dan had sauntered up. He was looking remarkably handsome in his dinner jacket, which I'd never seen him wearing before. Quietly taking his wife's arm and with a polite "Excuse me" to Simon, he masterfully steered her onto the dance floor. Jennie, luminous in her silver gown, glowed, and I sighed. If only men knew how simple we women really are, I thought. That all we wanted was to be shown some chivalry, made to feel special. Of course the road to forgiveness would be much longer for Angie and Tom, I thought, turning to watch them dance—not too close—but this was surely a start. And since you've got to start somewhere, a public show of affection in front of all your friends and neighbors—I saw a few people spot them and give Angie a delighted look, which she pretended not to see but the light in her eyes gave her away—was not a bad place to do it.

The party lurched on in a spirited manner. A band replaced the disco, and there appeared to be a free bar, a splendid idea as far as

I was concerned, and one I made regular use of. I had a bop with Felicity and Clarissa, who for some reason rocked with laughter at me. Frankie and Hugo had diplomatically stayed away, I noticed, so no haunted look for Clarissa tonight. She and her sister were sweet, though, finding me a seat by the wall after I'd more or less cleared the dance floor to "Brown Sugar," so that I felt like a dowager duchess in a Jane Austen novel. They kept asking me, rather anxiously, if I'd like a glass of water? Or some air? I declined.

It was late now, and some girls dressed as French maids were circulating with trays held above their heads bearing little blue glasses.

"Lethal," Peggy warned me, en route to the dance floor with my father as she saw me take one. She sighed as I knocked it back. God, del*icious*. I swiped another from a passing tray and knocked that back too. Then I went to the ladies'. Went twice, actually. Came back and found my chair. Then found the strap of my handbag incredibly interesting. Everyone was dancing. There were literally only a handful of people left in the dining room—I got up to pop my head round the door. A few people—including Bob, who, oh Christ, was making a beeline for me. I turned and fled. Scurried back to the library to lose him, muscling onto the dance floor.

"S'cuse me, sorry." I pretended I was looking for someone. It was heaving. Would anyone know I wasn't really dancing with anyone? Perhaps I should dance with Bob? At least then I'd have a partner. I turned back to see him leading Yvonne, from the shop, onto the floor. Right. Great. Yvonne had a moustache.

Disastrously pissed, I gyrated to the music anyway, but my handbag on my shoulder kept swinging into people who looked amused the first time, but not the second, so I put it on the floor. Ah yes, I could see why this worked, I thought, as I peered myopically at it. Why girls did it. You could look at your bag, dance around your bag, pretend you were in love with your bag…like so…I swayed, arms aloft—"Yooooo mye-eye, brown-eyed—oops!"

I was steadied by an irritated man who said, "For God's sake!" But I hadn't fallen over, only stumbled. Abruptly he caught my shoulders and I turned, annoyed.

"Look, I'm just dancing, OK?" I snapped. Only it wasn't the same man. It was Sam. And I was in his arms. He was dancing with me. Sam Hetherington was dancing with me, and not just jiggy-jiggy: proper hold-you-close dancing.

Right against his chest. I was in heaven.

"Sam!" I cried ecstatically into his left ear

"Are you all right?"

"Perfect!" I breathed gustily. "Just perfect." I nestled into his shoulder. We swayed in time to the music, or at least he did; I followed. And I felt so much better, supported. And suddenly, so full of wisdom. I gazed up. He was a bit of a blur.

"Sam, I know you're probably only dancing with me to make Hope jealous, but I want you to know it's fine by me. Really. I'm loving it."

His expression changed in a flash from amused to irritated. "Don't be silly, Poppy."

"She is very beautiful," I said dreamily, catching her in a swirl of white chiffon being twirled around the floor. By Chad? I couldn't see. I hoped so. "And when they came, Hope and Chad, we thought, well, we thought they were so perfect. The perfect couple. The blueprint for the rest of us. But nothing's perfect, is it, Sam?" My, those shots had been strong. Even I wasn't sure what was coming next. "Chip away at the surface and all sorts of cracks appear."

"Would you mind if we didn't talk about Hope?" Quite tersely, in my ear. I nodded sagely. Ah yes. Couldn't bear it. But the thing is, once my finger's hovered over the self-destruct button, I find it awfully hard to tear it away.

"I've got a terrible feeling I've fallen for you, Sam," I said throatily into his shoulder. I gave a cracked laugh. "How inconvenient is that?

When you're still in love with Hope? Hope. Hope springs eternal. Hope springs—" I dissolved into helpless giggles, for some reason finding this dreadfully funny.

He was steering me off the dance floor now. But I'd made a bit of a confession, would not be distracted. "Sam?" I had to shout loudly above the noise. "Did you hear what I said? I said, I think I've—"

"Don't be ridiculous, Poppy," he said firmly, depositing me on a chair. My old chair. Hello, chair. "Now wait here while I get your father."

"While I get your father," I repeated sternly, wagging a strict Victorian finger. Then I snorted unattractively and had to wipe my nose. But I sat demurely enough, sniggering only occasionally, as people drifted by. They smiled down, amused.

"Thanks for the tickets!" I called to Mark as he passed by with a pretty blonde girl.

"Nothing to do with me, Poppy," he grinned. "But I'm glad you're here. Having a good time?"

"Fantastic!" I gave him a broad wink. Well, of course. He wouldn't want to admit to sending another woman tickets in front of his girlfriend, would he? More people passed by on their way to the dance floor.

"Good evening," I greeted one or two. No, I would not sit. It was rude. I got to my feet. Just. "And thank you so much for coming." An elderly matron blinked at me, astonished. "Yes, it is a lovely party, isn't it? Not at all, my pleasure. Do come again." This, to Luke. "You too, Sue."

"Christ, love, what are you on!" Dad was suddenly beside me, alarmed. My father doesn't do alarmed. He's not a big man, but he was managing to hasten me, bodily, to the door. We passed a waitress. "Hey, hang on, Dad," I swung about. "There's this little blue glass, right, with this delicious—" But she'd gone.

"Schnapps? You drank that?" he said aghast.

"Three," I told him solemnly. "Wouldn't mind another." I made a break for it, but Dad's an ex-national hunt jockey, and his arms are strong. He was propelling me forcibly outside.

"Now what I'm going to do," he was saying in the patient tones one normally reserves for the educationally subnormal, "is pop you in the lorry, OK? Then I'll go back for the children, and then we'll potter off home, all right?"

"Righto," I said cheerfully, as he hustled me down the floodlit gravel drive. The night air hit me like a cosh, though, and suddenly I felt terribly, terribly light-headed. And a bit unwell. Was I going to be sick? I counted to twenty and somehow, having taken my shoes off to cross the paddock, found myself seated in the cab of a dark lorry in the middle of a field, shoes in my lap. Dad beetled off.

To stop myself being ill and the world going round, I sang. I sang, with deepest concentration, a verse from "Raindrops on Roses." So many favorite things to remember, though. Whiskers. Kittens. Kettles…Bugger. "Edelweiss," then. On I warbled. Beside me, a young couple who'd left the party early jumped into a Land Rover. They climbed into the back seat and started kissing. Ah well. I sang on. Everyone, it seemed, had found love tonight, except me. I sang on to the stars, just like Maria singing to the children, and somewhere during the third verse, my own children appeared. Just like the Von Trapps, but fewer, thank God.

"Darlings!" I greeted them exultantly, arms wide. Archie was fast asleep, wrapped in a blanket as Dad handed him to me through the driver's door. Then my own door opened and Clemmie was in Sam's arms, wide-eyed.

"Why were you singing, Mummy? We heard you miles away."

"Because I'm happy, darling! Well, hello," I drawled to Sam. "Can't keep away, can you?"

"Shut up and move across," said my dad, unreasonably officious for him. "Here, put this across the children."

"A seat belt," I boggled. "Didn't spot that on the way over. Coming, handsome?" I winked extravagantly at Sam.

"That'll do, love," said my father more gently. "And let go of his bow tie, there's a good girl."

"Why?"

"Because he doesn't like it."

I dropped it, disappointed. Sam's head retracted, and within a twinkling the cab door had shut on me. "Spoilsport," I pouted. Then I wound down the window and leaned out. Dad was already behind the wheel, though, and had the engine started. "Lovely party!" I sang, hanging out of the window as we reversed.

As we turned back toward the gate, the headlights from our lorry lit up the back of the Land Rover beside us. Bare limbs shivered in the yellow beam: two people were kissing horizontally and half naked on the back seat. From the waist down, in fact. A pair of pearly white buttocks gleamed, a broad back still in its dinner jacket, the back of a man's blond head, poised above a dark one. Suddenly Hope's beautiful but startled face was caught in the spotlight. As we rumbled off across the field, leaving Sam standing in the midst of his acres, it occurred to me that, while I hadn't recognized the buttocks, I had recognized the Land Rover. It rumbled through our village on a regular basis. It was Passion-fueled Pete's.

Chapter Thirty-one

THE FOLLOWING MORNING FOUND me a radically altered woman. No longer awash with champagne. No longer on top form. No longer singing in close harmony with an aristocratic Austrian family fleeing the Nazis. No longer in heaven. This woman was in hell, not with the sound of music, but the sound of throbbing temples. Unable to move from her bed, or unleash her tongue from the roof of her mouth, or crowbar open her eyes—I managed, briefly, then shut them again—never had a person felt so unwell. Staggered by the weight of my limbs, which I could just about coax into a fetal position, I lay doggo. Deado. Dead. And went back to sleep.

Sometime later I was awoken by the sounds of momentum gathering next door. A grumbling volcano. My children were bubbling under like so much molten lava, surely about to erupt. Ah. There it was. Archie gave a shriek of outrage, and Clemmie came running in.

"Mummy, I think Grandpa put Archie's nappy on back to front, but when I tried to do it he screamed. He won't let me."

"I'll come," I managed gnomically as, with a heroic effort, I heaved myself out of bed. I tested my feet for support, rocked momentarily, then lurched next door.

Archie was indeed wearing a back-to-front nappy as he stood gripping the bars of his cot, together with what seemed to be a T-shirt of Clemmie's. But at least they were alive; at least my father had had a go, I thought gratefully, as I heard him downstairs making tea. I lifted my baby son from his cot and nearly fell over. Had to hold the wall. Somehow I organized a clean nappy, and together we went downstairs, one hand in my son's, as he insisted on doing every stair himself, one on my throbbing forehead.

"Morning, Dad," I muttered, as my father caught Archie, who ran to him. He set him in his high chair. "Turn that down, would you?" I waved at the blaring radio.

Dad grinned, looking horribly chipper, clearly freshly showered. He made a long arm to the radio as I sank down at the table, head in hands.

"Morning, love!" he chortled. "All right?"

It's not often my father has the upper hand in the morning-after department; he was bound to milk it. I kept my head low and grunted non-committally.

"How're you feeling, then?"

"Marvelous."

Terrible. It was all coming back to me in glorious technicolor. Some little blue glasses. Bob leering at me throughout dinner. Chad's desperate eyes. Hope careering round the dance floor as the horn blew to "John Peel." Sam. Who I'd danced with, but—oh God, what had I said? I sat up slowly. Covered my mouth as my father put a cup of tea and two Nuroten in front of me.

"Oh God, Dad, I think I flirted outrageously with Sam Hetherington last night."

"No, no, love. Not so anyone would notice."

"Really?"

"Absolutely. Anyway, nothing wrong with a bit of flirting. Makes the world go round." He sat down opposite and sipped his tea.

"No, but the thing is, I think I might have overdone it…"

My mind was a blur. I tried to clear it. "Declared undying love, or something. God, d'you think I did?"

"No one takes that type of thing seriously at a party. Here, put some sugar in, get it into your bloodstream. Good night out, though, wasn't it?" He ruffled Clemmie's hair as she ran past to watch television in the other room.

"So, you don't think he noticed?" I asked anxiously, remembering…oh Lord, had I nibbled his ear? While we danced? I seemed to remember him brushing me off with a "No, Poppy." Surely not.

"Not for one moment," Dad said firmly. "Anyway, people like that get attention the whole time. It's like Brad Pitt, or whoever; they think nothing of it."

Brad Pitt. An A-list celebrity. That's how far out of my league my father thought Sam was. Interesting. Interesting too how, weeks ago, not so very long ago really, I'd felt he was not only in my league, but really quite proximate. At his great house, however, in his mulberry velvet coat, very much mine host, very much handsome bachelor of the parish, he was light years away. Bachelor. No, not quite. Divorced. From Hope. And thinking of Hope, some strange hallucinogenic memory struck me, to do with buttocks. I wrinkled my forehead in an effort to remember. Across the breakfast table, my father was optimistically setting a rack of toast before me.

"Dad, in the field, as we drove off, d'you remember a couple in a Land Rover beside us?"

"Too busy trying to stop you falling out of the window to remember a Land Rover. Now, are you going to be all right if I get off?" He shot his watch anxiously out of his cuff. "I've got to get back for the horses."

"Yes, yes, fine." I waved my hand dismissively, drained by the strenuous effort of recall. "Go. Be gone."

"The kids had breakfast a couple of hours ago and then I put Archie back down so he's had his kip."

I blinked. "Really? God, what time is it?"

"Eleven o'clock."

"Blimey. Right."

This surely was kind of my father. The horses would be crossing their legs in their stables by now. "Thanks, Dad." I looked up as he went to gather his keys from the side, his wallet. Then looked a little closer. There was quite a spring in his step. Quite a jaunty angle to the flat cap he was setting on his head. "Did you enjoy yourself last night?" I asked suddenly.

"I did, as a matter of fact." He turned as he went to the door, reaching for his coat on the back of it. "That Peggy's a nice lady, isn't she?"

"She is," I said cautiously. "But she's not on the open market, Dad."

"Oh, I know. We talked about that. Had a good old chinwag. And were getting on famously until I was told my daughter was— anyway. As I say, she's a lovely lady."

"What did you talk about?" I asked, curious.

"Hm? Oh, your mum. How I never got over her. Never found— or rather looked—for anyone else. And her and Roger. Funny. I always had her down as a scatty, frivolous bird, but there's a very thoughtful side to her. And the funny thing is," he looked pensive a moment, gazed contemplatively at the back door, "I got the feeling she thought the same about me. That I always play it for laughs." I kept very still at the table. "It's our armor, I suppose. Our protective layer. To prevent anyone getting at the soft underbelly. Anyway," he shook his head, like a horse ridding itself of flies: a regrouping gesture. Shrugged his coat on. "We thought we might go to the evening meet at Warwick on Friday. Just for a laugh, you know," he said quickly.

I nodded. "Good plan. She'd enjoy that."

"Only, sometimes," he paused as he got to the door, "it's dull doing everything on your own, you know?" He turned to look at me. "When the world is geared for couples. Restaurants, parties, cinemas—life. It gets tiring. Sometimes it's just easier to be two. To fit in."

He said good-bye. When he'd gone, I realized how I'd found that out last night. How, if you didn't want to look conspicuous, it was easier to be two. My dad had been alone for years, Peggy too, and I'd never appreciated the work behind that. They both did a brilliant job, presenting a breezy exterior to the world, but it was a job: an effort. A very conscious public face. For years they'd both climbed the stairs at night alone, got into bed alone, and I'm sure that got easier, more of a habit. But I couldn't see the public bit getting easier. And if you didn't want to disappear, didn't want to get a bit blurry round the edges, as some single people did, you had to put your back into it, didn't you? Into being fun. And interesting. And good to be around. Like Dad, and Peggy. Me too, now, of course. Lessons to be learned. Respect.

I hadn't realized I'd said it out loud, but my son, watching me from his high chair, echoed it gravely: "Rethpect."

I smiled and leaned across to take the squashed piece of toast he was offering me. Just then my back door opened and Angie stuck her head around.

"Coo-ee," she whispered, head on one side, anxious.

My smile became slightly wan. I dropped Archie's soggy bread. "Coo-ee, Angie. Come in."

"Are you all right?" She shut the door softly and tiptoed theatrically across the room. Sat down terribly carefully at the table making sure the chain of her handbag didn't make a noise. Annoying. Very dressed up, too, I noticed, in a little pink suit.

"Fine, thanks, just a bit tired."

"Blimey, I'm not *surprised*. You shifted enough to float a small flotilla last night. I've never seen anyone so plastered. Mind if I help myself?" She reached for a piece of toast.

"Do." I said drily, determined not to tell her the smell of the marmalade was guaranteed to make me heave.

"And there's nothing worse," she said firmly, buttering away, "than everyone avoiding you the next day and giving you sly looks in the village, so I wanted to pop round and say it didn't matter a bit. In fact we all enjoyed seeing you let your hair down for a change. Especially when you went on stage and grabbed the microphone."

I gazed at her horrified. "No."

"Mm," she nodded through a mouthful of toast. "Thanked everyone for coming. And then asked if we'd like to hear 'Climb Every Mountain,' but Sam wrestled you from the stage."

"Oh, God," I whispered, appalled, sinking my forehead into my hands. I had no recollection of that. Odd. Huge memory losses in some areas and wild hallucinations about buttocks in others. What was in those glasses? What was schnapps? It shouldn't be allowed.

"And whatever you do, you mustn't think the whole village is laughing at you over that man."

"Are they?" I yelped, jerking my head up.

"No, of course not. That's what I came to tell you. I knew you'd be feeling wretched—and of course I've been there myself, made a bit of a fool of myself in that department—so I came to say you absolutely mustn't worry."

"Yes, but you cornered him in his kitchen and stuck a rose between your teeth," I said testily. "I didn't do that."

"Well, you cornered him in the downstairs loo."

"No!"

"We thought you'd passed out in there, and Sam went to find you. You bundled him in and locked the door. He had to stop you swallowing the key."

I got up, horrified. Stared out of the window at the back garden. Then I swung back to her. "Oh God, I was thinking of moving to Clapham, but that's not far enough," I whispered. "It'll have to be Sydney."

"That's where Simon's going, apparently," she said conversationally, as if we were discussing popping to Ikea. "Jennie had a long chat last night. He's been offered a job, wants to make a fresh start. Getting a divorce, too."

Angie had clearly done the rounds this morning.

"I'll look into flights," I muttered, tottering across to the computer.

Ryan Air. Quite testing at any time. Particularly now. On second thought…I felt my way back to the table, holding on to the furniture.

"Oh, don't be silly, everyone drops a bollock now and again. It's very refreshing. Can't bear those who don't, actually. Pious twats. And he *is* very attractive, Poppy, it's not your fault."

"Whose fault is it, then?"

"God's," she said firmly, after a pause. "He's no business making men like that. Tom's back," she said, apropos, clearly, of attractive men. She reddened. "Or at least, he was last night. Whether or not he's still there now is another matter. Perhaps I shouldn't have given in so easily." She looked at me anxiously. Ah. So that's what this was all about. Ashamed of her own behavior, she'd come round wanting to remind me of mine. But why should she be ashamed of sleeping with her husband?

I voiced this, and she gripped my wrist across the table. "D'you really think so? I felt so cheap this morning, such a pushover, so I slipped out to see you and Jennie. Didn't want to seem un-busy. Told him I was going out for lunch, in fact."

Hence the pink suit. "Leaving him doing what?"

"Well, kicking his heels at home for a bit, then going back to his cottage, I suppose. Thinking how horrid and poky it is, hopefully."

I sighed. "Angie, he wouldn't be back if he didn't mean it."

"You don't think?"

"Of course not. It's too public. For God's sake, go home. He's the one that's made a fool of himself, not you. If you're quick he'll still be there, and if I were you I'd sit down at the kitchen table with a pot of coffee and some Hobnobs and iron a few things out. Then book a holiday."

She gave this some thought. After a bit she got slowly to her feet, replacing the chain of her Chanel bag on her shoulder. "Maybe you're right. D'you know, you're quite wise, sometimes, Poppy." She peered at me, surprised.

"It's always easy to be wise about someone else's life," I told her gloomily.

"Ain't that the truth," she agreed. Then she hesitated. "And I'm sorry I came round to, you know…"

"Gloat."

"You didn't really lock him in the loo."

"Didn't I?" I breathed, relieved.

"Nah. Just chased him down the corridor. You know how these things get exaggerated." She grinned.

I tried to grin back but my muscles wouldn't quite make it.

Angie gave me a quick kiss before exiting, rather speedily, through my back door.

Later that day I ventured to the shop for bread. One or two people smiled knowingly at me in the village. I smiled thinly back. Someone even hummed "Edelweiss" behind me in the queue for the post office. I wondered if this was a family thing? That just as my father thought he was Elvis while under the influence, I became Julie Andrews. Interesting. A psychologist would have a field day. Perhaps even suggest a nunnery. And wouldn't a habit be handy? To hide behind? I tiptoed home.

Three days later I got a message via e-mail from Janice.

Dear Poppy,

I hope you and the children are well. I so enjoyed looking after them. And I hope you're feeling better.

I cringed, toes curling in my trainers.

Sam has asked if you'd come in and sign some papers. He's away this week, but doesn't need to be here, apparently. I wondered if you could pop in on Thursday?

Away. I got up quickly from the computer. Well, obviously he was, miles away, if he had any sense. What papers, I wondered. I gazed above the screen to where the patch of damp had spread across the wall, flaking the paint. I picked at a bit, and a whole sheet came off in my fingers. I could fix that now, of course. Easily. Build a new wall. Not that the thought afforded much pleasure.

On the appointed morning, Jennie had the children for me and I duly drove into town. The first snowflakes of the year were falling, swirling down onto my windscreen, melting softly on impact. November. Soon it would be Christmas, my first one alone, I realized. I swept the snow away efficiently with the wipers, wishing I could sweep away so much else. Start again. With a heavy heart I parked, put my head down against the gathering blizzard and with a bitter wind sneaking around my neck, trudged up the high street in my old brown coat. Pushing open the familiar door, I realized I hadn't accounted for this: hadn't factored in the memory of this place causing melancholy to sneak over my soul, a lump to form in my throat as I mounted the stairs. I wondered if I'd need oxygen when I finally achieved reception. Or a hanky? Instead I plastered on a smile and handed my plant to Janice, hoping this wouldn't take long.

"Oh, you shouldn't have." She took it, smiling.

"Nonsense, it's the least I can do. It was so kind of you and I didn't even thank you at the time." Dad had obviously done that, when he'd belted up the stairs to spring the children from their beds, but still.

"I got terribly drunk, as you probably heard." Bare-faced honesty, I'd decided, was the order of the day.

"I heard you had quite a party." She grinned.

"To be honest I don't usually drink that much. My husband didn't, you see, so the odd tipple I had was on a night out with the girls, which wasn't that often." I shrugged. "It's no excuse, I know, but whatever the hunt was serving that night surely went to my head."

"Oh, I couldn't begin to drink one of those, let alone four or five as I gather you did. Go in, love, he's waiting for you."

I gaped, not at the four or five, but… "Waiting for me? I thought he was away?"

"He was, but he's back."

Janice's grin was widening. She was also ushering me across to his door; not exactly propelling me, but exhibiting the same sort of enthusiasm she had when she'd shooed me down to the party the other night, so that before I had time to think about it I was in his room, the door shutting behind me. I do remember wishing I hadn't got my old coat and boots on, and that my hair wasn't slicked quite so damply to my head.

Sam wasn't in a suit at his desk, he was over by the window with his back to me. He was wearing a dark red jersey and jeans, looking impossibly young and handsome even from behind. My heart was beating fast.

"Hello." He turned. Smiled.

"Hello. You're not supposed to be here."

"I know. But I didn't know how else to see you. And since I'm your solicitor, I thought a few papers to be signed in my absence might be just the ticket. Wasn't sure you'd come in so readily if you knew I was here. Thought you might be embarrassed."

"There are no papers?"

"No papers. Or at least—not yet. There may be later, to do with getting rid of me." He shrugged. "Depending on how you feel."

"Getting rid of you? Why would I want to do that?"

"Oh…a number of reasons." He looked hesitant a moment. Surprisingly unsure of himself. He crossed to his desk, walking around it, trailing his fingers on the green leather, eyes down. When he finally raised them, they were heavy with something I couldn't quite place. He gazed at me a long moment, appraisingly. Then massaged the blotter with a frenzied fingertip.

"I'd forgotten. You are...very lovely, Poppy."

I felt the breath rush out of me. Not what I was expecting at all. I waited, every nerve strained, every sinew tightening. But then he did an extraordinary thing. He continued around his desk to his chair and sat, which left me standing on the other side. I was dumbfounded. Surely after such a sentence, baffling or otherwise, a tumble toward each other, arms outstretched, was pretty much mandatory? Had I misheard? Had he perhaps said, "You are very lonely, Poppy?" Ipso facto a loser? No, I was sure he hadn't. Nonetheless I couldn't stand in front of his desk like a fourth former, so I sat, in my usual chair, heart pounding. He sat, too, in silent contemplation, it seemed, of his blotter, which he drummed lightly with his fingers. It was as if we were miles away from each other, and not just geographically; not just the vast leather-topped desk between us. The air seemed heavy with portent.

"Sorry about the other night," I blurted, the first to blink. "Getting so pissed and everything, chasing you down corridors. Singing. I don't remember much about it, to be honest. I don't drink a great deal, and I clearly overdid it."

He looked up and smiled; it reached his eyes. He sat back in his chair and looked at me properly, still retaining the crinkly eyes. "I liked it."

"You did?"

"Yes, I hoped it was *in vino veritas*. Some indication of how you felt. It's certainly how I've been feeling, although obviously I couldn't express it."

"Obviously," I whispered, thinking: why not? Why? In some senses this was hugely encouraging, but...was there another wife, I wondered wildly? Not just the one? Would number two spring from that cupboard by the door any minute now, head to toe in Chanel?

"Poppy, I've made a terrible mess of my life so far," he said softly, and all at once I knew. There didn't have to be another wife. One was enough. Hope was at the bottom of this. "I got married very young, fell madly in love, and it all went badly wrong. I got very hurt."

I nodded. "You're still in love with her."

"Oh, no." He looked astonished. "I'm in love with you."

More breath left my body. I'd be completely deflated soon, in the less than usual sense. And I itched to go to him. "Sam," I ventured, "must we sit here like this? Discuss…things like this, as if we're in a board meeting?" My eyes darted to his armchair in the corner. Not exactly a couch, which as we knew was the perk of the senior partner; and cluttered with papers, sure, but I could clear it very quickly. With one sweep of the hand, in fact.

"Yes, of course we must," he said, quite briskly. Sternly, even. "Hear me out, Poppy."

I nodded. Weird. Thrilling. Lovely, in fact. But weird.

He glanced at his blotter, then up at me, this time with an abrupt, defensive air. "Hope had an affair about ten months or so into our marriage. I found out and was devastated, naturally, but I reasoned that she was very young. And she was so sorry, assuring me it would never happen again, so I forgave her. Then less than a year later, she had another affair. With someone else. He lived next door."

"Good grief." I was fascinated in spite of my own inner turmoil.

"So I left her. Knew it was hopeless. That's when she hooked up with Chad."

"While you were married?"

"No, no, we were divorced by then. Chad wouldn't do that to me."

"Did he know about the other men?"

"Yes, I'd obviously confided in him at the time. He was my best friend. Is my best friend. He knew everything. God, I've sobbed on his shoulder often enough. But men are wired differently, Poppy. We have astounding arrogance when it comes to women. Think we can be the one to make a difference, make them change."

"Not just men." I thought of Phil. How I too had hoped for change.

"And Hope is...mesmerizing. Very beautiful, very charming, very captivating. If she sets her cap at you, if you're under her spell... well, I was lucky. I was captivated for quite some time, but I got away. Chad has not been so fortunate."

"She's having an affair with Pete the farrier," I told him, as it suddenly dawned on me. "I saw them together, in his jeep in the field."

"Yes, she is. I saw them, too. It's been going on a while."

Which was why Angie's advances had been rejected, it occurred to me: Pete already had somewhere to go after shoeing the horses of the village. And of course he and Hope had met at the book club. I remembered Hope appreciating his looks.

"Does Chad know?"

"I'm sure he suspects. But I haven't told him. I did tell Hope I might, though, if she doesn't watch out. If she doesn't mend her ways."

My mind flew back to Sam standing in his great hall by the window at the dance; Hope blushing at the floor, looking up at him through her lashes. No doubt agreeing she'd try.

"She's amoral, Poppy, so fat chance. Some people just are. A lot of men, but a surprising number of women, too. And I mind very much for Chad. I got out, but I don't think Chad ever will. And Hope hates that I've escaped. I wouldn't go so far as to say that's why they're here, but a bit of me thinks Hope brought him to England, to this area, knowing I was bound to come back. She'd like us to be in an eternal triangle for ever, killing everyone softly. But I'm not playing that game. I have to see her because I love my friend dearly, but I despise her now. And that took a long time. For a while I couldn't stop loving her. Was very hurt."

I swallowed. Felt very brown-coated suddenly. Very unmesmerizing.

"Why are you telling me this?"

"Because this is the first time I've felt anything again. When you first burst into this room, Poppy, with your baby son in your arms, struggling up the stairs with your pushchair, I felt something stir.

Something inside me relax and unwind, and each time I see you, it's with the same gathering excitement, the same surge of pleasure, and each time you go, I wonder when I'm going to see you again. You, with your sweet smile and your slightly chaotic way of tumbling through life."

This was more like me to be sure, and although astonished, frankly I was ready to vault the desk. I sized it up. Only four feet, surely, and I'd done long jump at school. I held myself together, though.

"You had no idea?" he asked.

"None!"

"Too busy letting that organ-grinder chappie sniff around," he said bitterly.

"Luke! How d'you know about him?"

"Oh…I know pretty much everything about you, Poppy, that's my tragedy. My affliction." He massaged his brow, in despair almost.

I gaped, astounded. "But—you've given me no indication, no suggestion!" I finally found my voice.

"I sent you tickets."

"What tickets?"

"To the ball."

"You did?"

"Yes, I put them through your door."

"But…I thought that was Mark! Why didn't you say?"

"How could I say? Don't you see how impossible that would be?"

"And—and when I tried to suggest things, mentioned the book club—"

"The book club!" He spread his hands desperately. "How could I come to the frigging book club?"

I stared. My head whirred. "What d'you mean?"

"You're my client, Poppy," he said patiently. "There's a professional code of conduct. I could be struck off. I know everything about you."

"Well, within reason."

"I know how rich you are."

It came as a bit of a shock. "Yes," I said after a bit. "Yes, you do, I suppose. But—"

"And everyone knows my house is falling down, is badly in need of a huge cash injection. Not that I'm sure I necessarily want it now," he said brusquely. Defensively, even. "I might sell it, so as not to be tied. I might go away." He got up from his chair and went to the window, hands thrust in his pockets, his back to me. My heart began to race.

"Go away?" I echoed.

"For a while. Paint, perhaps. Do something different. Not be squire of this parish. Master of foxhounds. Following in my father's inimitable footsteps. Italy, maybe. I'm told the light is wonderful."

"I didn't know you could paint."

He turned. Smiled. "I didn't know you could sing." I blushed. "Rather well, actually. Don't know why I bothered with a band."

"It's a family failing," I told him, getting up from my chair. No, I would not sit like this. Would not be still. "We sing in our cups."

"I shall look forward to that."

"So…there is something to look forward to?" I crept across the room tentatively. His eyes held me and he moved, too, but slowly; we seemed drawn imperceptibly together as if by an invisible thread. He stalled a moment.

"You'd have to fire me, of course."

"Of course," I agreed, halting too.

"And there's still the money."

"I don't want the money."

"You're stuck with it."

"I could give it away?"

"You could. I thought of that."

He did? "To charity," I said wildly. "Save the Children?"

"Well, no, your own children. In trust, until they're older."

"Oh, yes! How tremendous. And—and Italy. Well, of course I'm hopeless at languages, but I do love the sun. And pasta and—"

"No," he smiled, "it doesn't have to be Italy. Could be Wigan for all I care. Could be here, if you really love it."

We were close now, within feet of each other, and I felt myself aching for him. He reached out and took my hands.

"I don't want to be here." As I said it, I knew I didn't. Knew I wanted to get away. From the house I'd had with Phil, from the village, from the gossip, from everyone knowing my business. Not from my friends. I'd miss them sorely. And Dad, too. But they'd still be here, wouldn't they? When I came back? With Sam, and the children. To visit. And maybe with more children. If my mind jolted with surprise as this rogue thought crossed it, my heart didn't; it wasn't altogether astonished at my audacity. Because somehow I knew, having got it so terribly wrong—both of us having got it wrong—we'd now got it so right. I knew Sam knew that, too. As he let go of my hands and opened his arms, and I walked into them, I saw the light in his eyes; felt the surprise and delight in both our hearts as his lips came down to meet mine. At length, after he'd kissed me really rather thoroughly, we parted, hearts racing, breathing erratically, holding on tight and gazing at one another, shiny-eyed.

"You've forgotten something," he whispered at length.

"No I haven't." I smiled, wondering if my face might crack, so long had it been since I'd smiled like that, so rusty with disuse seemed my cheek muscles. "And I shall sign something to more dramatic effect just as soon as I can. But in the meantime," I linked my hands around his neck and brought his lips down to meet mine again, "consider yourself sacked, Mr. Hetherington."

THE END

READ ON FOR AN EXCERPT FROM

A Crowded Marriage

NOW AVAILABLE FROM
SOURCEBOOKS LANDMARK

Chapter One

By the time the suicide victim had been cleared from the Piccadilly Line and normal service had resumed, I was, inevitably and irrevocably, half an hour late. As the train lurched out of the tunnel where it had slumbered peacefully the while and picked up speed—quite alarming speed actually, and wobbling precariously, as if perhaps a shoe or some garment was still in its path—I glanced feverishly at my watch. Half-past one. Half-past one! I went hot. I mean, naturally my heart went out to the deceased man—or woman even; we hadn't been told the gender, just a rather macabre announcement over the Tannoy about a "person on the line"—but why did it have to be my line? Why not the Jubilee or the Bakerloo? Why, with unerring accuracy, did the severely depressed have to pick the blue one—for the second time this year? It was almost as if they saw me coming. Saw me happily applying the eyeliner and the lip gloss in my bathroom, chuckling away to Terry Wogan, merrily swapping grubby trainers for a pair of high heels, putting on my good suede jacket for a foray into the West End and thought—yikes, if she's getting out and about, if she's having a good time, that's it, I'm out of here, I'm toast—and hurled themselves into the path of an oncoming train.

Which is an extremely selfish and uncharitable reaction to a truly tragic event, Imogen Cameron, I told myself severely as I got off at the next stop and hurried up the escalator. Sorry, God. I raised my eyes sheepishly to heaven. Even as I did, though, I knew I was cutting a secret deal with Him. Knew I was admitting to being a guilty sinner in return for Him making it go well with the guy I was about to meet and oh, sorry, God *again*, but oh Christ—I was going to be so *late*!

I raced out of the tube entrance and down Piccadilly in the direction of Albemarle Street. Late, for my first meeting—first *lunch*, nay—with anyone who'd ever shown even the remotest interest in my work: a gallery owner, no less, who'd casually mentioned exhibiting my paintings in a private view and who'd offered to buy me lunch, discuss terms, but who, under the circumstances—I glanced at my watch again—had probably got bored of waiting and scarpered. In desperation I hitched up my skirt, clutched my handbag to my chest and for all the world like Dame Kelly Holmes sprinting for the line, jutted out my chin and hurtled through the pinstripes.

I'd met him at Kate's last week, at a seriously smart drinks party surrounded by her fearfully social friends. There'd been buckets of pink champagne sloshing around, and since Alex and I were on an economy drive and only knocked back the cheapest plonk these days, I'd got stuck in. By the time Kate sashayed up with the gallery owner, introducing me as "my artist friend across the street who does the most *fab*ulous paintings," I was practically seeing double. She'd then proceeded to lure him into her study—simultaneously tugging me along with her—to admire a rather hectic oil she had loyally hanging above her desk. Not one of my best.

"Yes…" He'd peered closely, then, as if that sort of proximity was a bit alarming, stepped back sharply. He flicked back his floppy chestnut waves and nodded contemplatively. "Yes, it's charming. It has a certain naïve simplicity—" or was it a simple naïvety?—"that one doesn't always come across these days, but which, personally, I embrace."

He'd turned from the picture to look me up and down in a practised manner, taking in my wild blonde hair and flushed cheeks. I was delighted to hear he embraced simplicity as there was plenty more where that came from, and I beamed back drunkenly.

"Tell me, do you exhibit a lot?"

I didn't, not ever. Well, not unless you counted that time in a pub in Parsons Green where me and three other painter friends had paid for the upstairs room ourselves and only our mothers had turned up, and once in a converted church in the country where I'd put the wrong day on the flyers so no one came at all, and was about to tell him as much when Kate chipped in, "Yes, quite a lot, don't you, Imo? But not so much recently. Not since that carping critic in the *Times* burbled on about the possibility of over-exposure."

She took a drag of her cigarette and blew the smoke out over his head as I regarded her in abject amazement. That she could *tell* such flagrant lies, standing there in her Chanel dress and her Mikimoto pearls, but then Kate hadn't just been named Most Promising Newcomer at the Chelsea Players Theatre, her very up-market am-dram group, for nothing, and continued to smile her sweet patron-of-the-arts smile and fix him with her baby-blue eyes. He buckled under the pressure, swept back his waves and turned to the painting again.

"Yes, well, critics are a loathsome bunch," he growled. "Don't know their arses from their elbows, and certainly don't know talent when it hits them in the face. I should know," he added bitterly. He drew himself up importantly and slipped a hand into the inside pocket of his tastefully distressed corduroy jacket.

"Casper Villiers," he purred, pressing a card into my hand, his dark eyes smouldering into mine. "Let's do lunch. I'm planning a mixed media exhibition in the summer, and I need an abstract artist. Say Tuesday, one o'clock at the Markham? Bring your portfolio."

And off he sauntered, just pausing to shoot me another hot stare over his shoulder as he relieved a passing waiter of a glass of Kate's excellent champagne. I hadn't liked to tell him that the "abstract" art before him was in fact an extremely figurative hay cart in an extremely figurative barley field and that I didn't even possess a portfolio, I'd just felt my knees buckle.

"Seriously influential," Kate hissed in my ear. "Knows literally everyone in the art world and can pull all sorts of strings. Rather cute too, don't you think?"

"Very!" I gasped back as, at that moment, my husband had sauntered up, looking amused, but never proprietary.

"Pulled?" Alex enquired.

"Hope so," I gushed back happily. "He's a gallery owner, in Cork Street. He liked Kate's picture and he wants to look at the rest of my work. At—you know—my portfolio."

"Terrific!" He had the good grace not to question the existence of that particular work of fiction. "About time too. I was wondering when my artist wife was going to be discovered and I could plump for early retirement. I'm looking forward to adopting Kept Man status. Oh, and incidentally, you can tell him from me, we don't want any of that fifty per cent commission nonsense either. It's ten per cent at the most, and if he's not interested, it'll be back to the Saatchis for us."

"Us?"

"Well, obviously as your manager I'll be taking a close interest in all financial arrangements." He waggled his eyebrows and twiddled an imaginary moustache.

I laughed, but could tell he was pleased, which thrilled me. Recently I'd started to get rather despondent about my so-called work and its lack of remuneration, and wondered if I shouldn't retrain as an illustrator or something. Something to get a few much-needed pennies into the Cameron coffers, something to make me feel like a useful working mother now Rufus was at school full time. It had begun to seem grossly self-indulgent to shut myself away in the attic with my oils, a broom handle wedging the door shut, yelling, "I'm on the phone!" to all-comers, producing paintings that no one except me had the slightest interest in. I'd even dutifully gone out and bought some watercolors and a sketch book with which to capture Paula the Pit Pony or Gloria the Glow-worm, but my heart wasn't in it, and in no time at all I'd found myself throwing on my overalls and squaring up to one of my huge canvases again. Casper Villiers' invitation, then, was the lifeline I needed. A boost to morale that had been far too long in coming.

As I hurried along the dusty West End pavements, my progress impeded by ludicrously high heels—I'd decided against the struggling-artist look since Kate had implied I was so successful the general public was in danger of being saturated by my talents— I tried to drive from my mind the summer exhibition he'd referred to. It was an increasingly pressing fantasy. The opening night: a private view on a warm evening, friends and family spilling out of the gallery on to the pavement, chattering excitedly, clutching champagne flutes; Alex looking heavenly in a biscuit linen jacket, stroking back his silky blond hair; my mother elegant in flowing taupe, my father…oh God, Dad, in that black leather jacket and cowboy boots. I moved smartly on. The press then: cameras flashing, lenses trained on my canvas in the window, my latest life drawing perhaps, that I'd rather pretentiously entitled *Nude in South London* (or as my sister, Hannah, had snorted, *Bollocks in Brixton*), and then my name in discreet grey lettering on the window: "Imogen Cameron—Solo Exhibition." No. No, that wasn't right because he'd said it was to be a mixed exhibition, and golly, not necessarily with me in the mix since he'd only seen one picture.

To broaden his knowledge, I'd spent the whole of last week feverishly photographing the rest of my paintings and arranging the prints in a leather portfolio—hideously expensive but worth the outlay, I'd reasoned—which I now clasped in my hot little hand, along with a couple of small oils, which I was sure he'd like, in a carrier bag. If only he was still there! If only he hadn't got bored with waiting and—oh, hello—here we are, the Markham. And I'd almost shot straight past! I gave a cursory glance to the rather grand pillars that heralded the entrance to a white stuccoed restaurant and hastened on in. As I pushed through the glass double doors I emerged into a sort of panelled lobby. Luckily there was a girl behind a desk directing traffic.

"I'm meeting a Mr. Villiers," I breathed, peering anxiously through the door to the restaurant. "But I'm terribly late and he might well have—oh! Oh no, he hasn't, there he is." And I was off, waving aside her attempt to escort me, and bustling through the packed dining room, weaving around tables with a "Sorry, oh, *sorry*," as I jogged a media type's crumpled linen elbow, misdirecting a forkful of risotto, intent on the solitary figure in the corner.

"I *do* apologise," I began breathlessly as he got up to greet me, looking much younger than I remembered and much better-looking. His chestnut waves flopped attractively into his dark eyes and his smile was wide and welcoming as he took my hand. "You see, there was this wretched suicide on the line—well, no, sounds awful, not wretched, although obviously for him, but—"

"Couldn't matter less," he interrupted smoothly. "I was late myself. I've only been here five minutes. Drink?" He gestured to a bottle in an ice bucket. "I took the liberty of ordering some champagne, but if you'd prefer something else?"

"Oh! No, how marvellous."

I sat down and reached for my glass eagerly, taking a greedy sip. Well, glug, actually. God, I was thirsty. I put it down thoughtfully. Steady, Imogen. Don't want to get disastrously pissed and start showing him your appendix scar or your cellulite, do you? Just... take it easy. But that was a good sign surely? Champagne? You didn't expend that sort of outlay unless you were interested?

I crossed my legs in a businesslike manner and smoothed down my skirt with fluttering hands. I was horribly nervous, I realised. "And, um, obviously I've brought along my Portaloo," I glanced down at it, propped up by my chair. No, hang on...

"Portfolio?"

"That's it." I flushed. *Shit.*

"Only I'm pretty sure this place is fully equipped on the sanitary front," he laughed.

"Yes, bound to be, ha *ha*! Oh, and plus, I've brought along a couple of small oils, but I don't know if you want to eat first or…?"

"Oh, eat first, definitely. Plenty of time for all that." He grinned, and twinkled at me as he flicked out his napkin.

Ah, right. A bit of chatting and flirting were in order first. Well, fine, I could do that. Could flirt my little socks off, if need be. Still smarting from my faux pas I managed to flick my own napkin out and twinkle back, then, taking the quickest route to any man's heart, plunged in and asked him all about himself.

Casper rolled over like a dream: he leaned back in his chair, stuck his legs out in front of him and launched expansively into "My Glittering yet Thwarted Career," whilst I leaned in, captivated, eyes wide, murmuring, "Really?" or, "Gosh, how marvellous," then later, "How dreadful!" when we got to the thwarted bit. It transpired Casper had been the most promising student at St. Martin's and a close contender for the Turner Prize, but his ideas had been cruelly stolen by jealous, inferior rivals. He'd reluctantly given up his dream of becoming an artist and opened a gallery instead, which was a tremendous success, and he now enjoyed great acclaim as a talent spotter.

"Benji Riley-Smith, Peter De Cazzolet—you name them, I've discovered them," he murmured confidentially, leaning right back in his chair. He was practically horizontal now, chin level with the table.

"Really?" I hadn't heard of any of them and could hardly make out what he was saying he was so far away from me.

"Casian Fartmaker, Barty Bugger-Me—" (I was lip-reading now so I may have got that wrong) he shrugged modestly—"I've been, well, shall we say, instrumental in their success?"

"Yes, let's," I breathed, sneaking a look at my watch under the table. I mean, granted this paean of self-congratulatory praise was being delivered with plenty of smouldering looks and lashings of champagne over a fashionable monkfish apiece, which was all very pleasant, but time was marching on. I had to pick Rufus up from school at three-thirty and Casper still hadn't looked at my work.

"So. You're a friend of Kate's," he said, lurching forward suddenly. He propped his elbows on the table, laced his fingers over the fish he'd hardly touched, and fixed me with his dark eyes. "She's kept you very quiet."

I'd been leaning right in to listen to his monologue so our noses were practically touching now. "Has she?" I inched back, hopefully not too obviously. "Oh, well, I suppose I haven't known her that long. Only since she moved to Putney a few years ago. We've been there a while."

"We?"

"My husband and I. And my son, Rufus. He's nine."

"Ah." There was something deeply disinterested in this monosyllable and I could feel his attention wandering.

"But Kate's lovely, isn't she?" I rushed on. "Sebastian too. They're great mates of ours. How do you know them?"

Nice one, Imogen. Back to him.

"Oh, Kate knows everyone," he said airily, and as he turned to wave down a passing wine waiter, I thought that, to an extent, this was true. Or to be more precise, everyone knew Kate.

Married to an eminent surgeon and with her very own designer label and boutique in the Fulham Road, Kate was one who attracted others. If I hadn't liked her so much I'd have envied her horribly—beautiful, fun, but kind too, and terribly self-effacing. I'd heard about her long before I'd met her. "Oh, you *must* know the Barringtons," people said when Kate and Sebastian moved to Hastoe Avenue. "They live across the road from you. *Every*one knows Kate."

Well, I certainly knew their house. Huge, red brick and imposing and on the right side of the Avenue (south-facing gardens and off-street parking), it was as hard to miss as our modest little semi opposite (north-facing pocket handkerchiefs and parking in the street) was easy to. And I knew the girl they meant too. Had seen her sailing off to work, blonde hair flying, calling out last-minute instructions to the nanny, and then returning from the school run later, hordes of gorgeous blonde children in the back of a gleaming four-wheel drive. I'd seen her in the evening too, going out to dinner with her husband, waving to the children at their bedroom windows, swathed in cashmere and pearls, long legs flashing out of a tiny skirt. But I hadn't met her, and might not have done either, had she not knocked on my door one Monday morning looking wild-eyed and desperate.

"Have you got a hacksaw?" she'd blurted urgently.

"A hacksaw?" I blinked.

"Yes, only Orlando's got his head stuck in the banisters, and I remember seeing you sawing up some boards in your front garden."

"Oh!"

My painting boards. Cheaper than canvas, but sometimes too big and unwieldy to fit in my easel, so requiring surgery.

"Oh, yes, I have. Hang on!"

I ran up two flights of stairs and seized it from my studio, then together, we'd dashed across the road.

The Barringtons' hall was about the size of a hockey pitch and had a grand sweeping staircase, up which marched hundreds of very expensive-looking balusters. Orlando's face was going a nasty shade of purple between the top two so I hastened up with my saw, but as I hacked away close to his left ear with Kate shouting, "It's either that or his neck!" I rather hoped Dr. Barrington didn't decide to leave his operating theatre early and come home to see me sawing his son out like some flaky magician. Orlando emerged unscathed, but causing wilful damage to a listed house left me in serious need of a sharpener. Since it was only ten in the morning Kate had hastened to her Present Cupboard and produced—oh splendid—we'd bonded over a box of Lindor chocolates.

Yes, everyone liked Kate, and it seemed my young gallery owner was no exception. He'd long been an admirer, meeting her first at St. Martin's where she'd designed shirts and he'd painted landscapes and…oh, he still painted landscapes, did he?…Really?…still dabbled in oils, and—oh Lord, we were back to him again.

"Even now," he confided over clasped hands, sotto voce, "when people come in to buy a Hodgson, or a Parnell, but find them too expensive, I say—hold on a minute," he raised a finger expressively, "you might be interested in a little-known artist I have out the back here, and then I take them out and show them one of mine, and do you know, they very often buy."

"How fascinating! Without knowing it's you?" I asked breathlessly but without the slightest interest. I really *did* have to collect Rufus soon.

"Oh, no, I never let on."

He winked and I looked suitably impressed and little womanish, but—oh, *please*, perhaps over a coffee, could we look at my work? Find out when this wretched exhibition was?

"So…coffee?"

I beamed. Finally. "Please!"

"And shall we take it upstairs? Where it's more comfortable?"

Oh, even better. Clearly there was some sit-soft area, a lounge or something, where we could spread the pictures out, stand up and view them around us.

"Good idea." I was on my feet.

In retrospect I suppose I did notice a flicker of surprise pass over his eyes; a faint startle, perhaps, at my alacrity, but he soon recovered. His face was naturally pink from all that champagne—either that or a rush of excitement at the prospect of seeing my work—and I let him guide me, his hand perhaps a touch too solicitous on my back, through the restaurant and back to the front desk.

He was talking nineteen to the dozen now, rather nervously in fact, about the new Turner Whistler exhibition, and it occurred to me this might be quite a big moment for him. A young star in the making? The new Tracey Emin perhaps, with him as my mentor? My Svengali? I smiled and nodded indulgently at his prattle, although I did pause to wonder why we were getting in a lift. That struck me as odd. Up it glided and on he chattered, smoothing back his waves and laughing too loudly and then, as the doors slid open, he ushered me out into a long corridor. A long, wallpapered corridor, with pink carpet at our feet, and lots of oak-panelled doors on either side. He walked me down it, rummaging in his trouser pocket, jingling loose change, but it was only when we passed a girl with a mop and bucket that it struck me...that this was a hotel. And that the jingling in his pocket was not coins, but keys, which he was bringing out even now, and fitting into a door with the number fifteen on it.

I gave a jolt of horror. Blood surged up my neck and face and to other extremities I didn't even know could flush. I stood there, aghast. Casper gently pushed open the door to reveal an enormous double bed with a bright red quilt in the middle of a dimly lit room. The curtains were drawn, and there was another bottle of champagne in the corner in an ice bucket. I half expected soft music to drift from the speakers, petals to float down from the ceiling. The bed seemed to be getting bigger, flashing alarmingly at me like the pack shot in an early TV commercial. As I gazed in disbelief, the saliva dried in my mouth.

"Shall we?" Casper murmured, indicating we should move on in.

"Oh—I..."

"We can spread your paintings out on the bed."

I panicked. And for one awful moment, was tempted. Tempted to believe the fiction: to go right on in—perhaps wedging the door open with my foot, I thought wildly—that's my foot on the end of my elastic cartoon leg—whilst my elastic cartoon arm flung open the curtains or dragged that passing maid in for moral support—but in the very next moment it came to me with absolute clarity that if I set foot in that room, I had also to be sure I could survive a leap from a third-floor window. Either that or be prepared—when I emerged via a more conventional exit, shouting rape—for critics to suggest that by entering such an obvious seduction suite, I had Willing Accomplice writ large on my forehead. I turned. Took a deep breath.

"There's…been a misunderstanding."

His smile wavered for a second. "I'm sorry?"

"Yes, you see, I had no idea this was a hotel. I was in such a terrible rush to get here I didn't pause to look. I thought it was just a restaurant, and when you said coffee upstairs, I assumed you meant in a bar or something. I had no idea you meant…" I trailed off, gesturing helplessly at the bed.

"Oh! Right," he said shortly.

I saw his expression change from one of incredulity that I could have misunderstood him, to one of anger that I could have embarrassed us both so. For a moment, I thought he was going to hit me. Then he did something far worse. His face buckled and he ran a despairing hand through his hair.

"This isn't me," he said softly. "This is so not the sort of thing I do."

Oh Lord. I swallowed.

"Look," I began, "it's fine, honestly. You don't have to explain."

"My wife and I—well, we've split up. Recently, if you must know."

Must I? I hadn't asked, had I?

"We—we're having a trial separation."

"Right," I whispered. I looked longingly down the corridor, to the lift, to freedom.

"But it's not permanent," he said defiantly, as if perhaps I'd suggested otherwise.

"No, no," I assured him quickly. "I'm sure it's not."

"And God knows I loathe it, *loathe* it. Seeing the kids only at weekends, not living at home, all that crap. But—well, I've got to get on with it, you see, and I get so lonely, and I'm staying here, at this hotel, while we sort things out, and I thought—well, we were getting on so well downstairs, so I thought—"

"It's an easy mistake to make," I said quickly. "And my fault too. I expect I missed the signs. The signals. Forget it. And now I really must be—"

"And when you said, 'Let's go and look at my etchings,'" he looked at me accusingly, "I thought—well, I assumed…"

Did I? God, *stupid* Imo. "Yes, yes, I do see." I blushed hotly.

"And the thing is, she's seeing someone else, I think. In fact I know she is."

His eyes, to my horror, filled with tears. I had a terrific urge to be in the Scilly Isles. On a little boat, perhaps, bobbing around the bay. I glanced around wildly. Where was that passing maid? Surely her shoulder to cry on would be more appropriate? More absorbent?

"Someone younger than me," he blurted out, "her personal trainer, such a cliché!"

Younger? Younger than Casper? How young could they get?

"He's Spanish, called Jesus, would you believe it, probably performs miracles, probably takes her to heaven and back," he said bitterly. "He's certainly been spreading more than the word. I expect he's hung like a stallion too—probably has to sling it over his shoulder when he gets out of bed."

I gazed around. *H-e-l-p.*

He pinched the bridge of his nose with thumb and forefinger to quell the tears. "He's twenty-four," he gasped, "with the body of an eighteen-year-old! The children call him Jeez. They ride on his back at the local swimming pool, he can do handstands on the bottom. Apparently he can make his ears waggle without touching them. Heaven knows what else he can waggle. With my wife! My Charlotte!" At this his voice broke and his shoulders gave a mighty shudder.

I stared at him aghast. He was struggling for composure but seemed to be losing the battle. I hesitated, but only for a moment, then plunged my hand into my bag for my mobile. I quickly punched out a number.

Casper leaped back in fear, his eyes wide with terror. "What are you doing?" he squeaked. "Are you ringing the police?"

"No," I sighed resignedly, "I'm ringing my son's school. I'm going to ask them to put him into after-school club and then I'm going to ask my neighbor to collect him for me."

"Oh!"

I put a hand on Casper's shoulder and swivelled him around in the direction of the lift.

"You, meanwhile, will come with me and together we'll find that sit-soft bar I've been fantasising about all lunch time. You will have a brandy and I will have a coffee, and whilst we sup our respective beverages you can tell me all about your wife and her scheming, faithless ways, and all about the dastardly Jesus too. On second thoughts," I muttered as I marched him off down the corridor, hobbling a bit now in my heels, mobile clamped to my ear, "I think I'll have a brandy too."

A Crowded Marriage

by Catherine Alliott

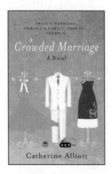

'Til death do us part just might cause you to wring someone's neck

Imogen Cameron can't quite figure out how she and her husband, Alex, have plummeted from living in their beloved London townhouse to scraping by in his exgirlfriend's guest cottage. But although the scenic pastures might inspire her flagging artistic career, and getting out of the city might do their son good, Imogen wonders if all the country air in the world could calm the crowds that are invading her marriage.

There's a gaggle of psychotic chickens, an infuriatingly bossy vet, that oh-so-sweet ex-girlfriend—and the feeling that her husband is preoccupied with more than just his job.

International bestselling author Catherine Alliott delivers an "intelligent, acutely drawn picture of a difficult marriage" (*Daily Telegraph*), crafting a witty, sophisticated, and poignant exploration of relationships and family.

Praise for Catherine Alliott

For more Catherine Alliott books, visit:

www.sourcebooks.com

About the Author

Catherine Alliott worked in London as a copywriter in advertising. She now lives in Hertfordshire with her husband, who works as a barrister, and their three children.

Catherine's first novel, *The Old-Girl Network*, was chosen by WHSmith for their fresh talent promotion in 1994 and became an instant bestseller across the UK, as did her subsequent novels, *Going Too Far*, *The Real Thing*, *Rosie Meadows Regrets…*, *Olivia's Luck*, and *A Married Man*.